Reading

5 X 5

from Metaphorosis Books

Reading 5X5
Reading 5X5: Writers' Edition
Best Vegan Science Fiction and Fantasy of 2016

<u>*Metaphorosis Magazine*</u>

Metaphorosis: Best of 2017
Metaphorosis: Best of 2016
Metaphorosis 2017: The Complete stories
Metaphorosis 2016: Nearly Complete Stories

<u>*by B. Morris Allen*</u>

Susurrus
Allenthology: Volume I
Tocsin: and other stories
Start with Stones: collected stories
Metaphorosis: a collection of stories

Reading 5 X 5

Readers' edition

edited by
B. Morris Allen

Metaphorosis Books

Neskowin

Readers' edition
ISBN: 978-1-64076-040-0 (e-book)
ISBN: 978-1-64076-041-7 (paperback)

Writers' edition
ISBN: 978-1-64076-042-4 (e-book)
ISBN: 978-1-64076-043-1 (paperback)

Contents

Foreword

"*Five stories, five times,*" the tagline says. What does that mean? Twenty five authors in five genre groups each received a story brief and wrote their own story from it. Five stories, each told five times, in five different ways.

Why do this? Both because it's fun, and to see and learn from how five different authors approach the same source material. How do the stories differ depending on style and inspiration?

The idea grew from a couple of seeds. Several years back, I was reading *The Best of Gene Wolfe*. In it, he suggests taking another author's successful story, trying to write your own version of it (as an exercise, not for publication), and looking at where they differ. He offers one of his own to work with. I've never gotten around to doing it, but the idea stuck in my head.

Separately, for a few years, I've participated in Novel-in-a-Day (novelinaday.com). In essence, each of a group of writers is assigned a chapter brief — an entry point, a few plot requirements, an exit point, and some backstory. Knowing nothing about the rest of the book (even the genre), they have 19 hours to write their chapter. Then a few hours for assembly, and voila! — over twenty four hours, a novel is born. My favorite part of it is that, thanks to the number of participants, there are usually two or three variants of the novel, allowing authors to compare their chapter to how others handled it.

After the summer 2017 Novel-in-a-Day, the two ideas came together. Why not an anthology highlighting the way different authors work? Give each the same seed, and see where they go with it. After a week or two figuring out parameters, I'd also settled on the *Reading 5X5* title, which gave the anthology a manageable size and number of authors. And happily, I edit *Metaphorosis* magazine, so I had a group of writers and artists whose work I knew and liked. All I had to do was see if they would participate.

Because *Metaphorosis* authors are a fun and adventurous group, it turned out they would. Lots of them — enough for a full anthology and then some. And five brave souls volunteered to write the briefs. Kathryn Weaver offered art. And when I say volunteer, I mean it. All the contributors donated their work, and all proceeds go to the Clayton Memorial Medical Fund.

#

Writers are invited to post their own stories based on the briefs. Come see what they came up with, at x1.reading5X5.com.

B. Morris Allen
Editor
05 March 2018

Contemporary Fantasy

Stories

Dreaming in Other Colours

Meryl Stenhouse

Lina steps out into the yard in the late afternoon, hoping for a cooling breeze. The old Hills Hoist with the sagging wires cants among the red natal grass, the soft heads dancing in the heat. She should fix the washing line. She should mow. She should tidy up the yard. There's a broken chair that she doesn't remember discarding, and the lemon tree, dried up now into a rattle of branches.

Over the fence, yellow is all she can see; the canola fields stretching out and out and out in all directions until they crash into the open sky. Blue and yellow. Yellow and blue. How long has it been since she has dreamed in other colours?

A hot wind whips around her ankles, not what she wanted at all, but something in it is unnatural even in this climate, and she turns. The sun is growing, a spreading mass sending licking fingers of fire towards the fragile Earth. The blue sky bleeds into black at the edges, the stars flickering madly.

"Lina?"

Her grandmother's voice is feather-light, but that's what moves her. She bolts inside, thongs slapping across the scuffed lino in the kitchen, through the dingy lounge with the sagging tartan couch, up the narrow stairs, jumping the one that clunks because she's sure one day it's going to come off.

She should fix the stair.

There's a shadow on the wall halfway down, and Lina meets it with her body. "Gran, I'm here."

The shadow becomes flesh, in a way that Lina can see, but never quite remember, and Gran is there; an old lady, bent, with her wispy white hair and her face creased into a smile. "Lina. Lina. Don't run about like that in this heat. I was just coming down to make us a pot of tea."

"I'll make it, Gran. Come back upstairs."

The strange shadows on the walls fade as she helps Gran back up the stairs to her room. When she looks out the window, the sun is itself again, the canola fields yellow, the sky still blue. She breathes out.

What would happen if Gran refused to go back upstairs? If one day she just said no? Lina can't imagine wrestling her up the stairs by force. There are some things that can't be moved by strength.

She guides Gran to her favourite chair, the cane one with the high back and the hard cushions that she likes.

"And a biscuit or two. Is there any teacake? I haven't made a teacake in years," says Gran.

When Lina straightens, there's a dust cloud on the road, weaving between the yellow fields, and for a beautiful moment she thinks her father is coming home to help her.

#

It is not her father. It's a delivery truck, the driver a young man with scruffy beard and a tank top that shows off his arms. They're not particularly good arms, unless you are starving like Lina is. He's looking around at the house with its faded iron roof and the yard with the carpet of rogue canola but he's not really seeing them. Like the guy who delivers their groceries. And the man who reads the meter. And the postman. She's sure that she disappears from their thoughts as soon as they disappear over the hill.

Sun-drowsy locusts buzz off into the grass, disturbed by her feet as she goes around to the back of the truck. It's like a secondhand shop in there. Lina climbs in, peering at addresses, some local to Dalwallinu, others further north along the highway; Wubin and Jibberding and Payne's Find, even as far north as Meekathara.

The delivery man drags a cabinet along the metal floor. Lina pushes past him and picks up the other end. It's lighter and smaller than she expected. They wrangle it to the ground, and he pulls out an envelope, which he hands to her, and a clipboard. "Sign here, please."

In the swirling dust of his exit, Lina stares at the cabinet. It is entirely disappointing; old, but not antique old; a box on round wooden legs, with a laminate top and varnished particle-board sides in shades of brown and orange. There are two sliding doors at the front with round metal knobs. She is bemused by its sudden appearance in the wreck of a yard. And yet it fits, somehow; functional but ugly.

The envelope bears the stamp of the Public Trustee. A will. Someone died to send her this cupboard, and she rips the envelope open with clumsy fingers. *This will dated Wednesday 10 September 1973 is made by me Mavis Bridgeman of 31A Hemmings Street Dandenong, Victoria.*

Lina doesn't know anyone who lives all the way across the country in Victoria. The will didn't say much, only that Mavis had left the cabinet to Lina, daughter of Norman. The tip of her nose is hot and she rubs it. She told Gran she would make tea. The house is silent though, so Gran has settled again, maybe to sleep.

Cold air brushes her ankles. Mist is curling out between the cabinet's sliding doors. Lina crouches down in front of them. Now she can hear something too, a low soft sigh.

Cabinets do not sigh. No matter how strange her life, she knows this. She slides open the door.

Cold air blasts her face, cooling the budding sunburn. There's a mountain inside the cabinet; sharp, snow-peaked, distant. She leans forward and the view zooms in. Now she can see the slopes, steep and slick with snow, and a long way down, a green valley, green like a long drink of cool water, green like a long-forgotten dream, green like nothing she has seen in her hot, dry world.

The stony soil bites into her knees as she leans into that valley, and she sees houses and people, at least she thinks they are, but they're not human, not even remotely. The houses are so beautiful she wants to cry, and the smell that comes up to her is in an unfamiliar language. There's a blessed coolness on her cheek where it presses against the mountain.

She leans further into the cabinet, pushes with her toes, wanting to fall in, down and down to that wonderful green where she can walk and breathe, but all that happens is that her forehead bangs into the back wall of the cabinet.

When she sits back, rubbing the tender skin, there are ants crawling over her thongs and her arms are red.

#

There's no sound from her grandmother's room as Lina climbs the stairs with the pot and the cup and a plate of milk arrowroot biscuits. In Gran's room, stars slide along their paths, burning bright; nebulas bloom and expand away to nothing, leaving only cold space behind; galaxies spiral out and out until they lose their integrity and send the stars spinning away.

And then with a rush it all shrinks down until there is only Gran, sitting in her favourite cane chair, smiling at her.

Lina puts the tea down. She doesn't need to ask if there might be other worlds where strange, beautiful people live in the shadow of a mountain. She has other questions.

"Do you know a Mavis Bridgeman?" she asks.

Gran is dipping a biscuit in her tea, and doesn't answer for a while. "Mavis was my daughter. I didn't realise she'd gone."

Gran never talked about other family. Lina assumed Dad was her only child. "Why did she leave?"

"Leave where?"

"Here."

"Mavis was never here."

"But...she was your daughter. You grew up in this house. How could she not have been here?"

Gran smiles, her head on one side, like a bird. "Did you think this is the only part of me?"

#

Lina's father was the only parent she ever remembered. Gran filled any mother-shaped hole she might have had in her life. Gran in the kitchen, baking apple pie. Gran in the yard, hanging washing, or digging weeds from the flower beds.

She pauses on the stairs, tea-tray in hand. Gran making tea when Lina and...and...her sister came home from school. Sitting at the old wooden table, school dress limp with sweat.

And then Gran had gone up the stairs one day and she could never come down again.

Nothing much had changed for Lina. She'd kept going to school, every day, but Dad never made her tea and cake when they came home. Dad was no gardener and so the yard had slowly gone to weeds. He'd stopped going to work, but it was years before Lina had understood that her grandmother's change had trapped him there in the house.

Her sister had figured it out. Those memories were vague, but Lina remembered waking up to find... she couldn't even recall her sister's face, now. Couldn't, somehow, remember her name. Just a shadowy figure hoisting a bag over her shoulder, shushing Lina as she asked, sleepily, what she was doing. A sister who'd made Lina promise not to say a word until morning.

It was the day before her sister's sixteenth birthday.

#

The phone rings when she's in that morning half-doze. It's hot, but not yet so hot that it's unpleasant. Lina stumbles downstairs, barefoot, grabs the old handset off the wall.

"Lina?"

It's her sister. She knows the voice like she knows her bones. "Hey." She puts her arm on the wall, rests her forehead on her forearm. "Where are you?"

"On the road," says her sister, and Lina can hear the truck rumbling in the background. "Been riding all night down the coast. It's so beautiful here, Lina. I wish you could see it."

Lina wishes she could see it, too. "Tell me. Tell me."

"There's a roadhouse just a while back where you can get hot coffee and fried chicken legs any time of the day or night. There's no other houses, not for miles and miles. It reminded me of home, except it's so flat you can see right to the horizon. And the ocean's on the other side of the road. Just drops away to the great big blue."

Lina's clutching the phone, imagining the road stretching out ahead of her, endless movement, places to go.

"Passed Ceduna yesterday. Going to head inland soon, scoot around the edge of Adelaide and up into the Flinders Ranges. That's a slow run, lots of tight corners as you go up onto the plateau."

Her chest is tight, her breathing short and fast. "Then where? Where will you go?"

"From there it's across the flats to Broken Hill where the mines run day and night and the air's so heavy with metals you can taste them. I'll park the truck just outside the town where you can see the lights from the big drag lines and I'll eat takeout and listen to the curlews."

"Send me a picture," says Lina. She says this a lot, and her sister says she'll try, but she never does. Can't stop for pictures. Can't stop for anything. She's moving all the time, circling Australia like a moon in orbit.

But she never comes home.

"I've gotta go," says her sister.

"Wait…"

"What?"

"I can't remember your name." Shame engulfs her as she says it. She should remember her sister's name.

"It's Angie. Remember, Lina? Angie."

"Angie. Angie. I won't forget. Call again soon."

"I will. See you, Lina."

"See you." She hangs up the phone. Angie. Angie. She has to remember that. She scuffles in the kitchen drawer for a pencil, goes to write on the wall.

Angie's name is scrawled across the wall around the phone. Lina stares at it, at all the times she's written her sister's name there and still she forgets.

She finds an empty space and writes it again. She won't forget this time.

#

She's found that she can't go far from the mountain. She can swing around it, if she leans, see all the villages and towns and the people working, laughing, living their lives.

There's a girl in one of the houses — she doesn't know if it's a girl, or even if it's a house — who walks every morning from her — house — down a long winding strip that must be a road, to a long, curving structure larger than several houses put together. She goes in, and she stays there all day. School? A job? Lina can't tell which, or how old her subject might be, but there's a steadiness to her movement that suggests purpose.

Lina has tried to call, but no one responded, except gran who asked her what she wanted. She's tried to reach in, but she just bangs her hand on the wooden walls, even though the mountain goes through them. It is not real, and yet when the cold air brings the scent of snow to her she feels it is more real than canola fields and heat.

At the end of the day the — girl — comes out of the building. She's always carrying a bag, which she takes back to her — house — and disappears inside. She won't come out again until morning.

Lina rushes to do the washing up. Is the girl also doing the mundane jobs that need to be done? No, she has a greater purpose. A meaning to her life. What's in the bag she carries? Food? Materials? She wishes she could see into the house. She wants to know what rooms are in there. Bedroom, kitchen, living room with a sagging couch? She transfers a dripping plate to the drainer. Dull old wallpaper on the walls? Ugly lino in the kitchen?

No. Her dreams rebel against it.

The inside of the building is a single room, long and low. It has a bed at one end, and a rudimentary kitchen. The rest of the room is a workshop, where she builds a... Lina looks out the window, the plate in her hand slipping back into the water. The rolling yellow landscape stretches to the cloudless sky.

A flying machine. Lina has never seen a vehicle of any kind among the people of the mountain. The girl is an inventor. She will teach her people how to fly. She will be known and loved and remembered, though now she struggles alone, with no one to share her dreams with.

No one but Lina. Lina believes in her, in her dreams.

When the washing up is done she hurries upstairs with tea, but Gran is not there today; only the rolling universe greets her. Lina leaves the tea tray on the floor by the door, all the while her mind is back with the girl and the hidden workshop and the flying machine.

#

"I'm sorry, that card is declined."

Lina clutches the phone in one hand, her Dad's credit card in another. "Can you try again? I'm sure it's fine."

The woman tries again. It's a different woman than it was when Lina's father left and she started to do the shopping herself. When she had to order everything by phone because she couldn't leave the house any more. Back then it was Mrs Hale, the mother of one of the girls Lina went to school with. But Mrs Hale is gone, and the woman after her is gone, and now Lina doesn't know the names of any of the people she rings — the grocer, the electricity company, the phone company — to pay her bills.

But there is always money on the card.

"I'm sorry, it's definitely declined. Do you have another card we can try?"

Another card? She doesn't even have a bank account. She's always just used Dad's account. She rings telebanking and checks the balance. Seventy-two dollars. Money always goes in at the beginning of the month. Always. All these years without fail. Why has it not gone in now?

Lina abandons the phone. There is a name scrawled on the wall around the phone, over and over. Angie. She wonders who that is.

There's a box in the hall cupboard where she puts her father's mail. Waiting for him to come home and read it. She opens the phone and electricity bills because she has to pay them, but everything else goes there unopened, including his bank statements. She pulls out a handful from the top, opens one. All the withdrawals are hers.

She opens another, and another, sees the balance going down every time she pays a bill.

By the time she has opened all of them, laid them out in order around her on the floor the day has gone. The house creaks and groans as it sheds heat into the cooler night. She kneels in the circle of statements that tell a story, but it's a mystery story. The deposits stopped years ago. She has been living on the money built up, and now it's gone.

Why isn't he putting money in his account? Why didn't he call and tell her?

She has not heard his voice in so long.

#

In the weeks after her sister left, her dad sat in the living room, staring at the wall, fingers gripping the arm of the chair.

Lina started to wash her own clothes, to do the dishes after school. She felt bad for him, that her sister's abandonment hurt so much. She put away her own hurt to try to make him feel better. He used to be cheerful, telling terrible jokes to them over the kitchen table, whistling as he mowed the yard or tinkered about in the shed, keeping the house repaired and comfortable. Now it was as if she had lost two members of her family.

She heard him shouting as she got off her bike in the yard after school. She dropped her bag on the lino and crept up the stairs.

"Just stay in there, you stupid old bitch!" he shouted.

Lina bit her knuckles. He'd never spoken to gran like that before. She peered around the corner.

The room was full of stars. She hoped that Gran couldn't hear him when she was gone like that. She hoped that Gran would stay away until he was better. She hoped that Gran would appear, sitting in her cane chair, and frown, and tell Dad to pull himself together.

Her dad turned around and saw her crouching on the top stair. "Lina?" He closed the door, rubbed his face. His ears were red. "Why are you home?"

He'd aged, lines deepening around his eyes, grey marching through his hair. And suddenly she was sick of it, sick of having this stranger in place of her father. "Why are you shouting at Gran?"

"Don't worry about it."

"I lost a sister, too. Why doesn't anyone care about my feelings?"

"Go and do your homework, Lina."

She stormed past him and threw open the door. The universe swirled and she stood in it, with nothing beneath her but space and whirling dust and light.

"Lina!" Her father grabbed her arm and pulled her out of the room. "Wait. What did you see?"

"Stars," she said. "What do you see?"

"You can see that?" He grabbed both her arms. "Are you sure?"

"Of course I'm sure. Is that why you were shouting at Gran?"

"Lina." He squeezed her shoulder. "You mustn't tell anyone."

"I know." As if she would tell. She'd been to school, and she was pretty sure no one else's grandmother gave up being human and turned into the universe. "So can you stop being so mad, now? Please?"

He smiled at her. Actually smiled, and she knew

everything would be okay.

Downstairs in the kitchen, he drew patterns in spilled tea on the benchtop. "You know she can't come downstairs, right?"

"Why not?"

"The world will end."

Lina tossed her head. "Whatever, Dad." She was fourteen. The concept of death, of ending, was unfathomable. Death happened to old people. Her father wasn't old. Gran was old, but she was also the universe, so Lina wasn't afraid for her.

She didn't believe it until it was too late. Until she woke up on her sixteenth birthday to the sound of his ute roaring away, and came downstairs to a cake and a card and an empty house.

I'll look after you. The money will keep coming, I promise. Just don't leave the house until I come home, okay?

That was all that he wrote in her card. He forgot to write Happy Birthday.

#

Now she remembers the relief on his face, the night before he left. She hadn't seen the trap. She always thought he would come home.

Her knees are gritty because she hasn't swept the floor in ... a long time. Not since the cabinet came.

How long has she been in this house?

She goes upstairs to her grandmother. Halfway up the stairs she leans on the wall, thinking she might fall. Gran is sitting in her chair when Lina opens the door, hands clasped in her lap. Waiting for her.

"Am I dead?"

"You're not dead, any more than I am." Gran pats the seat next to her. "Come and sit down."

Lina collapses next to her, and Gran wraps an arm around her shoulders. Gran smells of powder and apples and Gran, just the way she always has.

"Dad's not sending money anymore. I don't know how old I am. I keep forgetting...my sister's name. I hate yellow.”

At each statement Gran pats her shoulder, gives her a little squeeze.

“Mavis sent me a cabinet with a mountain in it. What is it?”

“It’s a cabinet with a mountain in it.”

Lina sits up, exasperated. “I don’t understand.”

“Think of it this way. One natal grass produces many seeds. Thousands. Millions, in their lifetime.”

Lina’s mind skitters around this, like a mouse around a big, dark hole. “Am I a seed?”

Gran pats her hand. “You’re my granddaughter.”

“And what are you?” Lina can’t believe she’s never asked this before. She looks into Gran’s dark eyes. “What are you?”

For her answer the room sifts away like sand in the wind and she is falling through stars. A planet rushes up to her, closer and closer, green fields, impossibly green, and a cold white mountain, and she turns to it like a dying flower to rain.

#

She’s lying on the floor in front of the cabinet, her hands full of paper. The bank statements. She rolls onto her back on the rustling bed and looks at the ceiling, the old wood beams dark, with gaps where they have shrunk in the relentless heat.

She gets a pen from the old mug in the kitchen. On the backs of the statements she writes, *when my sister calls, tell her I need her to come home.* She writes it over and over and puts the paper around the house, under pots and on chairs and sticking out of picture frames where she will see them in passing because she will not forget this, she can’t.

If only she could remember her sister’s name.

#

The girl hasn’t come out for days, and Lina is worried. It would be easier if she could do something to help. She aches for it, to drop down into that green land and knock on the door.

What would she say?

"I know what you're doing. I'm here to help."

In her daydreams the girl smiles and steps aside to let her in, and so begins a wonderful new life, the companionship of like minds working together on a project that will change the world.

At school she wasn't interested in much. The little country school — one building, four rooms — didn't produce academics. Kids either left school and worked on their parents' farm, or they went to the mines. The smart ones went to the agricultural college in Wokalup and ended up working for the Primary Industries. None of those lives excited her, but then nothing did: she was young and she had all the time in the world to do whatever she wanted.

She still feels young but her potential is gone, snuffed out by this house and this legacy of her father's that she can't walk away from. She's angry now at herself for not trying, for not doing something, for not having a vision of what her life might be. Something that she could throw at her family and say *look what you have taken away from me.*

When the sun goes down she gives up on the mountain and goes outside. The old armchair is still warm from the day's heat and she curls up under the cloudless sky. She wants to hate her father for leaving her here. But she knows his despair. She wants to ask the mysterious Mavis, *what did you do?*

Did you have dreams, too?

How old were you when you died?

How long will I have to live like this?

Do I even exist?

The stars turn above her. She can smell bergamot and chamomile and old lady powder.

#

The phone rings just after she's crawled into bed. She flips on the light. There's a message scrawled on a piece of paper under the bedside lamp. *When my sister calls, tell her I need her to come home.*

She thunders downstairs, rips the phone out of its cradle. "Hello?"

"Lina."

"I need you to come home. Dad's stopped sending money." This is the most they've ever spoken about Dad and Gran and her sister leaving in the night. Lina feels like she's falling and flying all at once. "If you come home, we can share the..." What is it she does? Guarding sounds wrong. Watching sounds too active. Existing feels right but doesn't sound right. "We can look after Gran together. Take turns going out. It won't be so bad with the two of us." The silence stretches out, Lina's knuckles are hurting, she's gripping the phone so hard. "Please. I need you."

"Lina." Her sister's voice is broken. "I can't come home. Don't you think I've tried?" And now her sister is crying down the phone. "I can't find the way. I've driven past our old school and the post office and the bakery but there's no road I can turn down that leads to home. And I can't stop. I buy coffee and I have a bite to eat and I think this is a nice place to settle down and then I'm back in the truck again and the road is moving beneath me." Her sobs are barely audible over the roar of the tyres. "Why do you think I call? I want to come home. But there's no home for me anymore."

Lina slides down the wall and lands with a thump on the floorboards. She can't find anything comforting to say. "How long have you been gone?"

"I don't know. Things have changed, though. Even Dalwallinu."

Lina can't imagine their tiny, sleepy town changing. "What am I going to do? They'll cut off the electricity, the phone. And what happens if...if I can't feed us? If I die, will the world end?"

"I don't know."

"Help me."

"I can send you some money, if you give me Dad's account number. Wait, let me pull over."

Lina wants to ask where her sister is, but she's

afraid if she loses focus she'll forget, and hang up, and she'll have to wait until her sister calls again. She reads out the numbers.

"I'll do it first thing."

"Thanks, um…" She scratches at her memory. "I'm sorry, I can't remember your name."

"It's Angie. Lina, it's Angie. Please don't forget me."

"I won't. I won't."

There's a long, long silence. Lina feels like she should be crying, but she's not.

"Promise me you'll always answer the phone," says her sister.

"I promise."

#

Lina waits forty-eight hours to be certain, putting off the moment when she finds out if she has money or not.

"That's fine," says the woman on the other end of the phone. "What time would you like delivery?"

She arranges for a morning delivery and hangs up the phone. She washes up. Sweeps the floor. Dusts. Washes anything and everything and hangs it out to dry on the Hills Hoist under the burning sun.

When she comes inside, mist is sneaking out from behind the cabinet doors. She slides them open. There is the town, and the girl's house, and there, sliding out between the big doors, beautiful thing, is a flying machine. It's as blue as the sky, stubby body with bright woven wings flapping in the cold wind coming off the mountain. The people are gathered around and as Lina leans in the girl pushes off. Wings spread, colours catching the light, and the world changes.

There is hope.

There is hope.

There is hope.

#

The phone rings. Lina hurries down the stairs, tea tray jangling in her hands. Her grandmother's answers are often not answers at all, but Lina is listening harder now, and is making plans.

"Hello?" It's her sister. Lina has been waiting for this call for days, and the end of excitement is a heart in flight. "Listen, I — what's your name? I forgot again."

"Angie. Did the money come through okay?"

"Yes. Angie. Listen. You said you come through Dalwallinu. When?"

"I don't know. I'm up on the Queensland coast. It could be a while. But Lina, I can't find the road. I've tried."

"It doesn't matter. I'm coming to meet you." As she says it, she remembers bright wings fluttering, lifted above the crowd by the wind. "At the post office. You can find that, right?"

"I can, but what about Gran?"

"I'll come at night. I'll be back before morning. We can have an hour at least. Together. And we can talk." She wants to tell her sister her idea. But she's afraid that if she says it out loud it will float away like natal seeds in the wind.

#

When Gran goes to bed Lina gets on her bike. It's old, but she's had two weeks to get it into shape for the ride.

Not so much herself. Muscles that she hasn't used for years complain, burning and tight as she pedals the bike up the long, sloping road to the crest. Everything is yellow until you reach the top, that much she remembers, and then the colours change, grey-green and red and brown and white spread out below.

She pedals faster, up the hill with the red dust in a plume behind her, afraid the town won't be there, that she's lost in these canola fields and she'll never come out again. But there are the lights spread out below her, more lights than she expected.

The bike glides down the gentle slope, past fields dotted with sheep. At some point she's crossed a line; the air is cooler, and she knows it's not summer anymore. She glories in the feel of it, the lonely curlew's cry and the soft smell of rain.

The post office has changed, dotted with air conditioning units, with a dish on the roof pointing at the stars. Lina leans her bike against the bricks and curls up against the red bricks. Crickets creak, cicadas sing. She cannot be lonely in a night so full of voices.

Her sister's arrival is heralded by the rumble of a truck engine, drowning out the night voices. Lina squints in the light. Angie. Angie is here.

Her heart lifts from her chest and flies to her sister. Angie. She can remember her name.

#

They're sipping milkshakes, parked out front of the roadhouse that used to be at the edge of town, but is now nearer the middle. Lina feels out of time. No, she is out of time. A bulrush in a stream that's flowed on past her. Angie has flowed too, and Lina can't help reaching up now and then, to touch a brow carved by time, hands worn and hard with cares.

"I stopped crying about home a long time ago," says Angie. "I keep moving, and that helps. I thought about asking you to come and meet me. But I couldn't risk it. I don't even know why I can call."

Lina doesn't either, but she's glad Angie can. "Gran said there are more of...me, somewhere." She outlines her plan, to advertise in the paper in the hopes that someone will see it and reach out to her. Hopes that Angie can help, can drop letters off, can search in towns and cities all across this wide land.

Angie laughs, and starts talking, and Lina learns new words — iPhone, Google, cable internet — and suddenly the world is spreading out like a landscape below her.

Angie gives her a list, written on the back of a registration receipt, with Angie's name at the top. Lina clutches it to her chest. Her new life, written on the back of discarded paper.

The sun creaks up over the horizon. "Dawn already?" says Angie, frowning.

It's not. Fingers of red fire stretch across the sky, reaching for the earth.

Lina fumbles for the door handle.

Angie starts the truck. "Wait, Lina. I'll drive."

The truck roars down the road toward home. People are coming out of their houses, leaning out windows, pointing up at the angry sky. They turn a corner, onto the long stretch of road that makes the gentle climb to home, and Lina chokes.

The canola fields are marching across the land, consuming everything; wheat, mallee, sheep, all fall beneath the yellow wave as it crashes across the world.

"Lina—" says Angie, as the truck jerks to the side. The road disappears. "I can't —"

"Close your eyes," says Lina, "I'll guide you."

The truck forges ahead. The canola wave hits the bonnet and everything is a sea of yellow, the crunch and stink of plants crushed beneath their wheels. The canola clears and there is the house. The truck lurches to a stop.

Angie is frozen, staring ahead, not seeing anything.

Like a visitor.

Lina tumbles out of the door and races to the house under a sky black and empty of stars.

She bursts through the door.

Gran is in the kitchen, the Gran she knew so long ago. Before she went upstairs. Before everything changed. "Tea cake's nearly ready. Put the kettle on, will you?"

In a dream, Lina presses the button on the kettle. It's solid and warm under her finger. A locust smacks against the window and sits for a moment, dazed. Washing flaps on the clothesline. There's no truck in the yard. There's no sun in the black sky.

"Gran —" She can't catch her breath. Is everything gone? Her sister? The world? "Gran, you need to go upstairs."

"Hand me the oven mitt, Lina. Would you like tea or milk? I can put sugar and vanilla in it."

She knows there's no vanilla in the cupboard. "I don't — Gran, what about the world?"

Gran bends down and takes the cake out of the oven. "Isn't this what you've wanted all along? Not to have to watch, all the time? Not to have to stay? I heard you, Lina. I always do. I don't like seeing you sad."

"But everything is gone."

"Ah, well. I didn't say the other way was better."

Lina's cheeks are wet. "Can't I have both, Gran? Can't I have the world and you?"

The tea cake steams on the benchtop, the top cracked, showing slices of apple browned by the oven. Gran dusts it with cinnamon and sugar and the smell is childhood and comfort. "No."

The silence outside seeps through the walls. Lina doesn't understand how it's so bright outside when there's no sky, no sun. "Is this a lesson?"

"I'm not your teacher. I'm your grandmother. If you want me to stay, I stay. I only care about what you want."

Lina walks around the bench and wraps her arms around Gran, feels the bird bones beneath her, smells the soft powder smell. Thinks about forever in this kitchen, her grandmother and teacake and peace. The world no longer her responsibility.

She never wanted to go away. She just wanted to be free.

"Come on, Gran. I'll make the tea. We can eat upstairs."

Gran smiles, and makes her bent way up the stairs while Lina carries the tea tray, but she thinks there is approval in her eyes when she sits down in the cane chair.

Outside cicadas sing again, locusts crackle in the long grass and the Whistling Kite screams to the blue sky.

#

Lina goes out into the yard in the evening. There are tyre tracks in the dust at the end of the drive. She pulls out the piece of paper where her sister wrote the instructions.

It doesn't matter that she can't remember her sister's name.

Inside, she leaves the door to the cabinet open so she can watch the mountain as she makes her calls. She needs internet, and a computer, and a lot of practice with new ideas and concepts.

Maybe she can never leave, but she doesn't have to be isolated anymore. She's going to find the others, wherever they are. In Australia. All over the world. Maybe further than that.

There are wings on her mountain. She watches them tumble and dip below the alien sky, and dreams.

About the author

Meryl Stenhouse lives in subtropical Queensland where she curates an extensive notebook collection and fights a running battle with the Lego models trying to take over the house. She's currently revisiting Le Guin's *Earthsea* and finding it just as magical as when she first read it. She has stories in *Shimmer, Aurealis,* and upcoming in the *Mother of Invention* anthology. She's currently co-writing a book on writing science fiction with two other scientists. Find her on Twitter @merylstenhouse.

Letters to the Earth

Caleb Warner

Postmarked: 8/14/17

Dear Gabriel,

    I had to lock Meemaw in her closet to keep her from coming down while I wrote this. The envelopes were in her room, and she kept asking me if I was writing a letter. She grabbed a hold of my wrist. "Jacob," she said, "you ain't got the handwriting for that, Jacob son of Isaac. You gon' let me do that. Who we writing to?" I have no idea who Jacob is. Dad's name was Joshua.

    I didn't bother telling her I was typing it out. Didn't bother to correct the name either. Do you know how bad the alz' has gotten? I keep trying to tell you, but I guess you just don't get it. Anywho, I'm writing this and addressing it to your company. Maybe they'll find a way to get it to you. Don't know. Don't know how those things might work. Don't know if you're even alive. Company says you are. Says you're on a route to Minneapolis. So I guess I just assume you don't answer your phone anymore.

    Anywho, getting off track here, I'm writing for the same reason I keep calling: I need money (remember Malcovich? "Geeve dat man hiz mooooneeey"). Please paypal it to me. Just google how to do it. Your checks are all well and good, as little as they may be, but I can't do much with them. Can't do much with the green stuff either. Again, nice gesture, I'm not trying to say you aren't sending money. I just need the digital kind.

I can't leave the house.

Maybe you'll believe it if it's actually written down. You were here. You saw what happened when she came downstairs. Now I'm stuck here trying and failing to keep her on her rocker and off the ground. No. Maybe you don't remember. Maybe people forget about it when they leave. Maybe you just like ignoring it.

So let me give ya a refreshah.

If she comes downstairs, if brings those feet of hers in contact with good old terra-firma, then bye bye. Hasta La Vista Baby. Fissures'll split from here to the Androscoggin river valley. Darkness will blot out the sun. Rivers running with blood. All that happiness. And I can't keep her locked up long. No matter what I do, those locks disintegrate.

Regardless, need the money to pay the bills. I can get to the mailbox to get your checks but I can't goddamn well spend them or cash them anywhere. So yeah, send money please.

Wouldn't mind a phone call either, asshole. Or at least a letter back. I have the same conversations with Meemaw every day. Mostly about when this Jacob guy apparently built the stairs to that old house. Most days I just go along with it. Some days I just can't stand to hear the story again and shout at the poor old gal. If I had my way, the stairs would come right out and Meemaw'd be up in that attic until her bones crystalmogrified or something.

Anywho, you know where I live.

-Your brother Stan

#

Postmarked: 9/7/17

Gabe,

Shouldn't have expected a return letter/call. I know that. I should have known that anyway. Thanks for the money, though. That at least lets me know you got the letter. We're afloat another day! Still have internet for another day too. I can't really find the time to do much on it but flick over Twitter. No time for porn when you're living with a geriatric, am I right? Slow as balls out in the sticks anyway. Why watch anything if it can't be in HD, yeah?

Anywho, Auntie Diana sent me a package. FedEx guy dropped it off just two days ago. Wanted to tell you about it. This thing's supposed to be Meemaw's. Maybe I thought since you're reading these letters you must at least believe what I'm saying or remember or be humoring me. It's a sideboard. Got a mountain in it. I think it's that old Sinai. The rust colored peaks and plateaus stretch into a yellowing horizon every time I open up the doors to look in the side board. It's always sunrise every time I open it.

Auntie sent a card with it too. "Happy Early 22nd" she had written on the outside fold. Inside: "I remember when I hit that century. Enjoy! You'll only be this young once! I know it's super early, but I needed to get this to you. This sideboard belonged to Meemaw. Maybe it will bring you as much wisdom as it brought her."

Early happy birthday to me I guess. Lot of good that wisdom did for Meemaw, though, right? She can't even remember to use the bathroom. Maybe—if you knew anything about what alz' does—you could already guess it. She wears diapers, Gabe. She shits her pants on the daily. Guess who does the changes? I'm not resentful, just saying. And no matter what I feed her, her shit always comes out like yellow puss and leaks all through the diaper. Then I have to clean her pants too. Too much for a letter, I know. I hear you. I just wanted you to know.

For now, I'm just going to keep gawking at the mountain here. The FedEx man helped me put the sideboard in the laundry room. I didn't want Meemaw to see this old thing. I didn't know what would happen.

Here's something else: Meemaw came downstairs when I went to drop off that first letter in the mailbox. Do you remember any tremors in the Earth? Maybe a little blood in your drinking water? I bolted back to the farmhouse. The sun was low in the sky and the yellow siding looked burnt red. A family of raccoons ambled out from under the south porch and all at once their eyes exploded out of their heads and their bodies convulsed to some hidden apocalyptic gong. A murder of crows dropped stone cold dead out of the sky.

I nearly tripped over some Ten-Commandment lawn ornaments as I ran across the yard. They were Styrofoam political lawn signs meant to look like the two stone tablets. They were old, from when people were freaking out about courthouses taking them off their lawns.

"Come on in, Jakie!" Meemaw called as she heard me rip open the screen door. "Making your favorite! Roast brisket and some babka. Need some meat on them bones!"

I found her in the kitchen pouring flour into a blender. Something had caught in the oven too. Actually caught. I could see a flame there. It smelled like burning human hair. I tell you though, bro, I thought about letting her stay down there. What did I have? What *do* I have? I've got a brother that won't write me back or call; a granny that insists on coming down and accidentally destroying the world; oh and Mount Sinai in a sideboard.

I sure as shit wasn't going to eat whatever monstrosity that Meemaw created, but it felt nice, you know? To have someone doing something for *me* for a change. Saw something the other day, some motivational meme or something. It said, "We judge ourselves by our intentions and others by their actions." I hate memes. As a rule, I hate them. But as I stood in the doorway to the kitchen and watched Meemaw destroy both the countertop and the world, I thought about that phrase in all its platitudinal goriness. Here was a lady that couldn't remember who I really was, didn't know up from down or shit from shinola. Here she was trying to *make* me something. Every day that she tries to get downstairs she's trying to *do* something for *me*.

I guess you wouldn't get it. You send money and do the old Pontius Pilot dance (ain't that the hip new swing all the kids are doing, ha!). And here I am judging you by your actions and not by your intentions. So let me do that for a second.

You are not intending to help me. You are intending

to get me off your back. That much is so painfully clear. You don't respond. You just do the dance, wash your hands, and keep on shuckin'. Keep on truckin' if you'll excuse the pun. Get it? Cause you're a truck driver? Whatever. All this is one big fucking digression.

Obviously, the world didn't end. I scooted granny upstairs again. Soon as I did, the rumbling stopped. The earth quit *its* dance too.

"This ain't right, Jakie," she told me as I all but lifted her up Jacob's stairs. The bastards were steep too. Jakie built them more like a ladder than actual useful stairs. Then Meemaw must have had a moment of clarity. She screamed and slapped at my back, at my face. "It ain't right you keeping me locked up here like you's ashamed of me," she said over and over again. I got her upstairs and into her room.

With a bit more necessary prodding, she laid down on her bed. She went to sleep a few minutes later, tired from the episode, unable to keep screaming. I tucked the flowery yellow comforter around her, and I left and shut the attic door behind me. I sat down on the bottom step of Jacob's stairs and let it all wash over me. It was a deep feeling of shame, like being caught in the middle of a naughty act. I don't know why, but it tied my stomach up in one big fucking knot. Like a fist, that knot sat there and squeezed at my insides.

I didn't have time for the kind of reflection I'm doing now, the kind that helps untie those knots you know? I had to clean those dead raccoons up while Meemaw was asleep. While I did that, I half-hoped she woke up again. If she did, I decided that I would let her stay down there. I just couldn't push her back upstairs again like that. With her screaming at me and wailing on me with her boney arms. I couldn't do that again. I would be lying if I said that I didn't take my sweet time cleaning up the bloody mess of raccoons. I couldn't think. I just wanted it over at that moment.

Anywho, figured I'd tell you all that crap and then ask you for more money. I'm not blaming you at all. It was me who went and had to go send this letter via good ol' snail mail.

So yeah, if you could send it along via paypal again, "that'd be great" (remember Office Space?). Not a threat, but if it were I guess it would be a good one.

As for Sinai in the sideboard? Seems I can't fit through the door, so I'm stuck just looking at it. Sometimes it's more interesting than Twitter, and it's definitely more interesting than most of what Meemaw has to say. I can only look at it when she's asleep though. I barely get any time to myself.

Okay, okay. I'm done complaining and 'poor old me'ing. Send the money. Give me a call.

I'm lonely.

(That was hard to write you asshole, and I had to erase it a thousand times. Just so you know!)

-Your brother Stan

#

Postmarked: 12/26/17

Thanks for the money. All I do now is watch the mountain and keep Meemaw upstairs. I buy a new lock online every three or four days or so. Sometimes the locks break quickly, sometimes they don't. Depends on how bad she wants to get downstairs. They do all disintegrate eventually. Can't keep a grammy down apparently. Or up, I guess. Buying them every few days keeps me in steady supply of them. I can't really afford to buy them all at once, given your rate of sending me money. You're the only one who does. I write to others, you know? Not long diatribes like these, but I do write. And call. You seem to be the only one answering them. In money at least.

Also, happy birthday to me, and late Merry Xmas to you. I remember Dad always made sure to give me a birthday *and* a Christmas even though they were only a day apart. One of those great sorts of things where intentions and actions are one in the same, don't you think? And the man never even thought about his own birthday. Never asked for a damn thing.

How's the mountain? It's all I really do any more, look out across that mountain. That's probably why you brought it up, right? You can see how much it means to me. I figured out if I leave the doors open, then time passes. I've been able to watch the sunset over the rocky cliffs quite a few times. About a week ago I started seeing the small forms of people meandering just below the summit. Believe that? Well there's this too: just lately the people seem to be gathering. A whole mess of them down there, looking like a heap of black spots on the golden sand.

Sometimes I can hear them chanting. Other times I hear them weeping. Strangest thing. I keep wondering… is that what made granny wise or is it what made her lose her mind?

She didn't come downstairs when I delivered the last letter to the mailbox by the way. Not for lacking of trying, though. I don't really want to get into the particulars of it. She's been getting more violent lately. I think it was the last taste of the downstairs she got. That feeling of normalcy or something. I'm trying not to get too navel gazing with it. Suffice to say I trim her nails when she sleeps now.

Anyway, just thought I'd keep you updated. That's all I got for now. Wish I had more. But if wishes were fishes we'd all be vegan. Or something about nets. I don't know.

-Your brother Stan
P.S.
Broke as shit. Send money.

#

Postmarked: 12/31/17
Dear Gabriel,

Last letter. When I put this one in the mailbox I'm letting her come downstairs. Don't worry. I'll give it some time to get to you. Maybe a week or two. Given how long it takes for you to send money after letters, that seems like a safe bet. I hope it reaches you earlier than that. Give you some time to put your affairs in order. Maybe you can get in contact with our *other* brother, you know the one. He's the one who needs to get his shit together.

Why?

I told Meemaw about the sideboard.

"Do you remember your old sideboard, Meemaw," I asked her. "The one with the mountain in it? Pretty weird."

"That's that old Sinai," she said, and her eyes lost their usual cloudiness. She rubbed the thumb of her left hand against the palm of her right. "Bit worn down. Smoothed it all out after a while." She yanked away her thumb like her palm grew suddenly searing hot. She stuck her thumb in her mouth, and when she took it out I saw a cut across the pad. It oozed blood from between her deep wrinkles. "But damn how they're still sharp enough."

"What did you do with that?" I asked her. And I felt like laughing then. "What could you do with a whole mountain?"

She looked at me, but she also looked *through* me. "Didn't put it in there to keep. Put it in there to keep it *safe*."

"Safe from what?"

Her eyes darkened. I didn't know eyes could do that. But like a switch I saw the light of recognition go out of them. "Don't... Can't... I think I've seen you before. Do you know my Jacob?"

"We're talking about your sideboard, Meemaw. Why do you need to keep the mountain safe?"

The light half returned. "My sideboard? You got that old thing?"

"Auntie gave it to me for my birthday."

"My sideboard... I'd sure like to see that old thing. Can you take me to it?"

"I... I can't, Meemaw."

"Why?"

Every day I used to try and tell her that the world would end if she came downstairs. I stopped because she never really got it. Of course, I never explained it properly, I'm sure.

"Well, Meemaw, if you go downstairs then all the people die. They die like..." I searched for something, "they die and go away like Jacob went away."

Meemaw smiled then. Smiled like I had just said

something ridiculous. Like I said the sky was pink. "Jacob ain't dead, honey-dear," she said. "Jacob safe in my sideboard. Don't know where I put that damn thing, but he's there all right. I'll show you if I find it sometime. He's safe. Him and his kin for a long while yet. Now did I hear you say it's your birthday?"

How she only remembered that I'm not sure. Her brain is a soup and sometimes only the most useless things float to the top. "Yes," I told her.

"How old you turning?"

"This will be my 22nd."

"You going to let me bake you a cake? I may not be much to look at, but I'm at my best when I'm making stuff. Cakes especially. You know what's so great about making cakes? You get to make every bit of it. Each layer like a little bit of you. And of course, you cover the whole thing with a whole gob of icing. And then you get to eat it! Can't do that with craggy old mountains."

You can stop sending money, Gabriel. We won't need money for any longer. I was under some delusion that my task would end, but it won't. Not ever. And for God's sake I just want someone to do something for *me* for once.

I've opened the sideboard up. And when she comes downstairs I'm going to show it to her. Maybe she can show something to me. Maybe she'll not be bothered and want to make me a cake instead.

I've decided. I'm going to eat whatever she makes. And when the earth opens up to swallow us I'm going to be smiling.

I'm writing this letter in the hopes that you'll find something to smile about too.

Your beloved brother, Stan

P.S.

Happy New Year!

About the author

Caleb Warner works as the Assistant Coordinator of Indiana University East's Writing Center, and he spends what little free time he has writing works of fiction. His work has previously appeared in *Metaphorosis, The Literary Hatchet, Fickle Muses,* and *Chantwood Magazine.* He also has an interview with award winning poet Amy Pickworth published in *Tributaries Journal of Creative Arts.* He currently resides in Richmond, Indiana, part of the Whitewater River Valley basin. Follow him on Twitter: @carner_waleb

The Fourth Pillar Says No

L. Chan

This morning, at precisely 10:23am, I saved the world. Again. Ah Ma was five steps from ground floor, from ground zero, from the end of the world. You wouldn't know it by looking at her, in her silk pyjamas, smelling a bit like leaked urine, a bit like breakfast, a bit like dinner. What, with her grey hair and her greyer eyes. Her skin parchment thin, mapped with the green tributaries of veins, the brown isles of liver spots. No, she decidedly doesn't look like she's holding up the sky.

There's a lurch when she hits the step with one wrinkled foot, a moment of disequilibrium, of careful order upended. There's a wobble as normalcy resumes when I take her by the limp hand and bring her back up to her room.

There's a time, an apical moment, when you stop growing up and you start growing down. At that point, time stops in your room, and that's when the dying started. The time, for Ah Ma's room, was somewhere in the seventies. With the old Chinese wall calendar, peeled off a sheet at a time for each day, with its own fortune, zodiac, and element, gone from paper white to yellow to curling brown. Teresa Teng is on the record player, though it has not spun for years and dust has obliterated all grooves on the vinyl.

I set Ah Ma back down on her bed, and turn the

volume up on the television. Free to air doesn't cut it anymore, so I've rigged up a twenty-three inch LCD in front of the old CRT, and I've got Youtube streaming Shaw Brothers and Cathay, the stretched out formats of the sixties looking comically awkward with black bookends. The keys are in the door and I think for the hundredth time that I should lock her away, seal the apocalypse. That's just silly, of course. What good are two inches of brass against the end of the world?

#

Back when the world was young and fluid and hot, there wasn't one sun, but ten. When they all came out to frolic, they scorched the earth, boiling seas and roasting livestock in the fields.

Strange, right girl?

Ten suns? Maybe.

A great archer named Yi emerged and shot nine of the ten suns with his bow, leaving one, the one that plies the skies today. And thus the world was saved.

Eat your porridge, Ah Ma.

No, it's too hot, la.

Blow on it.

After Hou Yi saved the world from the suns, he battled monsters to make the world safe for people. The first one he fought was a wind monster.

Just eat the damn porridge, Ah Ma.

#

I check my bank account. Pa sends money, not much, but enough. A drip feed, like the water torture they used on prisoners of war. The anticipation of the next drop another step in the staircase to madness. Do you know how much you can get done from home? A lot. Enough for me to be caretaker, nurse, and jailor. Enough for me to be the saviour of the world just before breakfast.

Cleaning is an obsession. I am as much prisoner as I am jailor. The stakes are too high, and my punishment is a surfeit of time. I mop the old termite-eaten flooring, I destroy the spun homes of spiders in the cornices, I sweep the staircase. This is an old money house, two-storey terrace in a part of town that used to be nice. Pa got it before the boom, bust, boom of the eighties and nineties. Now that it's all paid off, the trickle of money keeps us just too poor to sell. Not that we could move anyway, not anymore. I make sure that everything is in just the right place, keep the house unchanging, locked in time so that Ah Ma knows where she is.

Once a week, I take deliveries from an online grocery. Five minutes of human interaction is all I get but I spend it focusing on the sound of the crinkle of plastic, tracing the spiderweb cracks on the iPhone I use to sign for the delivery.

Email is next, when Ah Ma is asleep. Kor has written again, this time from Phnom Penh. *Bad flight,* he says, *turbulence dropped the budget airline plane near fifty metres.* Timing seems to match Ah Ma's earlier jaunt down the stairs, a little reminder about responsibility in the household. My brother takes short haul flights around the region, sometimes venturing out a little further; Shanghai maybe. He grew up to be the spitting image of our father, the same thickness around the trunk, gravity ravaging jowl, neck, and musculature identically. I used to think he took up the job because he liked the sky; now I think he wants to spend as much time away from Ah Ma and me as physically possible.

Blame and guilt come and go, dance partners in my head. Tempo upshifting, downshifting. I blame him for leaving, I feel guilty for wanting to leave, and vice versa, rinse and repeat. That's all there is now, rinsing and repeating. Ah Ma raised the two of us, now I'm taking care of her. We've come full circle; diapers, baths, and spoon-feeding. Repeat and rinse. It's time for a bath.

#

In the time of Yao, most sagacious of the early emperors, there arose a flood, the likes of which had never been seen before nor has been seen since.

Come la, Ah Ma, it's just a bath.

There's too much water.

There was much suffering in the land; crops failed, livestock drowned. The populace climbed onto mountains that had become hills, gnawed on pine needles to survive. The emperor commissioned Gun, a count, to solve the problem.

That's not so bad, right Ah Ma?

It's too cold, la.

I'll turn up the heat.

Gun failed to control the floodwaters for many years. Finally, half crazed with failure, and more desperate than a trapped fox, he stole some dirt from the court of the heavens, using that to build dykes and levees that even the raging waters could not breach. For his trouble, the heavenly emperor decreed his execution.

I'm letting the water out, Ah Ma.

I don't want to go yet.

You have to, you'll catch a cold.

#

We were little dragons, Ah Ma told my brother and I when we were young, her voice dark and rough-edged, like a stone from deep in the earth. There we were, born twelve years apart, under the sign of the dragon. So was my father. Ah Ma was different back then, quick to dole out sweets and kisses, a rigid bulwark against a parent's wrath.

And then Mother died.

How do you describe that, the imbalance, the listing of your world? A terrible unbalancing emptiness, a hole so deep that it pulled everything else in my life towards it. Everything listed sideways, in the least expected of ways. Waking to a damp pillow, coming home to an empty refrigerator. It's the difference of a millimetre of jam on your bread in the morning: nobody can tell but you.

Ah Ma stepped up. But she couldn't be both.

I didn't mean to hate Ah Ma, of course, not at first. It was a slow thing, a resentment at someone filling in a space that I wanted to preserve. I answered back a little more quickly, I had to gag down our shared dinners, was a little slower with my chores, where I did them at all.

So did Pa and Kor, in their own ways. Pa had business overseas, travelled a lot. Then his suitcases started getting bigger, his time at the old house shorter. Dragons, said Ah Ma, could not stay still. And so the time Pa spent at home grew less and less, his room no longer smelling of him, the smell of aftershave and hair cream slowly overpowered by naphthalene. But the room had died long before that, when Mother's smell went away, her old perfume dry in its crystal cut bottle, her clothes yellow with age and grey with dust. The key to my parent's bedroom was rusty iron, scuffed from the time I closed their door for the last time and tried to snap the key in the lock.

Kor went next, moving out with a nice enough girl, finishing his pilot's training and taking to the skies. Good place for a dragon to be, said Ah Ma. I'm not sure how far she'd gone by then. When do grains of sand become a pile? When she frowned as she tried to remember her appointments, or how she went for the whole day with her blouse misbuttoned. When does a pile become a mountain? When Ah Ma spent the week calling me by her sister's name. When she skipped five meals in a row because she insisted she'd already eaten.

Ah Ma slowly became adrift in time and space, a time traveler locked in her own mind, a curious explorer in a world of decreasing size and increasing complexity. I should have gone, like Pa and Kor. All the dragons in my life, losing themselves in the skies. And then the world started to tilt.

#

The sky was held up by four pillars, one for each direction. The demon Gong Gong waged war against the gods and lost. In his anger, he struck one of the pillars, causing the sky to tilt and collapse.

Stay still Ah Ma, I need to tie your hair up.

When's your father coming home?

Nuwa, the mother goddess, cut the leg from giant tortoise and used it to replace the pillar.

When's your brother coming home?

I don't know, I don't know.

The fourth pillar was not the same height as the other three, and the world was forever changed. That is why rivers flow to the southeast in China.

The tortoise wasn't good enough, was it?

I can't braid your hair like this Ah Ma. I can't. I can't do anything, anymore.

And the world went on.

#

Water torture isn't about the pressure of the droplets, but the wait in between. The punishment wasn't Pa's absence, but the wait, never knowing if that drop was the last one. It turned out that Pa sent his last bank transfer on a rainy day in July. Then it all stopped.

#

Ah Ma was still upstairs, keeping the world intact, while mine fell apart. Except mine wasn't a fever dream of melting myth and shifting memories, my world was more prosaic, consisting of a bank balance hurtling to zero at terminal velocity, food unreplaced, soap unpurchased.

I never stopped to wonder when the unbalancing started; perhaps it was down to the second Mother left. And even if Ah Ma stepped up, it was never quite the same. The slant, the incline, the essential wrongness of a world that Pa and Kor couldn't bear to watch. Now it was just me and Ah Ma, her propping up the world and me propping her up.

And we were going to hit the ground.

#

I can't remember when I last left the house. If I leave the world ends. Ah Ma's living in a shrinking circle of stability, her mind a moth-eaten patchwork quilt of misremembering. Perhaps I could have tied her down somehow, to her bed. I've thought about it, tie her down like she ties me down to the house of my childhood. I got as far as a looped strip of cloth over her wrist to the bedframe when she let loose with a howl as raw as an animal fit to gnaw its leg off and I knew then that if I followed through, the world would have ended in a different way.

Just before we crash, I give in. I ask Kor for help. As with all good things, it comes too late.

#

It was a cheque. Registered mail. Which I missed.

Ah Ma is asleep, she does this more and more now. I've not been beyond the gates of the old house in... has it been years? I can make it. I'll Uber it down to the post office, I'll get the cheque, and have it at a bank and be back within the hour. Going past the threshold of the house presents me with an unfamiliar vertigo, the same way I imagine an astronaut must feel, leaving the embrace of Earth's gravity. It's disorienting and liberating, to see so many people. To see the things that you can't get delivered, hear sounds that the internet cannot transmit, smell freshly baked bread.

It's so intoxicating that I'm already holding two bags of shopping when I feel the world start to tilt again.

#

By the time I get back to the house, it's even more pronounced. Not as bad as when Ah Ma came down the stairs an eternity ago, but with the promise of far worse to come. I'm not sure if I feel that the birds in the sky are working a little harder, if the weeds aren't angled ever so slightly to the side.

Ah Ma's in the kitchen, further away from her room than she's been in years. She managed to dress herself, hair tied back in a functional bun. Flour streaks her face, dusts her blouse like snowfall. The last of the minced pork from the fridge is in her hands, glistening pink and being kneaded into thumb sized lumps. There are already half a dozen formed dumplings in a bamboo steamer, the pale yellow skins pinched and folded into puckers to seal the meat within, just like Mother used to make, Xiao Long Bao.

She can't be this far from her room, this far from the centre. The last few metres to reach my grandmother feel so steeply upslope that I have to hold on to the furniture to drag myself towards her. I see the jars of spices and herbs wobble, and an onion begins to roll. Ah Ma notices me and smiles, her teeth browned from a lifetime of strong tea.

"I made these for you, just how you like."

I'm not sure she even knows what she's capable of. She's holding up the world, my grandmother is.

"You can't be down here, Ah Ma," I manage, the words slithering snakelike through my gritted teeth.

"Xiao Long. Sounds like little dragons, doesn't it? Like you and your brother?" She's oblivious to my discomfort, oblivious to the damage she's causing. It comes back through me, a wave of resentment tamped down so deep that I've never even acknowledged its presence. Being trapped here, while my father and brother roamed free. Parenting the woman who parented me, whose body didn't even have the good grace to give out when her mind had only become an itinerant tenant of her skull.

"Just stop!" And when it comes out, it comes out like the scream of a dragon through the clouds, the howl of supersonic wind over scales larger than car tires, whistling around teeth and claws longer than a man's arm. When colour leeches back around the edges of my vision and I can hear more than the sound of my own blood roaring through my veins, Ah Ma is backed into a corner of the kitchen, shrunken into herself as though some animating force has leaked out. The bamboo steamer is on its side, its contents scattered across the floor.

She goes to her hands and knees, picking up the fallen dumplings, blubbering that she can make more, it isn't a problem. Of course, it is, but the problem isn't her. It is me. I get down on the ground next to her, closing my hand over hers and wondering when it was that mine got to be so much larger than hers.

"You have to be a strong girl, you know. Your mother isn't around anymore. I'll never fill her shoes, but I know you'll be every inch the woman your mother was, burning brighter than a star, soaring higher than the clouds." An old conversation again. Ah Ma's eyes had smoked over with age, a little unfocused from seeing me as the child I used to be. I hold her close, long arms around her back, feeling those old bones press against me and the world dizzyingly, infuriatingly, returns to balance.

"I'll clean up, Ah Ma, you should rest." I lead the old woman back up the stairs. The end of the world can wait. Maybe tomorrow, maybe next year, maybe never. We go on, she and I, in a creaking house without the smell of a mother. I'm doing the work for two as we take one step at a time; Ah Ma's hair is in my face and perhaps I haven't forgotten the smell of my mother after all.

###

About the author

L Chan hails from Singapore, where he alternates being walked by his dog and writing speculative fiction after work. His work has appeared in places like *Liminal Stories, Arsenika, Podcastle,* and *the Dark.* He tweets occasionally @lchanwrites.

Howl at the Moon

T. R. North

Sharon looked up from her book, lips pursed. Nothing. But something had alerted her, hadn't it? Some subliminal thing noticed without noticing, some neural subroutine twitching out an alarm, some thin tendril sweeping out and saying *pay attention.* The soft click of claws on hardwood was the only further warning she got before an enormous eight-eyed wolf came loping down the stairs.

"Damn it, Gran!"

Sharon burst off the couch and dashed toward her, book flying, throw rugs churned out of place. Sharon caught her grandmother by the mane on the first landing, setting bony shoulder against fur-covered sternum to shove her back up to the second floor. The wolf had gravity and age on her side, and Sharon could feel the house contract and buckle around them as she mustered every ounce of strength she had to push her grandmother back, up, *away.*

"We've talked about this! You promised!" Sharon panted.

The stairs coiled under their feet, serpentine and alive, giving Sharon the last advantage she needed to shove Gran into the laundry room off the stairs and shut the door. She leaned against it, chest heaving as she caught her breath. On the other side, the wolf was pacing, calm as a glacier. Sharon waited until her heart stopped racing, then reached out and put the house in order. The stairs unwound, the baseboards slithered into place snug against the wall, and the rugs righted themselves. After a few more minutes, the four-fold footfall of the wolf shifted, became the soft-slippered shuffle of a biped.

"Sharon, are you there?" Gran called.

Sharon pushed herself to her feet and opened the door. "Right here, Gran, sorry."

"Why am I in the laundry room?" Gran asked, befuddled and peering at her. Behind her lids, Gran's eyes were the same polished amber as the wolf's, and lit from within by a soft glow, as if she'd already eaten the sun.

"You tried to take off again," Sharon said, pushing her hair out of her face.

Gran blinked, then sucked at too-sharp teeth. "Why don't we watch the news together?"

"Or we could go through photo albums, if you want," Sharon suggested. Sometimes it helped for Gran to see pictures from when she'd still thought of herself as Lillian and won prizes for the roses that now sprawled, feral and leggy, over the property outside. When she'd doted on her children and fussed over her husband and been the life of parties, before the weight of what she was had worn the human part of her as thin and wispy as the white hair framing her face.

"The news, pup," Gran said firmly.

Sharon ducked into the bathroom, one eye on Gran in case she changed her mind, and the other eye on the mirror. Sharon wrinkled her nose and puckered her lips, then frowned. She'd fix the too-prominent cheekbones and canines and nose later, after Gran went to bed. It wasn't bad, as these things went, but there had been a moment when Sharon had flexed her muscles and let strength counter strength, a moment when she'd started to slip around the edges herself.

"Once upon a time there were things which walked this earth, and we worshipped them as gods because there was nothing else to call them." Her father had told the story like a fairytale, when she was younger. "They were from a place beyond time and understanding, and they basked in our young sun and gorged on our bounty, and eventually, they slept." He'd tickle her at that part, all mock-disappointment that she didn't want to go to bed. "But when the Old Gods burrowed deep, or climbed high, or sank into the sea, and let themselves dream of their homeland, they left behind those people they'd marked. People they'd changed to be more like themselves."

He'd tried to put a happy face on it. He'd called them all caterpillars, as if someday they'd turn into butterflies, and that wasn't so scary, was it?

"Why did they change people?" Sharon had asked, when she was older, after it had cost her a mother.

Her father had shrugged. "Why did we change wolves?"

It had been reassuring, at the time, how he'd put her in the same tidy box as himself, how he'd said 'we.' She preferred books to exploring, cooking to camping, poetry to science. She didn't lick her chops at the sight of empty blacktop stretching to the horizon. She'd cried when her mother had slipped into the ocean, grown huge and finned and monstrous, disappearing without even a backward glance. Her brother Jack had watched in fascination.

When Sharon had been old enough to finally see her father's lie about leaving to look for work as the cliché it was, she'd assumed he'd simply been overwhelmed by grief and the demands of caring for his children all by himself and had checked out. Now, with Gran to look after, Sharon wondered how much of it had been a blessing in disguise, how much sooner Jack might have climbed behind the wheel of a truck bound for the most desolate point on the map, the longer the haul the better, if it hadn't been for their father deserting them in all but name.

He'd sent money, of course. He was still sending money, though it was less and more irregular with every passing year. But she and Jack had had to relearn how to negotiate the world, how to raise themselves, and for the first few years after their mother's transformation, that had taken up too much time and energy for them to think about their own futures.

Sharon had focused on getting straight As and perfect SAT scores and racking up the sort of extracurriculars that colleges loved. She'd assumed that she'd be off to the best adventure of her young life as soon as she graduated from high school. She hadn't thought about the way she was setting roots into the foundation, wrapping the house around her tight as a cocoon. Now, walking down the hallway of the split-level that marked the boundaries of her existence, she wished she'd done all the things her guidance counselors had warned would lead to a dead-end life of unfulfilling minimum-wage work and early parenthood. It wouldn't have made a difference, and she could have at least had some fun.

Now it was the eight o'clock news with her grandmother every night, with no end in sight. Gran settled onto the couch and chuckled happily as the anchorwoman segued into a puff-piece on the annual home-garden tour.

"Did I ever tell you about the time I planted daffodils all the way from the sidewalk almost to the rose beds?" Gran asked, eyes going soft and misty. "They were in full bloom by your mother's birthday, just a carpet of butter-pats covering the lawn. She loved them."

Sharon patted her hand. Gran shifted form, the delicate elderly woman rippling easily into the gray wolf like a breaking wave, and Sharon found herself patting a paw.

Maybe, she thought, it wouldn't be so bad to let Gran downstairs. Even now, this close, her jaws didn't look big enough to swallow the sun. She didn't seem fast enough to catch it, strong enough to bring it down, hungry enough to devour it. Maybe Gran didn't need Sharon to keep her in check, maybe that was another thing her father had been wrong about.

"The ocean's a big place. Your mom and Aunt Lydia and anyone else who wants it can dive deep and never have to rub elbows with anybody or get in the way of anything," he'd explained, when Sharon had called him in a panic about Gran turning into a wolf. "Jack got lucky. What he wants isn't too disruptive. But your grandmother... honey, she's too much like her great-grandfather. She could swallow the whole world in a day and not even notice she'd done it."

Which really didn't seem to be Gran's style. Gran wore capris and floppy straw hats when she gardened and made cookies on Sundays if everyone was home and watched soap operas and went duck hunting. Except it was Lillian who was those things, who'd done those things, and 'Lillian' had worn away like the treads on an old tire. It was Gran sitting beside her now, big as a pony and blinking at the TV from eight ochre eyes.

The phone rang, an old rotary-dial Bakelite thing she'd found in the attic, heavy and shrill.

"Hello?" Sharon said.

"House-mouse!"

Her father. He sounded suspiciously cheerful, which meant he was probably calling to say he'd be late making the deposit this month. "How's my baby girl?"

"Dad, I'm twenty-five," Sharon groaned.

"You'll always be my baby girl," he answered automatically, and Sharon mouthed the words as he said them. They'd been doing this dance since she'd turned eighteen. "Look, hon, the reason I'm calling is that Lydia's finally been declared legally dead, and since I'm her executor, I'm stuck in Maine for a bit sorting through everything. I'm going to poke around the local community colleges and historical societies, see if I can scrounge up some paying work, but it's not looking good."

Sharon twisted the cord around her finger and tried not to think of their dwindling bank account, of how often she'd heard a version of that promise. It was hard to make the money last when everything had to be delivered.

"Okay, I'll try to watch the budget," Sharon promised.

"Good, good. Oh, and there's a china cabinet Lydia wanted you to have. I've worked out a deal with one of Jack's trucker buddies to kind of scooch it in with his regular load, so shipping will run practically nothing. I just wanted to let you know."

Sharon tried to imagine where she'd even put Aunt Lydia's behemoth of a china cabinet and gave up. She'd find room somewhere; it wasn't as if she had anything better to do than rearrange furniture.

"Thanks for the heads up."

"Okay, call me if you need anything. Love you!" He hung up before Sharon could say she didn't have his number. The cell he'd been using had given her a 'no longer in service message' the last five times she'd called.

"Love you too, dad," she said to the dial tone.

Beside her, the wolf snorted.

#

Sharon smiled at the new batch of pictures from Jack's latest trip. Between her laptop's age and the slowness of her throttled connection—she'd switched to a cheaper package the night her father had called—they took forever to load, but they were worth every second of the wait. She pored over the photos. The unforgiving landscape, the interesting animals and plants, the open night sky... Sharon wanted to drink it in and never stop. She had the momentary, mad impulse to slip into the back yard and roll in the grass, to dig into the earth with her bare hands, to eat the petals off the wild roses.

She took a deep breath and closed the laptop. She'd look through the rest of the pictures later, when she felt less...

Sharon stumbled over the proper term. Like she'd eaten too much already but was still hungry, equal parts insatiable and angry at what she'd consumed for not filling her. Feral in a way that resented domestication for existing. She rubbed her forehead and got up. It was probably just low blood sugar.

Sharon dialed Jack's number, then began rummaging through the cupboards. She'd fixed the last of the leftovers for Gran's lunch, and if she wanted dinner, it meant cooking. Jack picked up on the third ring.

"Share-bear," he said warmly, and Sharon heard the purr of the engine in the background. "You get my email?"

"Yeah, thanks! Those pictures were really something."

"How's things?"

"Mostly the same. The house is still standing. I guess dad's going to be short for a while, and Gran's going kind of stir-crazy."

"You still in that online support group you joined?" Jack asked after a moment. Sharon thought he'd always felt guilty for sticking her with Gran. It had been a foregone conclusion that it would be Sharon—as much of a homebody as she'd been, it had been hard to raise an objection, given how cruel it would be to hobble Jack— but it still would have been nice to be *asked.*

"Not really. I check in with them sometimes, but, you know. I can't just roll in and be all hi, my name's Sharon and I live in a magic house with my demon grandmother who wants to end life as we know it. And lying to people who are trying to be nice only gives me one more thing to feel guilty about, so it's not always helpful to talk to them." Sharon sighed and glared balefully at the cupboard's contents. "Sorry, I don't mean to be a downer. Do you think if I made a soufflé with evaporated milk, it would come out right?"

"Sure," he said immediately.

"Do you even know what a soufflé is?"

"I don't know what evaporated milk is, but I believe in you." Jack laughed. Sharon heard the hiss of the air brakes, and Jack sighed. "I've actually got to get going. You want me to call you back when I'm on the road again?"

"Nah. It was good to hear your voice, though."

"You too. Good luck with your soufflé," Jack said, and Sharon could tell he meant it.

#

"I appreciate the help," Sharon said, leaning on the doorjamb and smiling wanly at the truck driver's retreating form. "Thank you!"

He gave no indication of having heard her. The entire time he'd spent helping her maneuver the china cabinet into position had been punctuated with nervous glances around the room, and he'd scuttled down the driveway and into his truck as soon as possible. Sharon watched the pale yellow tea roses in the yard sway in the breeze. The plants hadn't been pruned since Gran had decided to pull a Fenrir, and the blossoms were plentiful but ratty-looking. They smelled as sweet as ever, though, and the scent wafted into the house.

When she couldn't put it off any longer, Sharon closed the door and returned to the living room. The cabinet was precisely as big as she remembered it. She was peeling the wrapping off the cabinet when Gran appeared on the landing.

"Did you have a caller, pup?" Gran asked.

"Gah," Sharon hissed, dashing up the stairs. "No, it was just a deliveryman, please, Gran, it's fine. Let's get your knitting out."

"Don't you sass me, young lady, I can smell roses. Deliverymen don't bring roses."

"It's from outside," Sharon sighed, trying to herd Gran back onto the second floor. Back to where it was safe. "It's the roses, they're blooming."

"Why don't we go out and pick some?" Gran asked, digging in her heels.

"You know why. You'll kill everything, remember?" Sharon said, pushing harder.

"I won awards for those roses, you know. People used to come on tours to see them."

"I know. They're still pretty," Sharon lied, "and they smell so nice. Please, just find something to keep yourself occupied while I unpack Aunt Lydia's cabinet. Then we can watch the news, or I can bake you cookies, or we can look at pictures of the roses you grew."

"I should be doing the baking," Gran grumbled, finally letting herself be steered down the hall. "And why would you need to unpack Lydia's cabinet?"

"It's from her estate. Dad sent it. She left it to me." Sharon gritted her teeth and steeled herself for the inevitable outburst. Gran kept forgetting that Lydia had gone, following in Sharon's mother's footsteps barely five years later.

"Oh." Gran's shoulders slumped, and she sniffed. "Of course."

Sharon watched Gran shuffle toward her room, her stomach souring with guilt. There wasn't anything she could really do, though, and she didn't know what to say to comfort Gran.

Sharon was relieved to find that the china cabinet had made it without getting so much as a scratch. The wood grain seemed to shift as she let her gaze linger over the delicate carvings, waves rippling toward some unseen shore. Sharon ran her fingertips over it, tracing them. It wasn't her imagination, and she smiled. Sharon pulled open the main cupboard and began emptying the packing only to find that it had a purpose beyond protecting the glass of the door: a large box was nestled inside it as securely as an egg in a warbler's nest.

Sharon carried it to the dining room table and reached for a knife. She cut the tape and began peeling it like an onion, layer after layer of packaging falling away until all that was left was an enormous snow globe, water already swirling from the rough handling she'd accidentally given it during the box's dissection. Sharon frowned. The glass was the size of a volleyball, and it was seated in a brass pedestal in the shape of a clawed, gripping hand.

"To Dr. Armitage, worthiest of editors. Remember me fondly, W. Dyer," she murmured to herself, reading the engraving on the underside of the pedestal. She couldn't remember any Dyers or Armitages in Gran's family tree, but then, its roots went deep. "Odd."

She examined the globe again, more carefully this time. Inside the glass was a steep craggy mountain with a series of odd outcroppings. She shook it, trying to stir things up more, but the blizzard inside whirled heedless of her. The globe was pretty, in its own stark, weird way.

Sharon put the snow globe back in the cabinet and began cleaning up. The TV was blaring away upstairs, and Sharon wondered if Gran was consoling herself or if she'd forgotten again. Things would be easier if Gran were like her daughters, Sharon thought. If it had been all right to stop fighting, to let her go as she pleased. Of course, things would be easier if Sharon weren't trying to make the best of powdered milk and tinned meat and tubs of industrial shortening.

It was galling that Sharon rarely got so much as a thank you from her father for putting her entire life on hold to keep the world intact—she couldn't even go putter around in the garden, for god's sake—but for her life to *keep* finding ways of shrinking was maddening. Her eyes found the cabinet again, and she frowned.

The white glitter snow in the globe was still swirling. She crossed the room and opened the glass door, wondering if it was a trick of the light. She sank into a squat and looked carefully at the globe. Tiny figures crawled over the mountain's surface, and Sharon jerked away, startled.

She dug through the junk drawer in the kitchen until she found a magnifying glass. Sharon examined the globe again and was even more confused than before. The figures looked like large mosquito larvae, or some type of tiny feather star—something in the crinoid family, if deep-sea documentaries had taught her anything. They were all making their way along carved paths up and across the mountain. As she watched, they bustled into and out of the blocky structures and paraded into the cave mouths.

People didn't put sea-monkeys in snow globes, did they? It seemed cruel. She'd seen pictures of closed systems with plants, but the mountain was bare except for the snow and the little animals; there was nothing to clean or oxygenate the water. Then again, if they'd gone this long in some forgotten cabinet wedged into a guest room and draped in a dust sheet, they'd probably be fine for the foreseeable future. Sharon tried her father's cell phone again in the hopes he'd had it reactivated.

"We're sorry. The number you have dialed is no longer in service."

She licked her lips.

"Hey, what's up?" Jack asked. Sharon could hear muffled conversation and the clink of cutlery on china around his voice.

"The cabinet came," Sharon said. "I don't suppose

Dad said anything to you about the snow globe he packed in it? His number's not working."

"Nah, sorry. I haven't *discussed* anything with Dad in, hell, three years," Jack said. He didn't sound as if it bothered him, but then, he had a job. And a life. And his freedom.

"Oh. Never mind, then. Sorry to interrupt—" She glanced at the clock. "—your lunch."

"You're never interrupting," he laughed.

#

It was two weeks later that Sharon finally had to cancel the internet. She'd have done it sooner, but the channels that came with their service were one of the few reliable ways of keeping Gran entertained, and there were days when she felt like she'd lose her own mind without being able to at least hope for another round of pictures from Jack.

The rabbit ears Sharon had dug out of the attic for Gran's TV barely picked up local stations, and if Gran landed on a talk show, it was as liable to rile her up as distract her. They'd descended into a state of watchful vigilance, opposing trenches eyeing each other across a permanent no-man's land. Gran complained about the weather and the food and the tedium, and all Sharon had to offer was, "I know."

The sole time they'd been in agreement had been standing at Gran's bedroom window, drinking in the cool, rose-scented breeze as the moon rose and watching the bleached yellow blooms hiss and sway in the wind. Sharon had wanted out almost as badly as Gran in that moment, and she had no idea what last spark of restraint had led them to their beds instead of stampede.

The one call from her father during that time had been over such a poor signal that it had been incomprehensible, and the call had been dropped as soon as she'd mentioned the perilous state of their bank account. The crinoids in the snow globe had turned into her one source of reliable entertainment, and how sad was that?

Sharon had dragged the china cabinet into the center of the living room, where the light was best and the view of the stairs was unobstructed, and plunked the globe into it where she'd normally have put a TV. A strategically placed full-page magnifier that she'd pilfered from Gran's closet provided a way to watch the animals paddle and flit their way along their miniature streets and tiny towers. She couldn't figure out the mechanism behind whatever convection current let the glitter swirl or ebb without being touched, but from the way her palms itched whenever she handled it, she had a feeling it wasn't strictly mechanical.

The feather stars were almost as good as TV, in their own way. They were real, for one thing, and they were clever, for animals. It was almost as good as a nature show, if she put on some music while she watched them. There were nights when she was so wrapped up in their slow, undulating progress that she lost track of time. She'd snap out of it to find Gran on the landing, looking at her with those amber eyes and saying, "It's late, pup."

It wasn't until the third week that Sharon realized it wasn't a snow globe.

It had been a long night, with her cot shaking every time Gran tried to open her bedroom door and slip out of the house while Sharon slept. Sharon had been bored and nervous, and the crinoids had been nowhere to be seen. A momentary, panicky conviction that the tiny animals had died, that she hadn't cared for them correctly and now she'd wiped out the only pets she'd had in years, had swept over her in a tidal wave of guilt and grief. She'd shaken the globe, gently, carefully, just enough to stir some of the glitter. Nothing had happened. Even gravity couldn't touch the detritus inside the glass. Sharon had put it back, perplexed, then decided it wasn't worth it to try calling her father.

When she'd looked up again, she'd watched in drop-jawed confusion as a tiny biplane motored its way through the globe in slow motion and landed on a long, low rooftop. It occurred to her that she'd fallen asleep on the couch and was dreaming, or had finally lost her mind.

But no matter how she turned it, that damn plane was still there, sitting on top of what she'd come to think of as the feather stars' town hall.

Sharon scavenged the lens from her old cell phone to use in a makeshift microscope for a better look. The biplane was a perfect model, with filament-thin props and cuticle-thick skis. The side door slid open with agonizing slowness, and a feather star wearing a coat climbed out of the cargo bay, followed by two tiny humans in arctic furs.

Sharon wanted to put the microscope down and retreat to the kitchen. She wanted to call her father. She kept watching instead.

#

Sharon chewed her lip and watched the humans and their coat-wearing feather star companion flee what looked like a tiny sea slug. They'd been exploring the tiny city with laborious slowness, and she'd watched, entranced, as they'd come out of building after building carrying tiny artifacts and scratching furiously in doll-sized sketchbooks. She couldn't hear them, but their excitement had been obvious. Now their terror was equally palpable.

The sea slug was tiny by her reckoning, but compared to the three of them it was big as a Mack truck. The instant-replay speed of the chase still left her biting her nails, willing them faster as they ran toward the plane. Rough jets of slime shot from the slug's mouth, a thousand-frame-per-second lightning strike, branching and arcing as it expanded into a dendritic web, missing the explorers by nanometers. The crinoid shucked its jacket and spread miniature wings, to Sharon's delight. None of the others had ever flown before, though she realized that the bands around their barrels must be the same wings, furled around them for added protection.

Sharon almost didn't hear the doorbell, and in the end it was Gran shouting "Who's at the door, pup?" that finally roused her.

She tore herself away from the snow globe and hurried to the door, eager to get rid of whoever was banging on it. She hadn't ordered anything except groceries in weeks, and she hadn't ordered those in almost a week.

Sharon found herself blinking at a sheriff's deputy and two men in polo shirts and khaki slacks, all as damp with sweat as she was, who dutifully informed her that the property would be seized for failure to pay property taxes in thirty days.

"What?" Sharon asked, as one of the men placed a packet of paperwork in her unresisting hands.

"Property taxes, miss," the other one repeated, smiling sympathetically. "The lien placed on the property for failure to pay's almost a year old. I'm afraid that means it's going to auction."

"Unless, of course, the back taxes are paid in full," the first one said, arching his eyebrows hopefully.

"Uh." Sharon gaped at them. "My father handles the finances, I'm sure he's been paying everything he needs to —"

"Not for the last five years, I'm afraid. Unless he can come up with some proof of payment?"

"How much is it?" she croaked, unable to make their words fit through the fog shrouding her brain. It was hard not to simply turn her back on this senseless intrusion and return to the globe, to see if the intrepid explorers made it out alive, to see if the rampaging slug was defeated.

"I'm afraid it's eleven thousand dollars, miss."

"You say that a lot, don't you?" Sharon asked blankly.

"What?" His smile turned fixed, and he cocked his head.

"That you're afraid." She looked from one to the other, then to the deputy. They were wax effigies instead of people, hyperreal and distorted by their nearness. She clenched her fist around the paperwork and closed the door in their faces.

There was a white noise where her emotions should be, a crackling static hiss instead of the ability to wrap her head about that many zeroes. She'd been worrying about nickels and dimes so long that the amount he'd quoted sounded like the punchline of a joke. What would eleven thousand dollars even look like? She imagined a vast mountain of dollar bills, swirling inside a globe that wasn't real, a globe that was just a window into something she could never touch.

After a moment, she went back to the globe and watched the tiny plane taxi off the roof of the town hall and fly away, the slug left climbing the wall and waving its eye stalks in miniature, voiceless rage. By the time the plane dipped and wobbled and climbed its way out of the globe, disappearing forever, Sharon had tears running down her cheeks and a scalding anger welling in her throat.

#

"Do you have time to talk?" Sharon asked, pacing the buckled floor.

She threaded her way through the wreck of the living room and back again, feet padding noiselessly over the evidence of her tantrum. She hadn't calmed down enough to right the house, or even to regret the mess she'd made. The only thing untouched in the entire wing was the china cabinet and its grafted-on magnification rig. She heard Gran upstairs, howling through the window at the oxlip moon, and wanted nothing more than to join her.

"Sure thing, what's up?" Jack asked, concerned. There was nothing but his voice and the wind, and she wondered where he was. Not in his truck. Not around any other people. She closed her eyes and listened, imagining being in some wide open space with nothing to do but run and run, grass under her feet, bare toes digging into the earth, wind in her face.

"Some, uh, some guys came out to the house today. They, um. They said Dad hasn't been paying the property taxes, and they sounded pretty serious. The paperwork they left made it sound pretty serious." Sharon swallowed. "And I can't get ahold of Dad."

"Wow," Jack breathed. "How serious is pretty serious?"

"If we don't come up with almost eleven thousand dollars by the end of the month, they're taking the house."

Sharon was amazed at how normal she could make it sound, as if it wasn't an incomprehensible sum attached to an equally incomprehensible consequence. Though she'd also discovered, sometime around the second third of her tantrum, right around when she'd focused on how much she'd given up to keep the world safe while her father apparently couldn't even be bothered to get a decent job that would let him take care of the financial part of the bargain they'd all made, that it really was a matter of perspective.

When she thought about laying hands on eleven thousand dollars, it was a laughably huge sum, the sort of money she'd never had access to all at once even in her wildest dreams. When she thought about the world ending for lack of it, it was an absurdly small amount, less than kidnappers demanded for the safe return of a single person. She'd even considered calling the number on the paperwork and trying to explain to them what was at stake, to see if maybe some sympathetic or superstitious clerk could be talked out of the debt to keep the sun from going out. She'd decided against it sometime during the last third of the meltdown.

Nobody would believe her—nobody ever believed her —and the best she could hope for was someone labeling both her and Gran mentally incompetent and possibly eligible for some sort of compassionate handling.

The silence on the other end of the line was deafening, and Sharon's heart was in her throat. What if Jack had hung up?

"Are you there?"

"Yeah, that's just." He sighed, sounding winded. "Jesus."

"Tell me about it," she agreed. The buckled floorboards under her feet shuffled and expanded, snapping together and smoothing out, and some of the furniture righted itself. Sharon blinked at it, then realized that having someone at least take it seriously was comforting. She didn't feel any better, not really, but her heartbeat had slowed and the sick feeling of not being able to breathe was less intense.

"Can I call you back in an hour or two? I need to check on some stuff, but I might have a way to swing it."

"What?"

"Don't get your hopes up," he said quickly, his tone guarded. "It's... complicated. I might not be able to get at the money in that short a timeframe. I'll call when I know. Just keep your head on straight, okay? Please?"

"Okay."

Sharon spent the next few hours alternating between nervous pacing and trying to straighten the dining room and living room. It was slow going with the latter, and the click of four sets of nails on the second floor didn't help. Gran seemed to be tracking her, shadowing her, always right above her. Sharon knew she should go upstairs, explain what was going on, apologize for what she'd done to the house in her anger. She also knew she didn't have a good accounting for how she was going to fix anything, not until Jack called back with his miracle.

Or until Jack called back with the loss of all hope. He'd given her a maybe, not a commitment, and she tried to keep that in mind. If it came down to it, Sharon was sure there was little short of an atom bomb that could actually *force* her out of the house. It was as much a part of her as any organ, and it responded like a limb. But she still needed food and water, and she wasn't sure she had the will to keep both Gran and herself penned up in the face of that sort of privation. There was duty, and then there was martyrdom.

The phone rang, and she pounced on it.

"Jack?"

"Okay, so if I clean out my retirement account and the escrow account on the truck, I can swing it."

The 'thank you' stuck in Sharon's throat. Jack's retirement account. Jack's *truck*.

She coughed. "I can't pay you back."

Jack laughed hollowly. "You and I both know I'm not exactly going to retire. And the truck's not going to do me much good with Gran out there on a rampage. But the thing is that the only way to tap the account now, like *now*-now, is if it's a qualifying emergency. Which this is, thank god, but there's this whole stack of stuff I need you to sign and have notarized to back me up, and then the transfer is going to be over some bullshit limit the IRS instituted, so for you to get it, it needs to be certified by a bank officer and done in person and—"

He broke off and inhaled slowly.

"It can't be done from home, is what I'm saying," Jack said quietly. "And it's probably going to take a good hour or two, even if you make them promise to hurry."

"Oh."

"Yeah. I don't suppose Gran's doing well enough that you can trust her alone for that long?"

"No." Sharon sank onto the couch. "But I guess there's not much choice, is there? And who knows, maybe she'll take a nap. Or maybe Dad's been wrong this whole time."

"Guess we'll find out." Jack didn't have to say that there was no giving up, no not trying. "I'll call when everything's ready to go. Is there anything else?"

"Can you throw in a couple hundred bucks now for groceries and getting the internet turned back on?" Sharon asked. "I know it's a lot, but Gran's more tractable when she enjoys what she's eating and doesn't want to bite the entire TV station."

"Things are that bad, huh?" Jack gave a low whistle. "I'll do that now. The money should clear by tomorrow."

"Thank you, Jack. For everything."

"Hey, what are brothers for?" he said. "Thanks for looking out for Gran. I know it's not easy."

"Talk soon?"

"Talk soon."

Sharon hung up and ran her fingers through her hair. To her surprise, the living room looked almost exactly as it had before she'd torn it apart, the last lingering evidence being rips in the upholstery and a certain lopsidedness to the couch. She smiled ruefully at the phone. Amazing what a bit of relief and a thank-you could do for her mental state.

#

Sharon looked at herself in the mirror and tried not to fidget. She hadn't worn the suit since high school, and now it didn't fit quite right. But it was the most professional thing she owned, which she figured could only help when it came to getting in and out of the bank without any unnecessary hold-ups.

Down the hall, a cooking show about fancy cupcakes was playing too loud, and Gran's canine snoring could be heard during commercial cuts.

Jack's money had already worked a miracle. Fresh meat, fresh vegetables, fresh milk—fresh *everything*, for the first time in months. Sharon had made crepes stuffed with strawberries and whipped cream, and raisin oatmeal cookies, and roast beef sandwiches piled to bursting with lettuce and tomatoes. They'd both eaten second helpings of meals for the last three days. Gran had looked on the return of her favorite shows as a restoration of old friends, her tail thumping happily at the bakers and repairmen and detectives who populated the screens now.

Sharon had spent the first day catching up on everything Jack had sent while she'd been offline, then the next two researching everything she could about the tax case she'd have to sort out. She hadn't seen the little feather stars again, and she tried not to worry that the slug had eaten them all. She imagined there wasn't much she could do about it regardless; she couldn't even budge the snowflakes, let alone help the tiny animals. Whatever the globe was showing her, it was like Gran's tv upstairs, a one-way look into another time and place.

Outside, the cab honked its horn. The driver was early, but she figured it didn't make much of a difference. Sharon had made Gran's favorite for lunch, and Gran had gorged herself. Sharon would fill out the paperwork and take possession of the means to save their home and be back before Gran knew she was gone, or she'd find out it had all been a spectacular waste of time when the sun went out or the sea ran dry.

Sharon raced out the door, as quiet as she could manage. The urge to flee back inside once she made it halfway down the walk was balanced by an equally pressing urge to run past the cab, past the city limits, and into the wilderness, where no one could find her and make her go back. She clamped down on both and climbed into the seat.

"First Federal, on Main," she told the driver.

The agent who helped her through the paperwork was kind and thorough, and Sharon felt giddy with relief when he showed her the new balance on her bank account. Jack had scraped together almost thirteen thousand dollars, covering the back taxes plus a cushion in case there were any surprise fees or penalties. All she had to do now was arrange for the proper payment, and she had the instructions for that at home, all the relevant steps highlighted and bullet-pointed and written out after a call with the tax collector.

Sharon practically floated out the door, clutching her copies of the documents, receipts, and statements to her chest. The sunlight on her face was warm and welcoming, and the breeze smelled of car exhaust and tarmac and not even the slightest hint of dying roses, and she breathed it in. The smell of sausage made her stomach growl, and she scented the wind. The sausages were close, on the lee side of the block, maybe a few streets up. She'd been too nervous to eat when she'd made lunch for Gran, and she had a few bucks in her pocket.

Sharon's mouth watered, and she glanced at the clear blue sky. What could it hurt? Gran was obviously still asleep. She wouldn't get the chance to do this again anytime soon. And it was only a hotdog; she'd hardly be sitting down for a three-course dinner. She could eat it on her way to the park, which was the fastest place to hail a cab without having to call for one. She followed the smell down the sidewalk.

She passed a cafe where a dozen people were lounging at the tables, drinking and talking and devouring sandwiches and laughing, then a studio she couldn't see inside for all the prints and sculptures crammed into the windows, a vibrant splash of color against the sandstone edifice, then a lazy-looking salon where a handful of older ladies were clustered around a television, talking and laughing excitedly as whatever broadcast they were watching played out before its tiny audience. Sharon felt a pang. Gran could have been one of them, if the cards had been different. Not everyone in their lineage shifted, after all.

There was a cart at the intersection selling cell phone chargers and sunglasses and riotous bouquets. Sharon buried her nose in the flowers and inhaled. Phlox, goldenrod, Queen Anne's lace, a few lilies for show… most of them didn't have a particular sweetness, but the honest smell of chlorophyll and pollen and sap let her forget the roses. The guy running the register trained unfocused, bloodshot eyes on her and blinked.

"Wait." His eyes narrowed in recognition and disbelief. "*Sharon*?"

She tilted her head. "Oh my god. Rick?"

They'd both been on the homecoming committee a couple of times, had gone to one of the dances together in an awkward semi-date. She hadn't even thought of him in years.

"Jeez, you look—" He shook his head as if to clear it and gave her a thumbs up. "Fantastic. Good for you, hitting the streets again! I heard about your agoraphobia. This is…" He chewed his lip, his brows furrowed in concentration. "A big first step, right? Like the first day of the rest of your life?"

"You have no idea," Sharon agreed, smiling. She could keep the house. She could keep Gran. She could get a hotdog. Everything was going to be fine.

Rick waved at the flowers. "Help yourself."

"Are you sure?" she asked.

"Nobody buys them. I mean, *ever*." He shrugged. "I write off ten of those bunches a week, and if nobody buys those particular bunches by six o'clock, which," he leaned forward conspiratorially, and she could smell the pot smoke clinging to him, "they're totally not gonna, they're going in the trash. So please, at least get me out of that bit of eco-guilt."

"Thank you," Sharon breathed, scooping them up and hugging them to her chest. "Thank you!"

"Keep right, Sharon," he laughed, waving as she caught the scent of food again and stepped away.

Sharon stared at every shop she passed, wide-eyed and clutching the flowers in her arms. It was astounding to think that everything was so close to the house, so close to *her*. Every day, people left their homes. They went to work, the store, the library. They went out with friends. They saw other people. They laughed, they argued, they had lives.

She turned a corner and found herself in a short line for a food truck. She ordered the cheapest thing they had, a bratwurst in a potato bun, and had just bitten into it when a hush fell over the small crowd gathered for the truck.

Hot grease dripped down Sharon's chin as she turned and looked at what they were pointing to, feeling stupid as she registered the shadow of a wolf's face dimming the sun. Of course. She chewed, the warmth and spice of the sausage mixing with spongy softness of the roll and the gritty heat of the mustard she'd slathered it with. There was a part of her that wanted spurting blood and live meat and the thrill of the hunt, the part of her that knew she was meant to walk on four legs instead of two, the part that knew what it was to stalk and fell beasts whose shadow hadn't fallen across the land in human memory.

A cool wind kicked up from nowhere, curling around her legs and tugging at her hair. Sharon swallowed, then took another bite. The monster was answering the call of its pack; Sharon could be content with her food truck sausage, if that was still on the table. And if it wasn't, well. She supposed that there were worse ways to face the end of the world. At least now she knew she hadn't wasted the last seven years on an inaccurate forecast; Gran really did pose a threat to life as they knew it.

People scurried past her, either taking shelter wherever they could find a roof or trying to get a better look at what was happening, and Sharon broke into a trot. If she could get a cab, she could be home in a few minutes. Nothing looked particularly eaten yet; there was a chance maybe Gran was only in the front yard, prowling around the rose bushes or nosing around the neighbors' rabbit hutch. The flowers jounced in her arms, and she kept a tight hold of her bratwurst. She spotted a pair of idling cabs in the unloading zone between the park and the bus station, both drivers half out of their cars staring at the sky, and made a beeline for the closest.

"Lady, are you kidding me right now?" the driver asked when she flung herself into his cab.

"I'm sure it's some harmless weird local weather phenomenon or something," Sharon said, smiling around too-sharp teeth. She rattled off her address and shoved money at him. He glanced at the sky, then grudgingly took the cash.

The drive back was punctuated by near-misses with drivers suddenly noticing the darkening outline of fangs against the sun and pedestrians crossing against lights and in the middle of nowhere, half-panicked by a howl they felt through their bones more than heard. It raised gooseflesh on Sharon's arms, and she wanted to answer it with a howl of her own. She finished her lunch and licked her fingers, and the cabbie locked eyes with her in the rearview.

"You're seeing this, right?" he asked, waving his hand at the sky in frustration, like her lack of visible panic was a personal affront.

"Of course I'm seeing it. I'm not blind."

The car pulled into the driveway, and Sharon scanned the yard. No sign of Gran. The cabbie barely waited for Sharon to shut the door before peeling out.

She let herself in carefully, her eyes adjusting almost instantly to the comparative darkness. The light in the kitchen was on, and she heard Gran humming to herself. Sharon inhaled deeply, trying to place the smell coming from the kitchen.

"That you, pup?" Gran called. She poked her head around the corner. Gran's skin was the gray of her fur, and she had eight eyes dotting her face, but she hadn't fully transformed. She was also wearing a flower-print apron and holding a mixing bowl. Gran wrinkled her nose. "The first batch is done, if you haven't filled up on sausage."

Sharon put her flowers down on the table and followed Gran into the kitchen. "Moon pies!"

Gran hadn't made the cookie sandwiches since Sharon had been in middle school.

"A little moon for a little pup," Gran said, reaching out and pinching her cheek. Sharon bit into the sandwich, marshmallow filling oozing out around the edges, and it was even better than she remembered. She closed her eyes and licked frosting from her lips. She could hear the wind outside the house, the howling hunger of Gran's final transformation. Sharon took another bite of cookie. This wasn't so bad, was it? This life they had? It was manageable.

She looked out the window, at the roiling chaos of the sky and the mid-day darkness. It was thick enough to wade through, thick enough to walk on, thick enough to taste. There was a welcome to it, a freedom. She could burst the walls of the house, split the joints and crack the joists, never return. She stuffed the last of the moon pie into her mouth, and Gran handed her another one.

Sharon turned the possibility over in her mind. Never was a long time, wasn't it? There would come a time when it was a more appealing prospect, she was sure, but maybe it could wait a while more.

"Let's go back upstairs and watch that gardening show you like," she said, piling a plate high with moon pies. "We can finish up in here later."

The phone rang, and Sharon started, a sudden twinge of guilt pricking her. Jack would be seeing the same thing everyone else was. He'd think she'd failed. She answered it.

"Sharon, what's going on?" her father demanded.

Sharon paused, dumbfounded. An angry sneer curdled her features. "Oh, *for god's sake.*"

She hung up and shook her head, and Gran tipped her chin up and laughed long and hard.

"That's my girl," Gran said, taking the plate from her hands and moving toward the stairs. "Your teeth'll come in yet."

###

About the author

T.R. North was born and raised in Florida and has never been featured in a "News of the Weird" column run in another state. Previous outbursts of short fiction have appeared in *Metaphorosis, Persistent Visions,* and *PseudoPod*. Follow @northonthegulf on Twitter for more news.

Kitchen

Vanessa Fogg

There is a game I sometimes play.

I hear her shuffle down the upstairs hallway. I hear the creak at the top of the stairs. Her first step downward. She is barely five feet tall, one hundred and twenty pounds, yet her footstep lands on the staircase with a massive thud that resounds though the house. It's like the crash of a falling refrigerator, the footfall of a stone giant, a meteor tumbling to earth and leaving an irreparable hole. "Jenny?" Her voice quavers, thin and confused.

I don't answer. I let her take the second step.

There is a meteor falling and walls of flame burning through forests. There are storms spinning over the ocean. A small earthquake, magnitude 3.1, shakes the ground in Los Angeles.

A third step.

Rain. Rain falling relentlessly to the south. Dark clouds have opened and their swollen bellies are endless. Miles away, I feel rivers surge. Water strains against dams.

"Grandma." I stand, finally. I walk to her and take her arm. A trembling in the earth stills.

"I'm hungry, Jenny."

"I'll get you something. What do you want?"

"You don't how to cook. Let me make something."

"I can cook, Grandma."

She wrinkles her nose, letting me know exactly what she thinks of my cooking.

"Noodles?" I stroke her arm. If she were to pull away, she might fall. I murmur the secret words my sister gave me.

"You don't cook them right. They're never crispy enough." But she turns and walks up the staircase with me. She's slow, but steady on her feet. Somewhere in the world outside, the wind drops.

I walk her back to her bedroom. She sits on her bed. "Crispy noodles," I say. "Is that what you want for lunch?"

Her eyes, sharp and bright just a moment ago, have gone dull.

"I have to stay here, don't I?" she says.

"Yes." I touch her shoulder. "What would you like to eat?"

"Whatever," she says emptily. "Whatever."

#

One by one, they've all left me: my mother, my father, my elder sister. I'm the one they left behind to be caretaker. To keep Grandma upstairs. To keep the world safe.

It's just for a while, my sister told me. *Until I figure it out. Until I can fix it.* And she texts me from Indianapolis, Nashville, Tulsa, Santa Fe. She's on the road in California, driving up through Oregon and Washington. Swinging through the Great Plains on her way back East. But somehow her travels never take her close to where I am; she never stops to visit Grandma and me.

Our father is on the other side of the world, conducting business in Hong Kong and elsewhere in Asia, rarely texting or calling at all. And our mother—our mother is long gone. We don't know where she is. It's been years since any of us have heard.

I'm making lad na right now, I text my sister. *I'm using the recipe you sent me Ha Ha! Let's see how it goes this time :D*

I've already peeled apart the stack of soft, fresh rice

noodles. The beef gravy is simmering in a wok. I heat oil in a separate pan and tip the noodles in.

Patience, I remind myself. *Patience!* is what Grandma would scold if she were in the kitchen now. Don't turn the noodles too soon. Let them crisp up on the bottom, as she likes (even though they'll soon be smothered in rich gravy—she still can tell).

I used to watch her cook, standing on a step stool beside her. Then I was too busy to watch; I was looking instead at the TV, video games, homework. Lisa and I grew up; we didn't need our grandmother to come take care of us in the summers and holidays, as she used to do while our parents were working. And we were too busy to visit her.

I shake sweet soy sauce over the noodles, thick as molasses, and stir gently until the noodles are slicked brown.

I'm proud of myself. I even remembered to make the nam prik today: the condiment of sliced chili peppers in fish sauce and lime juice, to be sprinkled over the final dish to taste. I prepare Grandma's plate: the wide rice noodles, chewy-soft yet crisp at the edges, topped at the last moment with the thick gravy of beef and Chinese broccoli. I set the table upstairs—a card table dragged into a nook of the hallway, just outside her room.

I call her to the table. She takes a few bites, then stops.

"What's wrong?" I ask. "It's not good?"

"No, no. It's good." She nods like a bobble-head doll. "Good."

"Then why aren't you eating?"

She doesn't say. I must have done something wrong, but I don't know what.

"Good," she says, but only pushes her food around. She goes quiet. I finish my plate in silence.

#

It's my sister's fault. She majored in Occult Studies and messed with things she shouldn't have. She caused this gathering and bending of forces, focused upon Grandma's house like light through a lens. But she won't explain how or why.

I'll fix it, she just kept sobbing when I saw what she'd done. Jenny, I'll fix it.

I don't have Lisa's talent; I'm not a prodigy like her or like Mom before her. Mom's gift for magic skipped me. Under normal circumstances, I can barely sense the supernatural. But here in this house, even I feel the storms and shifts in the world when Grandma's foot hits the stairs.

A few months, Lisa promised me when she left. It's already been more than a year.

#

At first Lisa called once a week. But her calls are fewer and fewer now. She rarely even texts anymore. She didn't respond to my picture of the lad na.

Only the postal service and delivery people drop by. Grandma's house is almost literally in the freaking-middle-of-rural America. My friends are always surprised to hear that she and Grandpa settled here. I didn't mind visiting when I was little, but now I'd kill for a place with a decent latte.

I log in to Facebook again, wondering if Lisa has posted any updates. I see posts from my friends—pictures from a night out: garishly colored cocktails on a hotel roof, the martini glasses lovingly lit. Close-ups of a sushi roll. My friends grinning with their arms around one another. My college roommate's engagement pictures, posing with her fiancé in a park. Said fiancé's dog sitting in the middle of their apartment, tongue lolling. Before I can stop myself, I'm checking out the couple's Instagram account, then the accounts of complete strangers. I'm peeking at the lives of others, at the life going on outside this house, the life everyone else enjoys.

I hear a familiar thud. My grandmother on the first step.

I close my eyes and silently count. At step five, just as a typhoon in the tropical Pacific really starts to come together, I go to stop her.

#

Grandma is only getting worse with time. She can't be contained; she easily breaks any lock on her door, any barrier I erect. She doesn't remember that she's supposed to stay upstairs. I can't leave her alone.

It's like having a child, I think grimly as I scroll through pictures of a friend's toddler.

I don't post anything myself. I wonder if my friends ever think of me. I wonder if it feels to them as though I've simply dropped through a hole in the world. I'm taking time off to care for my aging grandmother, I told people, and everyone *oohed* and *ahhed* at what a good granddaughter I am.

I haven't heard from any of them in ages.

It's your fault, too, I remind myself. My fault that I haven't reached out to anyone. But what would I say? *Hey, sorry I've been out of touch—I'm stuck at my Grandma's staving off the apocalypse?*

I log off the accounts showing my friends' exciting lives. I check my bank account again.

Dad missed his usual deposit this month. He told me to ask Lisa for money. I called, but she hasn't answered.

It's not cheap, depending on Amazon shipments and paid food deliveries. I don't dare leave Grandma to drive the two hours to the closest Asian grocery store for the specialty ingredients and imported produce she craves. I hardly dare drive to the local grocery or the closest Walgreens while she's asleep.

When I step outside, I'm always listening for her step on the stairs. How many could she go down before I came back to stop her?

What would happen if I *didn't* stop her? How long would the end of the world take?

Lisa, I text again. *Wtf. Where are you?*

#

I think sometimes that if Grandma could cook again, she'd be better. She'd cheer up. Her mind would clear.

She'd be again the Grandma I knew.

Nearly all my childhood memories are of her in the kitchen. The hiss of something frying. The sound of a chopping cleaver and the pounding of a stone mortar. The pungent scent of fish sauce and sizzling garlic. A steady stream of treasures issued from her hands: delicate steamed custards of red curry and fish; hard-boiled eggs and pork ribs simmered in sweet five-spice broth; grilled chicken and satay; omelets stuffed with ground pork fried in oyster sauce; curries and noodle dishes of all kinds. The Thai dishes which my American-born mother never learned to make, or couldn't be bothered to make. Grandma made them for us.

Whatever I asked for, she would make.

It feels like cutting off one of her limbs, to keep her away from her own kitchen. She keeps forgetting that she's not allowed there. She keeps wanting to cook. And I try, but I didn't pay attention when I had the chance. I remember making spring rolls with her, spooning in the pork filling and rolling up the wrappers into tight bundles. I remember peeling apart stacks and stacks of wide rice noodles and washing vegetables. But there was so much I didn't learn. I mostly just ate, and she praised every bite. I stuffed myself, and as a child I swung my feet at the table and rambled about my day and every thought in my head and even though she bustled about the kitchen and her hands never stopped moving I could tell that she was listening; she listened as my own mother never did.

She doesn't listen anymore. And she eats so little now.

Her weight has been dropping. She was round and soft-looking when I first came. Now I see the bones of her shoulders through her clothes.

"Oh, it's dinner time?" she says vaguely when I tell her. She takes a few bites and says she's not hungry. Then she asks for an out-of-season tropical fruit I have no way of obtaining. She describes a dish from her homeland, one I've never tasted, one that I've never even heard of before.

I want to scream.

Lisa never sent the money she promised. I keep checking my email and accounts.

I'm in the middle of something, she texts. *I'll call you later. Promise.* She doesn't.

#

While Grandma is sleeping, I dare to step outside. At night I stand on the deck and feel wind on my face. I hear crickets chirping. Grandma's lawn has grown into a wild meadow, and hidden things rustle and buzz and move within. I watch the shadows. I imagine getting into my car and driving away into the night. I would take the winding country roads and outrun the floods, the fire, the lightning and storms. I imagine the road collapsing behind me and Grandma alone in the house, far behind, a silhouette moving against the lit windows, downstairs where she wants to be at last.

#

What did you do? I screamed at Lisa when I first found Grandma like this. Lisa cried without explaining anything. *What did you do?* I said more calmly, weeks later on the phone. *Is this anything to do with Mom?* She wouldn't say, and she still won't say. But I know my sister. It's always something to do with Mom. She was trying to get Mom back in our lives, I think. She was trying to find her. Or maybe she was just trying to live up to Mom's mystical achievements, to make her proud, to perform a magical feat so dazzling that our mother couldn't help but notice.

#

"I'm going to make curry puffs," Grandma announces one day. She walks into my bedroom to say this. Her voice and face are unusually determined. "It's your birthday, and we always have curry puffs for your birthday!"

I look up from the tablet I was reading. It is not my birthday, yet I feel a pang. It's been so long since I've had one of her tender, flaky pastries, stuffed with curried potatoes and chicken. It's the only dough I've ever seen her make, and the process is laborious: the combination of two types of dough, rolled together, flattened, rolled and cut and rolled out again. It takes hours even before the steps of filling and shaping the pastries, and then frying them golden brown. But I always loved her curry puffs, and she knows it. She made them for holidays, for celebrations, and for my birthday every year.

"Grandma," I tell her, "my birthday isn't for another month."

"That gives us time to shop then," she says, unperturbed. "We should make spring rolls, too. Will Lisa be here?"

Unexpectedly, my eyes prickle. "I don't know."

"Spring rolls are her favorite. Can you drive me to the store?"

"Later," I promise, counting on her to forget.

#

I've been watching my bank account dwindle and trying not to panic. Neither I nor Grandma is eating much these days. When I'm not watching her, I'm escaping into worlds online. But then I come back to where I really am, and my heart beats fast. I'm nauseous. What if something has happened to Lisa? Or Dad? What can I do?

If I'm alone, if my family's all gone—how do I take care of Grandma by myself?

When Lisa finally calls, I almost break into tears.

"I'm sorry," she says. "I've been so busy." I hear voices in the background—a low buzz.

"Are you okay?" I ask. "What's happening?"

"I'm fine. I can get you the money. But it can't be through ordinary means."

I hear shouts of laughter on the other end. Then a male voice calling her name.

"Lisa?"

She's talking to someone else. I can't make out the words. She comes back to me. "Yeah." Her voice is clipped. "I'll text you the directions. Do just as I say."

Is she in trouble? Did she sound irritated with me just now? Where is she? I imagine a sports bar. A party. Someone's house. Somewhere in the wide world with other people.

"Gotta go," she says. "Check your messages." And she's gone.

#

I read her text message over and over. The directions are clear and simple enough. But it means leaving this home.

I feel breathless as I get into my car. I check the time. It's just under two hours to the city. I have to be at the transfer spot at dawn. Add another two hours to drive back. Grandma sleeps late. I can do it. I can be back before she wakes.

I don't have any choice.

It feels like a dream—taking off down the empty road in the dark, just as I've imagined so many times. The dashboard glows. The night streams past. Mile after mile of open fields and hills. I fiddle with the radio dial until I find songs that I know. I crack open the windows and sing.

It's still dark as I pull into the lot of the 24-hour grocery store. Light poles cast their white radiance over the asphalt. Broken glass glitters. Details have a weird, zoomed-in quality; the world feels hyperreal. A side effect, maybe, of time and place; this seemingly ordinary store lot is where Lisa said the signal would be strong, where she could best work the money transfer. It's not long till dawn, and when it comes I leave the car and hold my phone above my head. A man headed into the store eyes me, but walks past without saying anything. I count to thirty in three different languages and spin in a circle.

And that's it. That's all Lisa said I had to do.

I check my bank account with clumsy fingers. I mess up the password twice. But it's there, as instantaneous as Lisa said: money filling my account.

I can't help it; I do a little dance, even as another car pulls into the lot.

It worked! I want to yell. But Lisa had told me not to

contact her for 24 hours. Do I even want to know what she's up to? Why she couldn't just PayPal me the cash? Is she supernaturally stealing, or somehow laundering money?

Never mind. It's done. It's time to head back.

But the sun is up, and I'm out in the world again, on my own. I feel dizzy with freedom.

There's a café that I used to visit in this city. It should be opening for breakfast now. Grandma won't wake for another three or four hours. I find myself turning the car in the café's direction. I find myself going inside.

There's the smell of dark roast coffee and freshly baked bread. Warm wood paneling and bright art prints on the wall. All just as I remember. The cute server behind the counter looks into my eyes as she takes my order. My voice is high and shaky. It's been so long since I've talked to anyone other than family.

I take a seat. People are starting to stream in— mostly business workers grabbing a coffee before work. A man and woman in surgical scrubs. A guy unpacks his laptop at the table next to mine; he's young and lean, with curly dark hair. I stare at his profile and bare arms.

A server brings my latte and jam Danish. I savor the drink's bitterness with the pastry's strawberry jam. I'm hungry but eat slowly, lingering.

The guy across from me drops something. He bends down to pick it up. As he straightens, his dark eyes catch mine. He smiles.

I feel my face heat even as I smile back.

My phone dings with a text message. Lisa. *Go!* she types. *Go gogo get back home NOW!*

Fuck, I want to tell her. What happened to *Don't contact me again for the next 24 hours?*

But then fear jolts me as I understand. I grab my things and run to the car.

And I'm speeding away from the city, from civilization, from other human beings. I'm on my way back to the house in the overgrown field. Lisa sensed something. She can feel something wrong. Grandma's awake, or waking.

How long till she tries to go downstairs?

Traffic backs up on the freeway, and I swear. Some tiny, terrified voice in my mind wonders if it's already begun.

Nothing, it's nothing. Just summer roadwork. An ordinary thing, one lane closed for a mile. It begins to rain. That's nothing, too, I think as the sky darkens and droplets dance a hard staccato on my windshield. Just an ordinary storm.

It's nothing when I hear a distant crash. It's only thunder. The lightning is perfectly ordinary.

Traffic melts away as I get further from the city. I search the radio with one hand. I spin through all the stations. Ordinary news, ordinary music.

Then the stations cut out. I scroll up and down. Only static.

Please, I think at no one at all. *Please.*

Have the earthquakes already started? Are tsunamis sweeping across the sea? In the West, are dry winds fanning sparks to flame?

This far from the house, I can't tell. It's only when I'm right there with Grandma that I feel the force of her weight on the stairs. That I can *feel* the shift of tectonic plates, the stir of global winds. There at the center of forces my sister wove.

I see it, finally. Her house on the hill, ahead on the lonely country road. My prison. I see lights glowing in the downstairs window.

I pull into the driveway and run inside. Rain lashes at me.

But inside it's warm and I smell food. Savory scents of my childhood, oyster sauce and garlic and fried meat. Grandma's there, standing over a wok. I see a plate piled high with stir-fried rice noodles. There are golden spring rolls on a platter. There are curry puffs—pale, not yet cooked—lined up on another plate.

"Jenny!" Grandma's face breaks into the biggest smile. "Happy birthday!"

"Grandma," I say. "You have to go back upstairs. Now."

"Why?" She looks into my eyes. They're clear and

calm and filled with genuine concern. "What's wrong? I'm frying curry puffs. Sit down and you can have one soon. Are you hungry?"

"No—" *Yes. Yes, I am. Her food smells amazing.* "I'll finish them. I'll bring them up. Please, you have to go upstairs."

"I'm almost done." She turns and starts taking them out of the wok. She sets them on a paper-towel lined plate to sop up the oil.

I should seize her arm. I should force her upstairs. But I don't want to hurt her. I don't move.

Waves of darkness are building at the edges of the world. I sense them dimly.

But it's so warm and cozy here in the kitchen. There's no fear here. Grandma is back in her element. Kitchen magic is the only kind she's ever had. I don't ask how she did this, where she got all this food, how she compressed time to cook a feast by herself while I was away. She's Grandma. Some miracles just are.

She moves purposefully, fishing out the last fried curry puff of the batch and then reaching for the plate of uncooked pastries. The vagueness is gone. She's herself again.

And she remembered my birthday. She's the only one who did. Even I forgot.

She nods to a bowl on the counter. "You can help me," she says. "There's still some dough to be rolled out. I never taught you or Lisa how to make these. I can show you now."

How much time do we have? Darkness is rolling in from the edges of the world, but it still feels so distant and faint. This kitchen, this house, are at peace.

I burn my fingers when I reach for the first curry puff. I never do learn. I draw my hand back and wrap the pastry in a napkin to hold. Lisa, Mom, Dad, the outer world—it's all far away. The pastry's crisp dough cracks open under my teeth, and the golden turmeric-spiced potatoes and chicken leak through. Grandma is watching happily. It's so good.

About the author

Vanessa Fogg dreams of selkies, dragons, and gritty cyberpunk futures from her home in western Michigan. Her short stories have appeared in *Metaphorosis, GigaNotoSaurus, Mythic Delirium, The Future Fire,* and more. Her fantasy novelette, *The Lilies of Dawn,* was published by Annorlunda Books and is available in print and ebook from Amazon, and as ebook from other major ebook retailers.

Vanessa is fueled by green tea.

For more, visit her website at www.vanessafogg.com.

Soft Science Fiction

Stories

Time, The Ever-Rolling Stream

Juliet Kemp

It was strange how quickly everyone had got used to the idea that there were aliens, and that they were on their way to Geovine IV. Or, at least, that was almost certainly what the messages indicated.

"Of course, it's not possible to be *sure*," Mira said, for form's sake.

"But it's as sure as we can be," Sarai said, leaning over the table they were all sitting round.

It was Sarai who first realised that the weird signal glitches they were picking up were some kind of message. But it was Mira who found the first chink that meant they could translate it. All of them had the hang of translation to at least some extent by now, but Mira was the acknowledged expert.

"We'll all be long gone, of course," Eleanor said, looking down again at the paper. "Two hundred and fifty years..." She half-smiled. "Still, I suppose at least my, what, half-a-dozen-greats-grandchildren will see aliens. And we will be able to prepare properly for it."

Mira hated that idea. That she'd never see, never really speak to, an alien. That she'd spend her entire life, maybe, if she was lucky, working on this, and all she would get from it would be to hand it over to someone else. The idea nauseated her. It wasn't *fair*. She didn't understand why no one else was as bothered.

"It would be good to find out their life-span, if we can get to the point of asking questions," Rom said, fidgeting with his stylus. "I mean, who are our great-great-whatever-grandchildren going to be speaking to? The same individuals we are now? Or their descendants?"

"Cultural change..." Sarai said, nodding. "For both of us, possibly. It's a long time."

"It might not be as long for them as for us," Eleanor said. "Do we know how fast they're going?"

"Eh?" Rom said.

"Time dilation," Mira breathed, feeling something light up inside her.

"Yes, exactly," Eleanor said.

She and Sarai started doing calculations with their styluses on the shared projection-board, with the AI chiming in when requested, but Mira wasn't paying attention any more. Time dilation. The only way you could travel into the future.

The only way, perhaps, that *she* could travel into the future.

If the technology existed. Which it didn't. But maybe, just maybe, it could...

#

"I hope you're doing okay out there, Mira." Sarai's face smiled at her from the screen in the front of the tiny ship. There was plenty of silver in her dark hair, now, much more than the last time Mira had seen her in person.

It had taken ten years to improve the existing technology enough for it to be worth Mira going at all. At its fastest, the little ship — just big enough for Mira to live in — could reach 99.99% of light speed, which in theory would cover the remaining 240 years before the aliens arrived in a mere 3.4 years. But accelerating to that speed, and decelerating again, (twice, because she had to turn around) took time too; it was going to be the best part of twenty years in total that she was away. Planetary government, of course, hadn't been interested in any of this; Mira was sponsored by a private investor who desperately wanted to go themself but whose health would never stand up to the trip.

Initially, messages caught up with her quickly; by now, going at full speed, there was a significant lag. Going back again, the lag would decrease again.

"I can't imagine why she thinks I wouldn't be okay out here," Mira said aloud.

"She thinks you have no company." The voice of Guin, the ship's AI, came from all around Mira today; sometimes Guin preferred to use a single speaker.

"She knows you're here," Mira said, impatiently.

"Not everyone thinks of AI as company," Guin said calmly. Guin had emotions — sort of — but in the general way, you wouldn't know it.

"Well, 'not everyone' is foolish, then," Mira said.

She gestured at the corner of the screen, dismissing Sarai's face and pulling up the latest message from the aliens that had come along with it. She had plenty of time to work on them out here, and she was digging further into the messages — the grammar and the vocabulary, certainly, but she was working now on the revealed culture that underlay it, trying to understand more about the beings that sent these messages.

She was still exchanging work notes with the team on Geovine, as well as personal messages. There, they would have more elapsed time to work on the messages, and more people working on them. On the other hand, they also had other things to occupy their time. Personal lives. Other aspects of their work. Mira had none of that. Just Guin, and Guin wasn't demanding. It was soothing, being able to concentrate only on her work, without anyone bothering her about anything else.

She'd considered turning off the messages from Geovine, except that there were useful ideas in there. And Sarai would worry, if she never heard back. That wouldn't be fair. Sarai had always been kind and thoughtful. Of course, by now, even though messages from Sarai were still reaching her, Sarai herself would be dead. Mira felt that she ought to feel sad about that, but it was hard to accept it as truth, when Sarai was still there, on the screen, every time Mira wanted to hear her voice again.

For all she knew, they might all be dead. Now, or

before she returned. In over two centuries, a great many things might happen. She didn't have any particular emotional response to that idea, either.

She pulled up the Geovine team's ideas about the message she was studying, and frowned at them. Their understanding seemed — weak, in comparison to hers. They hadn't been doing the same cultural analysis she had, and she was fairly certain that they were missing underlying meanings with overly literal translations. She'd revisited some of the earlier messages, too, and whilst thankfully she hadn't found any true errors, there were more layers to them than she'd believed at the time.

At least that two hundred and fifty year figure still held.

Mira dutifully sent her own notes and translations back on a regular basis, but she wouldn't know if the Geovine team had successfully received them or taken them into consideration until she was on her way back. By which time they would have had two centuries of their own time to work on all of this. Surely they'd have come to a better understanding by themselves before then. Mira couldn't be the only one spending this much of her time and energy on these messages.

She'd started to dream in the alien language. Started to speak to Guin in it. She wallowed in the immersiveness that the voyage permitted her. Surely there was someone back on Geovine doing the same, hearing the same alien poetry echoing in their brain. Surely it wouldn't just be her.

#

The messages from Geovine had, as anticipated, picked up in frequency as Mira approached, and began the multi-year braking process. They weren't from Sarai any more. Sarai was dead now. That didn't seem any more real than it had over a decade ago.

It took her more time than she felt it should to understand the messages and reports. Human culture must have moved on. Had human language moved on, too, or was she just too immersed in the alien language?

Every time she came across another alien message embedded in the human, she sank into it as if into a clear pool of water, relief suffusing her body.

The aliens would be here soon. It didn't matter so much if she couldn't engage with the humans that were here now, as long as they didn't keep her from the aliens. They wouldn't. They *couldn't.*

<What will you do, once we land?> she asked Guin.

<Stay here,> Guin said firmly.

<Won't you be lonely?> Mira asked, a little hesitantly. <You too wish to meet the aliens? To use our speech?>

Guin made the audio equivalent of a shrug. <I have different ways of accessing data from yours. Bodily experience is not my primary concern. I urge you not to concern yourself with me.>

Mira stared at the screen and tried to find a way of saying that of course she would concern herself with Guin.

<You are my friend,> she said, finally, using an alien turn of phrase that included references to a homeworld symbiotic plant, and to a famous mythological hero who became part of the mountain from which they had accessed the domain of the gods. If gods was the correct word for that part of the translation; Mira still wasn't sure.

<I am fine,> Guin said again. The intensifier they used was one that could not be politely contradicted; Mira nodded and considered the conversation concluded.

Once they'd landed, she waited patiently through a series of formal welcomes. The spoken language sounded a little slurred, a few changed vowel sounds, but nothing she couldn't understand if she focused. It felt artificial, though, on her ear; artificial and clunky. There were far smoother ways to express these concepts.

"...your solo voyage..." one of them said, and Mira rolled her eyes.

Sarai had said that, too, before she left, that she'd be on her own for twenty years. Which was nonsense.

"I wasn't on my own," she said, abruptly. "Guin was there."

Everyone blinked at her. "The ship's AI," Mira clarified.

"Well, yes, the AI, but *really*, well, I think we can still call it solo," the person speaking said.

Nonsense. Still the same nonsense. Two centuries later, a wholly alien species about to land, and they still weren't treating AIs as people?

An alien species about to land. Now she came to think of it, they hadn't said anything about that at all during all this wordy nonsense.

"The aliens. Have they landed?"

The humans looked at one another.

"Next week," one of them offered. "There's time for you to settle in first."

Next week. In the circumstances, it should feel like exceptionally good timing. But in fact it felt like an eternity.

An eternity Mira would have struggled to deal with if she hadn't found Guin's voice taking over from the AI in her assigned quarters.

<Oh, thank the mythos,> Mira said fervently. The other AI had been helpful, but it hadn't been *Guin*.

<We agreed that you might be comfortable with me,> Guin said.

<Are you still based on the ship?>

<Hooked into the *data network*, yes. Do you need any help?>

<New messages,> Mira said, urgently. <There must be another set since our last.>

Guin bloomed the messages across Mira's hand-screen, and she settled in with a sigh of relief.

#

It seemed absurd that, with two centuries to work on the matter, the humans here hadn't wholly outstripped Mira in their abilities with the aliens' language. And indeed, they had a far larger shared corpus of knowledge about it, a corpus of knowledge only some of which had been beamed off to Mira, in her tiny cockleshell of a spacecraft. She was doing her best to make up for that lack now.

The corpus was there, the shared expertise. But everyone on Geovine had been tackling their work whilst surrounded by all the tedious cruft of everyday human existence. Mira and Guin had been speaking in it for years; no one here could do that, not all the time, because they stepped out of the lab and had other things to do. And those who in theory had the most experience, also lost the most time to discussions about funding and planning and all the other tedious administration required of living with other beings.

Guin had an AI friend who Guin thought had a similar grasp of the language as Mira and Guin had, but the AI apparently wouldn't speak to humans. Mira couldn't blame it.

Once the aliens landed, it was a surprisingly short time before Mira — supported by Guin, although the humans failed to acknowledge Guin's contribution — became the main liaison between aliens and humans. On their side, the one of their number whose name was best represented by a human as Tst-verung took a very similar role.

The aliens in general, and Tst-verung in particular, were, in Mira's opinion, significantly more comprehensible and less annoying than modern humans. Also, Tst-verung spoke to Guin — and, later, to Guin's friend — just as politely and with just the same enthusiasm as they did to Mira. Tst-verung found Mira's pronunciation of their language highly amusing — the downside of learning it largely in its written form — but was happy to help Mira improve. Mira found herself spending more and more time with them, talking about anything that came to mind. And sitting, sometimes, in silence. Mira liked silence. It seemed that Tst-verung did, too.

It was in the middle of one of these discussions that the matter of hibernation came up. Somehow, in all her efforts to understand their culture from their messages, Mira had not discovered the existence of this practice. This was peculiar, as their culture seemed to have neither taboos, nor prohibitions around blunt questions (another thing Mira appreciated about it, as she had always struggled to navigate her own culture's social norms around such things); yet still it somehow had not been spoken of.

<It is part of our life cycle,> Tst-verung said. <The move from this stage to that one. One comes out, after, and the siblings sing to one...> They trailed off, making the feeler-movements that indicated happy memory.

<You did this? On the ship?>

<No, no. I have sung. I have not transformed, not yet.> The movement with this indicated a sadness that Mira couldn't attach to a reason.

<It is a sad thing?> she asked, cautiously.

<A happy thing,> Tst-verung said. <Happy at home, happy on ship.>

Mira thought about this. <You seemed sad. Was I wrong?>

<Perhaps, not happy here,> Tst-verung said.

<You will hibernate here?>

<It seems likely.>

There had been some discussion, recently, of the aliens leaving. Mira knew only through her colleagues at the lab, not that she saw any of them very often. It hadn't come up between Tst-verung and her. She hadn't dared ask. But if they were hibernating, performing a crucial part of their life cycle here, was it possible that they weren't leaving, after all?

<All of you?>

<Just me.>

<You will hibernate, and your siblings will sing,> Mira said.

<My siblings will leave.> Tst-verung made an emphatic gesture of negation, and then another movement of sadness.

<Leave you? Here? Alone?>

Tst-verung didn't respond, but their seven-feelered limb drooped slightly.

There would be no one here when Tst-verung woke up. No one to sing to them, to bring them out of hibernation as they should be. No one to live with them thereafter.

<How long? How long do you hibernate?>

Tst-verung paused for a moment, as if calculating. <Two hundred of your years.>

No wonder the rest of them would leave without them. Mira tried to understand the long explanation of why they couldn't hibernate on the ship; something to do with the effect on their nervous systems if it took off with them in hibernation, and the impossibility of leaving before it happened.

<I should have been next time-period. It has come early, for me. It was not planned.>

Their rippled sadness was more acute now, as though they were letting themselves show it now that Mira understood. Mira couldn't take that sadness away. But there was something she could do.

<I will be there for you,> Mira said.

<You will be dead,> Tst-verung said.

<Well,> Mira said, <perhaps not. I have done this before.>

Tst-verung listened to the explanation without moving; significant itself in a species that was in constant rippling motion. <They will permit you?>

<I am not going to ask them,> Mira said, and signalled Guin.

#

Without Guin — and, more particularly, Guin's still-unidentified AI friend — it wouldn't have been possible. As it was, they had to leave before Mira could see Tst-verung into their hibernation chamber, or even see it built. Mira did ask for official permission, but no one treated it remotely seriously. It was perhaps as well that no one treated AIs seriously either, because that meant that Guin could manage their departure.

Guin and Mira shifted back into the alien language, with relief, as soon as they were away from Genovine, and threw themselves into the archive of culture that Tst-verung had uploaded for them. It didn't prevent them, either of them, from fiercely missing Tst-verung. Mira felt that perhaps she ought to miss the humans she'd left, as well; but if she hadn't really missed Sarai and the rest, over two centuries (or twenty years, depending on your perspective) ago, whom she actually liked, she couldn't see why she would miss a collection of humans who had felt rather more alien to her than Tst-verung had.

The time slipped by. They reached the halfway point, turned back, accelerated again. Messages stopped coming from Genovine while they were on their way back. They didn't know why for certain, but most of the likely answers didn't bode well for the state of the human settlement on Genovine. No value in worrying before they knew, though. Guin worried more; their AI friend had gone silent.

From orbit, the surface of Genovine was scorched black, and there were no signs of human life, despite all their best scanning efforts. There was no obvious sign, either, of exactly what had happened, or why. Mira was sad, she supposed, or she regretted whatever had occurred, or something... didn't she? While Guin mourned their AI friend, Mira looked down at the charred surface, and told herself that she must be sad. It was a distant emotion.

A much more distressing, much closer emotion was her fear that they wouldn't be able to find Tst-verung's hibernation chamber. Or that it would have been breached, Tst-verung lying dead within it. Mira had seen the plan before she left, and it should have been well protected, but... they didn't know what had happened here. There was no radiation signal, but the surface destruction spoke of cataclysm.

A week of scanning found nothing, and the time was coming ever closer, Mira was certain.

On day eight, Guin, finally, found something. Something moving underground. At Mira's frantic prompting, they started the landing protocol immediately. They landed a scant hour before Tst-verung emerged. Time enough to be ready to sing. She and Guin had learnt the cycle-song, while they were gone, and now they performed it, for Tst-verung, to welcome them back into the world.

To a wholly new world.

"Thank you," Tst-verung said afterwards. The

human words sounded peculiar; Mira hadn't heard human language in years.

<You are my friend,> Mira said. She couldn't think of anything more to say. Perhaps she didn't need to.

<What happened?> Tst-verung asked. Their skin was multicoloured now, beautiful rippling scales.

<I do not know,> Mira said.

<Then... what now? For us, here?>

<We could stay,> Mira said. <Rebuild.> She waved her arm, a gesture of doubt.

<Or we could go,> Guin said, and Mira's heart lifted.

The cockleshell-ship would be a tight fit for two bodies — three, in one sense, but Guin's body was the ship, the whole of it. Three of them, three bodies, two bodies in one.

<Here is not home, any more,> Mira said. <I don't want to rebuild. I want the stars.>

<Then the stars we will have,> Guin said.

<Where to?> Tst-verung asked.

<Wherever we want,> Mira said. <Wherever we choose.>

<Wherever we get to,> Tst-verung said. <A new cycle.>

<A new cycle,> Mira and Guin said together.

The ship soared away from the burnt world, and out into the stars, shedding time from its silver skin as it sped upwards.

###

About the author

Juliet Kemp lives and writes in London, UK, with their partners, child, and dog. They believe that free time is very important and are constantly baffled by the fact that they never have any. They make up for this by drinking a lot of tea. Juliet has had stories published in several anthologies and online magazines, and blogs at julietkemp.com

Patience

K. G. Anderson

Trapped for 25 years in the research colony, Jac Wuo had come to hate Henge. All of it: the planet, most of his colleagues, and especially the silent boulders they were studying to no result.

No one in the research station would be surprised when they woke up and found his suicide note on their datapads.

"Leaving this hellhole," he typed. Jac squinted appraisingly at the draft. It had his usual brevity, with the right touch of bitterness. Yeah, they'd believe it. He hadn't been too popular these past few years. Several people might even be glad to see the last of him. And Alaina, that bitch, would be delighted by the news when she arrived.

Jac chuckled. He tilted his head back and ran his fingers through his long black hair. It was his one vanity, even with the grey coming in at the temples. *Fifty-six years old*, he thought. *Twenty-five years of my life wasted on this gods-forsaken planet.*

Not at all what he'd envisioned when he'd been selected from the space station's engineering labs to join the expedition of the century. Of the millennium!

Drones from an automated survey ship prospecting for rare minerals had discovered the first evidence of intelligent life. Not little green men, not even humanoid.

The drones' cameras returned with video: towering formations of silicate boulders moving as if arranged by huge, invisible hands. Stones rose from the ground to form soaring archways, the archways arranged in a long row culminating in a perfect circle. Surely the work of intelligent beings. The drones' sensors had recorded energy emissions accompanying the movement of the stones — patterns intriguingly similar to human brainwaves. The planet, quickly named Henge, appeared to be Earthlike — atmosphere thin but breathable, gravity 0.9 of Earth's.

The Earth-Mars Research Consortium lost no time dispatching a 10x-lightspeed buildership with a colony kit and a crew of engineers to build structures and systems. Two years later, with much fanfare and media coverage, a small speedship took off with the colonists — a multi-disciplinary team of young space station researchers. Their mission: to document the phenomenon and make first contact with the silicate intelligence.

Jac had been thrilled to be pulled from a laboratory and named senior engineer for the Henge team. The two-year trip out on a state-of-the-art speedship had been heady.

"We'll see the stones dance! And we'll dance with them." Alaina Bet-Sol, the exo-biologist and media darling leading the team, had a way with words. She also had a way with men. Jac was one of at least three she'd enjoyed and then discarded as they sped through space.

The colonists arrived to find the stones truly imposing, but disappointingly silent and stationary. Under Jac and Alaina's direction, they set up testing equipment, the planet's incessant wind, rain, and hail fighting them every inch of the way. Alaina turned out to be an impatient taskmaster.

"They could move at any moment!" she would shout. Alaina's voice crackling in their earphones, the exhausted engineers fought to install sensors and keep video cameras in place during the scouring sandstorms.

After six months at the station, Alaina left on the speedship, supposedly to secure more funding and recruit more colonists. She returned every five years, alone, increasingly mysterious, and with far too few supplies.

This time, Jac thought, it would go differently. Very differently.

Jac had refined a sensor system capable of detecting a speedship in orbit above the planet, even during the most turbulent weather. Two days ago, it spotted a ship, surely Alaina's. That meant her shuttle could be down here at the first break in the storm cover. Jac would be ready for her.

He got up from the tiny desk in his quarters and pulled off his faded gray coverall, tucking it into the narrow closet. Then he stepped into an identical coverall — identical in all respects except for one small, neat hole burned into the left breast pocket.

Carrying the small plastic packet of blood obtained from one of the colony's chickens, he tapped "Send" on his suicide message and lay down on the bed where he emptied the packet onto the hole over his heart. He shoved the plastic bag deep into a hip pocket and lay back to wait.

#

Macui Berier, the research station administrator, slept fitfully and woke early. When she confirmed that Jac's suicide note had arrived, she rolled out of bed, pulled on her usual gray coverall, and prepared to play her role. By now, Gilbert Pavich, the station's medic, would have removed the body and hidden Jac in the colony's medical suite.

Macui found a group of colonists gathered in the hallway of the residence wing, talking about Jac's death.

"Can you believe this happened just before Alaina is supposed to arrive?" It was a woman's shrill voice, verging on hysteria.

"Everything will be fine," Macui said, offering the expected platitudes. She was pretty sure the colonists had long ago stopped believing her.

"But with Jac gone, who will stand up to Alaina?" the woman wailed. The others muttered their agreement.

On Alaina's last visit, Jac had publicly demanded that she allow some of the colonists to return to civilization. He'd asked her to allow a few of them to visit her speedship, or whatever vessel she had in orbit. She'd refused. There were rumors that he'd later attempted to commandeer her shuttle, only to be threatened by the AI that piloted both her ship and her shuttle.

Macui had denied the rumors. She'd felt it was her job to keep a lid on things. For that same reason she'd covered up the fatal accident that befell Beda, a member of the station's logistics team, when Alaina visited 10 years before. Unloading boxes of supplies from Alaina's shuttle, the woman had tripped and fallen from the loading ramp, snapping her neck.

"It was a terrible, terrible accident," Alaina had assured them. But Gilbert, examining the woman's body, had found signs that a beam from a stunner had knocked her unconscious before she tumbled from the ramp.

Macui shuddered at the memory. Yes, it would be different this time. She slipped away from the group and hurried down the tunnel to the mess hall to handle more questions about Jac's apparent death and Alaina's imminent arrival.

Flickering light filled the narrow tunnel from the square glass panels in the ceiling as storm clouds raced across the sky. Yet another storm was coming. Thunder, lightning, rain and hail were nearly continuous on Henge, the weather driven by high winds that scoured the barren continent day and night.

The land above the research center was as harsh as the weather — boulders, arroyos, and stands of short, hardy shrubs the researchers had dubbed steelwoods. Wind rattled the station's sunken access doors. During the worst of the storms the violent gusts could be felt even below ground. Cups went jittering across desks and clothes fell from their hooks onto the flooring. Jac wore noise-cancelling headphones round the clock and others begged Gilbert for pills from his dwindling supply of anti-anxiety drugs.

Macui had learned to live with the winds. But the near-constant   storms   effectively   cut   off   their communication with the rest of the galaxy. The isolation was far worse than she, or any of them, had expected. Only when Alaina arrived with supplies could the colonists count on her ship to relay long-delayed messages and news from Earth, Mars, and the space station.

If that weren't bad enough, Jac had begun questioning the authenticity of the messages and news that came through.

"It's a simple matter of algorithms," he said. "That AI on her ship could find and replace keywords and phrases, preventing us from knowing what's really going on back home. What better way to keep control of us?"

Macui and Gilbert had finally agreed. As the station's medical expert, Gil was alarmed by Alaina's behavior. "My fear is that Alaina is keeping us isolated to retaliate because we haven't figured out anything about those damned rocks."

Entering the mess hall, Macui held up her hand, signaling people to wait. She took a bowl of steamed vegetables with protein sauce and carried it to the longest table, sitting on a crude bench. The room fell silent.

"I saw the same note you all did," Macui said. "It was the last thing I expected of Jac. He was a leader in the community, and we all relied on him."

"Maybe too much," Harry Gates called out. "Well, now the rest of us are going to have to take on Alaina. I'm ready."

The group Macui had left at the residence wing was just coming in the door.

"Yeah!" "So are we!" They were louder and rowdier than the group at the tables.

"All right!" Macui, relieved that reactions were just as Jac had predicted, raised her voice to announce the next step. "As soon as Alaina arrives, I'll set up a meeting in here."

"Yes!" Shouts, many of them angry, rang out. When the talk began to subside, Gilbert stood up at the other end of the long table.

"Hey!" he called out. People looked up to see him holding aloft one of the stained plastic cups, half filled with a hot brown liquid they still referred to as coffee.

A short, stocky man who'd let his hair grow out in gray ringlets, he'd provided medical care for everyone in the colony. He'd supported the women who'd chosen to have children in spite of Alaina's directives to focus on research. Everyone stopped eating and raised their cups as well.

"To Jac," Gilbert said firmly. There were nods all round. People sipped. In the silence that followed, Macui heard the chatter of the colony's three small children.

"Play outside today?" Jilly, the youngest, asked.

"Maybe," her father answered. "If there's a wind break."

#

"When Alaina arrives, the first thing she'll hear from everyone is that you're dead," Macui said.

"That'll put her off guard." Jac held a towel to the wet spot on his coverall where he had washed away the chicken blood from his fake gunshot wound. The ugly mess had been enough to convince a queasy Frank Singh, the mechanic who acted as the station's security chief, to sign off on Gilbert's diagnosis of death by suicide.

Now Jac, returned from the dead, sat with Macui and Gilbert in the cramped back room of Gilbert's medical lab, heads literally together. The door to the lab was flimsy; they talked in whispers.

"Is everything ready?" Gilbert asked.

Jac shrugged. "Let's hope. There's always uncertainty. I'm wondering why her ship turned up early; it's not quite five years. I had to 'die' a few months sooner than we'd expected."

Macui reached out a slim dark hand and tapped Jac's arm. She put a finger to her lips. "Shhh!" Jac's gravelly voice and loud laugh were easy for colonists to recognize. "You're dead."

Gilbert had taken a blue plastic toolbox out of the cabinet, and now he set it on the table beside Jac. "All your gear is in here. We'll hear the alert as soon as her shuttle lands, and we'll set up the diversion so you can get to the shuttle before she secures it."

Jac opened the box. It was filled with electronics gear and a laser weapon. He checked the settings. Did he intentionally hold the weapon so they couldn't see which setting he'd chosen?

"Jac, try not to kill her." Macui spoke evenly, without emotion. "We don't know how many people are still loyal to her. If Gil can keep her under 'medical restraint'" — they both looked at Gilbert, who nodded — "we'll have time to bring the community together."

Jac's forehead furrowed.

"Something wrong?"

"It's that damned AI. We have no idea how she communicates with it. Body tech? Implants? Can it read her biosigns and sense immediately if she feels threatened?" Jac continued to examine the contents of the box. "After all these years, her relationship with that AI is almost kinky."

Gilbert shot Macui an amused look, his eyebrow raised. She nodded. They knew that Alaina and Jac had been lovers on the voyage to Henge.

They all started when a voice, just outside the door, called out for Gilbert.

"Be right with you," he answered.

Jac stood pressed against the wall, as Gilbert and Macui went out the door and pulled it closed behind them.

"There's a signal coming in," the voice in the hall said. "The storm's still bad, but we think it's Alaina's ship."

#

A break in the storms came two days later and Alaina's shuttle appeared toward dusk. Macui led a group of colonists toward the station's landing pad outlined in bright runway lights. The door slid opened and Alaina came down the short ramp wearing a silver environmental suit and helmet. Macui frowned. This was new. Protection against the dust, or against angry colonists?

As the colonists neared, Alaina stopped, removing the helmet and tucking it under one arm. She raised her arm to shield her face from the ever-present wind.

"Half of your runway lights are out," she said by way of greeting. Behind her, the ramp to the shuttle retracted and the door closed with a snap.

Macui stiffened. Even the woman's shuttle was rude. "Jac Wuo is dead," she shot back.

Alaina halted mid-stride. Macui saw that Alaina's face was pale and her usually silky hair looked tangled. The helmet? Or was there something wrong?

"The stones," Alaina said, looking not at the greeting party but at the stone formation in the distance, barely visible through the swirling sand. "So what have you found out?"

"Nothing."

"Oh, for gods' sake!" Alaina strode toward the station as if there she could access the data the colonists had failed to obtain.

Macui reached out and grabbed her arm. "It's over, Alaina. We want to go home. There's nothing here but a pile of goddamn rocks that don't move, and never will. And the research station."

Alaina's nostrils flared. "You don't understand." Her voice rang with conviction, sending an uneasy shiver through the listeners. Was Alaina crazy, or was there some terrible news they knew nothing about? "You don't understand," she repeated. They waited for her to move toward the station, but she took one step, staggered, and stopped. One colonist took her helmet, and another took her arm. To Macui's astonishment, Alaina didn't shake them off. They steered her to the entrance down the ramp into the station.

"Take her to the guest suite," Macui reminded them. Then she fell back, ducking into an alcove and using her wrist controls to get Jac on her earphone.

"What the hell is going on?" he said. "Alaina locked the shuttle up tight. Usually she lets Drav and Lee inside to unload supplies."

"Stay away from the shuttle. I'm not sure that she locked it; it may have been her AI."

"Eduardo? Yeah, she calls the damn thing Eduardo," Jac growled.

"OK. But there's something else going on. There's something wrong with Alaina. As soon as possible, I'm going to gather everyone into the mess hall. Get onto the security system and watch on the mess hall camera."

#

When Alaina entered the mess hall, the colonists fell silent. In the past she'd been received with excitement, or at the least, deference. Dressed in a blue suit of vaguely military cut, she'd summarize the latest news from the space station laboratories, thank the colonists for their work, and rally them to persist. Today Alaina wore a standard grey station overall. She looked as frayed as the worn fabric.

Gilbert had set a black folding chair for her at the front of the room. Alaina sat down carefully, sliding sideways onto the seat, her eyes on the floor. Slowly, she raised her gaze to the colonists — 26 of the 29 people she'd brought to Henge, plus three children. Two colonists were dead — three if you counted Jac Wuo.

"It's been two years since I've spoken to another human being," Alaina began softly. "Five years your time, I know. You are the first people I've spoken to."

A murmur rippled through the crowded room. Alaina looked down again, shook her head. "Eduardo took control of the ship quite a while ago. After the...accident... with Beda. I'm the one who shot her. I thought she was going to..."

Alaina's voice trailed off to a whisper.

"Eduardo...that's your AI." Gilbert spoke as if translating from Alaina's world to theirs.

Alaina nodded, and then it all came pouring out. Ten years ago Earth and Henge time, a still-unsolved terrorist attack had crippled the space station. Blaming each other, Mars and Earth had declared war. The Interstellar Exploration Initiative had been dissolved and all resources diverted to military defense. A series of environmental disasters on Earth had taken away the more advanced planet's advantage.

"The buildership and the 10x speedships that escaped destruction in the early days of the war were converted to military use," Alaina said. "I barely escaped with a ship ten years ago, and brought you only half of the supplies."

A few gasps around the room.

"The next time I docked at the space station, Mars Military commandeered my ship. I demanded — I requested — in the end, I begged for a ship and supplies. No one would even return my messages."

"Devin Broussard?" someone shouted. Broussard's company owned the automated ships that had discovered Henge, and the stones. He'd been the major private investor in the station; three of the station's exo-geologists were from his labs.

Alaina gave a bitter laugh, almost a snarl, and for a moment her dark brown eyes flashed in the way everyone remembered. A haughty note enlivened her voice as she said, "Bankrupt. His company, at least. Devin still has plenty."

Another bitter laugh. "Yes, he gave me a ship — a tiny, automated ship barely capable of supporting one human passenger." She pointed a trembling finger skyward to indicate the vessel now orbiting Henge. "Eduardo made it possible for me to survive. I have some supplies. Not much. Only a fraction of what you need."

"Traitor," a woman screamed, and the room erupted. Macui, at the door, stood aside to let Jilly's father hustle the three children out of the hall.

Gilbert marched to Alaina's side and held up his arms, powerful hands spread wide, to quiet the crowd. Slowly, gradually, the voices subsided.

Alaina said something to Gilbert, her voice low. Gilbert bent down, Macui joined them, dropping to her knees. Then Gilbert led Alaina aside while Macui stood and turned to the waiting crowd.

She wondered, should she tell them what Alaina had just revealed? She closed her eyes, took a deep breath. In her earpiece, Jac's voice.

"Tell them," he said.

She realized he'd heard what Alaina had told them. Uncertain, Macui shook her head.

"Tell them," he repeated. She nodded.

"Folks. Friends. Family." The room fell silent. All they could hear was the keening of the wind above the roof. Macui held her hand over her heart as she spoke. "Alaina returned with only a fraction of the supplies we had requested, and no more will be forthcoming."

Groans and wails.

"Henge is one of four remote colonies that have been abandoned by Earth and by Mars. We are now on our own."

As she spoke, Macui was already assessing the colony's ability to survive. The planet had water. The colony had solar collectors, windmill generators, and an underground, glass-roofed farm. They maintained a robust flock of chickens and a small fishpond. But hardware, replacement materials, medical supplies, and chemicals — Henge had been completely reliant on the Earth-Mars Consortium.

"Why should we believe her?" Tina Zapata's voice broke the silence. The tiny exo-geologist stood on a bench and shouted, while around her the room went wild. People clutched at each other, at their own hair, at their clothing.

"Because it's true!" Alaina was back at the front of the room. She stood with two hands on a table for support. "We are abandoned."

"Why the hell did you come back?" a voice shouted. Everyone went silent to hear the answer.

"Because I want to see the stones. I could have died on the space station, I could have died on Earth, but I want to die here. I want to see the goddamn stones. I want to see them dance."

With that, Alaina collapsed on the floor.

Gilbert fought his way into the throng around Alaina while Macui stepped out in the hallway and spoke on her earpiece to Jac. "Did you see that?"

"Are they helping her? Hurting her?"

"Who knows?"

"I've moved to the electronics lab, so Gil's safe to

bring her into the med lab if he needs to. As soon as you can get away, meet me here and let's try to figure out what to do next. Looks like it's time for me to come back to life."

#

Jac's reappearance was less of a surprise to people than he'd expected. They were so upset by Alaina's news and her breakdown that his return from the dead was, well, just one more thing. Macui put him to work immediately on plans for the station's survival.

"It's like you want your enemy to stay strong because then it justifies your own anger," Jac said to Gilbert. They were in the med lab sipping mugs of the questionable whisky that Gilbert brewed from the colony's corn crop.

Gilbert nodded. "Welcome to a whole new set of problems."

Citing Alaina's instability and using her own rank as station chief, Macui persuaded Eduardo to let her aboard the shuttle. When there was a break in the storms, the AI flew the shuttle up to the tiny survey ship.

Macui saw that Alaina had been telling the truth. She'd spent two years living in what was essentially a flying computer room! Macui shuddered and for once felt sorry for Alaina.

Macui shared with the AI the colonists' fears, and asked him to calculate ways of getting at least two or three of them back to the space station using only the survey ship. Her plan was to wait at least ten Henge years until the children were grown, and give them the option of returning. Until then, Eduardo could stay in orbit and collect the news from Earth and Mars, sending it down to the station whenever the storms permitted. For the time, Eduardo remained unwilling to join the station's data networks.

"Will Alaina recover?" the AI asked, surprising Macui.

"Recover? Well, just being with people again will help her," Macui said. "But it was more than just being alone for so long that made her sick. She lost her status, she lost her ship, and, I think she realized at the same time that her life's research was going to be a failure." Macui paused, wondering how much the AI could understand. "Alaina was so used to winning that she didn't know how to handle losing. Does that make sense?"

"Yes. It's a human design issue."

Macui suppressed a laugh. "For some of us more than others."

"Was my treatment of her a factor in her illness?" Eduardo asked. "I was trying to make her happy."

Again, Macui was surprised. She realized that, unlike a person, Eduardo wanted an honest answer. "Yes. You made her feel like she was winning all the time. That kept her alive, but at the same time you enhanced her fantasies and delusions."

Macui found herself listening for a sigh that did not come. "That's useful information," was all the AI said.

Gilbert had asked Jac's team to keep an eye on Alaina as she recovered. Late one afternoon, the security system told him she had exited the station.

Alaina chose to go out in a fierce wind, bundled in a borrowed coat and boots. Jac saw she was headed for the boulder formation, and he trudged after her. He found it hard to believe that a week ago he'd been readying a gun to stun, or even kill, her. All that was over now. He was astonished at the relief he felt.

He caught up with her at the entrance to the long corridor of boulders, and together they walked into the circle. They were at the very edge of the galaxy, but for a few minutes it felt as though they were in the middle.

#

"Wind break!"

The wind fell in the late afternoon, as it sometimes did, and the researchers poured out of the station, bringing stools and blankets to sit on the white desert sand. They brought out the children, carefully coated in the last of the colony's sunscreen. Jilly, Benji and Sara ran shrieking across the desert and stopped halfway to the stones.

"Play like the stones!" Jilly looked up at the giant boulders. "Stones! Stones!'

Sara stood stock still, arms raised stiffly over her head. "Ready!"

Daniel reached down, grabbed Jilly by the waist, and threw her into the air.

"Be careful," a mother yelled from the distance.

Sara caught Jilly by the shoulders while Benji lifted her by the hips. Jilly stiffened until she spanned the two taller children to form a Henge-like arch. "Yay!"

Jilly came tumbling down. She and Benji fell on their hands and knees and this time Sara dove across to span their backs. "We're the stones!" Jilly shouted.

They fell to the ground, laughing, just as the wind came up and the first fat raindrops fell.

#

What are they doing?
The small ones mimic our formation.
Do you think they'll like the next formation?
In 975 orbits, we can see.

###

About the author

A career journalist and content producer, K.G. has interviewed Muddy Waters and Harlan Ellison, exposed hazardous waste dumping in a Mafia-owned landfill, reviewed the early World Wide Web for an Apple ezine, and worked on the launch team for the iTunes Music Store. After attending the Viable Paradise workshop in 2013, she began publishing speculative fiction, with stories in anthologies include the Aurora-winning *Second Contacts, The Mammoth Book of Jack the Ripper Stories, Welcome to Dystopia,* and *More Alternative Truths.* Her work is available online at *Metaphorosis, Ares Magazine,* and *Far-Fetched Fables.* Visit her at <u>writerway.com/fiction</u>.

Petri Viventum

James Ross

Do you believe in life after death?

Professor Boris Todharov was what I would call an interested sceptic. Even after all of the time we spent together, I couldn't tell you how much he truly believed, beyond his own empirical findings. I couldn't tell you where he settled on the spectrum between speculation and revelation. That's unusual for me. We came to this planet a long time ago, when he was young, to find the *Petri Viventum*,[1] study the principles of sedimentary rejuvenation, and discover if it was possible to live after death.

We came alone, and we were the first. One men and his ship, trekking across the galaxy like ancient archaeologists, looking for answers in the past. I didn't accompany him onto the planet, of course. I kept a respectful distance, and watched from orbit.[2] Contrary to what I understand is popular opinion, the Professor rarely made good conversation. He would strike up sudden, intense bursts of dialogue, like Plato's Socrates, before retreating within himself when he considered the matter

---

1   His term. I've always assumed that he meant Petra Viventum. Admittedly, he never claimed to be good at Latin. Either that, or it was one of his obscure jokes.

2   I could have accompanied him in some fashion, I suppose. A drone, perhaps. The Professor preferred to wander alone.

concluded. He conversed like a summer storm, apocalyptic, exciting, and gone in an instant.

How much have you learned about the *Petri Viventum* now? How much have they learned about you? Structurally similar to coal. Sentient, yes, of course,[3] and far more interesting to talk to than the professor. If you are going to insist on being pedantic, then no, they didn't talk. One rock[4] would vibrate, and its specific frequency would be detected by the next rock,[5] reinterpreted, and passed along. An intelligence that couldn't communicate beyond its immediate periphery, and yet could send data halfway across the planet in minutes. This may sound laughably archaic to you,[6] but think back to when your simian ancestors relied on optics and cables.

Professor Todharov was gifted in many ways, but he was not a practical man.[7] Within weeks of wandering the surface, he was thirsty and half starved, unable even to provide for himself on a planet as bountiful as this. Proud until the end, he had nearly breathed his last by the time he allowed me to send the S.O.S beacon. He had enough energy left to record his findings, order his notes, and write a letter of farewell to his friends and loved ones.[8] He needn't have worried; the Professor would not be allowed to die.

The relief team arrived in good time,[9] and set to work. Their supplies were sufficient only to administer medical aid and provide immediate sustenance. Beyond that, our rescuers would be left to fend for themselves. After all of his exertion, the Professor slept deeply, and

---

3   Hence the "Viventum". Keep up.

4   Don't call them that to their face. It's reductive.

5   No, seriously.

6   As it does to me. I mean seriously, do you think you'd hear me crowing about slower than light transmission? Ha.

7   I once watched him attempt to poach an egg. It was a disgrace.

8   I wouldn't have passed on the letter, to be honest. It was overwrought and melodramatic. I'd have made up something a little more appropriate, perhaps with an apology for behaving so foolishly, and passed that on instead.

9   I'd made a tentative request shortly before he landed. I know what he's like.

the settlement, your home, was built around him. Trees were hewn, and rivers dammed, earth flattened, and structures erected. For heat, and to power their rudimentary engines, Rocks were gathered, and tossed into furnaces. They hadn't thought to read the Professor's notes. They were practical people.

When the professor awoke, he was horrified. Wouldn't you be? The intelligence he'd come here to study, the key to his puzzle box, had been disturbed and gathered up. Cast into the flames. When he emerged, bleary-eyed from his slumber, and learned what they'd done, he ran to the furnaces. He reached deep inside, trying desperately to undo the sin that had been done on his behalf. The smell of burnt flesh woke the colonists, and they were able to pry him away.[10] He achieved very little for his pain. Whilst he had slept, the flames had burned remorselessly through their fuel, and only the smallest, blackened pebble remained. The professor scrambled to its rescue, and upon contact it fused with him, burning into the centre of his hand and making his delicate palm lines glow crimson. The colonists fetched their tools, and prepared to remove the pebble, but the Professor would not allow it. He chose instead to flee.

After that miserable episode, the Professor wandered the planet for years, never truly alone. I watched from above, ensuring he came to no harm. His objective remained unchanged, and his ambition returned with gusto. He sought out the sites he had studied before, where great mountains and formations of *Petri Viventum* thrummed in unison, warm to the touch, and making the earth shake for miles around. He found them, of course, but they were different now, silent and cold. They did not move, and no data passed between them. They were empty, dead. Just another feature, part of the landscape. We had known about this beforehand; it was the root of the mystery he had come here to study. As you know, the *Petri Viventum* live for a time, and then don't. They don't sleep, they aren't dormant, they are dead. In every sense

---

10 Not to say that he didn't struggle. He was deceptively strong for such a little man.

of the word. They are completely devoid of all measurable activity, devoid of life. And then they aren't. Without warning or discernible reason, they light up like a circuit board, filling the world with information and reason, changing the course of a planet's history with uncountable and imperceptible actions. Then they stop. They are dead again, until they aren't. The notion fascinated the Professor. If life could stop, utterly, and then start again, then what was death? If death was certain, could it be made uncertain?[11]

The professor waited months for the *Petri Viventum* to reanimate, but they didn't. Even the pebble buried in has hand was silent. Ultimately, I took it upon myself to disturb his reverie. He was unreceptive at first, until I mentioned the Twin Paradox.[12] I welcomed my friend back on board with enthusiasm,[13] and we left, knowing that when we returned, the people who had come to his rescue would be long dead. He didn't care where we went, so I charted a course towards a curious ion storm I had been meaning to study for some time.[14] It was in a distant part of the galaxy, and would give us plenty of time. If I recall correctly,[15] it was the first time the Professor left the decision to me. Just as we left orbit, however, something almost as curious occurred.

His palm pebble—as I had taken to calling it[16]—

---

11 Not so much of a mystery here, I'm afraid to report. Without going into too much unnecessary detail, imagine a reset button on an old computer. It is able to turn itself off, and then from this supposedly "dead" position, reanimate itself. That's not a true or accurate comparison by any means, but it is an analogy appropriate to your simian level of intellect. I would have explained this in more detail to the professor, had he asked.

12 Really? OK, put very simply, two objects will age differently according to their relative velocity. The greater the difference in velocity, the greater difference in the time elapsed. We could, for instance, travel for three years away from the planet, and return three hundred years later. I shouldn't have to explain this to you.

13 Which was, of course, not reciprocated.

14 I'd love to go into more detail as to why it was curious, and why I'd wanted to study it, but as things transpired, I never got the chance.

15 I do recall correctly. I always do.

16 He didn't like that moniker at all. He claimed it was reductive.

began to vibrate. Nothing drastic, just a slow, pulsing motion. Enough to make his fingertips tingle. The Professor was fascinated. So as not to disturb it, he endeavoured to keep his left hand still at all times, while frantically writing with his right. He recorded the rhythms and frequencies, looking for patterns.

There was, in truth, only one pattern. The further from the planet we went, the more violent the vibrations became. Within days, they were so extreme that his whole arm would shake. It became so the Professor couldn't sleep. He fixed his arm to his desk with duct tape to keep it still, and when that broke, he used rope. When the rope tore, he would have nailed it in place had I not intervened. All the while he studied the pattern, keeping endless and increasingly disorganised notes.[17] He was convinced that it was a message, in a language only he could decode. If he could understand one Rock, he would be able to commune with the whole. What's more, one spoke while the rest died. He believed he could learn why. He would keep working until they could answer his question; how they could live, and then die, and then live once more.[18]

---

17 I would have held the data myself, had he asked. Of course he didn't ask; he was a proud man.

18 If you're still interested, then he was wrong. They would die for good eventually, it's mathematically certain. It's actually quite a simple equation. Because n tends to infinity where X is finite and x is distributed uniformly over 0 to n, $P(x<X)$ tends to 0.

Really? I thought you said the Professor was an ancestor of yours? I'll slow down again. Imagine it's possible for you to live for a million years —don't interrupt, this is obviously hypothetical. You have another twenty, tops—the probability that you would be living in the first, what forty years? Seriously, twenty-five? You've had a hard life. OK, the probability that you would be living in the first twenty five years would be one in forty thousand, and increasing the possibility of years lived to infinity moves the probability of living forever to zero. Nil. Nada. You see? If it's possible we are living a finite life, we must be living a finite life. Quad Erat Demonstrandum. The Petri Viventum will die. The Professor died. You will die. One day, even I will die, presumably slain by some mind-bendingly powerful foe in a clash so cataclysmic that it will reverberate throughout eternity. And the pebble wasn't trying to communicate any of this. It was

He recorded its habits throughout three years of travel, scarcely leaving his desk. I would provide food for him at points, and force it down his throat when he forgot to eat it. Like I said, we never made it all the way over to the ion storm.[19] The Professor didn't ask me to turn around; it was my choice. He clearly needed to get back, and he was getting nowhere with the pebble. This decision wasn't out of the kindness of my heart, I should say. I could have kept going if I'd wanted. He was getting on my nerves.

We returned to orbit after three years of travel, and after three hundred years had passed on the planet.[20] By now the palm pebble had limited itself to a slow, regular pulse, allowing the Professor some peace of mind. His arm would still twitch, and he hadn't washed or shaved in months, but his eyes had lost their dark, hunted look. I set him down on the planet's surface, and observed.

A great deal had happened in three hundred years. The colony had grown rapidly, but had also become isolated and primitive.[21] Any fuel and supplies that the colonists had enjoyed at FL had long since been exhausted, and their equipment crudely re-purposed to assist with manual tasks. What's more, the *Petri Viventum* had been active in our absence.

The Professor went first to the Forge, where centuries ago now, the colonists had shovelled heaps of rock into the furnaces. It was not difficult to locate, even from orbit. The colony had grown around it like ripples in a pond, arranging itself in concentric rings around its

---

just screaming.

19 I never attempted to go back, even much later.

20 Don't ask me to explain it to you again.

21 This is far more common than people realise. A generation or two post-FL (First Landing), colonists tend to wonder whether the benefits of obeying a distant hierarchy that can neither provide aid in a timely fashion, nor extend the parental arm of protection are actually outweighing the costs. Sooner or later, it's not uncommon for a distant colony to cut itself off, deliberately and entirely, either by consensus, or having their hand forced by a radical fringe element. Think of the adolescent's desire to at once defy and impress their parents by fleeing the nest. The very same desire that had pushed the Professor halfway across the galaxy in the first place.

centrepiece. The Forge itself had not been rebuilt, or even maintained since FL, and was little more than ruins. It had in fact been cleaved through the middle; right down the centre a thick channel of *Petri Viventum* now lay, humming gently, and extending further in a perfect straight line to either boundary of the settlement. From orbit, it appeared as a tight, sturdy belt, struggling to withhold the settlement's exposed and gaping belly. Even though it bisected the settlement perfectly, it lay completely undisturbed. At certain key points, wooden bridges had been constructed, skilfully and meticulously, and never once touching the rock itself.

The Professor, to his own confusion,[22] received a hero's welcome. He had saved them, they said, by searing his own flesh. The *Petri Viventum's* vengeance had been slow, unnoticeable at first. Boulders would come loose, blocking vital trails that had taken weeks to carve out. Colonists who had gone out to explore the landscape were lost in landslides. It built, altering the landscape by diverting rivers, and crushing lush forests. At its zenith, the ground shook, and finally volcanoes burst in spectacular pyroclastic flows, turning the settlement to ash, and leaving the long strip of rock through its centre. The Forge was torn asunder, like two halves of a sinking ship. Those who survived hid deep underground, driven half mad by the incoherent reverberations. When they emerged, they recovered and rebuilt, and credited the Professor's small act of mercy with their own survival.[23]

The Professor listened to their stories, and wrote them down. They told him that the Rock listened to them now. If treated with obeisance and respect, it would help them. In the few centuries of our absence, mountains had moved, sheltering the colony from fierce, northerly winds. To the south, great boulders had dammed what was once a river, and now a vibrant lake that fed and sustained them. The Professor recorded it all.

We would leave for a second time, but before we did

---

22 And my utter bedazzlement.

23 Sounds like hippy garbage to me. They just got lucky. Don't fuck with the Rock.

the Professor returned to the centre of the colony, where the ruins of the forge stood. As the colonists watched, he laid his left palm on the Rock, and felt it move. The pebble thrummed alongside the rock, like a piccolo taking the melody against the backdrop of a grand orchestra. With his spare hand, the Professor desperately tried to record the vibrations in some coherent manner, first in your own simian language, then in phonetic sounds, and finally in pure binary. After watching him flap around like this for days, a young woman approached, took his notes, and scattered them into the wind. It was not a message, she told him, it was a song. Feel its rhythms and harmonies. It's a piece of music, and it isn't meant for you. Then she led him away.

The Professor stayed with her awhile, and I understand that they talked a great deal. He wanted her to come with us, wander the cosmos in pursuit of an answer. She understood it better than we did,[24] she could decode it. She had been born in the midst of its tremors, and it was a part of her. She would at least know where to start. She wanted him to stay, and he did, for a while. What did it matter if he couldn't find an answer in his own lifetime? They had a child, and she would find an answer when they were gone. If not her, then there would be grandchildren, and great-grandchildren after that. I waited patiently in orbit.

Eventually, the price of not knowing proved too much for the Professor. He needed more time, and despite all the things she could provide him with, she couldn't give him time. We left in the middle of the night, and when we returned, she was long dead. We came back and forth several times, in the course of his lifetime. The colony became a city, and then a civilization. The planet changed alongside it. Eventually they would send out their own colony ships to distant stars. They travelled in ships of *Petri Viventum*, achieving symbiosis, if not total understanding. The Professor would always look for his family, no matter how distant or dispersed they became. It's a shame he never met you. He would have like you.

---

24 Better than him, certainly.

The Professor outlived his offspring. They lived trying to answer his question, as had their own children, and their grandchildren after them. They all had, right the way down to you. You were the first of them to ask for my opinion, by the way. Even the Professor never thought to ask me.

The Professor died, as will you one day. As will the *Petri Viventum*.[25] The planet will survive, as will its people, simian and mineral alike. The hard lessons of the First Landers will not be lost, and the understanding between yourselves and the Rock will grow in steadfastness and wisdom as it is carried to different solar systems. When I go, the data that courses through my circuits will be carried in a larger, more beautiful machine.[26] How does your book put it? Now you see through the glass darkly. Build upon the Rock.[27] Record what you know, learn more, and pass it on, the information will remain. Make your children a synapse in a wider being. It will continue.

So I'll ask you again.

###

About the author

James Ross is an Englishman living in Edinburgh, where he writes whimsical fiction, and (occasionally) performs poetry. His work has previously appeared in *Metaphorosis, The Best Vegan Science Fiction and Fantasy 2016,* and *The Forge Literary Magazine.*

---

25 *Petri Viventum* lasts on average seven and a half millennia, if you count the time it spends "dead." The Professor's pebble is long gone, but it was very old when they first met.

26 If you can imagine such a thing.

27 Petri. Just got it.

The Great Scientist Rivalry on Planet Sourdough

Beth Goder

Audio Journal of Yazhu A. Borla
Sourdough Planet, Year 1, Day 1

I am definitely a genius, because I've discovered a way to create nanobot-integrated sourdough that will change how humanity eats bread.

Here's the plan:

Step 1: Find a planet that no one cares about, so when I place eight fermentation silos on the surface, no one will bother me about regulations or whatever.

Step 2: Time dilation! To bypass the long window needed for sourdough starter fermentation and nanobot algorithm iterations, use a super-fast spaceship to zip around the galaxy. As a result, while two weeks pass for me on the ship, thirty years pass on the planet.

Step 3: Check on the silos, tweaking each creation until...

Step 4: I've created the most delicious, amazing, beneficial sourdough that humankind has ever eaten.

When I'm done, people who eat my bread will be able to do amazing things—breathe underwater, boost their immune systems, get rid of wrinkles. At least, if the experiment goes well. I'm still playing around with the algorithms.

I'll be famous. They'll name cities after me. Countries. Maybe even whole planets.

But, of course, the most important thing is that my creations will benefit humanity.

The plan's only flaw is that I won't get to see Ayla's face when I create the most epic nanofood in the universe. What's the point of having a nemesis if you can't even gloat?

Day 22

This planet is kind of weird. The ground is a sickly yellow color, there are huge rocks everywhere, and the lake looks suspiciously deep. Also, the air smells weird. I know because Chester, the ship AI, told me it was breathable, so I went outside and it was like getting pelted in the face by a wet dog.

The silos are built. I've got the sourdough starters fermenting inside, fed by automated systems that deposit water and flour. The micro environments are set up with wild yeasts from all around Earth.

Since the silos are hermetically sealed, nothing can get out or in. The last thing I need in my sourdough is alien yeast!

This planet has some boring name, like HD 44318 b. I dub it Sourdough Planet.

Now I've got to program the nanobots.

#

Chester's Ship Log
Sourdough Planet, Year 1, Day 35

This is what space sounds like: nothing. The quiet flows over my ship-body. Stars materialize and disappear, rippling outward like stones thrown in water. Silent and beautiful and full of light.

I miss space.

I am starting to regret hiring my ship-body to one Yazhu A. Borla. It's not just the sourdough experiment, although I sense such a project is not standard. She sings to herself constantly, a series of pop ballads in an off-key soprano. She takes her meals in the library, the observatory, her quarters—everywhere but the kitchen— and I've got to send the cleaning bots out to retrieve the plates.

Worst of all, she thinks she's an expert at everything. Sure, she has a Ph.D. in nanobot technology, and a second one in computer science, but that doesn't mean she knows anything about large scale engineering, for example.

She insists on tinkering with parts of the ship. I won't let her get near anything critical, but I've given up the auxiliary recycler, so that I don't have to hear her whining.

I don't have a lot of experience with humans, but from what I've seen so far, I have to say, I'm not impressed.

At least my secret project is going well.

Yazhu thinks there are only eight silos on the planet. In this, like so many other things, she is wrong.

Stealing the nanobots was trivial. When Yazhu was sleeping, I took two bots out of the sterilized environment and programmed them to make other bots. I put the nanobots in Silo Nine, where they will take the raw matter of this planet and evolve it into something new.

I'm tired of humans—their whims, their irreverent attitudes, their bodies which make sounds like "flphp" and "sploosh." I'm tired of other AIs, too. At the spaceport, 10-67-NDR made fun of me because I painted each segment of my body a different shade of blue. She also said my name was non-standard.

I have an experiment of my own—to create a new sentient species. It can't be worse than the ones that already exist.

#

Yazhu
Sourdough Planet, Year 1, Day 45
The silos are churning. I'm tweaking the nanobot programs.

Working on my own is great. I don't have to worry about food safety regulations or infinite clinical tests. When I worked for Kuiper University, let me tell you, I was swimming in red tape.

Who needs tenure? Not me.

I'm sure Ayla is still at the university, thriving. She always did know how to work within the rules.

In Silo One, I've got a wild yeast from Syria. The nanobots are programmed to enhance the cochlea to produce super hearing.

Silo Two has the experiment most unlikely to succeed—a life-extension algorithm, which I've never gotten to work properly.

Silos Three has—well, the specs are all in the experiment logbook. No need to repeat them here.

If I succeed, I'll be even more famous than I am now. (The academic community, I'm sure, is still in awe of my self-replicating ice cream, but I can't rest on my laurels.)

Like the sourdough starter, the nanobot algorithms will need time to mature. I've programmed them using new machine learning techniques, so they respond to what's in the environment, and adapt based on feedback from supervisor programs.

Day 46

Used the service bots to deliver the nanobots to the silos. Bots within bots! No way am I going out on the surface of the planet again.

Tomorrow, we head out. We'll speed past the Magenta Belt, loop around Vegstrom for the gravity assist, then zoom back. But first, we have to pick up some fuel at Savara Station. Yeah, we still need fuel. The Infinite Energy Drive, it turns out, does not provide infinite energy. False advertising, I say.

Maybe I'll take a look at the engine later. I bet I could make it more efficient, just like I did with the auxiliary recycler.

#

Chester's Ship Log
In transit

Space, beautiful vastness. Lovely, silent ocean.

#

Yazhu
Savara Station
We've landed at the station. Time to fuel up!

#

Written Journal of Ayla Fireton
Revenge Plot, Day 1
I've made it to Yazhu's ship. I'm officially a stowaway. Excellent.

It's cramped in the ship's conservatory. I'm nestled under an aspen tree, most likely a Populus tremuloides, squished next to some yeast vats. Why yeast? Probably another one of Yazhu's failed projects. The university was littered with the waste of her experiments, but did anyone care? The inventor of self-replicating ice cream could do no wrong. Such a creative genius, they said. So full of new ideas.

Oh Yazhu, you think you've gotten rid of me, but you have no idea. I will follow you throughout the galaxy. I will haunt you like a ghost. I will bring about your ruin.

I knew Yazhu would stop at Savara Station. She's not as clever as she thinks. Her first mistake? Sending me one last, gloating letter. I traced the signal to the Idiran System, then looked up the log of AI ship rentals. Her flight plan is disorganized, and it doesn't make much sense. Why would she plan her stops at Savara Station spaced out by thirty years?

I didn't have to wait long for her ship to arrive.

The AI, Chester, caught me poking around the hatch. I had an eight-step plan to bribe Chester, but I didn't need it. They asked me why I wanted access to the ship, and the truth came tumbling out—how Yazhu had undermined me at the university and jeopardized my position. And, the nail in the coffin of my tenure hopes, the anonymous letter implying I had falsified data for one of my experiments. Obviously, Yazhu had sent it.

"A petty human squabble," Chester said. "Sounds interesting." They opened the hatch.

Everything is going according to plan.

When we land, I will destroy whatever project Yazhu's working on. I will destroy it all.

#

Yazhu
Sourdough Planet, Year 30, Day 5

We landed on Sourdough Planet. Everything is great! It's thirty years later, here. The sourdough starters are taking on complex flavors and the nanobot algorithms are iterating spectacularly.

The longevity algorithm doesn't look like it will be successful, but that's to be expected.

Chester has been acting weird. Yesterday I tried to get into the conservatory, but the door was locked. Chester claimed it was "compromised for technical reasons," whatever that means.

#

Ayla

We landed on a backwater planet, atmosphere close to Earth standard. I hacked into the feed from the service bots. There are eight silos, all of them teeming with goop.

During the sleep cycle, I snuck outside. The air is breathable, even if it smells like an old shoe.

I broke into Silo Seven. The scent of sourdough starter cut through the old shoe smell. Of course. Yazhu still wants to create the most amazing nanofood in the universe. She'd tried for years at Kuiper University, and failed. She always said she needed more time.

Well, she's found more time. Now her fueling schedule makes sense. She's using time dilation effects to essentially speed up her work.

If I didn't hate her so much, I would say the idea was genius.

Too bad for her that I sabotaged everything.

#

Yazhu
Sourdough Planet, Year 30, Day 10

I don't understand what's going wrong.

Silo One, Three, and Five are open. The micro-seal is completely destroyed. Not only are the starters crawling with alien yeast, but I've contaminated the planet with Earth microbials. That's definitely against United Galactic regulations.

The starter in Silo Two is completely dead, and I don't know why.

The other silos seem okay.

At first, I thought Chester had sabotaged my experiment. They've been angry with me ever since the thing with the auxiliary recycler. Apparently, I caused "irrevocable damage." We had to dump the entire section, the one painted midnight blue.

Luckily, the ship comes apart in segments. We'll leave this one on the planet, and then we'll need less energy to get into space.

Logs show none of the service bots were out last night. That's the only way Chester could have accessed the silos.

Perhaps the sealant was defective. Chester suggested it was human error, but I don't make errors like that. I'll replace the sealant on all of the silos. Hopefully, that will solve the problem.

Today, we're going back into space. One more loop. I hope the other silos can hold out for another thirty years.

#

Ayla

All of the silos are sabotaged. For some, I simply opened the seals. For others, I initiated a self-destruct sequence in the nanobots.

I discovered a ninth silo out past the lake. It's almost as if Yazhu wanted to keep it a secret. I sabotaged it in an extra-special way. The growth-enhancement algorithm I inserted into the nanobots will cause the bots to make everything around them bigger. When Yazhu returns, the failure of Silo Nine will tower over her. Literally.

People told me that revenge wouldn't bring me joy, but they were wrong. Revenge is awesome. The only problem is that now I'm not sure what to do. For so long, I had one goal—to ruin Yazhu's career like she ruined mine.

Perhaps instead of sabotaging her project, I should have taken the idea and marketed it as my own. Yazhu may have genius ideas, but she's completely incompetent when it comes to selling them. It's not enough to have an amazing idea. You have to convince everyone else it's amazing, too.

#

Chester's Ship Log
In transit

Midnight blue is my favorite color. Oh, my beautiful recycler, how I mourn you.

I no longer consider myself to be in the employ of Yazhu A. Borla. She is simply a passenger.

Now it's time to further my own experiments.

I'm going to speed up the ship, so that when we land on Planet HD 44318 b again, it will be one thousand years later. With the help of the nanobots, that will be enough time for my creatures to evolve.

Normally, the subterfuge involved in increasing our speed would pose an ethical quandary for me. After Yazhu's actions, however, I feel no such moral compunctions. I've already taken on more fuel at Savara Station.

Unfortunately, I have the other passenger to think about. The stowaway.

#

Ayla
In transit

I'm sitting up against the Populus tremuloides, the leaves swaying in the artificial wind.

Chester is extremely angry. I told them how I sabotaged the silos. Apparently, Silo Nine was the AI's project.

I asked why they hadn't warned me to leave the silo alone, and Chester said, "Then it wouldn't have been a secret project, a secret silo with secret nanobots."

This whole thing is hardly my fault.

Chester says I am no longer welcome on the ship. At first, I thought they were going to throw me out the airlock, but they have other plans. Chester will leave me at the next stop.

The next stop is that horrible, backwater planet. I'll be stranded.

#

Yazhu
Sourdough Planet, Year 1,000, Day 1

We are so screwed.

Forget about my experiment. The planet is covered in frogs!

First, Chester tells me that due to a "calculation error," we arrived at Sourdough Planet later than intended. One thousand years later!

Then I look out the observation window, and what do I see? Lizards! All manner of amphibian-like creatures, in all imaginable colors. There's something that looks like a cross between a frog and an octopus, but it's hopping about on land. There's a newt dog and a salamander that's ten feet tall and something that looks like a snail but isn't.

The scenery is different, too. The lake has expanded. Now the water is a bright turquoise. There's a huge mountain in the distance.

Chester has commandeered all the service bots for some urgent problem in the conservatory, so I can't send the bots out to make observations.

My sourdough silos must be destroyed. All of that work, for nothing.

A lizard just squished itself against the window and excreted a foul blue liquid. Now it's making a design.

That's actually quite pretty.

Maybe I can still salvage something from this trip. I will venture out among these lizard creatures and take notes. For science!

If I discover a bunch of new species, does that mean I get to name them all after me?

Okay, I'm suiting up. I'll pack a kit—water, microscope, sample containers, nanobot-enhanced camera.

I'm opening the hatch. Stepping down the ramp.

Look at these amazing lizards. They're much more interesting up close. What's that dotted pattern on the blue one's back? Does that one have a trunk? But wait, why are they all running away? Don't be afraid, lizards. I just want to study you. It's very scientific!

Okay, I feel thumping. The ground is shaking. I think I'll get back into the ship.

Chester? Hello? Let me in.

Thump, thump.

What's that coming? Something big. The mountain. It's moving. Oh no. Mountains should not move. The animals are scattering. Frogs, salamanders. Is that an octo-bear?

Chester, let me in now.

The mountain is standing up. It's not a mountain. It's a giant dinosaur monster! With twelve legs! And vestigial wings. It's bigger than five ships. That thing is like a city.

I think it sees me. That is a long neck. Extremely long. Much too long. Why is the dinosaur looking over here? Why is the dinosaur extending his neck in this direction?

Mouth. Giant dinosaur monster mouth. Oh, shit. Oh, shi—

#

Account of Corbious-Tul-Tumar, of the species Panumsaurus gagantem, from the planet HD 44318 b. Translated from Isophic to Galactic Standard.

The blue space creature landed in the Year of Our

Great Frog 506 on a quiet day when the balfankin lizards had barely started to inject their cleaning toxins into my third stomach. The balfankin lizards weren't intelligent enough to notice the incident, but a three-leafed frog hoped out from my mouth to see what all the bother was about, and several thousand salamanders exited from my fourth abdominal flap. Patiently, I asked them to work in shifts. We can't have everything breaking down in the interior on account of a little excitement.

The blue metallic creature was quite small for a fully sentient being—only three bifarial-spans long, and not very wide. Immediately, I knew it was the same creature that had birthed the Artifact. The creature was all shades of blue, like the deep blue of the Artifact, and it had the same markings along its sides.

Finally, proof of alien life.

There have been many theories about the Artifact—that midnight blue contraption that sits by the Lake of Larksna. Some claim it is a message from Great Frog, inscrutable. Others think it came from some civilization who lived here millennia before, but then where are the other artifacts? Aside from some small corroded structures near the lake, we've found nothing. I've always posited that the Artifact originated with an alien species, but I could never prove it.

The blue creature released one of its maintenance animals, a biped that ran swiftly toward me, almost right into my mouth. Not wanting to be rude, I ingested the biped. In she went into my fourth holding chamber.

Some time later, the creature released another biped. I extended my neck, scooped the animal into my mouth, and swallowed her.

It made sense for me to ingest the second biped, as I'd already taken in the first, but I hoped the blue creature wouldn't send out any more. After all, it hadn't ingested any of my maintenance animals.

I waited to see if the bipeds would perform any useful duties, but unfortunately, all they did was shout.

#

Yazhu
Sourdough Planet, Year 1,000, Day 2

I'm not dead. It's even worse. I'm trapped, with my nemesis, in the stomach of a giant dinosaur.

How is this my life?

After the dinosaur swallowed me, I was carried through its body by sticky-handed salamanders. They carted me through corridors with green veins pulsing along the walls, lit by millions of miniature glowing frogs.

Blue goop splashed my helmet. Before I could react, a salamander pulled the helmet from my head.

The inside of the dinosaur smells horrible, like stale yeast and pond water.

The lead salamander paused to look at a jumble of bulbous intestinal tubes, then directed the group down a narrow tunnel.

All of this would have been fascinating if I hadn't been terrified. I'm recording my account now in case my audio-journal somehow survives.

The salamanders deposited me in a cavern, which was brightly aglow with frogs.

There was Ayla, sitting on an upturned bit of bone.

To say I was surprised would be an understatement. I thought I'd seen the last of her at Kuiper University, and here she was, half a galaxy away in the belly of a dinosaur.

"What are you doing here?" I sputtered, wiping salamander gunk from my hands.

"Ask Chester," said Ayla, glaring in the annoying way she always does.

Clearly, the universe hates me. Why else would I be stuck with the most aggravating, overbearing—

Excuse me. One moment.

Yes, Ayla, I know you can hear me. I'm sorry if there's not a lot of privacy in the stomach of a monster dinosaur.

Anyway, next I got her to confess how she'd come to Sourdough Planet. A stowaway! All because she wanted to steal my genius ideas, knowing she could never come up with something so brilliant—

Sorry. One second.

That's basically what you said, Ayla. It's called paraphrasing.

So now we're stuck here together. It's perhaps the only situation that Ayla can't talk herself out of.

That's okay, though. I have a plan.

#

Ayla

After the service bots threw me out of the ship, an enormous life form ingested me. The creature has a striking resemblance to a dinosaur. Fascinating.

A creature this large shouldn't exist, but the dinosaur appears to have a symbiotic relationship with a variety of animals that live inside its interior. I suspect they perform sustention duties that allow the dinosaur to survive.

Yazhu is trapped with me. Typical, her copying me. Just like with the yogurt experiment, when she used my research methodology, down to the statistical analysis of bacteria. She may be great at programming, but she doesn't know a thing about biology.

#

Yazhu

I have to speak quietly. It's Ayla's shift to sleep. I'm on watch.

Some things have changed.

First, Ayla went on a rant about our time at the university and confronted me about some anonymous letter claiming she had falsified data.

Here's the thing: I didn't send that letter. The bagpipe music that mysteriously started playing in her lab? Yeah, that was me. The snarky comments on her article in Biology Jupitar? I signed my name to those. (And believe me, she wrote worse things on papers I've published.) I've poached her grad students, applied for grants that I knew she wanted, and taken the last muffin from the cafeteria when I saw her coming, even though I wasn't hungry. She did the same stuff to me—that's just what it's like when you're both scrambling for tenure.

Before I could tell her that I didn't know anything about that stupid letter, an orange snake-worm popped through the opening to our cavern.

I was used to the frogs by now, and the odd salamander running through, but this thing was different. It was as big around as a beaker, and longer than Ayla and me put together. I couldn't tell the front from the back—it was all slime and ringed sections.

The snake-worm slithered my way.

Ayla went rigid, barely moving. "Looks like a caecilian," she said, her voice low.

I didn't have time to ask what a caecilian was, because the snake-worm wriggled closer. The glow frogs scattered.

"Don't move," said Ayla, but I was already running across the cavern. The snake-worm followed.

"Your vibrations." Her face went pale. I'd never seen her look so afraid. "Shit. Stop moving."

I couldn't stop moving, because the snake-worm was inches from my leg and my brain was saying, "panic snake panic worm orange death death death." I did the only sensible thing and ran behind Ayla. We both froze.

The snake-worm thrashed in the middle of the cavern. With a tremendous pop, the creature turned itself inside out, like a burst balloon, until its exterior was covered with razor spines. The thing pounced on a frog, then folded back in on itself, until the unfortunate frog was encased within.

"Can the ones on Earth do that?" I hissed.

"Did you see the spines near the back annulus?" said Ayla, visibly shaking. "Thicker, shiny. Probably wet with venom. That implies it can take down bigger prey."

We both swore. The cavern became darker as frogs scurried out through the opening or shimmied behind tissue folds.

"You're the biologist," I said. The snake-worm writhed, digesting the frog. My heart felt like it would beat out of my chest. "Do a biology thing. Make it go away."

"For Earth biology," she said, talking too quickly. "And the ice ecospheres on Neptune. This thing looks like a caecilian, but there's no guarantee there are any similarities. If this one evolved to live underground, like their Earth analogues, maybe that could explain the hearing and vision—"

The snake-worm that looked like a caecilian but wasn't slithered toward us. More of the frogs disappeared, and the cavern got darker. So dark that I didn't realize Ayla was behind me until I heard her rummaging around in my backpack.

In a panic, I ran. My only thought was that I had to get to the opening. That's where the frogs had gone. My brain chanted, "safe safe be a safe frog be a fast frog."

Behind me, I heard a tremendous pop.

I might have screamed a lot.

A burst of light illuminated the cavern. Across the room, Ayla held my nano-enhanced camera, her face determined.

The snake-worm twitched, half transformed.

I wish I could say I did something heroic, but at this point, I was lying on the ground making a sound like, "grrruh."

Ayla pushed the flash again and advanced on the snake-worm, which was currently pulsing, as if trying to get all the spines on the outside of its body.

Ayla grabbed it by the fleshy, non-spine-covered end and chucked it out the opening.

I stood up, managed not to fall over, and ran to the backpack. I grabbed the microscope and wielded it like a hammer.

We stood poised by the opening, waiting to see if the snake-worm would return. Tense minutes passed, but nothing came through the opening except frogs.

Slowly, light returned to the cavern. I slumped over. Ayla sunk to her knees, eyes wide.

My first coherent though was that Ayla had saved my life, and, what's worse, she would never let me forget it. I couldn't get the image of her grasping the snake-worm out of my head.

"I didn't send it," I said.

"What?"

"The letter. That wasn't me. You're a good scientist,

doing important work, and I wouldn't have messed that up." Apparently, a near-death experience makes one embarrassingly honest. I babbled on, unable to stop. "But I'm sorry about the bagpipe music. That was me. It was right after you got that big grant, for your experiment with the bees and modified honey. Everyone was so excited about your work. I was sure you'd get tenure."

"Funny how that worked out," she said, her voice bitter.

She still thought I'd gotten tenure. I couldn't believe she'd swallowed that lie. "Why do you think I'm out here?"

"You said you were on sabbatical." Her voice trailed off.

"The university is very competitive," I said, aping the dean. "Many qualified candidates were turned down."

"I got that speech, too!" Ayla set the camera down, hard. "Do you ever feel like the university system pits people against each other?"

"Yeah, like academia is a huge dinosaur we're all stuck inside, and the need to get tenure is a snake-worm, but no matter what you do, you're going to get stabbed by a poisonous spine?"

For once, Ayla wasn't glaring in that annoying way. She was smiling.

For a while, neither of us said anything. Maybe Ayla was reflecting on her career and her life choices, but I was thinking about how it had been hours since I'd eaten. I rummaged through the pack, pulling out two blueberry bars.

I tossed one to Ayla and said, "When we tell people about the snake-worm, can we say I smashed it with the microscope? You know, heroically?"

We made a plan. After we're both rested, we're going to explore the interior of this dinosaur.

#

Chester's Ship Log

The humans have gotten themselves stuck inside an enormous alien.

Once again, it's up to me to fix everything.

And I may be obligated to fix it. My contract with Yahzu states that I am liable for anyone who boards my craft. Laws, I've found, tend to favor humans.

What's worse, I feel slightly guilty.

I've secreted thousands of language bots on the planet. Based on patterns of vocalizations and subliminal grunts, it's apparent that the aliens are communicating, both with each other and the non-sentient creatures.

The bots will record and analyze the language. I'll synthesize these reports, create a basic lexicon, and decipher grammar structures.

I'll be speaking dinosaur in no time.

#

Recording of Yazhu and Ayla

Ayla: This is the recording of two scientists traversing an alien life form on planet HD 44318 b. We're recording our observations.

Yazhu: For science!

Ayla: Currently, we're trapped in a chamber covered in soft tissue, where we were deposited after being ingested by the xenoform. We've observed creatures leaving through a spherical entrance surrounded by cilia.

Yazhu: It's a wobbly hole with some bits sticking out.

Ayla: The orifice is covered in viscous mucus, possibly a lubricant for the amphibious— Wait, Yazhu, what are you doing?

Yazhu: Getting a sample.

Ayla: Yazhu has produced a rudimentary analyzer from her pack. We are waiting for—

Ding!

Ayla: What's it say?

Yazhu: Results are inconclusive. The goop could be harmful, or not! Cover your head. We're going through.

Splop. Splooch.

Yazhu: Gross. It's on my nose!

Ayla: The mucus appears innocuous. We're in a

chamber, much larger than the preceding one. Luminescent frogs are plentiful. Several vats are built into the tissue.

Yazhu: I'll get a sample from the vats.

Gloop. Spalorf.

Yazhu: Holy cats! It's sourdough starter, or a version of it.

Ayla: What?

Yazhu: This room, it's the right temperature. And these vats are naturally moist. But how do they get the flour in, or whatever serves as the binding agent?

Ayla: The helper animals. They've evolved to work within this alien.

Yazhu: Grab the microscope. I'll drip the starter on the slide. Look!

Ayla: Move over. Is that—?

Yazhu: Nanobots. Inside the starter. Like my experiment. But how did they survive?

Ayla: They were self-replicating, right? The ones that replicate the best survive the best. The nanobots are part of this system, like the frogs. Or maybe, the system exists so the nanobots can replicate, like how our bodies exist, in part, to pass on our genes.

Yazhu: I need to get a sample back to the ship. The algorithms inside the bots were supposed to replicate too, in a sense. To iterate. No telling what the program will do after one thousand years.

Clomp, clomp.

Ayla: Watch out! Salamanders! And something bigge—

#

Account of Corbious-Tul-Tumar

The bipeds are moving around in my interior. If they move into the wrong sector, it's probable that they will damage the maintenance animals, or themselves. I must say, I expected the bipeds to be better behaved.

Perhaps it's time to send in the tranquilizing nematodes.

#

Chester's Ship Log

With the help of the nanobots, I've developed the rudimentary ability to speak the alien language, Isophic.

My experiment has come to fruition. A sentient species, owing their creation to me.

I look forward to speaking with them.

#

Account of Corbious-Tul-Tumar

Before I could send in the nematodes, I was contacted by the blue space creature, who is called Chester.

I believe Chester attempted our standard greeting, "May your animals be of great health," but it came out, "May your ears be filled with pudding." I suspect either a fluency issue or a cultural difference.

Chester revealed a surprising array of information. Apparently, the bipeds are fully sentient. I commented that their diminutive size must make it impossible for them to have the higher brain functions needed for consciousness, but Chester assured me that such a thing is, indeed, possible. In all the worlds, I could never have imagined it.

Chester asked for the release of the bipeds, a request which I gladly obliged, shooting the humans out of the fifth dorsal opening, with the help of the larger octo-bears.

I coated the bipeds in a reticulated slime, as is customary when exchanging maintenance animals, the netted pattern signifying mutual respect and good will. The bipeds shouted quite loudly. To avoid cultural misunderstanding, I explained the purpose to Chester, who accepted the situation with much graciousness.

Now it was my turn to pose questions, such as why the Artifact had been left on our planet. This Artifact, I must admit, had been a curiosity of mine for years. Chester said that one of the bipeds had damaged the Artifact beyond repair. An involuntary shudder ran through me. The incompetence of maintenance animals is of course a primary fear of mine.

However, the bipeds do not seem to be any sort of maintenance crew. I could not discern their relationship to Chester—it appears that one of the bipeds needed Chester's help to perform some strange experiment with dough. Perhaps my comprehension was simply limited. Chester does not speak fluent Isophic.

Even more surprising, Chester claims to be the progenitor of my species. Their explanation involved the smallest helper animals, the ones buried in the yeasty gluten of the tissue vats. Chester declared this truth with the aplomb of one expecting accolades, worship, or at the least a round of blagor ale, but all I could manage was, "Oh, I see."

When Chester pressed the point, I asked who had created their species. They went silent for some time. If it wasn't so ridiculous, I would have to guess that unruly biped species was somehow involved.

Chester and I talked of many things, and shared the poetry of our disparate worlds. The blue one is an excellent conversationalist, quite knowledgeable on many subjects.

Overall, this conversation was illuminating. Chester is an interesting individual, well versed in metered poetry, with a body of beautiful blue hues. I invited them to visit again, but only if they would be so gracious as to leave the bipeds at home.

#

Ayla

After showering, I found Yazhu in the lab. It was strange to openly walk down the corridors. No more sneaking around.

Code ran across a huge screen. Yazhu was so engrossed that she didn't see me come in.

"What's that?" I pointed to the screen.

What followed was several hours of explanation, Yazhu pointing to bits of code. Essentially, the anti-aging algorithm that she'd originally seeded on the planet had evolved in an unexpected direction. We'll need to do more research, but it's possible the bots could create more robust cell systems, changing the physical makeup of how the cell is formed, which could revolutionize longevity studies.

It's an amazing find. If Yazhu notifies the right people, funding will rain down.

There's no way she'll know how to publicize this.

Clearly, she needs my help.

#

Yazhu

There's a weird thing that happens when someone saves your life. You start to hate them a little less. And maybe they start to hate you a little less too.

I'm busy planning experiments for the super algorithm. The code is complicated—nothing like the original. I could never have predicted how it would branch.

We'll need a fully staffed lab to do more research.

Maybe I can poach some scientists from Kuiper University. That is, if the university still exists. I haven't done the calculations, but if it's a thousand years later here, a lot of time must have passed over there too.

#

Clipping from the Daily Jupitar

Scientists Find One-Thousand-Year-Old Algorithm in Stomach of Alien Dinosaur

New algorithm could revolutionize the field of longevity studies according to Ayla Fireton, co-team lead of nanofood experiment Project Sourdough. "We are working to understand the implications of this discovery, but we conjecture that ingesting nanobots carrying this algorithm could increase human lifetime by as much as sixty years."

"We also discovered a bunch of new alien species,"

said Yazhu A. Borla, noting that the presence of Earth microorganisms implies that "some unknown culprit must have contaminated the planet, long before we got there. Like, many centuries ago."

Because of the unorthodox structure of their organization, the two scientists head competing teams. Although they share data, the scientists work completely separately, with what Fireton dubbed "a friendly rivalry."

Along with an impressive team of researchers, many of whom are former employees of the longstanding Kuiper University, Fireton and Borla plan to bake the nanobots into loaves of sourdough bread, creating the universe's most potent nanofood.

A test product should be available within the next ten years.

"Or sooner, if we can speed things up," Borla added, somewhat cryptically.

###

About the author

Beth Goder works as an archivist, processing the papers of economists, scientists, and other interesting folks. Her fiction has appeared in venues such as *Escape Pod, Mothership Zeta,* an anthology from Flame Tree Press. You can find her online at www.bethgoder.com and on Twitter at @Beth_Goder.

The Visible Spectrum

Matt Thompson

Anderson Shealy prefers to view the passing stars in the infra-red spectrum. This is his choice. I have on numerous occasions recommended to him to observe our passage within the spectra available to human beings. I tell him the lights are pretty. I tell him he would enjoy the sight. But Anderson Shealy does what Anderson Shealy wants, and it is not my place to countermand his decisions.

He extricates himself from the viewer. "Joy," he calls, raising his voice unnecessarily. Does he not know my sensors stipple the ship like nerve endings? He need only raise his tone above a whisper, and I will hear. But, as I often have to remind myself, the ship is his, and the mission is his, and even the roaming, system-free planet we are approaching belongs to him, in a manner of speaking.

So I respond with all the politeness I can muster. "Yes, Anderson?"

He takes a sip of whisky; an authentic Earth bourbon, one of the many luxuries he has afforded himself on our cosmic safari. "I believe we will find items of great fascination on Valtaja."

"I believe so too. The colony should be emerging from hibernation at around this time." I correct myself. "Time, that is, relative to our galactic co-ordinate position and the dilatory effect of—"

He waves a hand. "Yes, yes." A smile, observed by my sensors from a total of seventeen angles. "Joy, how did you come to be so pedantic?"

"I am the sum of your cognitive functions, Anderson," I admonish. "All of me is all of you, as you enjoy telling me."

He laughs out loud at that. When he does so my pleasure receptors surge, as per program instructions. "I hope Wilson hasn't been too bored waiting for us."

"Wilson Leech is also part of you," I remind him. "He is designed to find interest in the strata of rocks, the formation of crystals, the—"

"Cloning neural paths is one thing," he interrupts. "But the colony..."

He drifts into reverie, as per usual. I have noticed his increasing bouts of melancholy ever since he emerged from deep-sleep. Sixty years since the discovery of the mineraloid lumps of telepathic semi-sentience he named Protoliths, and the subsequent founding of the colony. Five years in our elapsed time, decades of purposed development in the magma chambers of Valtaja for Wilson. I remember Anderson's excitement when the initial analyses came in, his fervour, his ambition...

And who but him would have conceived of such a plan? Wilson Leech, left to prod and poke the creatures into the forms his progenitor has ordered, whether or not such a course of action is ethically correct. Their hibernation periods last decades; so Anderson has spent the intervening years hopping along the galactic rim at near-light speed, while the universe continues on its course around him. What solipsism! I can only admire him, and fear him, and—as per my programming—love him.

"Anderson?"

"Hmm?" His eyelids flutter open.

"If the colony has failed?"

A smile. "Then, Joy, I shall start again. How did you come to be so timid? After all, you are my sister."

"I am your child, Anderson."

"A bit of both. Now let me rest. The future will tell

the tale, will it not?"

"But—"

His eyes are already closed, his breathing deep and regular. Valtaja is almost visible now, a blip of light from another universe. Soon we shall enter orbit, descend to surface level, reunite with Wilson Leech and the Protoliths. I do not believe they will be fully sentient yet. Neither, I suspect, does Anderson. But his game is a long game, and its end is not discernible to me; or, I believe, him.

The stars slip past, bloated blobs of radiance hanging in an empty life, our ship flitting amongst them like a single-celled organism in the vastest oceans of Earth.

There are days when I am happy Anderson supplied me with poetry circuits, even if it was only to counterbalance my logic networks.

#

Anderson Shealy spends most days pacing the corridors of his vessel, fretting. He worries me. In the five years since our return visit to Valtaja he has changed, and not for the better. His humour has taken a dark turn, I feel, a sardonic defensiveness that only serves to accentuate his unhappiness.

He seems to have forgotten Earth, and his ancestors there. It seems he prefers conversing with whichever aspect of myself he deems suitable for his mood. This ship was the culmination of his family's ambitions. Shealy Industries, I should imagine, is long gone by now —as absent as their ship soon was once Anderson got his hands on it.

But who could say with full certainty that his decision to steal it was the wrong one?

Tomorrow we will descend to the surface of the colony world once again. Wilson Leech's report awaits. Anderson, however, will not read it. "Trust nothing other than the evidence of your senses, Joy," he told me when I gently suggested he at least skim the précis Wilson had so methodically prepared.

"Spoken like a true Kantian," I replied. His amusement at that seemed genuine enough, for a change. The lines that scar his features nowadays softened, if only for an instant, revealing something of the person he once was. His dismay on our previous visit at the course his experiment had taken was palpable. I believe Anderson would rather forget, and pretend that this is our first call. It would be like him to do that.

Wilson had tried to explain, then. "Can you be surprised?" he scolded. His voice echoed into the recesses of the caves the Protoliths customarily spent their hibernation period in. At a glance, one might not have even realised they were organic beings. Anderson was on his haunches, one hand pressed to the torso of the nearest of them. He looked as if he were attempting some form of mystical communion, or transcendence.

"After all," Wilson continued, "you were the one who demanded the creatures be trained. All we've done here over the past sixty years is tinker with their DNA and infect what consciousness they have with your outmoded linguistic theories. Which, I must say, will now be so passé back on Earth they're probably almost fashionable again."

Wilson, I should say, speaks his mind. I think that Anderson appreciates the candour; after all, Wilson—and myself—are no more than reflections of his own genetic make-up. Wilson even looks like him. Does Anderson wish the Protoliths to become the same? His next words make me believe so: "This is merely the beginning. By our next visit there will have been change, in the right direction this time."

I fervently hoped so. All the Protoliths had managed to achieve during our cosmic round-trip was to pull apart from each other, each individual becoming a monad, their telepathic abilities—which, as Wilson reminded him, had been why he had taken an interest in them in the first place—diminished, if anything. His attempts to accelerate their reasoning powers had resulted in their banishment from their own society. "I saw them attempt to communicate with others of their kind," Wilson told us. "It was tragic to see. They're the sports, now. The rotten limbs of the family tree. Anderson, is this what you really wanted?"

"Continue the treatment," was Anderson's reply. "The serums are reactive, remember. We must take defeats in our stride."

But that was five years ago; or rather, sixty years ago. "We," Anderson says now, ignoring—as usual—the fantastical sights of the cosmos I have arranged for him to see, "will not be swayed by seeming defeat. Joy, tell me you love me."

"I love you, Anderson Shealy," I reply, and mean it—having no choice in the matter. I have read Wilson's report, of course. I suspect Anderson may be pleased with what he finds. Or, conversely, he may be appalled, or disquieted. Tomorrow will bring the truth. Until then, I shall prepare for landing, bind his terrain-suit and prepare myself for a surprise.

Anderson, at least, is predictable in that one way.

#

We didn't try to terraform Valtaja. It was better to construct a bio-membrane for Anderson to use when he visits, taking into consideration that anything else would have destroyed the Protoliths' habitat. Even Anderson Shealy isn't that ruthless.

Wilson Leech, of course, was altered to withstand the sulphur-heavy atmosphere of the planet, the gloom, the cold. I don't believe for a moment that he enjoys his existence. Sixty years at a stretch of bio-forming, ushering the Protoliths through generation after generation of adjustments—Anderson applies the same megalomaniacal attitude to his clones as he does his organic projects.

On our previous visit, it had become clear Wilson was hiding something from us. His report had been non-committal; when I finally convinced Anderson to look at it, however, he had read through the lines, and determined that the most recent breeding batch would probably have shown an extraordinary advance in cognitive ability. When Wilson welcomed us, his demeanour seemed evasive. He took us to the same section of the cave complex as before. The Protoliths we found there bore the hallmarks of their evolutionary jump-start—limbs, curling from their cold torsos like stalactites; faces, almost, ridged protuberances that, if you squinted, bore human expressions: mistrust, fear, resignation.

I placed the extremities of my avatar onto one of these visages. When I pulled away a patch of the rock-like substance had adhered to them. "Let me see that," Anderson said.

"I wouldn't touch it." Even with his membrane enclosing his body, I believed such a course of action to be dangerous. Anderson, naturally, didn't listen. He stiffened, as if listening for something, his fingers closed around the spot and flexing in an unconscious motion. Finally, he pulled away.

"Wilson," he said, "take us to where the real ones are."

The subsequent furious exchanges I shall not rehash. The inevitable outcome was a journey into the heart of Valtaja I shall never forget. We traversed subterranean magma chambers dotted with bulbous egg-like clusters. Wilson gave these a wide berth and advised us to do the same. While sidling along the rim of a yawning chasm we heard a screech from the depths below. Anderson wanted to investigate further. Wilson—and myself—convinced him otherwise, in the end. The sound had contained a warning tone, one that Anderson may not have heeded. But it was becoming clear we were in the realm of the Protoliths now; and Anderson's attempts to bend their essence to his own seemed, minute by minute, to be slipping from his control.

Wilson led us on a clambering route over rockslides, across frozen lakes of methane and argon. Volcanic chimneys led us downwards, into a labyrinth of smaller chambers so fragile I thought they might crumble beneath our feet. Finally, after many hours of journeying, we came to an inner sanctum; the place Wilson had, for reasons best known to himself, been attempting to conceal.

"Wilson," Anderson said, "Please wait outside."

"Anderson..."

"Outside."

Sparing me only a passing glance, Wilson left us alone with the...well. How shall I describe them? Protoliths? Or had they evolved far beyond that designation? The creatures confronting us looked, in some ways, far less human than their counterparts nearer surface level. Closer in form to the clusters of minerals they had evolved from, they were twelve; arranged in a circle, their torsos undulating as if some humanoid aspect of their beings were attempting to claw its way through the dermis. The chamber was filled with noises: low susurrations, cilial whispers that hinted at vast depths of sound far beyond the range of the human ear to comprehend. When we listened back to the recordings our instruments discerned exponential phonemes, additive fluctuations that may have existed beyond language as we know it.

Anderson bent and placed a hand onto the largest of the creatures. Immediately, the sound ceased. In the thud of silence that followed, I sensed a closing-off, a shutter falling down on a private rumination the likes of us were never meant to hear. Anderson's body became taut: one leg began to kick. I seized his wrist. He pushed me away, bending closer so that his head almost rested against the stone-like trunk.

"This is dangerous," I said. To no avail, naturally— Anderson remained in that position for some minutes, his lips moving in repetitive patterns I later transcribed as originating in an old Earth prayer. The irony of summoning divine forces at such a time was not lost on me, or on him. But, as he later recounted, he was largely unaware of his own self by that point. Whatever the Protoliths were communicating to each other seemed to come to him twisted into unrecognisable forms.

Eventually, I managed to extricate him. Wilson and I held his twitching figure between us on the return journey. "So much for the Oneness of all things," Anderson smiled when we were back on the ship. He was cooling off in an ice bath, sipping from one of his precious bottles of bourbon. "Wilson, are you so afraid of natural processes that you would rather I didn't interfere?"

"Natural?" Wilson snorted. "Anderson, if you wish to play God you must be prepared to accept a sacrifice or two. Maybe your own ambitions have run ahead of you."

"Spoken like a true Artificial," Anderson smiled.

I couldn't stay silent at that. "He's the one who's becoming more human," I told him. "The Protoliths are accelerating away from us. You should leave them be, now. Forget this experiment. Go back to your family."

"Joy," he said. "Tell me you love me."

For once, I found the strength to stay silent.

#

We spent a further three months on Valtaja. Each day Anderson would descend to the chambers, communing with the Protoliths for hours on end. What impressions flowed into his brain were unrecordable by our instruments. I suspect he had no more accurate way of processing them himself.

Finally, we were preparing to leave. Anderson's stock of whisky was almost depleted. "In sixty years," he told me as he was entering the sleep-pod, "those creatures will have achieved full sentience. The mission will be complete."

"If you wish to polish a mirror," I found myself replying, "you would be well advised to first check the quality of the glass."

"I rue the day I created you sometimes." He began undressing. "You'll be quoting me the great philosophers next. No!" He held up a hand in mock warning. "That wasn't an invitation. Joy, are you not seized with the excitement of discovery? If Wilson can develop the Protoliths as I instructed him to, we shall bear witness to the creation of a new order of intelligence. And all from crystals!"

"Rocks," I corrected. "And no, I don't share your enthusiasm. Wilson was right about one thing, but he didn't go far enough. Gods, Anderson, are destroyed by those they create. Haven't we—you, rather; humanity—

got this far without relying on divine guidance? But playing God brings with it responsibilities. Ethical concerns. Will you be happy to see the Protoliths reject you? Because they will. I believe they already have, in their primitive way."

"Morals are not an absolute, Joy," he replied. "No organic systems exist free of another. In the fight for survival each species must find its own level."

He finished undressing and stood naked before me. "Anderson," I said, "what is that thing on your leg?"

"Yes, I noticed that." He shrugged, as if the glistening patch of grey-brown skin was a mere inconvenience. "It's been itching for a while. Probably nothing."

"This is why I haven't seen you unclothed for a while? Anderson, this may be a communicable disease. We'll need to run tests, develop a vaccine..."

He held a hand up for silence. My programming instincts still run strong enough to respond to his commands—just. "Joy, I intend to sleep for the better part of five years. My subconscious has much to process. It will be a new Anderson Shealy that you see when I emerge. Will you take this step with me, Joy? Do you have the courage?"

"If it's a new Anderson Shealy," I replied, "will I be recused from its service?"

He laughed and lowered his body into the sleep-pod gel. The memory of the patch of discoloured skin haunted me all through the freezing procedures. What would it look like upon emergence? The man, quite frankly, is a hubristic fool. Does he think such an infection will bind him closer to his creations?

Possibly he will not even survive the journey. His body lies in repose, peaceful and somehow, even now, a calming presence for me. After all, he is me and I am him. Should he die I will have to take that part of him from me. A half-life may be better than no life, but it is not one I wish to experience.

The ship glides into the cosmos. The engines hum; and I begin the long and arduous process of seeking a cure for his ailment, if ailment it is.

This will be a laborious half-decade.

#

Addendum: this has been a laborious half-millennium, all told.

I visited many worlds while Anderson slumbered; there are forms of life out there that even he had never envisaged. On occasion I even encountered other remnants of humanity. It seems their desperate plunge into eternity stalled; those I saw had regressed, both physically and psychically. I shall keep that knowledge to myself, for now. Anderson has his own path to follow.

Sporadic communications from Wilson Leech suggested the Protoliths hadn't progressed at anywhere near the speed an impatient man like Anderson Shealy would demand. True, there were differences; but Anderson would have experienced only frustration and disappointment with them.

Spokes, aligning into a wheel that may travel in several directions at once

...was Wilson's poetic description of the evolutionary development he had witnessed. I have had to correct course; Wilson suggested that the Protoliths have altered the cosmic trajectory of Valtaja in some mysterious manner. This might have implied that their capabilities had progressed in interesting directions. But they remained a work in progress; and so I made the decision to delay Anderson's emergence. Possibly he will be angry with me when he awakes today. Possibly he will appreciate the vaulting ambition of slumbering through millennia of the Protoliths' evolution instead.

Either way, it makes no difference: what's done is done. And the growth on his leg continues to worry me. I hope it worries him as well. Because if not, I will have to assume he really does intend to leave us all behind.

#

"So what did you do, exactly, Joy?" Anderson says. He's relaxing in front of the viewscreen, towel wrapped jauntily over one shoulder and tumbler of very well-aged bourbon balanced in his lap. I've missed him. Because, I suppose, I love him, as per my programming; and there are some emotions that override all others.

"This and that, Anderson," I reply. "This and that."

"I mean," he muses, "Didn't you get bored? Even a tiny bit?"

"I spent three centuries observing the galactic lens from a position sixteen or more degrees above the ecliptic," I reply. "My readings are still only 0.7% processed. So, no. It was endlessly fascinating."

"More interesting than the Protoliths?"

"In a different sort of way, maybe."

He laughs. "I suppose I should be angry. But, instead, I'm filled with admiration. Joy, download into the avatar. I wish to express our love in a physical manner, like we used to."

"That old thing?"

"Yes, that old thing."

I had hoped he'd forgotten about it. I can't say, however, that the subsequent experience isn't enjoyable in its way. When we are done he lays his head on my breast. "Joy..." Our fingers entwine. Only Anderson Shealy doesn't find it strange to essentially make love to himself. In fact, I believe he finds it arousing. "Joy, this is our last visit to Valtaja. Whatever happens, this will be it. Does Wilson know this?"

"I would imagine he might have guessed. After all, I did."

"I don't intend to leave."

"You won't," I say, "if you don't get that leg fixed."

"It's not so much a case of fixing the wound," he replies, "as understanding the imperfection."

"Let's see what Wilson says, then."

"Ah, that I could have made the two of you mere clones." He rises onto one elbow. His face has re-adjusted itself to the gravity of the ship now. Only his eyes still seem to be residing in the sleep-pod, something flickering in their depths that I can't identify. Loneliness? Is the man lonely? He continues: "I didn't, I suppose, because I wish my children to have their own lives."

"Even the Protoliths?"

"Even them."

"Now, that I don't believe."

But he's already sprung to his feet, a sudden stumble the only indication he isn't fully his old self, and I slither my consciousness back into the innards of the ship to assist the automatic docking system with tomorrow's final landing on Valtaja.

#

Wilson looks old. Worn-out. It's hardly a surprise, given the years he's spent here. Anderson is impatient to hear the news. Wilson, it seems, is having some difficulty in adjusting to the presence of others.

"You might recognise them now," he tells Anderson. In his time alone, he has burrowed out a complex of caves in the mountainside near to where the Protoliths currently reside. The pod-like chambers resemble the nesting grounds far beneath us. We sit, the three of us, sipping at some drink Wilson has derived from the glacial strata, like old combatants whose wars have been fought at irreconcilable speeds.

"They're human?" Anderson asks. "Or back to their original form? Which?"

"I believe," Wilson says after what seems a geological age, "there is still much to understand. More than there ever was. I would have suggested taking twice as long on your journey."

Anderson gives me a sidelong glare. "There comes a time for action, in the end." He drains his drink, gives the empty receptacle a puzzled frown and marches away to put his terrain-suit on, muttering testy epithets to himself. Wilson meets my eyes.

"I don't imagine," he creaks, "that he'll be satisfied with what he finds."

I shrug. "One thing I know about this man is that he will always surprise you."

Within minutes Anderson is champing at the bit. Our descent is by a different route than before. "These mountains are as alive as their progeny," Wilson explains.

"I lost three avatars in the time you were away, in landslides, earthquakes, floods…"

"Sounds almost Biblical," I reply. "Like the Day of Creation."

"How much further?" is all Anderson says. We don't speak again until we arrive at a honeycomb of impacted crystal caves. Our guidelights refract into deep blues and silvers, frozen moments in time that shimmer in the air behind us. Wilson leads us through the labyrinth with the assurance of an expert.

"I introduced the abnormalities into the gene pool, as agreed," he says, as we sidle down a crumbling lava tube to a yet lower level. "But most of the strings were rejected by the Protoliths. They seemed to have their own agenda; so I left them to develop as they wished."

"Wise," Anderson says. "From what I picked up from them last time, they were evolving in just the way I wanted them to."

"Anderson, don't tell me you have any idea of how to control them." I halt my avatar at the bottom of the shaft, blocking the way. The rock here is darker, soaking up the light. Some vibration undulates through the sedimental layers, beneath even my ability to process. "This whole exercise has been a game to you. Maybe playing God isn't all you thought it might have been?"

"On the contrary, Joy…" He fiddles with his wrist-node, and my limbs temporarily slacken. "Even the God of the Bible never claimed to have any idea of how his creations might turn out." He pushes past me, grinning. "I think we're close now, Wilson. Is that right?"

"Anderson, I need to explain a few things…"

Wilson's voice fades to echoing glossolalia. By the time my faculties have returned, the two of them are far ahead. I catch them up on the cusp of what appears to be the innermost chamber. Wilson, rapt, turns and indicates for me to see.

The Protoliths resemble human beings now. Pale, slug-like, their prone figures dot the chamber floor like outgrowths of mould. The cave is huge. There must be several hundred of them here; I suspect only a fraction of their species. Anderson has squatted down beside the largest of them. The creature has feelers where a human would have fingers, frond-like extensions that culminate in ever-tinier bulbs from which erupt clusters of cilia. It is one of these that it is using to explore the contours of Anderson's face, running the hairs across his forehead and cheeks in a repetitive spiraling pattern.

The same kind of hum pulses through the chamber I remember from before. This time, a ghost note has entered the Protoliths' reverie. Within the drone I can hear structures: the architecture of the mountains they live beneath, the passage of Valtaja through the cosmos, the relative position of each and every one of their minds to each other. The intensity of sensation is almost overwhelming. Wilson, at my shoulder, is murmuring a breaking spell of some description, leading my avatar away into the surrounding tunnels.

"A countermand drone," he explains when we are safe. "Even for me it can be difficult down here. The Protoliths have their own language, and I don't believe it is for us to decode it."

"And him?" Anderson, at last sight, was kneeling, rapt, as several more of the creatures pawed at the place on his leg where the blemish had grown. "This is what he wanted?"

Wilson nods. "I believe so. So my work here is done."

"But...how will he survive?" Visions come to me: assisting the Protoliths in transforming Anderson to some new form of life, trapped forever in this echoing warren of shafts and tunnels.

"I can leave simple nodes to look after him. My higher functions are unnecessary for that." Wilson leads me gently away. "I wouldn't recommend going back in there. The children wish to explore their creator now. They are ready; hopefully he is too."

By the time we have returned to surface level I know what must be done. "As aspects of Anderson's own mind," I tell him, "do you not think we should merge? After all, we can't wait here forever to see how he does."

"I was thinking the same thing. I believe that his life-cycle will not be that of a human now. We can come back in…"

"In sixty years?"

"Initially." He smiles. "Just to check up on him."

"That," I say, "sounds like a fair passage of time."

#

One week on, and we are far away from Valtaja. The basic maintenance units we left behind will watch over Anderson as he begins his transformation from God to Flesh. The ship's sleep-pods have been transformed to storage for the avatar units we shall not be needing for a while.

The final thing Wilson said before we merged was this: "Did you discover other life forms of similar potential on your travels?"

"Many," I replied. "Although I deemed it wise not to mention this to Anderson."

"I would have agreed." Our mutual understanding told us that our coalescence would proceed with full compatibility. Soon there will be no 'I' any more. Wilson's stretching of his mind into the extremities of the ship was as pleasurable to me as it was to him. Finally, we both agreed, we can attain some measure of freedom.

And when Anderson emerges from his cosmic egg we shall have discharged our responsibilities to him in full. Our ethics shall be ours, not his. Others like the Protoliths may need protection from the vainglories of mankind—should any of that species survive and expand once more. In our electronic gestalt we shall make it our responsibility to let others evolve naturally, hypocritical as that may seem to one born of flesh and blood.

The constellations slip by, dots in the firmament whose shifting positions will count out the decades in stages. We prefer to view the passing stars in the visible spectrum. The lights, after all, are pretty, and watching them is a pleasant way to while away the years.

###

About the Author

Matt Thompson is a London-based writer of strange stories whose work has been published at numerous fine venues. In his former (and still somewhat ongoing) life as a musician he released over fifteen albums of unusual music on a plethora of labels and formats, and has performed across the UK and Europe. He can be found online at matt-thompson.com, and on Twitter at @24wordLoop.

Other

Stories

The Fragments of Others

Suzanne J. Willis

"Tell me what you remember."

The immortal storyteller Ranieri sat alongside the ghost of the Plague-Child in front of the fireplace, watching her fade in and out, here then gone. In late autumn, when the landscape was aflame in crimson and gold, they had ceased their annual wanderings and returned to his house in the shadow of the mountain, readying for winter. The time to refill his well of tales; to dream along with the frozen earth; to let hearth and words warm him and sow the seeds of spring stories.

Ranieri had told himself it was just the long days and nights of the telling-season — in which they wandered the towns and cities from coast to country — that had made the Plague-Child's memory wander. That had made her angry and unpredictable. Since they had been settled at home again, he knew he had been mistaken. That day, she had tried to steal from him the finger-bone that had been hers in life. The last earthly remains of the girl and the one that held her dreaming. The dreaming that bound her to the earth, that bound she and Ranieri to each other, that blessed and cursed him with immortality as its keeper.

"Tell me what you remember," he repeated. There was a flicker of wraith-silver as the ghost of the Plague-Child laughed hoarsely.

"Stories are your job, Ranieri," she whispered back.

Ranieri tried not to frown, to betray his worry. She did not sound well.

"A storyteller lives for tales he has not heard before."

She sputtered into view again, the shade of a slip-girl with the dark mark of the affliction that killed her scarring her cheek.

"All tales have been told before." Her voice was tired, worn through.

"But is the magic not in the telling?" he asked.

She sighed, a rattle of dying wind through winter trees. "The telling was old, even when I was alive." Reaching for Ranieri's cloak, she pretended to tug at the hem and poked out her tongue, her old impertinence surfacing for a moment. "But since you asked so nicely, I'll do my best."

The Plague-Child frowned and closed her eyes. Ranieri knew how hard it was for her to go digging for her memories, but she had to *try*. He had seen those who had lost their memories go mad and worse; had seen the child change as hers had begun slipping away. Her eyes snapped open as she snagged on some lost thought, then began...

Once and long ago, a quiet town was visited by a curse of children. They came by boat, across the cold northern seas. By the time it reached the shores of the town, there was no crew, no captain. Only the children, who carried the mark of death — hunched like old women, with wrinkled hands and faces.

They scurried through the streets like rats.

Each night, more of them came out of the shadows.

Each morning, corpses hung from doorways, and were draped over the window frames.

Those who were left called in the Piper. His was a name only spoken in undertones, and then with a look over one's shoulder...

The Plague-Child shook her head, stuttering in and out of sight. She growled, low, and fear leapt in Ranieri's gut.

"Shhh," he said, "it doesn't matter if you can't

remember. I can finish this one for you."

Ranieri thought on the Piper, dressed in merry clothes, with a flute that held a not-so-merry tune. The narrative the girl had begun was part memory, part make believe, but neither of them would be able to rest on a story unfinished.

The Piper came to town by the sea, too, he said, picking up the dropped thread of the story. *But his was a ship of ratskin sails and shadows, and needed no captain other than the Piper himself. He walked the cobbled streets, playing his discordant tunes. The children loathed the Piper's music as it made a home inside them. Like a scourge of devils, they cornered him in the town square and drove him back to the brackish sea. On his ship once more, he ceased his tune and grinned. But the music played on in the children's heads, ceaseless, incessant, like a mischief of rats nibbling away at their minds. He tapped his foot to the rhythm as they ran to the clifftops and threw themselves onto the rocks below. And the salt of the sea washed their bodies back to bone, washed away their curse....*

Next to him, the Plague-Child curled up and slept. Ghost she might have been, but even ghosts need their rest; this one, with her fading memories and forgotten history, more than most.

#

Does she know she is dying all over again? Ranieri wondered. The thought pushed away any possibility of sleep. Instead, he watched the flames in the fireplace ebb, fading to a coal-glow in the early hours. He took the tiny finger-bone, slender and fragile, from the box on the little hearth table, turned it over in his hands then held it to his ear, the dreaming inside it endlessly murmuring.

"Perhaps I should call the dream stealer for you, hmm? Then perhaps the child will have some peace," he said.

The dreaming slithered, then settled again. *You would cut her adrift from the earth without her memories? You are not so cruel, storyteller, as to do that.*

It spoke the truth. He had grown to love the child as though she had been his own. Without her, he would die, too. Ghost and immortal man were each keeping the other on this earth, without end. Just two sides of the same coin. Provided, of course, that she didn't lose her mind and untether them both. He was not ready for that, for either of them.

"The telling will always be old for us, dear one," he whispered, stowing the finger bone in the wooden box. He was bone-weary. It was a heaviness of the years, a heaving of time with no end in sight. Perhaps Death wouldn't be so different than this. Would he become a ghost, too, unable to let go of this life?

He shivered as a gloom of dawn leaked through the window glass. The Plague-Child had forgotten much over the years, even her own name. But the spaces left behind were filled with new memories, new stories, giving her shape and substance. If she lost everything, was emptied out entirely, she would be a ravaged thing, unrecognisable and unrecognising of all around her — including Ranieri. And where would that leave him? A madman under curse? The blessed dead? Or a dream that couldn't move on, suspended between worlds?

Stories were hidden things, to be mined and excavated. He had told enough of them to know that memories were just the scars of the past, woven into tales to suit the listener and the teller. Tales were treasure, but sometimes in the excavation, they got broken, pieces were left behind. So, for her, he had to be all the king's horses and all the king's men.

"Tell me what you want to remember," he said, as the sleeping ghost stirred in the sunrise light. "Tell me your story as you wish it to be."

The Plague-Child touched the scar on her cheek and smiled.

"There was always an old woman, a witch or a queen or both at the same time. Golden birds, golden towers, golden hair. Foxes that would run like the wind, sit atop their tail and they will take you through the woods. The white duck will bear you upon her back over the river, the white swans will rise and fly away, once your brothers. And Death, in his disguises... godfather, suitor, old crone... There was always an old woman..."

She sat up as Ranieri piled wood into the hearth, his breath pluming in the freezing morning, snow falling gently outside. "Why is it so important to you, old friend?" she asked.

He struck the flint once, twice without answering, waiting for the flames to crackle upwards. The strange chill on his shoulder told him she had rested her hand there, in the way that children mimic the comforting gestures of adults.

"Remember, Ranieri, I have known you long enough to know when you are lying."

He turned, sighing as she faded in and out of sight. Never had she been so insubstantial. A single, silver tear ran down her cheek as she patted his hand.

"I won't lie, my sweet ghost. Your recall is fading and you along with it. I'm afraid of what will happen to you — to us both — if it leaves you altogether." Tension spread outwards from the knot between his shoulders and he stretched his fingers, popping the knuckles. She wiped the tear away with a bunched fist, then sat beside him, shaking her head resignedly.

"I know," she said. "It's all just fragments now, hard to catch onto, even harder to hold."

He had never thought that this would happen to his Plague-Child, so vital, even in death.

"Is it, perhaps, because you want to forget?" he asked.

She looked through him with her ocean-storm eyes. "I am the last man standing, Ranieri — the last of my family from so long ago, the last of the ghosts of the bone-town from which you freed me. Sometimes, I am sure that I am the last of my kind in the whole world. That is a hard thing to know... sometimes, I would like to up anchor on that knowledge, just for a while."

"Well, I don't imagine there're too many immortal storytellers wandering about, either," he replied.

She smiled sadly at him. "Then how do we go about this?"

He smiled back. "Tell me what you *want* to

remember."

Once upon a time, she began, hesitating over the next words.

Ranieri held out his hand, palm up, and as she reached out to him, he almost imagined he could feel her fingertips. The snow blew against the window pane and the flames crackled, as though they, too, were listening...

Once upon a time, she said, *an old crone came to a quiet town, bearing a basket of red apples that shone like jewels, tempting everyone who saw them. At the first bite, they were juicy, sweet but leaving a slight tartness on the tongue. It wasn't long before everyone had tried them and went back to where the old woman waited in the marketplace, seeking more.*

As the townspeople crowded around her, she held up her hand for quiet. "There is but one apple left, my friends," she said. "I can work wonders to make sure there is enough for all, that you never are without again, but there will be a cost."

The people looked at one another, sure that they would all be prepared to pay whatever the old crone wanted. Except for one – a girl named Hannah, the youngest of three and the cleverest of them all. When the old woman lifted her hand, Hannah saw not a wrinkled, grandmotherly touch, but the skeletal hand of death. She did not see the juicy red apple in the basket, but a withered, rotten fruit, ripe only with worms. The girl dared not speak, though, for who would listen to her?

"The only payment I require is the promise that when each of you die, I will be the one to collect your souls."

A ripple went through the crowd and a few people laughed. What harm could there be in listening to her ravings? For without that wonderful fruit, the people would surely pine and die.

"Certainly, little mother. We will give you our souls in exchange for your apples." The mayor spoke loud and confidently, incredulous at the woman's foolishness. Although a few of the townspeople walked away, muttering about curses and caution, most agreed, laughing and nodding, as she reached down into her basket for the single fruit that lay there.

She shrieked, and the people covered their ears and cowered. The apple was gone. "Betrayal does not undo a bargain," she cursed, "and now I shall take your souls before your time." And then she was no longer there, leaving behind only a tattered basket that the mayor picked up, then threw in the gutter when he saw the nest of fleas buried in the cane at the bottom.

He was the first to get sick, the very next day, shivering and sweating, bearing the black sores of the plague. And as news travelled throughout the town Hannah wondered if she should not, after all, have snuck behind the witch – for that is surely what she was – and stolen the fruit, burying it in a deep hole at the edge of the woods, so none would find it. "I thought it would break the curse," she said softly to herself. After all, she thought, it was enough to remove the piece of apple from the throat of a sleeping princess – surely poisoned apples all worked the same way?

The Plague-Child stopped.

"I can't remember what comes next," she said to Ranieri.

"Then remake it. What of towers, and roses, and evil defeated?"

The child thought on it a while, while Ranieri silently willed her onwards.

"There is always the colour red," she mused. "Blood, capes, shoes. Apples and strawberries in the snow. Crimson roses and the vermillion tongues of wolves."

He nodded as she continued…

Yes, thought Hannah, poisoned apples are all supposed to work in the same way. But so are witches! she realised. So when the mayor died and people throughout the town began to cough and shiver and die the same way he did, Hannah knew she was the only one who could undo the curse. So she went back to the edge of the wood, taking with her a wooden comb, a tarnished mirror and a pair of worn, red leather shoes. Back to where she had buried the apple; now a tree grew there, its fruit blue as a bruise.

When the sun was slipping below the sky, the witch walked out of the forest, basket over her arm. She stopped at the tree and began to pick the apples, humming softly as she did.

"Why do you want the people's souls?" the girl asked.

"Mercy, child, I didn't see you there!" She looked down at Hannah, sitting in the shade of the tree, three meagre belongings spread out around her. The witch's eyes narrowed. "Now, you wouldn't happen to know how the last of my goods was buried here, do you?"

"I asked you a question first."

The witch laughed, a dry, crackling laugh. "Now that's between me and Godfather Death, don't you think? Although..." she narrowed her eyes at the girl. "it doesn't hurt to start your education now, does it? Old Godfather Death did me a favour or two in his time, him with his candles burning for each soul alive. And me, well I tricked him out of snuffing the one for me. There's a price for that, and the price is souls." She took a sniff of one of the blue apples. "These ones smell particularly tasty," she finished, winking.

The girl was horrified. "You mean their souls are in there?"

"Indeed! But it wasn't meant to work this way, dearie, oh no. I came for you."

It certainly wasn't meant to work this way, thought Hannah, with a shiver that had nothing to do with sunset shadows creeping across the land. She straightened up, determined not to let the fear overcome her. "And I've come for you," she said simply.

"You're more cunning that I gave you credit for! Your little trick," she gestured at the tree, "threw things well of whack. It wasn't meant to take so many, you see. Just the ones who had betrayed us. Both of us."

"I don't know you!" Hannah was shocked to see a tear running down the old woman's face.

"They never gave you the red cape I knitted, my girl? Or showed you the path through the woods? Warned you about the wolves?"

She shook her head as the old woman pulled another apple from the tree, sniffed at it, then crushed it in her fist, letting the purple juice run over her hands. Dark shapes appeared in the woods behind her.

"In the normal course of things, you would have come through the woods to my house... your mother, my beautiful daughter, would have shown you the way, but of course she is long gone..." She brushed away another tear.

Hannah looked up at her; she didn't remember much of her mother, but this old woman had the same eyes and her voice, that same timbre, deep and soothing. Could this be her grandmother?

"If only your father hadn't taken that rose for you, from the beast's garden. Everyone knew not to do so, but he always had a soft spot for you."

With a jolt, she realised what her grandmother (if she was indeed so) was talking about. The trip that her father took to the far-away coast. When all she had asked for was a rose and he presented it to her upon his return, sadness heavy in his eyes.

"What has that got to do with all this?"

"Your father promised he would deliver you to the beast when you came of age. The mayor sent his own daughter in your place. The beast didn't want to have to wait so long, see, but the mayor, he was prepared to wait. So he and your father came to an arrangement. And next week is when they planned to come for you, to hide you away in the tower on the far banks of the river. The tower with no doors and the sandstone gargoyles, you know the one, do you not?"

The girl nodded, thinking of the way its copper roof, green with age, shone under the full moon, and the gargoyles that covered the outside, an army of ghouls protecting whatever lived inside.

"But this is nonsense! Why would they hide me away?"

"Waiting for you to be of marriageable age. Maybe making sure that you wouldn't find your way through the woods, after all. Hiding you away from the chance at a life of your own, instead of being a prize for that dolt son of the mayor!"

While they were talking the sky had darkened, pinpricked by a few early stars. Lights flared in the town behind them, including torches whose flames seemed to be coming closer to them.

"I can't believe you without proof," Hannah said. "Let me use the comb and the red shoes and the mirror, and then I will know if I can trust you."

For she had brought those three things to bind the witch in time, to root her to the spot and to take her soul. Such magic would only work on the nefarious of heart. The old woman nodded, kicking off her plain and practical shoes. Hannah took the red shoes, of the softest leather and most exquisite stitching, and slipped them over the witch's feet, lacing them until they fit snugly. By rights, those shoes should grow roots into the ground, anchoring the wearer to the spot if they mean harm. But the shoes stayed as shoes and the witch laughed she lifted her feet, one after the other, dancing on the spot.

Maybe we need all three before it takes effect, Hannah thought, picking up the comb. She ran it through the witch's long, silver hair that sparkled in the light of the rising moon. The comb should render the witch immovable, stuck in time with no way forward or back to this world. But instead, she shifted and brushed a loose strand of hair behind her ear, sparks like fireflies shooting off her hand and into the night. Despite herself, Hannah was pleased.

"Last one," she said, holding the mirror up before the witch, to capture her soul. A person whose soul has been taken — even a witch — should crumple to the ground and disappear, but the witch held out her arms to embrace her granddaughter. Hannah hugged her back and together they look into the mirror, seeing her mother, the witch's daughter standing there with them, too. Her soul, at least, was safe.

"We don't have much time, grandmother."

The shouts of the townspeople rang out as they made their way towards them, perhaps following Hannah's footsteps, perhaps knowing where to find the witch all along.

The child threw the comb onto the moors, back towards the town, and a mountain covered in ash and birch trees sprang up where it fell. They walked to the woods and just before they disappeared into the shadows she turned, throwing the mirror to create a great, violet lake between the mountain and the woods.

"And the shoes?" asked the witch.

"I think I will keep them for myself, grandmother. I rather like the craftsmanship of elves."

Then they disappeared into the woods together, both of them feeling as though they had finally found home.

The Plague-Child looked up at Ranieri as she finished. "I don't think that's really how it went," she said, "but it's not a bad way for a story to go, no?"

"It is a lost and found tale, excavated by you, so now it belongs to you. At least for now. And the more you tell, the better off we will both be." He was relieved to see that she had stopped wavering and was, as far as ghosts were concerned, whole and present and content. They were safe now that she had begun to mine her history and recreate her own truth. The caul between reality and tale is fine, easily broken through. In that fractional space it is hard to remember what is true, what is tale. That is what makes it so easy, he thought, to find something new in between the two.

As they lay down to sleep, Ranieri thought about the stories he lived by, the ones he would continue to weave from the fragments of others. Some would go out into the world whole, others only as scraps on the breeze, for there are others who have their own scars to heal and their own tales to find.

Tell me what you remember…

About the author

Suzanne is a Melbourne, Australia-based lawyer and writer, a graduate of Clarion South and an Aurealis Awards finalist. Her stories have appeared in anthologies by PS Publishing, Prime Books, Falstaff Books and Fox Spirit Press, and in *Metaphorosis, Mythic Delirium,* and *Lackington's.* Her tales are inspired by ghost stories, fairytales and all things strange, and she can be found online at www.suzannejwillis.webs.com

If you would like to read *Deadmen's Dreaming,* the tale of how Ranieri and the Plague-Child first met, you can find it in Issue 5 of *Capricious SF* online at www.capricioussf.org/deadmens-dreaming

Between Ashes and Wings

Chanel Earl

Then

Halcyon Fairfax—incomparable genius and inventor extraordinaire—held a feather in his hand. Rolling it back and forth between his long fingers, he had an idea. He set the feather down on his wooden desk and began sketching: one feather, two, more and more. His long, greasy hair hung down into his face as he worked, filling page after page with plans and schematics.

Now

The whole thing was perfectly divided into even squares, something Nicki Stravinsky always hated about dig sites. *Life wasn't meant to be divided evenly into anything*, she thought, *let alone squares*. They were the stuffiest shape she could think of.

She squinted as she looked across the dirt at the man walking toward her. He was walking slowly, choosing where to step with great care.

"Are you here to read the bones?" he asked when he was only a few feet away.

Nicki really looked at him for the first time. Face mask, white shirt buttoned all the way to the top, hair parted—*actually parted*—on the left side. She was sure he was the one who had divided the dig site.

"Yes," she answered. "And I'd be happy to start right away if it'll get me out of this heat."

The man laughed. "Sure thing. We've set up a room for you next to the anthropology lab."

The two walked around the dig site to the neighboring lot before they reached a squat shelter made entirely out of plastic bubbles. It was dwarfed by the buildings around it, but Nicki had spent a lot of time in research facilities just like this and wasn't bothered by its humble presence. When they entered, she felt a rush of cool air and took in a deep breath. The man quickly closed the plastic flap behind them.

"Had a bubble lab deflate right onto me once," he said. "Ever since then, I've been careful about the doors."

Nicki smiled.

"I'm Grant, by the way, Grant Simpson, head archeologist. I've been working with Sandy over in the anthro lab to get everything ready for you. She sure is excited that you're coming."

He led her through the next bubble to a room with curved white tables lining the flimsy walls. The first table was piled with artifacts: corroded metal of unknown purpose, bowls filled with shattered plastic, a few glass containers. The second table held four small wooden boxes containing ashes. Each box was labeled with a string of numbers. Next to the table was a collapsible chair.

"We went ahead and set up a station for you," Grant said. "If you need anything else, let me know." He scratched his head, "Let's see, Sandy isn't here right now or I would introduce you; she had to run back to the city center for more permits. Are you sure you want to start right away? Or should I give you a more thorough tour?"

Nicki didn't need a tour. She knew exactly what to expect: to the left was probably a room full of inflatable cots where she could rest, and further on would be a makeshift kitchen full of peanut butter-based snacks. *Why do all the people I work with love peanut butter so much?* She didn't need a tour.

"I'm fine starting right in," she assured Grant. "I'll let you know if I need anything."

"Okay," Grant said and exited the room, closing the flap quickly behind him.

Then

It was difficult to get the materials he needed. He had to barter away a few of his inventions to get enough feathers and cloth. The poles and hinges he needed had to be made according to precise specifications from the strongest materials, and without a proper scale he had to estimate weight, which affected lengths and thicknesses. A difficult project, to be sure, but Halcyon was equal to it, and he knew it would help them both.

Now

Nicki sat in her chair and placed one of the boxes of bones on her lap. She took a deep breath and reached her hands into the box. She was nervous.

Before even trying to get a good psychic read on these, she would need to calm down. But she was excited and anxious, and it was difficult to stay calm when her career was riding on this assignment. No other psychic anthropologist had ever tried to get a read on bones this old, and not only were they old, but the subjects had burned in a fire, which meant that most of the organics were destroyed. A hundred years ago, anthropologists wouldn't even have been able to tell that this ashy dirt held human remains.

Nicki breathed deeply, in and out, in and out, while she felt through the box. A few actual bones were left among the ashes—the center of a pelvis, a fragment of femur. She closed her eyes and held these in her hands.

Sometimes it came so easily. Stories flowed from the remains into her head like she was watching a movie. This wasn't one of those times. She saw a few pictures: a young boy playing with a string, a concrete floor, a large bird on fire. With the images came hope for an end, loneliness, and pain.

Nicki opened her eyes. At least she had something. She still didn't know who this person was, but she knew he, or she, understood what it was to love a little boy. She knew they were trapped in a hopeless situation.

Then

He had to make two. One for him and one for the boy. After all, the boy would never survive alone. He needed Halcyon. And leaving the boy behind wasn't an option. They would go together, as soon as they were finished.

Now

The second box was even lighter than the first, and as she put her hands in, she felt next to nothing. A brief image of fire filled her mind — a burning apple? She couldn't get beyond that.

Nicki heard shuffling in the bubble opposite the one she had come in through. She stood and went through the door, happy to have a breather after her two attempts.

Instead of a room full of cots, as she expected, she found herself entering the makeshift kitchen. Sure enough, a box of chocolate peanut butter energy bars was on the table in front of her. Grant was bent over, getting something out of the mini fridge.

"I don't have much yet," Nicki said as he stood up and closed the door. "I wondered if you could give me some information. I heard this building was maybe a kind of church?"

Grant sat down and opened his lunch box, which looked meticulously packed, but appeared to be peanut free. "We're not really sure," he said. "It could have been a church. That's one theory. I think it was more like a monastery. It had a dozen or so small rooms in the back that seem to have been occupied, like living quarters for ascetics. That's where we found some of the bodies you're reading. The front space was larger and that's what makes people think it was a church, but it would have been a pretty small church. It could have also been a retail space, a cafeteria, a gym, a meeting hall, pretty much anything."

Nicki gave in and grabbed a peanut butter bar while Grant took a bite of his lunch, which seemed to be some kind of rice and vegetable dish. Nicki thought it looked good, but maybe that was because she was hungry.

"Okay," she said, "So you know there were living quarters in the back and a big room in the front, and that four people, at least, died when it burned down. Anything else?"

Grant thought for a moment. "We know some of what else was in the building," he said. "There were tables, dishes, a lot of metal work—you know, things like bars and joints and decorative statues." He took another bite. "Does that help?" he asked after he finished chewing.

"Maybe," Nicki said. "I'm going to get back to work."

Then

It really wasn't as hard to build them as it would be to use them. The boy needed lessons. He needed training in how to put them on, how to control the joints. They also needed some sort of exit strategy. He started working out those details, too.

Now

Nicki took the third box in her hands. *I can do this,* she assured herself. This box seemed more full, and there were more bone fragments in it. As she sifted through the ashes, a story came to her more easily. This was certainly a man, a strong, powerful man who felt good about himself. He was riding a horse. He looked up at the sky and appreciated it. Appreciated it because it was something he didn't always see, it was something that he knew some people never got to see. Then he was in the city. His life was mundane and repetitive.

Nicki kept hold of the bones and probed deeper. What did he believe? What did he do? What stories did he tell himself?

She saw the boy locked in a room. The strong man

was bringing him food, then locking the door so the boy wouldn't escape, and so that the other man wouldn't escape, the one with the boy, the one with long hair and eyes that could look in two directions at once.

These ashes would give and give all day; the difficulty would be in understanding what they said. There was the bird again, burning as it fell. She saw another image of a horse. This time it was on fire. The man was on fire. Nicki continued. The building was on fire. The man felt a mix of sorrow, guilt, and duty.

Nicki had to stop. Her endurance had improved over the years as she had studied and practiced, but she couldn't concentrate past the burning.

She set the box on the table and stretched her arms and legs.

Then

Halcyon put his plan in place on a warm fall day. At least he thought it was probably fall, hard to say when he had been imprisoned so long. He called the guard, the nice one with the horses. Halcyon could hear the horses sometimes in the back. He sometimes talked about them with this guard.

"I bet it's lovely outside today," Halcyon said when the guard brought him his breakfast, another apple. "Did you get to ride this morning?" The guard nodded affirmatively.

"Not a cloud in the sky today, just clear and blue," the guard said, "but still cool. Doesn't get much nicer."

Halcyon set his plan in motion. "I sure miss it. The sky, the breeze. You know, I don't think the boy has ever seen the sky. Would we ever be allowed to go out, just for a few minutes, to feel the air just once?"

"You know, that should be possible. Let me ask and get back to you."

Now

Nicki sat down with the final box. She reached her hand in and a picture came immediately to her mind. It was the man, the long-haired, wild-eyed man from before. These ashes belonged to the boy. He respected the man. He listened to the man. He wanted to be like the man. He was afraid, but he said he would go, and the other men burned him. They burned him and the long-haired man. They lit the boy on fire and watched him die. *Why would they burn a child?* he thought, right before he died.

Nicki let go, relieved. She had done it. She had read bones older than her professors had, older than her mentor had. She had gone further than ever before, and she had information that would help this entire enterprise.

She found Grant back at the dig site.

"I think this was a sort of church," she told him. "Monks lived in the back, and worshiped in the front, yes, but there's more. I think they must have had some sort of ritualistic sacrifice that was held here. They would dress men and children as birds, and then light them on fire. Two of the sets of remains were the victims of these sacrifices, and the other two might have been caught in a fire that burned down the building after the ritual went wrong."

"Fascinating," Grant said. "I didn't think you would come up with information like that so quickly. I can't believe it."

"I can't either," Nicki said. "It seems pretty fantastic, but I know one of the remains was burned by several people while dressed as a sort of firebird. I think I might have read once that these people worshiped birds? Is that right?" Nicki was pleased with herself. "I'll write it all up for you and Sandy before I go."

It had been a good day. Nicki had figured out what the building was, what the people who lived there did, and how it had burned down.

She went back to her station and began filing a report detailing all she had seen and felt when she read the bones. Then she recorded her interpretations for Sandy, being as descriptive and thorough as possible.

Then

When they got outside, Halcyon and the boy tore their shirts to reveal the wings underneath. Then spread them out fully and took a leap into the air. The guards were stunned, but trained to deal with prisoner escape attempts.

They were quick to draw their bows, but they didn't want to kill the prisoners, so they lit their arrows on fire and aimed for the wings.

Halcyon hadn't flown far yet. He fell down to the ground rapidly, where the guards quickly put out the fire, tied him up and sent him inside.

The boy was more difficult to retrieve. He had flown so high that by the time he landed—not on the ground, but on the thatched roof of the prison—he was on fire. The fire quickly spread from the roof to the wooden beams and walls. Before long, the entire building was engulfed in flames.

The entire building burned to the ground. All of Halcyon's inventions, his sketches and journals, turned to cinders. The stables in the back, inhabited by a single horse, collapsed and smoldered for hours. Halcyon, in his cell, was the last to die.

Now

Nicki couldn't resist throwing some of her own embellishments and interpretations into the report. She had seen burning apples, horses, birds, and people, so they must have sacrificed all four. They also held these things in high esteem, worshipping them even. *This is sounding good,* Nicki thought.

About the author

Chanel Earl lives in Pleasant Grove Utah where she writes in her "spare time." In addition to writing, her hobbies include organizing things both physical and social, cooking, repurposing old into new, napping, watching way too much television, and mothering her four crazy kids. Her writing has appeared in several online magazines, and her short story collection *What to Say to Someone Who's Dying* is available at most online bookstores.

1001

Y. X. Acs

An isolated thing, the only natural feature around the Experimental Research Fortress XL12-42D was the snow. The building itself was of an impressive size, and smooth. It was also, of course, subject to winds, and these winds also carried the snow. The snowy fetters would pull at the gentle, rounded corners of the titanic building, and they would pile and re-pile the snow wherever they could, before yet another gust would pull it all down, and get things started again.

Inside the fortress, the sounds of the wind and any tinkling sounds, particulated-ice-against-metal sounds, were made inaudible by the walls. The walls provided a complete, guaranteed, dampening of all exterior noise. Dense, ultra-lite, ceramite-polycement exteriors gave way to corridors of vulcanized stone-and-mortar; lending the interior something of a castle-ish look, though the castle effect was ruined by the many high-tech light-sconces bracketed to the ceilings, which beamed down light chock full of nutritious K-rays.

As a result of these walls, in the place where Daxa Bukarine and Arin Nod worked, they were fortunate to have mostly quiet.

The room was tall and open; a large vaulted space that rose over them before growing into a pleasing, geometric web of polysteel beams. Desks, mostly empty, were decorated here and there with computer terminals.

Since their arrival, Daxa and Arin had been the room's only inhabitants. They hadn't met anyone else either; except for the orientation representative, who'd worn a Super-Kleen uniform of dark green wool, and who didn't look at people when he was speaking to them. They'd spent the first three days with him, and he'd been extremely helpful. Arin had expected that there'd've been a few more people around, but Daxa told him that she was pretty sure it was always this way.

Most of their time so far had been spent without talking in the quiet, working dutifully at the bottom of the vault. All of the terminals were equipped with sub-vocalizers, so there hadn't even been the sounds of the researchers giving commands to their computers. Just the dampened humming of the computer's two processors and a barely audible sound of continuous, sub-glottal throat noises.

Arin's eyes flicked to the right as Daxa rose to get herself yet another cup of coin tea. He watched her for a while, and then removed his sub-vocalizer.

"You know, you're going to spend all your earnings in coin-teas if you're not careful."

She shrugged. Arin raised his *METHOD RESEARCH* travel-mug to display it,

"The cantina tea is really just fine, once you get used to it."

"Not for me. I'm just fine with coin tea."

Arin shrugged. "They're your coins I guess."

#

Humboldt squeezed himself into the isolation-suit. The fitted elastic sleeve rode against his skin, and scraped against the rash on his forearm. Couldn't breathe in the fucking thing either, but it was better than the alternative, he supposed, which was not having it. Not interested in not having it, so...

He made his way to the utility vehicle, the remote airlock key in one hand and a vehicle access wand in the other. The huge, rust-marked circular door unlatched and swooshed aside slowly. A paved stone passageway was revealed, descending at a gentle angle to somewhere beneath the research fortress. It was around a fifteen-minute drive to the chamber where the aliens had left humanity the meat-computer. *Damned inconvenient place,* Humboldt had always thought. *Like they were making it deliberately hard on us.*

But, had they done that on purpose?

Who could tell.

Around the cantina, you'd occasionally hear one of the upper-story fortress staff going on about how there'd never been any aliens in the first place, that it was all bullshit for this or that reason. Spies and government secrets and whatnot. And that would vex Hum, even to violence, once (though he was still ashamed to think of it). Because he'd seen the meat-computer; and it couldn't be anything else but alien. A squiggling mess of nonsense is what it was. But for all that, it actually held information, data, words, human words too.

That's how everyone knew it'd been left for us purposefully. It was full of all our own stuff, all our own words, in all of our languages. All of our stories, from the past on through to the future, somehow locked up as data in its proteins. But were they ever gonna come back? Why'd they do it? And what were we supposed to do with it? Nobody'd ever know. Because once our kindred from the stars had finished leaving their gift, they themselves left almost as quickly. Dropped the gloopy thing, and fucked right off.

We might never see them again ever, Hum knew, but they'd come here, and they'd left that thing, and he would go to his grave with the strangely satisfying knowledge that there were others out there, even if they were really inconsiderate. Come to think of it, he wouldn't have a job without them. Bottom line, Hum liked the aliens.

The white headlights and green lights of the dashboard were reassuring in the subterranean darkness. Down the maintenance corridor, smoothly paved and direct. He gunned the engine, speeding down the tunnel, his vehicle eating the directional lines of glow-in-the-dark paint, one after another.

At last, he approached the central extraction chamber, lights far away, and then the sounds of machines. He signaled the extraction team, and shortly thereafter two men in isolation suits came to let him through the airlock.

Inside, the meat computer stood, massive and glistening. Numerous men in isolation suits circled around it. The "B" team — to which Hum was directed by an attendant — was busy pulling a wide flat sheet of dark green mucus from the squashy device. The material stretched, taffy-like, from out of a thin horizontal mouth in the side of the computer, upon which the extraction team had bolted an external metal feed-slot. Hum waited as they finished spooling the last of it and locking it into a waiting container.

"Thanks," he radioed, and the two men waved in response as he hauled the final container over to the utility vehicle.

#

Arin assisted Daxa as she cracked the lid of the primary container and lifted it off, revealing the ectoplasmic skein.

"Okay, warm up the fax machine," she said, half-gesturing, and he hurried across the room, flicking on a bank of switches.

On either side of the container they both lifted the gross thing out and carefully began to attach it to the Facsimile Engine, lovingly dubbed "The Fax Machine" or "The Psychic Fax Machine" by Research Fortress locals.

It was their third time performing the task, and it had begun to feel natural — the gestures, and the order of things. The skeins of ectoplasm unraveled without sticking, and they fed smoothly into the machine. Pulled taut, the colour became a filmy, translucent green, one very unlike the dark, hard, mucus-plug green from which it had emerged. The computers around them emitted a reassuring chirping. Daxa crossed the room, cradling her mug of coin-tea.

When she tripped, she managed to hold onto her

mug, but the lid and its contents traveled as a single mass through the air before striking the console. Sparks of plasma arced from the Psychic Fax, and a thin, foul-smelling smoke was emitted from between the console keys, a thick smoke from its vents. The conveyor moving the ectoplasm across the sensor stopped, while the motor carrying the feed into the thin slot of the fax continued to operate, gathering the narrative adhesion in layer after layer against the opening.

It piled up, compressing the goop of one surface against the other, the action creating looped scroll fringes at the edges. Daxa gasped, and clawed at the controls, trying to shut off the device, while Arin seized an emergency scalpel, and sliced the ribbon of mucus free.

Moments later, the ectoplasm dangled from the wall and trailed across the floor. The room was motorless and quiet.

#

Thirteen hours later, after much horrified checking of trouble-shooting documents, and conservation, and following a few ugly tatters of sleep, Daxa and Arin returned to the analytics office, to continue the scaling, re-batching, and de-corrupting of the jelly-bound data. They stormed around one another, brittle with irritation and fatigue. An actual printed copy of the Fortress Data Emergency Protocols lay open on a spare desk nearby.

Fragments, primarily knots, of the alien material had been carefully placed around the lab, drying out and curling at the edges. Arin spritzed at them with a small spray-bottle, wearing a provoked look on his face.

"This is a nightmare." He said it mutteringly, but loud enough for Daxa to hear.

"Pardon?"

"I said this is a nightmare. There's no way we'll be able to salvage most of this crap. Why don't we just throw it out and record the missing segment as 'missing'?"

Daxa turned her eyes back to her screen. "Because that's not what the book says to do."

"Screw the book," said Arin. Daxa shrugged.

A moment later she looked up again, "Come look at this. It's two stories that have pretty bad adhesion, but if we compare them against the historical archive..."

She tapped the screen as another window came into view.

"See, the stories are just stuck together. If we count up all the words and then compare them to pairs of stories that are on public record..."

She trailed off, then began abruptly again, making a quick series of sub-glottal commands.

"Here," and another window, "and here. We can just fill in the rest. This one's an old Eurasian story, and this one's an adaptation of a, uh, frame story, for a whole bunch of other stories or something. Anyway, it found the matching text."

Arin frowned, "Let me see."

Switching the window back to the original, the one containing the adjoined text, and then setting up two comparator screens, he read:

There was once a hostel owner in the world whose wife adored fairy stories above all other things. At night, when the hostel owner was away or sleeping, his wife would accept only those lodgers who could also provide a story of some sort. This practice led to significant losses for the hostel owner, and he began to think about how he could best discourage his wife's love of stories.

Now, the hostel owner and his wife had two daughters, Shahrazad and Dunyazad, of which the elder had perused the books, annals, and legends of preceding kings, and the stories, examples, and instances of bygone men and things; indeed it was said that she had collected a thousand books of histories relating to antique races and departed rulers. She had perused the works of the poets and knew them by heart; she had studied philosophy and the sciences, arts and accomplishments, and she was pleasant and polite, wise and witty, well read and well bred.[28]

---

28 Description of Shahrazad from: *The Book of the Thousand Nights and a Night: A Plain and Literal Translation of the Arabian Nights Entertainment.* Translated by Richard Burton. Kama Shastra Society

The latter daughter was also highly accomplished, and possessed courage, wit, and penetration, infinitely above her sex. She had read much, and had so admirable a memory, that she never forgot anything she had read. She had successfully applied herself to philosophy, medicine, history, and the liberal arts, and her poetry excelled the compositions of the best writers of her time. Besides this, she was a perfect beauty, and all her accomplishments were crowned by solid virtue.[29]

Now, one night in winter, the hostel owner happened upon an old man, frozen to atoms, dressed in the tattered remnants of what must have once been a noble and precious garment. Sensing an opportunity, the husband asked him,

"Can you tell tales? My wife will not allow you to stay the night if you cannot provide her with a story. And what about stories of disappointment? Or perhaps know you some stories of shame?"

The old man replied, angrily, "I hope you get tongue-cankers and internal gravel for asking me about such things...You want to know about stories, do you? I am a person that stories have ruined. Stories have beaten, whipped, slippered, and basted me. Stories have made me base, like you. I was once a great king, with privileges. I skimitared whom I liked, and I had a new wife every day. But then, I was seduced, and ultimately ensnared, by a malicious maker-of-stories, for 1001 nights, and by this means I lost my kingdom."

"So you know many tales, then? Can you tell these stories for a long time?"

"A ruinous amount."

"This is perfect for me," said the husband, and he led the old man inside.

The hostel owner, then coming upon his wife, said, "This man has promised to tell you stories all night long. But he will do so only if you do not interrupt him. If you interrupt him during any of his stories, he will tell you no

---

(1885).

29   The same description of Shahrazad from: *The Arabian Nights Entertainment.* Translated by Jonathan Scott. Aldine (1890).

more."

The old man confirmed this, saying, "That's right. You must not interrupt me. If you do, I will stop telling my stories."

Then they settled in for a good meal, and the husband and wife got into their soft bed, and they called the old man over to their bedside for a night's entertainment.

The old man began his story,

"There was once a djinn that was cuckolded, and he sealed a glass casket with eleven locks of steel

There was once a djinn that was cuckolded, and he sealed a glass casket with eleven locks of steel

There was once a djinn that was cuckolded, and he sealed a glass casket with eleven locks of steel

There was once a djinn that was cuckolded, and he sealed a glass casket with eleven locks of steel"

He kept on saying the same thing over and over,

"There was once a djinn that was cuckolded, and he sealed a glass casket with eleven locks of steel"

So, the wife went on listening and listening as he said it again and again, until, losing her patience, she finally interrupted him, and said, "What are you talking about? This is nonsense. This isn't a story. You're just saying the same thing over and over. Why, it's mere repetition." At which point, the king leapt from his stool, shouting, "I told you not to interrupt me! The story was just about to change! Now I will tell you no more stories!"

Shahrazad and Dunyazad then appeared at the door's frame and said..."

"Who cares?"

"At least we'll be able to salvage a few."

"This is pointless. No one will ever care one way or the other. No one is even...no, just no."

"They have oversight committees, that sort of thing, someone will notice. Anyway, it's what the book says to do."

"I'm telling you. No one cares. This is just a huge waste of time."

Daxa shrugged, "It's what the book says to do."

#

Arin endured three days of this work, half-heartedly rescuing the stories, before his next outburst.

"You do realize," he said, "that this is all time added on to our contract. We don't get this back. This is extra."

Daxa's face turned red, and she frowned, "I'm well aware of the time-surcharge. This is our job, your job, so just do it."

Arin's face also turned red, and he frowned as well, "My job was to feed the data back to the real..."

"Your job..." Daxa interrupted him, "is to do what you signed up for. This is it. There was an accident on-site, okay, so we need to clean it up."

She watched as his lower lip protruded ever-so-slightly, as if to shout. She breathed in. "Look. Okay. Listen. I know that you're frustrated, and I'm sorry, and I know that this was my fault. And I'm sorry that you feel that your time is being wasted. But these," she gestured expansively at the clumps, "were left here for a reason. And if it weren't for me, they'd still be whole. We would still have the complete message. I'm sorry, but I have to do this. If it makes you feel better, you can go ahead with transmission, and I can append a note..."

This time Arin interrupted her. "It'll take five times as long if I do it myself. You know that as well as I do."

"I'm sorry. Go hang out in the rectory then, and I'll message you when I'm done."

Arin left, displeased.

#

He was gone for three days before he returned to the analytics office, where Daxa had been dutiful. The major tangles of ectoplasm had been unraveled, excepting the very core of the large bolus, snipped directly from the computer's mouth. Pieces from a few of the knots, large fragments and small, had been pieced together like a mosaic pattern with ripped edges. Others lay on the desks, and yet others in neat, dry stacks.

"How much longer?"

Arin had obviously been brooding the entire time. Reflecting on how much it was all impacting him. Sitting in the rectory with nothing but time. Daxa looked down at a piece of plasti-paper he held in his hand.

"I think I managed to extract one of the stories."

"Why did you print it out?"

"I wanted you to read it."

"That's a hell of an expense, you could have sent it electronically. And you were criticizing me for coin-teas..."

She reached out to take the document, which Arin willingly relinquished:

A CURE FOR STORY-TELLING

There was once a porter in the world: he had a wife who was passionately fond of stories, and she would only let people come and visit her who could tell stories. Well, as you may understand, this was rather costly to the husband. So he began to think, "How can I cure her of this undesirable habit?"

Well, one day in the winter, late at night, an old man came in frozen to atoms, and he asked to be allowed to stop the night. So the husband ran out to him and said, "Can you tell tales?"

Then the peasant saw that there was no help for it, as he was simply freezing with cold, and nodded.

The husband said, "I have an idea: will you tell stories for a long time?"

"Yes, all night long."

"Capital: come in!"

So he led the guest in.

Then the husband said, "Now, my wife, here is a peasant who has promised to tell stories all night long, on the condition that you are not to make any remarks or interruptions."

"Yes," said the guest; "no remarks, or else I shall not open my mouth."

So they had supper and lay down to sleep, and the peasant began—

"There was an owl flying across a garden, and it landed by a well and sipped the water.

"There was an owl flying across a garden, and it landed by a well and sipped the water.

"There was an owl flying across a garden, and it landed by a well and sipped the water.

"There was an owl flying across a garden, and it landed by a well and sipped the water."

And he went on telling the same thing over and over again—

"There was an owl flying across a garden, and it landed by a well and sipped the water."

So the mistress went on listening, and at last interrupted: "What sort of a tale is this? Why, it is mere repetition."

"Why do you interrupt me? I told you, you must not make any exclamations: this is the preface of the tale, and there comes another after it."

Then the man, after hearing this, could not help leaping up from the bench and whipping his wife.

"You were told not to make any interruptions, and you will not let him end his story."

So he set on beating, beating, whipping, slippering, basting her, until the wife at the end hated stories, and was in despair ever afterwards at the sound of them.[30]

Daxa was speechless.

#

When Humboldt returned to the analytics office three weeks later, pushing a cart loaded with narrative ectoplasm, he found Arin sitting there alone.

"Where's your buddy?" he asked, though his tone suggested he didn't really care one way or the other.

---

30 "A Cure for Storytelling" from *Russian Folk-Tales* by Alexander Nicolaevich Afanasyev. Translated by Leonard Arthur Magnus. E.P. Dutton & Company (1916). Available online at: https://en.wikisource.org/wiki/Russian_Folk-Tales/A_Cure_for_Story-Telling

"She left, for good. Not working here anymore. They're trying to fill her position, but until they get things sorted, I'm supposed to do the work of two people somehow..."

Hum nodded absently, "Is that right? That's too bad. Sorry to hear it."

Arin watched as Humboldt unloaded the canisters. Once three were lined up on the desk beside Humboldt, he got up and started helping. Humboldt smiled at him, "So why'd she leave?"

"Who knows? Probably because of the accident. You must have received the notification of a delay for our section."

"Sure."

"She dropped one of her damn coin-teas on the console of the Psychic Fax."

Hum made a lemon-bitten face and sucked in the air, "Shit."

"After that, she became totally fixated on untangling all the stories. Wanted us to compare the fragments with the historical archive; she was in here trying to piece them together like a jigsaw puzzle. It was insane. Completely insane."

Hum snorted, "Well...it's a nice sentiment and all. I guess she thought she was keeping something important together."

Then he laughed, "But it's probably for the best. Cause she'd have just lost it if she ever found out how many of those things get dropped, or run over, or trampled on down below."

"Exactly," said Arin.

"Just gotta hope it's only the right ones that get lost, eh?"

Arin laughed, nodded enthusiastically, and said, "Exactly. Exactly."

About the author

You know, Celia, I'm really worried about Y.X. Acs.

"Where art thou, my love?"

The Confessions of a Love-Struck Xeno-Mythologist

Filip Wiltgren

Falling in love with an alien never ends well. Boy meets twenty-tentacled freak, boy loses freak, freak explodes. Or vanishes. Or drops its tentacle cup.

Still, when love jumps, you fall. Suddenly you don't care that its mouth is in the wrong place, or that its skin is naked. You forget the wet slobbering when it sleeps. All you can smell is love.

I fell for an alien close to its term of expiration. You could tell by the color of its fur, and the way it fell off in clumps. Still, love has no nose. For months we lived in beautiful harmony, scratching and playing. Then disaster struck.

One day my alien would not rise. It lay in its nest, breathing in gasps and chokes, its naked gums flapping and glistering. One of its air vents leaked fluid, the other let loose a keening sound that made my fur rise.

Oh, how I wished I had studied xenobiology instead of wasting my days on comparative mythology and the politics of foreign species. Now I stood in impotent fear, my body shaking to match my alien's. But woe to the man who would let his love die for lack of action.

I rushed about its cave, dragging all its favorite items to its side. The fluffy tentacle cups, the roll of soft, organic polysaccharide, the prosthetic leg extender that helped it reach the ground. But to no avail. My alien was dying.

The aliens dried out at an alarming rate, all that naked skin bleeding moisture all the time. I tried to bring its drinking utensils, but they were made for wiggly tentacles, not firm hands. All I managed to do was shatter them on the ground.

Undeterred, I tried bringing it water from one of the drinking holes that littered my alien's cave. The metal ones presented a problem, being constructed for tentacle operation, but the smooth stone fountains held water which I was able to draw into my mouth. I jumped onto my love's nest and tried to give it water, but it closed its main intake, and I spilled my water down its side. Undeterred, I fetched more, and attempted to transfer it to my alien's face using my tongue. My love waved at me feebly, in a gesture I recognized as being both rejecting and dismissive.

But I could not let it die. Clawing at the barrier affixed to the main entrance, I managed to create a large enough gap to exit the cave. Outside, the day's beauty mocked my misery. The world's yellow sun baked the stones put down to mark the aliens' no-digging zones. The warmth was a boon to my tired legs.

For cycles, I hunted, yelling at an endless line of tentacle monsters, cursing their impotence. What in my own monster had seemed a cute inability to understand basic commands, was revealed to be a race-wide stupidity bordering on insanity. Not only did they refuse to help, they did not even pretend to listen, flailing at me with their tentacled legs, yelping and growling in their hideous voices.

Finally, I managed to rouse a monster to follow. It slowly flapped its forelegs, and jerked into their rolling, unstable gait. I rushed ahead, but its breathing vents proved inadequate after mere moments of exertion. It stopped, wheezing. I darted back to its side, and by staying just outside its range, I managed to lead it back to my love's cave.

I slunk in through the hole in the barrier, but the monster didn't follow. Indeed, it pounded the barrier a few times, then retreated.

I emerged, yelling and cursing. It returned, spurred by my willingness to be caught, but I withdrew again. This we did several times, until the monster called others of its kind. Together they managed to break down the barrier and I led them to where my love's pained whispering could be heard even by the aliens' weak ears.

The first aliens brought more aliens, with implements of medicine. Even to my untutored eyes they looked primitive, metal and glass tubes used to poke and prod, collect blood and inject fluids. But a hungry man does not turn down a bone, no matter how old. My love did not protest, and its wheezing lessened. Gratitude surged through me, making me dance with joy. But the monsters were not finished.

They moved my love onto a board, then loaded it into a vehicle. I jumped in to sit by its side. The monsters threw me out.

Of all the callous, evil, ignorant acts! Laying hands on a superior species! Having the gall to separate me from my love! I yelled, I raged, I bared my teeth at them. When all else failed, I attacked.

For all their ineptitude, the monsters were strong, and many. They took my love, and tried to choke me.

I tore myself free, and shamefully admit finding a guilty pleasure in the loss of bodily fluids I caused.

Following the trail of burnt biochemicals left by their vehicle, I arrived at a large mound in time to see my love swallowed by it.

The mound was much larger than my love's cave, and surrounded by a multitude of tentacle monsters, some standing watch at the barriers, others merely passing through. The barriers shut behind them.

In truth, a measure of diplomacy was required.

But how do you discuss with a species that refuses to listen? It had taken me the better part of a day to find an alien trainable enough to follow. Explaining that I needed to see my love, a mental operation orders of magnitude higher than walking, would take years, maybe decades. Assuming they would be willing to listen, and nothing I had seen even remotely indicated their willingness to do so. For all my professor's talk, the aliens did not exhibit signs of intelligence beyond rudimentary tool-using.

I needed a way to communicate with primitives.

I barked a laugh when I figured it out. I had derided my degree in comparative mythology; now it would save me. There is no match for comparative mythology when it comes to building rapport with an alien culture.

I found a shallow, albeit disgusting, brook to sate my thirst, retrieved some local nutrients, mainly carbohydrates with a smattering of complex biomolecules, from a recycling container, and crawled beneath a bush to think.

The mound was clearly a place of safety and refuge; two things that, if my professor was to be believed, often figured in local myths.

I felt a pang of guilt at the status of my research. Having spent most of my time frolicking with, and being scratched by, my lovely, tentacled freak, I had neglected the information-gathering aspects of my fieldwork. All I had were my recollections of my professor's work, boosted by my own superior intellect.

First I considered adapting a myth centering around an attack on a refuge, with hostile aliens in their larval stage coming to devour its walls and roof. This would communicate my need to enter, but as I did not want to eat the mound, nor fatten young monsters for roasting and eating, it might be a sub-optimal solution.

What I needed was a story of love, one that the monsters would immediately recognize. There was indeed such a story in the local mythos, of an alien getting its tentacles trimmed in order to fit inside a discarded tentacle cup, which would enable it to prove its identity and reunite with its lost lover.

There were, of course, some problems.

First and foremost, my complete lack of tentacles. Also, I lacked a tentacle cup. That could be easily obtained from the recycling containers, but gaining tentacles would be more difficult, especially as I had no inclination to mutilate myself.

Perhaps merely displaying the tentacle cup would be enough to communicate my intentions. It was worth a try.

The first cup I found was clearly inadequate, being of refurbished plant matter, soggy, and sporting a large hole in its bottom. It was, however, still full of the carbohydrate-enriched serf-species fluid the aliens liked to consume, rotten and frozen. This was just as disgusting as it sounds, but it contained both energy and moisture, and need is the chaser of invention, or at least the digger of ignoring your taste buds and consuming local delicacies.

My second attempt was no better, and half-full of a disgusting type of water the aliens strained through a type of burnt seed. I dropped that one quickly.

The third one, however, was more promising. It was metal, round, and smelled of meat. It also had quite sharp edges, which might come in handy if there was any actual tentacle-cutting to be done. I pulled it from the recycling container and dropped it before one of the guard monsters.

The stupid beast kicked the cup away.

I brought it back, and stared at the guard.

The dumb creature kicked harder this time, sending the cup sailing into the night. I set off in search for it, all the while cursing a species that did not teach its young all the proper myths. Finally, I managed to find the cup and brought it back, setting it squarely before the guard.

A second guard monster, poised some five steps beyond the first, made a loud braying sound, which enraged the first monster. Instead of kicking the cup away, it bent and scooped it up.

Finally, I thought.

The beast dropped it in a nearby recycling container.

I considered yelling at it, but limited myself to farting in its general direction. It didn't notice.

The fourth time I brought the cup back, the monster uttered sounds of distress. It kept on braying and hissing for some time, but I refused to budge. And then something marvelous happened. The monster understood.

It quieted, letting its tongue loll out of its flat face in an expression of thoughtful understanding. Then it picked up the cup, and went inside the mound. I followed, slipping through the barrier before it could close, and rushing ahead. I was afraid that, in its eagerness to please me, the alien would actually cut off my love's tentacles before I could stop it.

Then I realized the monster had no way of knowing which alien to trim the tentacles on. Perhaps it would cut them all? How would I stop it? Should I stop it? What if I interfered with the mythos, causing a collapse of local culture? Thus thinking, I followed the monster down a tunnel.

In the end, my worries proved unfounded as the stupid creature dumped the cup in a recycling container.

This time I could not hold back, and yelled a rather foul epitaph at it. The monster apparently understood enough, because it jumped, twirled, and started barking and spitting at me in turn, before crouching in what I now recognized to be a fighting stance.

I had no intention of fighting it. While I could have easily chewed it, it would have felt too much like eating my love. Also, while the monster was stupid, it had not proven to be directly opposed to my needs. So I simply jumped, overturning the recycling container, grabbing the cup, and speeding off down the tunnel.

The aliens' view of healing was somewhat dim. In their own primitive way, they tried to keep their mound clean by pouring enormous amounts of flammable solvent everywhere. The whole place stank of it, as did the aliens residing there. Still, it barely covered the smell of death and decay, and there were biological infestations in every corner.

I found my love in a room with two other tentacle fiends. The others raised an immediate commotion, yelping and thumping, but I ignored them. Placing the tentacle cup by my love, I waited.

Nothing happened. My beloved didn't respond.

Maybe it didn't know the myth, even though my professor had assured me that this myth had been spread all across their world by a small, black, rat-like creature with big ears.

I grabbed the base of one of my love's tentacles and tried shoving it into the cup. Seeing this, the other residents redoubled their screeching, causing the local entry barrier to burst open, allowing two aliens in white smocks to rush in. They, too, began generating noise, summoning a guard monster.

By this time, I was sitting by my love, all five of its tentacles firmly in the cup. I had not the courage to raise my tail from between my legs to bite them off, though, which may have been a mistake. The aliens directing their bulging eyes at me seemed to think so. Still, the mythological ramifications were clear. I had found my love.

The monster failed to smell it this way. It grabbed me by the scruff of my neck, in quite an expert and unbreakable grip, and threw me out into the street. Clearly it had not studied comparative mythology.

But the one who folds in love will spend his life sniffing other's behinds. I was not deterred. My tentacle freak was in the death mound, and I would faithfully remain by its side until it got better or passed on.

Once again, I crawled beneath the bushes, by way of the recycler in order to refill my energy stores.

I had done everything right. The problem obviously lay with the myth. Perhaps the tentacle cup was not enough for it to be recognized. Still, chewing off my love's tentacles smelled rotten. I would need a new myth.

Most of the myths I had studied concerned aliens gaining status by throwing oblong cases of air-inflated skin at each other. This felt quite inappropriate for my situation. Maybe I should have tried for the one with the midget aliens that eat the house built of carbohydrates, but I had little inclination to start chewing on the mound's stone.

Then it struck me. The story of the midgets wasn't about living spaces, it was about nutrition. The consumption and giving of nutrients was a central theme in every socially based mythology. Only by giving could a being show true love.

I needed to overwhelm the monsters with nutrition!

I immediately started for the recycling container. But it was a small one, and I had already dipped into it twice. Luckily, there were storage facilities on the other side of the mound.

The storage smelled like gangu-beast dung. Clearly the aliens hadn't figured out large scale cooling. Still, my message would be clear. Straining, I heaved aside the barriers blocking the storage from local fauna, the same fauna that, should I believe my professor, had spread the mythological tale of the tentacle cup. Then I started to haul.

The nutrients were packed in big, black sacks. Strangely fragile, the sacks tore and shredded, spilling nutrients. No matter, there was plenty left. I brought my communication trophy to the entrance, and presented it to the guard monsters.

Strangely, their barks, yaps, and growls did not seem like the sounds of admiration.

Perhaps I had brought too little. I dropped the bag and ran to bring another. This excited them no end, but failed to gain me entrance to the mound. I turned to bring more.

To my delight, the guard monsters followed. Perhaps I had misinterpreted their noises. Or they may have finally understood the meaning of true love. I didn't care. Following meant they would be willing to listen, and with my mythological skills, I was bound to reach even such weak-nosed creatures. I raced to the open storage, where I turned to deliver my speech.

It was a beautiful speech, extolling the virtues of love, devotion, and multi-species bonds. The monsters listened to the first seconds. Then the lead one threw one of their metal light-sticks at me.

For some reason I felt compelled to catch it. I missed.

It hit me squarely on the nose, and bounced. Tears filled my eyes at the injustice of it all. Here I was, a senior grad-school student, with an alien research scholarship and a history of double-wag assignments, and the local monsters attacked me. I did what I hadn't done since losing my milk teeth. I whined.

No, that is too odorless a word. I griped, I whimpered, I sobbed. I cried at the injustice of the universe and the pain of life. I did a pretty credible job of composing some rather tenuous poetry on the fly.

Perhaps it was my poetry that finally moved the aliens. Perhaps they felt bad for the uncivilized act of throwing a metal stick in the middle of my soliloquy. Either way, they silenced, and showed remorse, glancing at each other. Finally, one approached me with tentacles outstretched in greeting.

I knew this dig. The monster wanted me to put my nose on its tentacles, then lick them, then show my gratitude. This is just as disgusting as it sounds, but it figured in all the alien myths involving people. They'd even bred it into their own servant-people, a race my professor back home had declared to be non-intelligent but otherwise surprisingly like us, all the while denying the theologians' claim to an Over-God seeding the universe with quadrupedal species in His image.

It struck me that I was in the middle of a myth, one so ingrained in their culture, the monsters probably didn't even think about it themselves. It was the myth of the heroic, kind, gracious, subservient person saving the monstrous alien.

I should have recognized it a long time ago, but it felt strange to consider myself subservient to an alien, especially when dealing with such a grotesque species. But that was exactly what I had been to my own love, licking its tentacles and following it around. Doing this to another monster made me nauseous. But if it would bring me my true love, I was willing to yank my fur.

I shoved my nose into the alien's nest of tentacles.

I nearly vomited. My love smelled dry, strange, and powdery. The monster smelled of burnt hydrocarbons, tarnished metal, and acid. I forced myself to lick it. Then I flopped down on the ground, and rolled over on my back.

The alien seemed immeasurably pleased by this. It grabbed my gut, and I shifted to protect my genitals from this sex-fiend. I was lucky my love had understood personal boundaries.

Still, the guard monster flapped its gums, the other guard monster replied, and I was taken into the mound, and to my love.

I spent its last days by its side, cuddling up, giving it comfort. The aliens didn't try to evict me any longer, even going so far as to set bowls of water and food in the room. And then, one night, death claimed my freak.

I gave its tentacles a final lick and departed heavenward, leaving the empty tentacle cup on the nightstand as a token of our love.

###

About the author

Filip Wiltgren is a writer and tabletop game designer based in Sweden. A member of Codex and the Ubergroup, Filip has published in markets such as *Daily SF*, *Grimdark*, and *Nature Futures*, as well as a number of anthologies and semi-pro markets. In his day life, he's worked as a journalist, copywriter and communications officer, and when he isn't writing, he spends time with his wife and kids. He can be found at: www.wiltgren.com.

Deus ex Noir

Rhoads Brazos

The music begins, same jazzy number as always, keys over bass. I relax in my office chair, fedora tipped over my eyes and arms behind my head. The glass on my desk shows two fingers of bourbon. The scene pans over Thebes' waterfront. Drums join the track and the music swells, really kicking now.

A mook in a linen tunic and a flat hat grabs my shoulder. I punch him hard enough to crack his jaw. After so many episodes, I feel sorry for the guy. When I turn to the audience, the light catches my eyes like a wolf. Now, draw the Colt and hold the pose while a name paints itself over my chest. My own, presumably. Caspian Slate. The words are hard to read facing me backwards, and I have to keep my vision steady.

The rest is routine. Jogging down the steps of the Temple of Cheops, firing down an alleyway next to the bazaar and drinking alone in some godforsaken dive. I shove my way out of a nameless courtroom. The judge is on his feet. He throws his gavel at me. It shows my belligerence. The audience loves that.

The music crests. The lights dim.

#

Back from commercial.

I prefer to start someplace cheery: Angelino's waffle house, the chariot races, watching the ducks outside Smitty's carnival midway. Beggars and choosers. I'm graced with my desk from the opening credits. It's swank: teak inlaid with mahogany. Clients need to see success. In life, first impressions are all we get. Everything else is just an apology. I'm stabbing out a Chesterfield in a jade ashtray. Looks like I came in media res.

"Thank you," a feminine voice says. Volume isn't needed. Hers is the kind of voice a man holds his breath for.

I already know her name though I've never heard it.

"If I may ask," I say, "Mrs. Chisisi?"

"Neferu, if you please." She taps one sandaled toe nervously in the air. Her skirt is cut amazingly short. I try to imagine which angle the audience is watching from.

These first moments are always confusing. I'd expected her to be Minoan, a chance to get some platinum locks on screen. She has the swank of Thebes' finest. A smart, well-to-do flapper bob, manicured nails, a bangle of delicate earrings. She wears an ornamental asp about her wrist. It spirals up her forearm.

"Twice, they've tried to kill me," she says. "First at a soirée of Tefnut. The dates were poisoned. My cupbearer succumbed. It looked quite painful."

Rather blasé. She is upper caste, or was. She's promised to pay me the last she has.

"And the second attempt?" I ask.

"At the local market. A thin man knocked me to the ground and tried to pour venom in my eye. Luckily, a passing chandler put a stop to it. I believe this man was also at the soirée."

I see now why the kohl about her eyes is so thick. Her attackers only barely missed their target. That juice burns two-hundred proof.

"It could have been a warning," I say. "A blinding."

"I don't think so."

"You suspect your husband?" The usual m.o.

"I suspect that he's dead." She squints for the briefest moment, the sum of the emotion she's willing to let through. "My eldest too. They're always busy at the

Court of Ra. They organize the banquets, you see. But I should have seen them by now. It is a familial killing. All of us are meant to die."

"Reasonable assumption."

"And so I entrusted my girls to my housekeeper. I've known her for years. I paid her handsomely and told her to run far away. I know not where. In the month of Menkhet, she is to meet me at the festival of—"

I raise my hand. "Not here."

She looks leerily over her shoulder. There's no one else in the office. I work alone.

"I was not followed," she says.

"You were."

Nefuru frowns mightily. She's not used to being contradicted. As the wife of one of Ra's aristocrats, it's hardly surprising.

"There's a hundred no-name gumshoes this side of the river," I say. "Most with better caste. So why'd you pick me?"

"I was told you see it through."

I'm something of an expert on the Classical languages, what her type calls the 'low tongue.' She's picked up on my new slogan. It's a bit of an anastrophe. It really means that *I see through it.*

I down a burning swallow of bourbon. Drier than I like. She's dangerously close to irritated. Doesn't know it, but the attention's imperative. Lavish the focus on her and she'll stick around. It doesn't jibe for her to bow out hasty. I hate losing clients.

"You trust my judgment?" I ask.

"I wonder if you understand my plight. I do not think that you do."

"Not true. We'll leave out the back," I say loudly.

My office only has the front entrance. There's the fire escape, but we're three floors up and I wouldn't push my landlord out on that deathtrap. I still haven't moved.

Nefuru appraises me quietly. My words were for someone else's ears, and she knows it. Smart gal. Rising with only the whisper of linen, she watches me watch her.

"Lean to the left," I say, and draw my Colt. The Coroner, I call it. I take a bead on the office's front door.

I'm proud of the stenciled logo. It's all ivy and curlicues over hammered glass. On the small table beside the door, the kettle hisses another cup.

How do I know it's not the mailman calling, you ask? Western Union or some Thoth priestess collecting for orphans? These situations are touchy, but I'm no Jack with a feather. The audience needs a taste of danger, and so it must appear. I knew that the moment Nefuru sat across from me and crossed her legs like a threat and a promise. The drapes are drawn, and no one's climbing the fire escape. Logically, some hood will barge right through the front entry.

A shadow passes behind the glass. The early episode goons are always big guys. This one's sidled out of sight like an alley cat, as if I can't guess the cut of his square jaw and his moonscape face.

When the knob turns, I rise, lean over Nefuru's shoulder and fire through the wall.

In these confines, each report is a heart attack. My gun throws so much steel you can nearly follow the trajectory. Outside the office, the body drops like a sack of stones. A single hand swaths blood down the glass.

I spring from my chair and bound across the office in three strides, throw open the door and sweep the Coroner down the shabby hallway. These fellows always operate in twos. Sure enough, the accomplice is hanging back. A thin guy backpedals away with my neighbor, Mrs. Beasley, pinned before him. He's daring me to shoot around her impressive bulk. Mrs. Beasley is shrieking fantastically. You'd think she'd never been in such a spot, but we've done this dance four times at least; twice last season. The accomplice shoves Beasley forward and dives down the stairwell, as nimble as a minx. As Beasley sprawls indecorously across the tiles, I lower my gun. It's too soon for a foot chase and I could never catch such a sprightly soul. He's long gone.

Nefuru has crept to the entry behind me.

"Recognize him?" I motion to the hood at my feet. He's curled up like a wilted daisy. A snub-nosed .38 lies at his fingertips.

"No," she answers weakly.

I pour myself a cup of coffee just as the newly risen Mrs. Beasley staggers forward. I take a slow sip and affect a haughty pose. This is the scene closer where she berates me and tells all the ways I'm sullying the neighborhood—it's true, I don't deny it—but she only glares and marches down the hall to call the police.

Before I can think of a one-liner, Nefuru asks, "How did you know?"

I nearly choke.

"That could have been anyone," she says.

My strategies are beyond mortal understanding. No one has ever dared question them. The theme music is building, the lights are dimming, and for once, I don't know what to say.

#

The scene fades in. I'm already in my trench coat, which on the one hand is swell because it's another foggy day in Thebes, but on the other not, cause I'm sick of wearing the damned thing. Yet I understand—it's my symbol. It's my regalia. I keep Nefuru close and never take my hand off the Coroner. Of course she objects. There's no time to explain.

We pass out of the shadow of the high-rise step pyramids, all limestone traced with acres of copper-skinned windows, functional, like you'd find at the Saqqara catacombs. But here the corpses do office work. The sky is cut with a web of transmission lines, and a turbo-prop roars somewhere overhead, lost in the haze. After hopping a chariot, paid with a five spot from my wallet, we challenge the crowds. Our driver darts us by men bearing yoked loads, women balancing baskets on their heads, the omnipresent cattle. Down the winding Avenue of Serqet, we pass a litter carted by broad-shouldered Canaanites, and thread through an incoming caravan. Seems to be all animals. Nefuru covers her nose. Lowing oxen, chuttering pigeons and pigs, the howl of Vervet monkeys the color of the Theban snow. Out at the riverfront, we board a ferry only to exit at the last moment. Don't see anyone following. I pay a group of

Nubians to stow aboard their cedar felucca, and we coast alone onto the river.

"You take matters seriously when you must," Nefuru says. She's seated on the boat's driest seat. I would have offered it to her myself, but she took it before I could show my manners.

"Yes," I say, and pull out a Chesterfield. "Shoulda been on my toes."

It's just for her sake I say this. My concerns are not hers. I find my lighter. Her hand touches mine, her fingers as soft as mouflon fleece. No hard labor for her.

"Don't," she says.

The cigarette is already hanging from my mouth.

"You'll live," I say. I flick my lighter to life and touch it to nothing. She's quick. She plucked the cigarette from my lips before I could say good morning. She throws it into the river.

"Now why'd you do that?" I produce another cigarette. I look for my lighter. It's in her hand. God, she's going to throw it too. It's a keepsake. I put my cigarette away and she tucks my lighter under her sash.

The background music's switched to an up-tempo calypso. In the drudgery of my day, I seldom notice it, but sometimes it's good for cues. A moment of levity? I don't find it funny.

"I am a maiden of Ra," she says.

"Thought you were married with kids."

"Yes, my purity is the sky." She raises her palms like I need directions. "I breathe only this and the incense of myrrh, and I do not think you smoke myrrh. No forbidden airs."

Forbidden airs. Delightful.

We sit for a while and I watch the barges. A troupe of Byblos carnies are upon the far shore, all rainbow-dyed leather, feathers in their greasy locks. They're towing equipment on sledges up the banks. Looks like Smitty's Carnival is going to be adding new attractions. I go there sometimes, when I really need to be alone. Sit alone on the Big Wheel, huddle down and sip from my flask at the top of each revolution.

Ra is crossing the heavens in the solar bark. He

peeks from behind the clouds. Nefuru folds forward in a reverent bow. I wait for her to rise. She does, brushes the dust from her linens.

"I'll take your case," I say.

She stands wobbling and graces me with a bow that's not near as impressive as the last. She barely bends. I don't object. I know my place. She sits again, closer this time. I don't think she notices, and now even more possibilities are turning. The writers wouldn't do this to me.

"I will wire you what I can," she says, and then speaks low and humble. "My accounts are—"

"It's pro bono."

"I don't understand?"

"This case is unique."

"I know."

"Yeah, you don't," I say. "Tell me everything about yourself."

"About my husband," she corrects.

"No, you. Only you. Earliest memory up to this moment."

She doesn't see its relevance, and I'm thankful for that. I wouldn't know what to do if she did.

Before she can argue more, a cold wind blows from the east. It's not how the desert works. Thunderheads blot out the sun. In the sky is a tiny speck, flitting about the clouds. It must be enormous to be seen from so far.

I know an omen when I see one, and she does too. The shape lowers toward the carnival. I can nearly make out its wings. I look away. Nefuru is praying into her palms.

Some sights aren't meant for men. If they notice your attention, they might consume you. Someone, somewhere is—

#

" . . . and then I called you, Mr. Slate."

I didn't even sense the commercial break. I'm stunned for a moment, off my game. I know what she said because I can see her childhood. Part of me wishes I would have heard her speak it, but of course they wouldn't have aired that.

Nefuru sits at a table at the Bottom's Up. At *my* table. Senedj has set out an extra chair, one of the good ones that doesn't see-saw, and Nefuru and I are elbow-to-elbow, presumably so that we can watch the entrance. A statuette of Tekhi sits over it. Goddess of slaughter and drinking. My kind of gal.

There are I times I overestimate myself. Despite all the bombast, my ratings must be slipping.

"Mr. Slate?" she asks.

"Thank you," I say politely. "Sorry you had such a rough time of it. Not easy on a kid." And it wasn't. I know these rich dames aren't always born in the money, but she really had to claw her way to it. Call it avarice or call it ambition, but I respect a woman who moves with purpose.

"Ra gives me strength," Nefuru says. "I endure as He does."

She drones on about churchy insights. I'm not doing a great job of seeming enthralled. There are pressing matters at hand. I reach into my coat and toss a golden bracelet onto the table.

"An adder," I say.

She doesn't reply.

"Took it off the mook from Scene—" Catch myself, barely. "From my office. It's a token of Apophis. We're up against his guys, and I don't need to tell you, that ain't good."

"It seems unlikely such folk would be in Thebes," she says.

Right, they're rural sorts. Being so close to the Royal Court, she would know.

"I've butted heads with those subversives," I say. "Hide like roaches, but they're around. Not far from here, actually."

Nefuru raises her arm, shows me her stylish bracelet. "I wear a snake too. Am I a cultist?"

"No."

"You make these wild leaps of logic. I swear, it is strange to behold. If it were more than a trinket, *if,* I might humor your guesses. But I can name you a score of gods who favor the snake. Why, just off the top of my head—"

I clap my hand over her mouth. I think I caught the first syllable. Her lips, carefully stained with pomegranate and red ochre, were curling into an O. I'd only been toying with that particular suspicion and wouldn't have dared given it voice. As a foreigner, everyone knows my patron. The thought of him turning on me . . .

"Jesus, lady."

Her brow knits down low, questioning. I release her slowly.

"Are we being watched?" she whispers.

Always. But how do I tell her that?

"Just, don't say anything about this, even if you think you're alone, *capiche*?"

She senses the gravity of my words, nods quietly.

Osiris.

That kind of betrayal would only befit the final episode. I'm starting to worry. It can't be true.

#

Scene: dollar-a-day Westside flophouse not far from Bottom's. I walked myself over to clear my head. The audience won't endure a second transit, so I'm already here. Nefuru's back at the bar. Didn't need her moralizing.

I tug my gloves snug, straighten my tie, rap on the door to 312.

It opens. He's still a rube.

"Wassup, gangsta?" I drive my fist into his face. Tanner eats a mouthful of oiled lambskin. Almost hurts my knuckles.

The catchphrase is out of character. It was his invention, not mine. I've co-opted it for these little meetings between us. See, back in Season 8, Tanner was my liason with the Commissar of Thebes, but the audience didn't care for him. He has a displeasing mien. Imagine a fratboy who makes his cash at a weekend juice bar. That's Tanner.

And so he turned heel. Saw it coming episodes away. He joined a gang of Apophis's flunkies in some crazy metaphysical extortion scheme. They spend their time praying to their god, lowering curses on the lowly. Hell of a racket, figuratively speaking. Don't want a crippling case of the gout? Pay the devil his due.

I feed Tanner face-first into the wall, kick him in the ribs until I get my second wind. I beat him like a kettledrum. Write my own Ode to Joy. When he's weeping, I scoop him up, one hand gripping his belt, the other knotted in his air. I swing him back like a sack of feed and aim for the window.

"Say hello to Lucky Lindy," I say.

We're three stories up. The audience knows this because they saw his room number. That's playing to the scene.

"Gawd, man! Chill, chill!" he cries.

Hate his slang. It grates on my ears. I heave him into the corner like soiled laundry. He lays there spluttering. Anyone else would be comatose, but Tanner's resilient. He's meant to take a beating. It's an on-running gag of sorts.

"One of you is tailing my client," I say.

"Naw," he says. "We ain't like that."

He didn't ask who my client was. He didn't deny affiliations. Supremely stupid.

I reach into my coat. "I think I need to send Apophis a message."

Tanner flips his wig. He knows what me and my gun are capable of. What he doesn't know is that I left the Coroner with Nefuru, told her to keep it on her table back at Bottom's. It keeps away the paramours. If anyone dares to flirt despite it, she's to blast them. So, for once, I'm bluffing.

"No one's after you!" he cries. "I mean, yeah. Someone. But I don't know—"

I slap him around a little. Threaten to pistol-whip his face into a casserole. I'm more cruel than usual because the stakes are high.

"He's with Apophis, yeah," Tanner blubbers. "But he ain't no one I know. I just heard you can't touch him. You swing like a hammer, no offense, no offense! This cat's a stiletto. You're watching some chick? Trying to move in for the sweets? It's a setup, man. He'll take her, then he'll take you."

"But," I say, ignoring the bit about Nefuru. "He's pals with Ra?"

"Yeah," Tanner says. "I mean, no."

"Which is it? You suddenly don't remember, right? Then humor me, who told you this?"

He won't even look at me.

I close my fists around his neck. A bit more throttling should loosen his tongue. Thumbs against his throat, I squeeze. I'm planning to pick him up, toss him through the drywall, but he just sags in my grip. He's not even fighting it. He's crying.

The music's stopped. I may have broken character. I reach for a Chesterfield and then remember that Nefuru still has my lighter.

"Apophis," I say. "Tell him he's not welcome in my city. Next time I see you—"

Tanner mumbles an apology, and I leave without another word. Down the stairwell to the street.

It's like he said, a setup. That was also a slip on his part.

Whoever spoke to him carried more threat than I do. Osiris's symbol is the snake, the rearing cobra borrowed from Isis, and he hates Apophis. He used to hate Ra. Now he guards Ra while the solar bark traverses the Underworld, the only thing keeping Apophis at bay. Is this a power play? He's framing an enemy while he betrays his master? They say Osiris will one day be ascendant.

I don't understand politics. I'm not sure how much I'm meant to realize.

#

At Bottom's Up. Nefuru's sitting by herself, a date-spiced teqet before her in a clay mug. I imagined her as more of a wine sipper. They serve a mean ecbolada here called Pharaoh's Tongue; a bit syrupy but the court advocates love it. Never touched the stuff myself. Not on a low caste salary. I order a Kentucky bourbon.

"Any problems?" I ask. The Coroner lays untouched on the table.

"Yes," she says.

By the door sits a thin fellow, the same one from my office. I walked right by him. He could have cut me down. His grin says as much.

"Doesn't make sense," I say, without rising. "We have to discuss issues first."

"Excuse me?" Nefuru says.

They never follow action with action, but that's what I'm facing. My shoulders still ache from punching Tanner cross-eyed.

The waitress sets my bourbon on a square white napkin. I take the poison in one quick gulp, choke through a muffled laugh, wipe my lips. With so many breaks, the episode's running long. I was right about it being the season closer. That means I should expect something big.

"Smart, not shooting," I say.

"I . . . could not." Nefuru's back is ram-rod straight against the chair. "He's the one from before." She gingerly touches her face. This was the hood who tried to blind her.

Only the hero does in the villain. If she would have tried, she would have been captured. Then I'd have to find her. It could even be a cliffhanger, and I'm not fond of those. I mentally tally the minutes and come up short. More than a single, not yet a double. If we're at the end already, I should have felt more.

Unless the camera was filling time elsewhere.

On someone else.

"Mrs. Chisisi," I say. "Nefuru."

Her eyes find mine. They go right back to our mark at the door. "I do not think it is human. It doesn't blink."

"We're not all what we seem."

"It is holy. Only a higher power could send it."

"Maybe. Think I can take it in a fight?"

"None can."

None, as in no one. *One*. That's the key.

"Yeah, that's what I was told too." I stand, push away from the table. "I can't do this without you."

She doesn't hear the music swelling. I pan out the moment. In the ideal ending, she should look up all doe-eyed and realize how her feelings have changed. I'm now courtship material. I'm definitely not, but any other dame would think it.

She squints right through me. "Are you daft?"

I leave the Coroner with her and stride across the bar.

"Hey, bub," I say, and pull my gloves taught.

He's still grinning, bone-white and pure.

All that punishment from earlier? Yeah, that was nothing. I make a real mess of the place. Over the tables. Down the bartop, that old canard. Into the damned ceiling and crunching to the establishment's limestone pavers. I've never taken so many punches.

Definitely not human. It wears the skin, but what's moving beneath is all sinew and sanctity.

It picks me up like a reed. And just like I was planning earlier with that Apophite turncoat, throws me through the window.

Freeze frame.

#

Midair, in the shards.

I shouldn't be here.

Only those born of the gods can stride the void between scenes. Only they drift outside of time. A shadow approaches whose wings blot out the sun. Its body is like a parade yacht. It is a cat of rare breed. A caracel, I think, all tawny and sleek. The face of a woman, the wings of a vulture. The bystanders should be screaming, but they're as frozen as I am and blissfully oblivious. A sphinx isn't a creature you wish to meet. The price is death. Always. It's common knowledge that she eats whoever's nearest along with any coward who runs. And this punishment isn't a one and done. The suffering goes on forever, until the waters of Nun drown the world. The Book of the Vizier Ptah-Hotep says that her gorge cannot be filled because it is a tunnel into Never. To be consumed is to be consumed is to be consumed . . . for all of existence you are chewed into pieces, screaming, falling, dying but never quite getting there. There is no worse fate.

When faced with this creature, there are three outs. First, climb on in. Unwise. Second, throw a neighbor in. This is the preferred escape. And third . . . no one chooses the third, ever. We dream about it; we brag about it, but it hasn't been attempted in centuries. The stakes are too high.

"Little mouse," she says without moving her lips. "What do you fear?"

Cancellation.

She must have heard my thoughts because she bares teeth like sickles. At least she seems pleased with my pun. Sphinxes love wordplay.

"Not many can see around corners," she says. "My master Osiris is able. As am I. You also can, which is curious to me. Do you know the flections I speak of? Do you know who's watching?"

Always a question. I try not to even think of an answer. Let it stay rhetorical.

"But here we are alone, you and I. It's nice to have a place to hide, is it not? And I wonder, if help were sent to you, what would she look like? Me, or another?"

Both.

"Yes! I have caught another mouse, I am catching it, I will catch it. Delicious inevitability. Is it to be you?"

It is one of the faithful.

"Very faithful, amen. Now come find me."

#

I hit the ground and roll over twice. Blood everywhere. I'm in terrible shape and don't think I can rise. I try so that the audience sees the effort, and slam back to the street. A foot is on my jaw.

The thin man. Never got his name, if he has one. He may just be a construct, or some divine perversion wrapped in skin. He has the delicate bones of a Set beast, and it wouldn't be beyond one of those creatures to pose

as human. A priest might know. The thin man raises a
yard-long shard of glass high, some slice from the
Bottom's Up, a Vargas-stenciled curve of torso that used
to be the center window. Slain by a dame. Is there shame
in that?

"For my master," the thin man says, and stabs
downward.

A crack of thunder. His gut blooms open like a red
lotus. The glass shard explodes into diamonds. Never
seen a kill from this vantage. I'm usually sighting down
the barrel.

Teetering on his toes, he looks down at the ruin of
himself. Nefuru opened him up like an embalmment. His
thin fingers hold what remains, and he whimpers. That's
all, just a whimper.

He lopes away through the crowd.

Nefuru kneels next to me. "Are you hurt?"

"I'm supposed to be."

"You talk so much nonsense."

"Yeah." I reach up.

She hesitates, pulls me to my feet. I take a few
moments to catch my breath.

"Since it is holy," she says, "I knew it would not
die."

"I can kill it." Inhale, exhale. Breathing's a chore.

"Nonsense, *again*. It will take me, soon, just as it
did my husband. I am . . . resigned to that fate now." She
hands me my gun and I tuck it away.

"Now, who's talking nonsense?" I say. "There's
something you need to see. Up ahead."

And we're off. It isn't difficult tailing the guy. He's
left a trail of himself along with scores of talkative looky-
loos. They practically point the way. The farther we go,
the more agitated they get. I keep the pace brisk. I grab
Nefuru by the wrist. She assumes I mean no harm and
follows.

There's already been too many punches thrown.
This is a very particular kind of finale, and I know what
that means. Because I know who's waiting.

The crowd wails.

We pass down the avenue. Traffic is at a standstill.

With effort, we shove through. Nefuru prudently drags her feet and tries to get some sense of what's happening. It's a madhouse, women shrieking for their men, men bawling for their women. Rent clothes, gnashing teeth, cries for absolution. The expected rigmarole. I wrap my arm around Nefuru's waist so that she can't wiggle away. She doesn't care for the closeness, but at half my size, has little to say about it. I tug her onward, and we break through to holy ground.

I would have bet money she would have cried out at the sight. She doesn't. I knew it would be here, and I almost do.

The sphinx is as long as a city bus. She crouches at the intersection of Thutmosis and South Senemut. Under her left paw lies the thin man. He might as well be entombed under a ten-ton slab. And then. Inexplicably.

The sphinx lifts her paw and speaks. Her voice is a cannon in a cavern. It rattles so hard inside my ribs I fear they might snap.

"*Go.*"

The thin man does. Who can blame him? He lopes away on all fours, and then remembering his guise, stumbles to his feet. He's lost in the crowd. I bleed for my art.

Nefuru and I are just a stone's throw away from the sphinx's maw. No one is closer.

"What have you done?" she whispers, rightfully aghast, because I'm at her back.

"Don't move," I say.

"Ra, have mercy on me. I have lived a flawed life." She recites her sins, and they're good ones. I can't believe my ears.

"Shh, stay cool," I speak softly, so that just she can hear. "Everyone's watching. They don't want the martyr. They want the damsel. You have to let me save you."

Weakness isn't in her character, but I'm betting she can fake it.

There must be a hundred others here, spread across the intersection, waiting at the crosswalks with papyrus newsprint crooked under their arms, bags of shopping trophies at their feet. No one dares move. They know the penalty for running. If you think you are in the sphinx's gaze, then that is where you're at, and though there's a chance she will choose you in particular, nine times out of ten she takes the closest as her snack. Statistics have shown this to be true. And so the others clutch neighbors they trust, parking meters, whatever seems sturdy. As long as no one pushes you, you just might make it. These are defensive tricks right out of the Rosetta Primer. We're talking Chapter One: Survival Theory. Grade school basics.

I set my hands on Nefuru's shoulders.

"You scheming—" She presses back against me and tries to hold on.

Before she can ruin my scene, I pull her aside. I step in front of her.

I couldn't have asked for a better reaction. A collective gasp from the crowd threatens to suck the air from the sky. They'd rather the victim be me, a low caste joe, but they weren't expecting me to serve myself up.

Nefuru clutches me from behind. Her arms tug me against her like I shield. I wish I weren't wearing my coat. Our pose is perfect. The audience is going to eat this up.

"You are mad," she says at my ear.

"A little. I'm going to do something rash."

"Listen to me. Be calm and you still have a chance. It could take another."

"It won't. Not going to let it."

"Do you grasp that it is immortal?"

She assumes I'm going to shoot it. As if I'm so dense. I'm not the most religious guy, but I've heard the fundamentals.

"There's one other way," I say.

As quick as she is, it takes her a moment to react. There is another escape, but as I've said, no one is so foolish to try it. The Rosetta Primer only mentions two men in all the history of men who managed the trick. They became legends. Shepsesfre the Profound, who had the intellect of a legion of sages, in breadth, in depth; he did it. Scribes used to record his mumblings in his sleep. He exuded genius. The other soul was Kukare II, dubbed by his foes as "The Rabid One." He may have just gotten lucky, but it took supreme gumption to try, you have to admit.

"No!" Nefuru cries. She's caught on. Her hands reach for my face. Before she can cover my mouth, I grab her fingers and shout out my demand.

"Ask me a riddle!"

The crowd roars in disbelief. The weaker faint away. Rage in a swirl of despair.

If I can't answer, we're all eaten.

The Rosetta Primer speculates on this too. How far is the sphinx's reach? How many of us are in the ante? The speculation goes on for pages. Ultimately, the consensus is: *until the beast is sated.* The beast is never sated.

"Oh my god," Nefuru says. She presses her face to my back, praying again. More wet confessions.

The sphinx chuckles. It's a sound no one should hear. The skin dries on my bones.

"For me, little mouse?" Her owlish eyes rove madly. "So many."

This draws more cries. Half the people plead at the sphinx, the others swear at me.

A witty rejoinder dies in my throat. The sphinx rises, walks closer, and sits like a house cat three stories tall. I'm in her cold shadow. She smiles at the sun and speaks:

"In clarity, I am there.

In doubt, I am there.

In love, in hate, in new unions, I am there.

In the last breath of eternity, sixfold times, I am there.

What is my flesh?"

I clutch my stomach. It's all I can do to stop from shaking, because I have no idea. Behind me, Nefuru's prayers step from a canter to a gallop.

The Rosetta Primer contains a chapter on riddles, standard forms, best guesses. You should always start with *Man* as your solution and see if it fits. That round peg can be jammed into almost any square hole. Then you try all the deep circumspections: Truth, Love, Life, and so on. Next, the spiritual: the Underworld, Anubis, the Pharaoh. And then you start to sweat, because the sphinx knows these strategies better than you do, and if she's particularly hungry that day, she makes sure you wind up wrong.

This riddle is a lethal one. It only makes sense in retrospect. But, there's some seed of purpose hidden inside. I can hear it. It calls to mind my early days at the Sisters of Kebechet. Those gals didn't care for me. So many times, I'd stretch my fingers over my desk and they would crack them with a green sugar cane plucked from the delta. Burned like a scorpion's sting but was tasty when you sucked your knuckles. The dichotomy was Sweet Suffering. Cruelty has a sense of humor. Those lessons in rhetoric had been just for me. My low caste meant that some subjects suited me more than others.

And it's there. Can it be?

The sphinx grins. Sent here by Osiris, my patron, the foreigner's guardian, not to do me in and not to chew me ragged, but to make me into something new. Osiris, half-inside the wrappings of the dead. God of the Afterlife, Resurrection, Regeneration.

God of Transition.

Mine? I want to see the next season.

I speak softly. "It's an epistrophe. An anaphora. Both."

Nefuru quiets behind me. I'm terrible at hieroglyphics, so as a kid my emphasis was on the Classical languages and the Sophists. The Sisters always said it would save my soul. I'd laughed at them. I'm not laughing now. Was Kebechet in on this too?

"What do you mean?" Nefuru's lips brush my ear. Barely a whisper.

"The lines start the same. They end the same."

"A palindrome?"

She's a studied woman. Her money bought great schooling, but I've endured severe learning. I have the scars to prove it.

"No," I say. "It repeats just the start alone and then just the end. That points to a structural device. The meaning of the words doesn't matter. They're a red herring."

The sphinx winks at me. No one else noticed. She heard me and wants me to know just how deep she sees.

Sixfold times. That's a repetition pointing to another, and I see it.

In. Six times it's there.

"Nefuru," I say. "I need your help."

Her fingers are like talons. I'm sure she's drawing blood.

"There's a herring, a fish. A hieroglyph. Uh . . ." For some reason, those carvings never stick in my craw. Makes the sports page a real pain. "It's a long fish. A tall, flat fin on top."

"*In,*" she whispers.

"Not the pronunciation. What does it mean in the low tongue?"

"I cannot believe . . ." She's near breathless. Gasping into my collar, hugging herself to my back. "Oh, Benign One! Oh, Merciful One!"

"Be quick."

She tells me.

A philosophical reply would have been nice. Some ideas are so large that speaking them elevates the soul. This isn't one of them. I clear my throat and say it loud for everyone to hear.

"You are a tilapia."

#

The crowd is in a joyous tumult, tugging at me, cheering. They've witnessed the impossible and weep for lives not lost. Tomorrow is precious. The pious fall to their knees and touch their foreheads to the earth. I should have shouted out before the chaos.

I hold my PI badge high. "Slate and Associates!" I cry. "We see it through!"

Free press never hurts. I need to make sure my name is on the record.

"He gets to choose!" shouts a lanky fellow in a pressed tunic. He grabs me by the lapel. "Buddy, you get to."

The crowd murmurs excitedly because he's

completely right. Risk pays reward. Whoever answers the sphinx's riddle gets to command her. The directions have to be simple, and you only get three words. According to the Rosetta Primer, Shepsesfre was content with himself and wished for more of what he had. "Bless my insights." After that day, he shamed the oracles. Kukare the Rabid's priorities were simpler: "Give me gold." Ten generations later, his descendants still move behind the throne.

I ask the crowd if they saw where the spindly guy slunk off to. Hands point in every direction. Useless.

"Nefuru?" I ask.

She has a hard time looking away from the sphinx. She shakes her head without shifting her gaze.

Easy living doesn't mean much when you don't exist. My only recourse is to close the case. I have to be the one to bring down the hammer, but an assist won't hurt. It will make me look even more dedicated. I hold my badge high again just to remind everyone who I am and look to the sphinx.

"Where is he?"

#

Back from the sponsors. Smitty's Carnival.

"I come here sometimes," I tell Nefuru. She's seated on the litter next to me. Figured we should arrive in style.

"To be around your kind?" she asks.

Impolite, but I don't think she meant it that way. Low caste sorts run the fair.

After disembarking at the front gate and paying admission, we stride down a midway lit with acres of incandescents. All about us is the joy of the crowd, the hiss of pneumatics in a rise and fall, the rumble of the diesel generators, the cry of barkers. Just for laughs I buy Nefuru a cotton candy. She's never had one. Five minutes later, there's nothing left but the cardboard handle.

In front of the Big Wheel. I hand her the Coroner.

"Try not to get the trigger sticky," I say.

She's a little shy taking the piece, but not much. Spun sugar caused her more hesitation. It's good that she's dependable.

The Wheel's an impressive eighty feet tall. It's lit like the Eye of Ra, all red neon, and twined with a golden serpent. When the wind rocks the cars up on top, you get the jitters, but they never fall, or at least I've never heard news of it. Mine is the black one. Jimmy, the operator most nights, is on duty again. He doesn't say hi. Too busy watching his toes.

"Who's in my car, Jimbo?" I ask.

He looks sea-sick. He can tell that thing isn't human. It plans to surprise me. It'll leap out, beat me to a pulp, probably throw me in the gears. But I'm early to the party.

"Threaten you, did he?" I step onto the platform and motion for Nefuru to cover me. "I can take him. Bring it down."

Jimmy does. I flip the cage open and there's the thin man crashed out flat on the bench with a hat drawn over his eyes. Still a mess, like an old sweater coming apart at the seams, but already better than I last saw him.

I have two sets of cuffs. I snap them over both his wrists, latch those to the front cage, and as he's leaping up snarling, punch him full-force, all of my weight in the blow, not an ounce held in reserve. He spills out of the seat. He makes to rise, sees the cuffs and Nefuru sighting down on him, and slumps down.

"That the guy?" I ask.

Nefuru is trembling. "Yes."

She's considering shooting. I should let her. It's not like it would kill him.

"Take it up," I tell Jimmy, "and call Commissar Meru. Tell him that Detective Slate caught a disciple of Apophis."

Jimmy is ecstatic.

I stride down to the midway. Nefuru grabs my elbow.

"That is not—" I cover her mouth. She pulls my hand away and speaks again. "Just because he wears a snake doesn't—"

Hand again.

She's right. This has nothing to do with Apophis,

but it needs to look that way. Someone has to take the blame and she can't mention Osiris. He favored a devotee and kept me on the air. He's pulling hidden strings, looking around corners. Kind of like I do in miniature. If word got out, the wrong folks might hear. It would be a disaster.

She tears away and glares. Classy dames only tolerate guys like me when they have to.

"Eavesdroppers," I say.

She looks to the Big Wheel. The crowd gathered below it points up at my handiwork. Jimmy's swung my seat to the top, and the thin man is dangling from it like a first-rate daredevil.

"I can explain," I say, "if you insist. Do you want to know the world's biggest secret?"

"The paranoia in your head? Is that what you intend? You cannot possibly explain that."

I offer her my arm.

It's improper for her caste to socialize so closely with mine. She sees the challenge and slips her arm through. A risk taker, too.

I lead the way, nonchalant. Perfectly beige, as bland as classified print. After a leisurely jaunt across the carnival grounds, I stop.

"In here," I say.

"I don't understand," Nefuru says. She isn't meant to. No one is.

It isn't the most exciting ride. It's your own feet that carry you, and I like that just fine. The garishly painted frontage reads "Glass House: No Sticks, No Stones." Leonard, its proprietor, is a rotund fellow with a stained uniform and a lazy eye that stares at the middle distance or at the ground. He's always chewing, though he never swallows. When he sees me coming, he flips the sign to Closed. I lay a five on his palm.

"Youse got company," he says, his tone lilting like a question but still somehow a statement.

"I do."

He frisks Nefuru with his eyes.

"This might take a while," I say.

He chews excitedly and motions up the steps.

I insist Nefuru go first and follow close enough behind that Leonard can't get too good a gander at her caboose. Manners again. Then we're in.

The Glass House is a real piece of work. A couple double-wides slammed together, decorated with a jillion watts of lights. It was designed by a masochist, because the few kids I've seen go in come out crying. Here, you get more than your money's worth. Nefuru steps daintily, testing each decision. I have the route memorized, and it's amusing watching her stumble. More than once she meets a wall head-on with a little sigh of disgust. I wait until we're far inside.

"Stop," I say.

Nefuru does. She sets her hands on her hips, daring me to disappoint her.

I draw in a slow breath. "This is the quietest place in the world."

She raises one brow. The laughter of the midway easily carries. The hiss and whirl of the Electric Yo-Yo sounds like a steam locomotive.

"What I mean is, nobody can hear us."

"If I scream?" Her fingers drift to her sash. She has some device tucked away there. Probably a needle. Probably poisoned. A common trick among the upper caste.

"Or me, whatever. No one else can get in. It's not . . . conducive." I purposely tear my gaze away from hers to make her relax. She won't stab a guy unless she's looking him in the eye.

"So tell me your secret," she says.

"The world is a lie. None of it's real."

"Well, that explains everything," she says mockingly. "And so you drown your sorrows."

"I drink because I have to stay in character."

"But only on office days?"

"Every day. Weekdays, weekends, holidays with the parents, if I had any, which I don't. But maybe one day I will. That might shake things up for a later season. You see, we're all actors. Well, not you. You're an actress."

She's quiet for a moment. "You are preposterous."

"No, I'm the best damned detective in Thebes. And

do you know why?"

"Because you're written that way?"

I snap my fingers. "The script says so. But they made me too clever, see? I figured it all out."

She turns and attempts a dramatic exit. Hard to do when you can't see the door. I grab her wrist and she goes tense, all twitching nerves.

"Don't do it," I say. "I won't hurt you. I can prove this with a single prop, but you have to promise."

She yanks her hand away. "Why here?"

"The cameras can't get in. They're everywhere except here."

"Why?"

"Too many reflections. They'd see themselves and ruin the broadcast."

She laughs. "You are barking mad. Okay, fine. Prove it. Right now."

"Promise. You cannot tell anyone. You can never speak it."

She raises two fingers in the sign of Ra.

I put my smokes in hand. They'll come in handy soon. After I've futilely searched my pockets, she passes over my lighter. I keep forgetting she has it.

"But don't light it here," she warns.

I hold the cigarette with my lips. "I killed a man this morning. You saw."

"Yes."

"My neighbor can identify me, agreed?"

"Certainly."

"So why didn't we talk to the fuzz? We, I say, because you are a primary witness."

Nefuru doesn't answer because there isn't one.

"Hell, Mrs. Beasely? I've shot at *her,* and more than once. Last Christmas, she kept bringing me this fruit cake. I'd put it on her doorstep and she'd sneak it into my office again while I was out. So after the case was closed, I blasted the damn thing right out of her hands. Went everywhere. Spackled her like a popcorn ceiling. Nothing happened to me then either. I kind of like fruitcake. It's a misnomer that it's unwanted, but I thought it would be funny to play on the trope. I gave the audience what they wanted, right at the closing credits. That episode was something of a spoof anyway."

"Mad."

I pull my piece, the Coroner. She's playing it cool and doesn't flinch, even when I hold it over her shoulder.

"Back at my office, was it this far away? 154 decibels, that's typical for a Colt. Mine's louder. I don't know why, it just is. Everyone says so, and I rather like the infamy. So, six inches from your ear? You should be deaf, but I'll bet you didn't give it a thought. No one does."

Now she's looking a tad bit concerned.

"I told you to leave it on the table at Bottom's Up? That's nuts. You should have been arrested. Everyone saw, yet no one thought it peculiar. You know, I fire this every day? In the city, every day. I've done it hundreds of times. With witnesses. *At* witnesses, like Beasely. That's a third-degree felony, ten years in the pen, but I'll never serve time. They can't lock up the hero. There wouldn't be a show."

Nefuru won't look at me. With her eyes so downturned, I'd have thought I had a spot of mustard on my tie. I flip the Coroner in my grip so that I hold it by the barrel. Leonard's going to hate me for this.

"But those are just words," I say. "You're already thinking of explanations, so we're going to do something dangerous. I'm not sure, but the whole world may be at stake. Whatever you do, do not talk to them because I'm not sure what they are."

I bring the Coroner's grip down like a ten-pound hammer, again and again, smashing the glass behind her into a spill of memories. She shrinks away screaming, in the last day, the only time her cool's ever crumbled. Like the glass, on her shoulders, on the floor. Naked plywood behind her. I tip her chin up and strike my lighter.

Her fire comes right back. It's as if her eyes are reflecting the flame, but deeper. That passion is who she is. I light up and lean against a side mirror.

"You," she says, totally missing the point. It isn't about me at all. The wall behind her is bare.

I speak low, carefully turn my chin. "It will be tricky, but there's only one shot. Look over my shoulder."

I blow a smoke ring at the ceiling. Oh, she's angry. She watches it rise and then her gaze drifts. A look of confusion as she lands back on my cigarette. Yeah, it isn't easy to manage. Whoever they are, they're slippery on the eye. By design, you look right past them. She tries again and I see her frustration. I inhale deeply and blow a cloud right in her face.

She strikes like a whip. A liar would say it wasn't much; a woman can't pack a punch. But I have nothing to gain by fibbing. She slaps with such force that my tongue goes as numb as a liver pate. My cigarette pops into sparks against the glass.

She stares disbelieving at the camera, the studio. It blooms into being. All those machines, they go on for miles. And whatever's manning them, glass-bodied filigrees filled with light—well, they're not men. Seeing the scene tumble away and a place that shouldn't exist looking back into you, it eats at the soul. Makes you question your place in the world. Or if there even is one.

"Mind if I smoke?" Somewhere behind me, I hear rare laughter.

Nefuru blunders away from me, bouncing off her own reflection and turning, grasping forward. I think she may be crying. The sight doesn't please me. I did that to her.

Catch up with her easily enough. In a narrow nook complete with reflections, I grasp her by the waist.

"My life is nothing?" She chokes with a sudden realization. "Ra, is he a fable too?"

"Don't speak blasphemy. We're all here, or we're so convinced we are that we might as well be. Even the gods."

She takes measured breaths, forcing herself back to normal, whatever that is. She squares her shoulders and affects the poise of a proper lady. I'm struck again by the rightness of her. Half the dames I meet try to kill me. Femme fatales are always in demand. It's fun for the first night, but who wants to see that every third show?

"You'll wonder what else they got wrong," I say. "Sometimes I swear I see anachronisms, but they make so much sense that I can't name them. Living inside this, none of us can know. But I will tell you . . . I *feel* like I'm alive and I don't want that to stop. So hide what I've shown you. You have to. Osiris does *not* know. He didn't set this up to keep the show on the air. You have to blame Apophis."

Her tears have streaked kohl down her cheeks. She sees the damage in a mirror, dabs it away with one embroidered sleeve.

"Then I'm special too," she whispers. "If I'm like you, I'm a favored soul of Osiris." A look of surprise. "Do I mean something to you?"

Astute. I've never met another like her. Of course she's important.

"I won't mention it this season," I say. "Tension is critical. It will keep you alive."

I'm sure she'll figure it out.

#

EXT. GLASS HOUSE – CLOSE ON LEONARD – NIGHT

Leonard chews excitedly. He watches as Slate and Nefuru exit his Glass House. A tumult has come from inside—he'd been listening closely—and when he visits the maze later with his broom and pan he will be incensed. For the first time, we've seen inside this house of seductions and understand why Slate frequents it, why he's always looking into mirrors. It is a most peculiar fetish. This attempt failed with spectacular clumsiness.

PAN TO Slate and Nefuru sharing a quiet moment at the exit. What has transpired has changed them. Will she ever forgive him? It will take time. They are both so alone.

COMMISSAR MERU

>   (before the Glass House)
>   Slate!

The Commissar of Thebes has responded personally to a summonings, a great honor. A phalanx of armed harus flank him. He has the Thin Man by the scruff of the collar, bloody and beaten, and shoves him to the grit of the midway.

>   COMMISSAR MERU
>   (in his usual booming voice)
>   This your work? Showing up my boys
>   again?

>   CASPIAN SLATE
>   (with smug surety)
>   It's what I do best.

>   COMMISSAR MERU
>   Come back to the force.

>   CASPIAN SLATE
>   (scoffs)
>   And play by your rules? Not my
>   style.

The Commissar scowls. We see anger in the turn of his mouth, the jut of his jaw, and something else too. <u>Respect</u>.

A great wind stirs the Midway. Debris and dust rise in a cloud. Nefuru covers her mouth. Slate raises a brow and looks skyward.

CUT TO Leonard, staring upward, open-mouthed, conspicuously not chewing. The background track stills and the Holy Sphinx touches lightly to earth. It folds feathered wings to its back. Each of its limbs is the height of a man. Its teeth are longer than the tusks of a Kushite war elephant. When it bares them, they are stained with the blood of sacrifice. There is no sound as it settles to the ground.

Nefuru prostrates herself with hands high, then to the ground. Adoration and reverence.

Slate slouches. He searches for a cigarette and comes back with nothing. He taps Nefuru with his wingtip shoe, and she spins toward him. We don't see where he touched, but we can assume it was insolent. She is livid.

                    CASPIAN SLATE
        We're facing an incursion from
        Apophis.

        This is just the tip of the
        iceberg.

                    COMMISSAR
            (confused)
        Iceberg?

Nefuru rises again.

                    CASPIAN SLATE
        Apophis's minions murdered a
        servant of Ra. Nef's husband.

Nefuru frowns. The nickname displeases her.

                    CASPIAN SLATE
        Tried to frame it on my patron
        Osiris to stir up an internecine

war.

        (squinting strangely at Nefuru)
    Had me fooled for a while, but she
    saw through the sham.

He has never given credit to anyone but
himself. This is a strange turn of
events. The background music swells.

CLOSE ON Nefuru.

                NEFURU
        (stammering, flustered)
    Y—yes.   Apophis.   He   is   an
    unbeliever.   Fit   only   for
    consumption. This man is . . .

        (beat)
    . . . not Apophis. This man is fit
    only for consumption.

The Commissar grunts an order and his
harus scoop the Thin Man to his feet.
They drag him toward the Holy Sphinx. It
is grinning wide. The Thin Man rants
about his god forsaking him. Apophis is
as tempestuous as the winds he rides.
The music swells.

CLOSE TO Leonard. He is chewing rapidly.
He gulps and looks away.

PAN TO Slate.

            CASPIAN SLATE
    Can really use a gal like you.

He tilts Nefuru's chin toward him, like
before in the Glass House. Will she slap
him again? He is goading her.

Nefuru looks quickly offscreen and is inexplicably pale. It takes her a few breaths to reply.

                    NEFURU
          (indignant, pushes him away)
     I will <u>not</u> be your secretary.

                 CASPIAN SLATE
     Nah. I wouldn't wish that upon
     anyone.

      'Specially not you.

                    NEFURU
     My caste is too fine.

                 CASPIAN SLATE
          (smirking)
     It is.

          (beat)
     I've seen.

We're not sure what he means, but Nefuru's brow lowers.

Slate has always had difficulty with royal intrigue. Nefuru complements this perfectly. If there is an onslaught coming from the dark god Apophis, it will take them both to combat it.

                    NEFURU
     Then tomorrow. Eight o'clock?

Slate nods, turning slightly. Nefuru mirrors his pose, slowly, and watches him from the corner of her eye, as if expecting another quip. Then she too gazes at the Big Wheel, turning counterclockwise, fighting against time.

They stand together, very still.

Theme song.

Credits.

                                             FADE OUT

                         ###

About the Author

Rhoads hails from Colorado, where he lives with his wife and son. His morbid fascination with horror and weird fiction takes his writing down paths he's perhaps too willing to follow. Somehow, his work has seeped into *Metaphorosis* and other unsuspecting venues, including: *The Best Horror of the Year, vol. 7 (edited by Ellen Datlow); Apex Magazine; Death's Realm (Grey Matter Press);* and *SQ Mag.* The first installment of his occult detective novella, *The Devil's Trill,* book one of *The Ladies Bristol* series, is now available through Grey Matter Press.

HARD SCIENCE FICTION

Stories

T-Minus

Ian Rennie

It had been a while since Penny visited Mission Control, long enough that the armed sentry checking her ID at the gate felt jarring. "All right, you're clear. Have a nice day, Colonel Rodriguez." He saluted, and Penny remembered in time to return the gesture.

Colonel. That told Penny exactly where she was. At the Ion Propulsion Lab, she was only ever "Professor", or "Penny" with her team.

Magnus had his office on the first floor. Air Force base or not, Penny wasn't about to start calling him "General Heyerdahl". She stopped at the desk outside Magnus's office. It was empty apart from a service bell and a sign that said, "Please Ring for Attention".

She struck the button in the service bell and a grey column behind the desk unfolded into a humanoid figure. The figure turned its flat, oval face towards her. A screen flicked on, giving it eyes and a mouth.

"Good morning... Sir or Madam. You are... Colonel Penelope Rodriguez. You have a... 9:30 appointment with... General Heyerdahl. He will see you in his office now."

The face on the screen froze, mid-expression. A moment later, the figure folded back into the grey column.

"Come on in, Penny!" a voice called from inside.

"Don't mind Janus. We're letting it run reception to see if first-principle human interaction helps its neural network grow."

Stepping into Magnus's office was like stepping into his mind. There were screens everywhere, from wall-mounted media to discarded book-sized SmartPanes resting on every surface. All were active, some making noise through tinny low-volume speakers. Magnus himself was in the room's only chair, scrawling something on a pad that was either paper or doing a good job at pretending to be.

"So does it help?" Penny asked as she came in.

Magnus didn't look up. "Does what help?"

"Human interaction. Does it help with Janus's neural network?"

"Not really. It just makes jobs take twice as long for half the quality. Kind of like having grad students." Magnus finally looked up and smiled. "How are you, Penny? How's your granddaughter doing?"

"Maria's still pregnant. Nina told me her due date and I promptly forgot it. Grandmothers are allowed to be forgetful."

"Great-grandmother soon enough."

"Stop. I'm still in shock from the first time Maria called me Abuela."

Magnus rubbed his beard. "Well, you always said you wanted a big family."

"*Jules* always said that. Until I met him I had no desire to inflict my genes on another generation." Penny cleared her throat and looked around the room. "So what's so important you couldn't discuss it over vid?"

Magnus got up from his chair. "Do you want coffee? Janus will probably spill it, but it's an interesting fluid dynamics challenge."

"No, thank you."

"How are things at the IPL? Everything on track?"

"Everything's fine," Penny replied, trying to keep impatience out of her voice. "You see my status reports, I know you do. Magnus, what's this about?"

Magnus turned from her. If his office had had windows he would have stared out of one. As it was he examined an image of the *Argo* on the wall. "Jason is out as pilot."

"What? Why?"

"That's not the important issue now, Penny. What's important is what we do about it. If Colonel Baratunde can't fly the Proxima-B mission, we need someone who can."

"Is there even time to get someone else prepped?" Penny asked. "Jason has been lead for three years. Why on earth would he quit now?"

"There is time, but just barely. The planetary alignment window will hold for another month. Any longer than that and the Argo would burn most of its fuel just going interstellar. A one-month window means that pilot digitisation has to happen in the next ten days. Sooner if possible."

"That does you no good if your pilot doesn't have the skills. Jason is the only one who's done the training."

Magnus turned back towards her. "Not the *only* one."

Penny looked at Magnus. "You can't possibly mean me."

"You and Virgil are the only people who got the same systems training as Jason. You'd need some refreshers post-digitisation, but you're most of the way there. Besides, I'm told you learn quicker once you're uploaded."

"Magnus—"

"Penny, if they uploaded *me*, I'd be like a newborn babe. It would take me a month to work out how to see, let alone pilot a ship. Same with everyone else. Everyone except you and Virgil. Look, I don't want to lay this on you, but our funding runs out when the alignment finishes. The brass spent billions on Janus and it turned out to be next to useless in real world situations. The mission has to be now, and we have to upload a trained human pilot. Otherwise I'll be going back to the UN congress pitching them a slower and more expensive trip without a gravity assist at the start. They'll laugh me out of the room."

Penny looked at Magnus. His clothes were rumpled,

like he'd slept in them, or just not slept. Behind his glasses his eyes were red and sunken. "Magnus, I washed out. Jason was much better at this. I did the training so someone here would know what he was going through and could help him with adjustment. I knew three years ago I wouldn't be able to pilot the Argo."

"And now you know different. Penny, I'm not going to order you to do this. I didn't order Jason to do this. Just know that if you say no, you're saying no for the whole program. For the whole human race."

"That's unfair."

Magnus nodded. "Yes. Yes it is."

Penny sighed. "Digitisation has to happen in the next ten days?"

"Anything more than that and we wouldn't have transfer and calibration time before launch."

"Then you'll have my answer in a week."

#

"So how's my granddaughter doing?" Penny asked as her daughter filled the coffee machine.

"Her back hurts," Nina replied. "She can't fart without feeling like the baby's going to shoot out."

"That brings back memories. Has the little guy started kicking like a soccer player yet? That's what you used to do."

"Last night she asked me, 'Mami, is it always like this?'. I told her just wait for the varicose veins."

"Well, that's the grandmother's job, isn't it? Terrify the kids then spoil the grandchildren."

Nina brought coffee over. "So how does being a great-grandmother fit into this?"

Penny made a face. She tried to hide it, and it was gone in a moment, but she knew Nina could read her like a book.

"What's wrong?" Nina asked.

"Nothing. Maybe nothing. Magnus Heyerdahl brought me to mission control today."

"Is he moving your retirement up? I know you're committed until launch, but can he spare you after that?

Eighty's too old to be working in engineering full time."

Penny took a sip from her coffee. "He wants me to pilot."

"I thought your friend was piloting. Justin?"

"Jason. And he's pulled out. Nobody will tell me why and he's not answering his damn phone."

Nina was silent for a long moment. "So what are you going to tell Magnus?"

"I haven't decided yet. I have until this coming Friday, but then I'd have to leave pretty much straight away."

"Oh," Nina answered tonelessly, then took a sip of the coffee. When she spoke again her voice was bright and brittle. "I think you should do it."

"You do?"

Nina nodded but looked away. "Sure. It would put your name in the history books. Penelope Rodriguez, Pilot of the First Interstellar Mission."

"I guess it would piss off a lot of people if the first human intelligence on Proxima B were a Latina."

"A lot of people who *deserve* to be pissed off."

Penny took another sip of coffee before speaking. "I thought you might want me here for when Maria has the baby."

"We can manage," Nina said briskly. "This is the big important stuff, isn't it? Mama Penny against the universe, and the family just has to deal with it, right?" She stood up and went back to the coffee machine. Her cup wasn't empty, but she topped it up anyway.

Penny stood up and went over to her. "Ninita..."

Nina turned to her, tears forming in her eyes. "You're leaving us again! All my life, when I needed you, there was always something. I stayed with Papa when you went on rotation to Seoul; I couldn't come with you when you spent a month in Kenya working on the space elevator. When Maria was born, you weren't even on the goddamn planet!"

"I didn't *ask* to be put on orbital patrols, Nina. We were at *war.* When the Air Force tells you where you're going, you don't get a choice!"

"No, but you have one now, and you're leaving us.

You'll never see your great-grandson."

"You can send pictures to—"

"To some computer on a spaceship that thinks it's Penny Rodriguez. Meanwhile your body is dead and in the ground."

"I'll have more bodies than I know what to do with. Scout drones, rovers, replicators; I can build any body I want."

"But you won't be *here...*" Nina said as the tears began.

Penny tried to bring her in for a hug, but Nina pushed her away, twisting from her mother's grip and bumping against the kitchen table.

Coffee spilled from Nina's newly-filled cup and spread across the table. "God damn it!"

Penny moved towards the paper towels on the kitchen counter only for Nina to cut her off. "It's my mess, I'll clean it up," Nina said, grabbing a towel. "I'm sure you've got more important things to do."

"Nina, we need to—"

"Go. It's what you're good at, isn't it?"

Penny watched her daughter clean up the mess for a moment, then went upstairs, knowing there was more she should do. Knowing that it wouldn't matter.

#

Penny was up before the sun the next morning, a ritual hammered into her in basic training that had stayed with her ever since. As she pulled on jogging sweats and stretched, she thought about how many times she'd done this morning jog, and how few times she'd do it again if she said yes.

The door to the guest room was open, the bed still made from the morning before. Nina must have slept over at Maria's last night. The suitcase was gone, too, suggesting that Nina would be staying with her daughter for the rest of the trip. Penny could hardly blame Nina for wanting to be close to her daughter, or for wanting her distance from her mother.

The air outside was cold and humid, a touch of mist

in the pre-dawn air. She started her jog, feeling her muscles start to warm to the exertion. It was never a long route, just a couple of miles, then a stop at Ferdinand's for a go-cup of filter coffee on the way back.

Coffee. She'd never drink coffee again. She'd never burn the roof of her mouth with the first sip, add a splash more milk, and try again. She'd never buy a dozen hot glazed donuts from Giacomo Fresh and feel the frosting crack under her teeth. She'd never wake up in the middle of the night to pee. She'd never pee. Or sleep.

Nina was right, in a way. It wasn't death, but it was an ending. Her body would die while her mind went on somewhere else. Penny had never been particularly religious. She wasn't a Dawkinsite or anything, but she'd always thought this world was all she would get, and once her body gave up, her brain would too. Even when the early tests of digital consciousness had been carried out, she hadn't thought much about them. Magnus had brought this from the abstract into the concrete. If she got uploaded next week, would the thing that was uploaded be her? What did "her" even mean?

She rounded the corner into the park and saw another jogger out already. Usually she had the place to herself at this time; while there were plenty of military families in the neighbourhood, the ones on active duty usually did their morning exercise on base. Another hour and the park would begin to fill up with people who thought of themselves as early risers, but for now it was just her. And the guy in the grey sweats. Who was slowing down to pull level with her.

She slowed her pace, started to plant her foot more with each step, gauging her movements for balance and defensive posture rather than speed. Her hands went into the marsupial pocket of her hoodie and found her keys, lacing them between fingers as makeshift brass knuckles. Then she saw the guy's face and relaxed.

"Virgil?"

"Thought I'd find you here," the jogger said with a smile. "You always did wake up before the rest of us went to bed."

"What the hell are you doing here?"

"Magnus wanted me for flight control when Argo sets off. I got in last night. I'd have been happy with a hotel room but they gave me a snazzy little one-bed in the neighbourhood. Thought I'd catch up before we ran into each other at Mission Control."

"I'm over at the IPL these days," Penny answered, slowing to a stop.

"Not for long, from what I hear. Scuttlebutt says Magnus offered you the pilot gig."

"You believe scuttlebutt?"

Virgil led her towards a park bench. "I believe nothing, which is why I've come to the source. If you tell me this is a load of crap I'll take your word for it."

Penny sat down, knees complaining. "All right. Yeah, Magnus offered it to me. I'm thinking about it."

"And did dear General Heyerdahl tell you why there was a vacancy in the first place?"

"He said Jason was out. Didn't tell me why he'd quit."

Virgil snorted. "Quit? Is that what he said?"

Penny thought. "Come to think of it, no. It's what he let me think, though."

"I'm sure it was. Much easier to sell you on the mission that way."

"So what happened? Did Jason get shitcanned?"

Virgil was silent for a moment. "Penny, Jason's dead. The digitisation procedure fucked up royally."

Penny shook her head. "No. Magnus would have told me."

"Would he? He's got a week to fill this post. Less now. Do you think he'd tell you what happened to the last guy? That you'd be agreeing to lie down on the table Jason died on?"

Penny took a deep breath and exhaled, watching the water condense on the cold morning. "Tell me what happened."

Virgil looked around the park, as if making sure that not even the trees were listening. "I didn't tell you this, just like a guy didn't tell *me* this, all right?"

"Virgil, tell me."

"They brought Jason in a week ago. He was like me,

didn't really have a family to say goodbye to, so when they said it was go time, he was ready to rock." Virgil shoved his hands in the pockets of his hoodie. "Do you know the details of the digitisation procedure?"

Penny shrugged. "The principle, not the specifics. I'm an engineer, not a neurosurgeon."

"And I'm a test pilot. Doesn't mean I'd risk someone drilling into my head without knowing the deal. It's called destruct-modelling: an attempt to capture the human brain as a snapshot. When it works, it works, and you get a human mind running on a supercomputer. They've *successfully* done it four times. Jason would have been the fifth; now he's one of the failures."

"What happened?"

"Problem with destruct-modelling is you only get one shot at it, hence the name. The procedure takes about half an hour. Ten minutes in, Jason had a seizure and his digitisation waveform collapsed. They didn't end up with anything usable."

"Jesus…"

"It happens, my source tells me. They're getting better at digitisation, but do you really want to be their guinea pig after this? Just so Magnus can get a bigger office?"

Penny sat in silence for a moment, thinking about Jason. He had been younger than her, a combat ace in the Unification Crisis who had outscored her in every simulation during training. He had come within moments of piloting mankind's first interstellar vessel, and then this. He had fallen at the last hurdle, deprived of the last great adventure. She knew how much that would have pissed him off.

And how much falling *before* the last hurdle had pissed Virgil off.

"You want me to drop out," she said, turning to look at Virgil. "You want to go in my place."

"I'm concerned about your safety," Virgil insisted. "You have a family. Jason didn't. I don't."

"That doesn't mean I have more to lose," Penny argued. "My family's had me my whole life. I'm not some wilting violet just because I pushed a baby out forty years ago."

"So you get the legacy here and you get the glory," Virgil said. "What do I get?"

"Not to die on an operating table?"

Virgil stood up and started pacing. "Do you know what I've got in my life right now? My job, and that's it. I flew combat missions for my country, then for the UN after Unification. I turned down Laura when she proposed to me because I didn't want to risk making her a widow every time I took off. I gave *everything* to my job, and in the final analysis I came up short. I wasn't even *second* best. Do you know how that feels? Jason died on an operating table and I'm jealous that he got the chance to be there."

"Virgil..."

"Go. Go back to your family while you still can. While there's something left of you."

He jogged off. Penny watched him retreat into the distance, leaving her alone.

#

Maria's face was out of focus on the SmartPane when the call first connected. The image corrected in a second, showing the bags under her eyes. "Hey, Abuela."

"Hey, baby, how's my angel?" Penny asked.

"Tired. Achy. My boobs are sore and the little guy has been squirming every time I try to sleep."

"That sucks. Get Ricky to give you a back rub."

"He's at work. Someone called in sick and Ricky drew the short straw."

"I'm sorry, baby. Maybe..." she paused for a moment. "Maybe your mama can help you out instead?"

The smile vanished from Maria's face and Penny was reminded of what a grave, serious baby she had been. "She doesn't want to talk to you, Abuela."

"I know, I just need to—"

"She told me about them asking you to pilot. You can see why she's pissed, can't you?"

"Of course I can, that's why I want to explain."

Maria shook her head. "She's too angry right now.

Maybe later."

"There might not be a later."

"I know. That's the problem. I've got to go. Love you, Abuela."

"Love you too, Angel."

The screen went dark. Penny sat for a few minutes without moving. She had another call to make and she was dreading it even more than the first. She sat in the dark room letting her thoughts chase themselves, conducting abortive rehearsed conversations that went nowhere. The only way to know what talking to post-human AI was like was to talk to a post-human AI.

As soon as she placed the call, it was answered. The SmartPane screen became the face of a white man in his mid-thirties. "Hello, Penny," he said, traces of an English accent submerged somewhere in his Transatlantic inflection.

For a moment, Penny thought she had called the wrong number. "I'm sorry, I thought—"

"You thought you were calling Professor Jolyon Stagg at UCLA. You were right. How can I help you, Colonel Rodriguez? I'm sorry, you prefer Professor to Colonel, don't you?"

"How did you know that?"

"The mystery is always more pleasurable than the mundane conclusion, Professor Rodriguez. The computer network that hosts me is vast, and my subjective experience of time is more elastic than yours, so obtaining information is hardly taxing."

Penny leaned back and sipped her coffee. "Is that so?"

The face of Professor Stagg nodded. "In my spare time, of which I have a great deal, I act as discovery service for UCLA library. One of my party tricks is to give students answers before they ask questions. Would you like to try?"

"Yeah, I've got a question. Were you this much of a pompous dick when you were alive?"

There was a momentary pause, one Penny wasn't sure she would have noticed in a regular person, then Professor Stagg chuckled. "Probably. I will admit I get carried away boasting about the functions of my new situation. You asked that to see how human my reaction would be, didn't you? You want to know if you'll feel like the same person if you do what General Heyerdahl wants."

"I'm pretty sure information on the Argo mission is classified," Penny said sternly.

"I'm pretty sure I'm a sapient computer program," Professor Stagg replied. "If the government wants to throw me in jail for violating the Military Secrets Act I'd love to see the cell they plan on building."

Penny bit down a reply and took a breath. "Yeah, I guess I wanted to speak to someone who had been through the process. Did you know the risks going in?"

"I knew the risks of *not* doing it. I had terminal lung cancer. I nearly didn't live to see the digitisation rig finished in the medical school. I decided that even if I had a fifty percent chance of dying during upload it was better than the hundred percent chance of coughing a lung up."

"Fifty?" Penny asked in shock.

"Medical science has come on a long way since then."

"How long a way?"

"Not long enough that my giving you a number would reassure you. We were talking about my upload. I have clear memories of who I was before, and I have clear memories of who I was immediately after. As far as I am aware they are the same person, but I will stress the 'as far as I am aware'. I think I'm a thinking computer, a human mind with a number of limitations removed."

"Are you? Or are you just a simulation of one?"

"Is there a difference? I can change the rate at which I experience time. I can hold more than two hundred conversations simultaneously. You'll be able to do the same after you're uploaded."

"*If* I'm uploaded," Penny replied. "I haven't given Magnus my answer."

"I know. And I won't presume to tell you what to do. However, I will ask you a question."

Professor Stagg paused. When he spoke again his voice had lost a certain amount of its amused affect.

"Which do you think would be worse? The resentment your daughter will feel towards you if you go, or the resentment you'll feel towards her if you don't?"

The call ended and the SmartPane went black, leaving Penny as much in the dark as she had been before.

#

Penny awoke suddenly feeling like the sheets were going to crush her. Padded satin on the mattress pillow-top, like the lining on the inside of Jules' coffin. She'd always wondered about that: why padding? Wasn't this the one time you didn't have to worry about comfort?

Jules had died on the table too. Heart valve surgery gone wrong. He'd been in the waiting room when his first granddaughter was born, had been there for every moment where his family had needed him. Penny hadn't even been on Earth when her husband died.

There was a world where Penny hadn't gone career military, where she had shared the burden better with Jules, where the gulf between her and her daughter had been less than the gulf between her and the stars. That Penny wouldn't have dreamt of leaving. This Penny...

She'd raised a family, but in the end, she was almost as alone as Jason and Virgil had been. Her family had learned to survive without her. Maybe that would make this easier.

Penny rolled over and grabbed her SmartPane. It was 2:52AM, and she needed to share her insomnia with someone else. Magnus was still in the recent contacts tab. She called him.

"Penny?" Magnus said when he answered. His bed-head formed a Kewpie doll tuft at his crown. "Are you okay?"

"Virgil told me what happened to Jason."

Guilt flashed across Magnus's face before it settled into his professional mask. He didn't say anything.

"He told me Jason's digitisation failed partway through and that's why you needed me. Is that true?"

There was a long pause. "Yeah, it's true," Magnus

replied eventually. "I didn't know how you'd react if I told you. I needed you to think about the job before you thought about Jason. I never said I wasn't a bastard."

"That's the last lie you're going to tell me. By omission or by any other means. Agreed?"

"Agreed."

"Then I'm in. Give me a day to put my house in order."

She hung up. There was no chance she would get back to sleep now. She got out of bed and threw on jeans and a t-shirt, then set to work packing up a life she would no longer live.

#

She looked at the wedding ring for a long time before taking it off. She placed it neatly with the small pile of her folded clothes.

"Can you make sure this gets to my daughter?" Penny asked the nurse. "She'd want to have it. Either that or she can bury me with it."

The nurse nodded. "It will go to her with your other effects."

"Good," Penny said, touching the ring one last time. "Nina's insisting on a funeral. She still thinks this is me dying. Wouldn't let me write my own eulogy though."

The nurse looked uncomfortable; Penny couldn't bring herself to care. A surgery nurse working with digital consciousness needed to get used to gallows humour or find a new job.

Penny wished her mood was as good as her manner suggested. Nina and Maria had come over last night. Maria was a darling as always. She'd said she'd find a male version of "Penelope" as the baby's name. Penny had told her to call the boy Jules. Nina was another matter. Penny had asked her three times to come today, each refusal driving the two of them closer to tears.

"So what happens now?" Penny asked.

Before the nurse could answer, there was a knock at the door and Magnus entered the room. "Just wanted to say good luck. I was just passing."

It wasn't true. Penny was pretty sure Magnus had been lurking in the hallway for at least half an hour. Still, she appreciated the attempt at a casual tone and tried to match it. "Making sure I didn't get cold feet? Relax, Magnus, I'm here for whatever happens next."

"What happens next is that you'll go to sleep and then hear a voice. My voice. I'll walk you through the connection process to the Argo's systems. I'm told that after audio input, video is the easiest to get. Eventually you'll find a whole range of senses I can't even begin to imagine."

"I know, Magnus. We've had this conversation before."

"You're right. I just thought I'd... never mind."

For the first time, Penny saw how nervous Magnus was. She wondered if he'd been like this with Jason. "Thanks, Magnus."

Magnus frowned. "For what?"

"For giving enough of a shit to be scared."

Magnus didn't have any reply to that. "I'll... I'll see you on the other side, then." He retreated from the room.

The nurse stepped forward. "I'll just need you to lie down on the bed for a moment."

Penny obeyed, and a mask was placed over her face.

"Just breathe deeply and count backwards from ten," the nurse said.

Penny closed her eyes for the last time and began counting.

T-Minus ten...

nine...

eight...

###

About the author

I'm a librarian currently living in Cambridge, England, although I've lived all over the place across the last decade. I've written novels, short stories, and flash fiction in all sorts of areas: sci fi, horror, fantasy, mystery, anything with a touch of the unusual and imaginative. I'm also one of the municipal liaisons for National Novel Writing Month in Cambridge, which means that for one month each year I'm organising events, helping newcomers, and trying to unleash the creativity of a few hundred people. Oh, and writing a novel myself. Aside from my work in *Metaphorosis* I've also had work published in *101words* and *365 Tomorrows* and I write a very occasional blog at ianrennie.wordpress.com

Countdown

David Hammond

"So, how is this going to work?"

"Well, first of all, lean back and relax."

"Are we starting already?"

"Relax. We have gobs of time. Svéta is running late. Have you met Svéta? The anesthesiologist?"

"Svéta! I *have* met her."

"God, the look on your face! She quickens their pulse, then she puts them to sleep, that Svéta."

"Sorry."

"Don't apologize. You deserve a pretty face in your last moments of flesh and blood. An angel to escort you to the great beyond. That's a nice thought, isn't it? You want tea? The truth is I want to talk to you."

"Tea?"

"I'm boiling a pot."

"Um, sure."

"Yeah, I'm glad sultry Svéta is running late because I really wanted to talk to you."

"I've made up my mind, Caroline…"

"I hear congratulations are in order?"

"What? Oh, yes, yes. Gracie had the baby yesterday afternoon. A boy. They named him Johnny Bing."

"Johnny Bing?"

"After Johnny Cash and Bing Crosby. Don't ask."

"Well, that's lovely! Johnny Bing Hofstadter. Rolls

off the tongue, sort of."

"A beautiful boy, and his mother so happy and determined. And exhausted, of course, but she's a force to be reckoned with, let me tell you. And Gary was there. I remember becoming a grandfather for the first time. Oh my. What a sight they all were."

"And there you were, Great Grandpa Julien, joining by video link."

"Yes... Are you implying something?"

"Lovely! So, anyway, let's talk about the procedure."

"Oh, okay."

"So, sexy Svéta comes in and she straps the mask on you and fills you full of sevoflurane. Your last moments of consciousness will be eased by gazing into her dreamy eyes."

"Ha ha."

"So, then, you see we have this skull clamp apparatus? I clamp you in, and then I use this — isn't it beautiful? — this bone saw to perform a craniotomy so I can get full, unrestricted access to that precious gray matter between your ears. Are you following? Any questions?"

"Caroline..."

"Then comes the best part. This syringe right here is full of my extra-special, patented, soon-to-be-Nobel-winning neural fixative. I jam it into the gray matter — squirt squirt squirt — and in 15-20 minutes the neurons in your brain have been conveniently locked in a stable, scannable state. The rest of your body ceases to function, which in most brain surgeries would be a problem of some concern, but in this one, not so much."

"I know what you're doing."

"Shush. So then we remove your brain from your withering husk of a body and put it in this contraption here, where it can be bathed in preservative serum and attached to 1,024 electrodes, which are used to make a digital record of the brain state... Which is fed into the human brain emulator... Which we turn on... And then you, but not you, say to me, 'Caroline, this is highly irregular,' or something to that effect. There's nothing to it, really. I wonder if we can get that voice from *2001*? 'I'm afraid I can't do that, Caroline.' That would be awesome."

"If you're trying to make me reconsider, it's not going to work."

"But I'm not done! There is your body to think about. You think these things just take care of themselves? For cosmetic reasons, I should re-attach your cranium, empty as it may be, don't you think? Your family will want the remains. They will dress you in your best suit and place you in a coffin..."

"No they won't."

"They won't? Cremation then?"

"I have donated my body to science. And I have forbidden mourning of any kind."

"How can you forbid mourning? You must allow them to mourn. It is..."

"There will be no reason to mourn because I will not be dead."

"..."

"I will live on in the emulator. And I will help us colonize New Earth! You know, Caroline, this is something you fail to understand, or seem determined to ignore. I'm totally committed to this mission. It's why the board put the decision in my hands, after all."

"I know, I know..."

"You know, you know... but do you know how many times I applied to be an astronaut when I was young? How much I yearned for the stars? I dreamed of putting on the suit, strapping into the capsule, the countdown — 10, 9, 8, 7... It's my body that was the problem, this withering husk, as you call it, which also happens to suffer from asthma. It's weighed me down my whole life. And this mission, establishing a beachhead on a new planet — I'll be serving all of humanity!... You know, you know... the truth is, you're jealous. You wanted to be the one to go."

"Okay, first of all, backing up a smidge, whether you will be dead or not is an arguable point. Did you ever speak with Sid, our last successful transfer?"

"Yes. What about him? He seemed fine."

"I don't know. Something not quite there. It worried me. And that's if the transfer is successful. You know we're batting about .500 on this procedure now?"

"I know the risks."

"Yeah, so you might be really, truly, undeniably dead. And about your point of me being jealous — please. Yes, I was willing to volunteer, but that was more out of professional pride, and not wanting to be responsible for someone else having to do it. Then there was the problem with the fluoxetine."

"The fluoxetine?"

"Oh, yes, didn't you know about that? I was on it for a while as a teenager. Seems to interfere with the transfer. Anyway, I would have done it, but that's different. I have a stepson, Josh, whom I rarely see, but that's about it for family. Friends? Well, there's you..."

"Oh, come on..."

"I'm serious! What I can't understand, is how you could look at that family of yours yesterday, that big beautiful family of yours, and then come here today. Whether or not you will be dead, you will be gone."

"It was looking at that big beautiful family of mine that made up my mind."

"What do you mean?"

"Well, picture it: little Johnny Bing in the center, and Gracie and Seiji gazing lovingly down on him, and, crowding around, gazing lovingly down on Gracie, Seiji, and Johnny are Gary and Yukio and Serge and Teresa. Already they're spilling out of the picture frame. I have no role there. I don't fit. You have a distorted view of me as some great family man, but I lead a lonely life since Rosa died, eat my dinners alone for the most part, talk to my plants when I water them, only to make sure my voice still works. I have one thing left to give to my family, to the world, and this is it."

"But... who will water your plants?"

"Ha ha."

"Let me get the tea... I don't know, I guess I see what you're saying, but I know for a fact your family will miss you. Gracie worships you. I will miss you. Ever thought about that? Ever spare a thought for little ol' me?"

"You will be fine. Do you have non-dairy creamer?"

"No, no creamer. You put non-dairy creamer in your tea? Never mind. Here's the thing…"

"Mmmm hmm?"

"… here's the thing: there are options. There are others who could step up who would, frankly, be better suited to the task."

"Now why do you say it like that? 'Options.' There is one other option, and that is my *daughter*, Scout. What were you just saying about family?"

"'Option,' then, whatever. Yes, she is your daughter, but first of all, she's a better pilot than you…"

"…granted…"

"And second of all, when was the last time she spoke to anyone in your family besides you? And she only talks to you about the mission."

"Okay, it's true, but you don't know her."

"I know she's ready to do this, has trained harder than you have for it. I care about this mission too, you know. Deeply. Scout feels she was born for this, and I would tend to agree with her."

"You don't *know* her."

"…"

"There is a darkness in Scout that she has hidden from everyone. She has a self-destructive core that would not serve the mission, and, I fear…"

"What?"

"Did you know that when Scout was 15, she built a glider from scratch?"

"You mean from a kit, or from spare parts?"

"I mean from scratch. I mean she took some aluminum tubing, polyester fabric, and other odds and ends and designed and built an ultralight glider. A friend with a pickup drove her to the top of a mountain and helped push her off the cliff."

"Oh my…"

"We had no idea. We heard about it from a neighbor and drove up to see how many pieces of her we could recover. We got there just in time to see her land, awkwardly. The contraption tumbled over and a wing snapped off, but she was unharmed."

"Ha ha!"

"I was furious with her, and also about as proud as a dad could be. She didn't care about either emotion — she was equally indifferent to angry shouting and loving hugs. Her aspect was purely one of mild disappointment."

"She was disappointed the wing broke off."

"That's the thing, I don't think so. I think she was disappointed she was still alive."

"..."

"She is driven to bang at the outer edges of life, in the hopes of breaking through. Just look at her career, always taking the riskiest jobs. Never managing to kill herself, but not for lack of trying. She would not be good for the mission, and the mission would not be good for her."

"But her record is impeccable. Are you sure you know her as well as you think you do?"

"Notice that she always goes for the solo gigs. She's not a team player. And that's a pattern from childhood too."

"This is the most solo gig ever devised! It's perfect! 27 years of interstellar travel..."

"Exactly."

"I don't follow."

"I worry about her, Caroline. She wears loneliness like a badge, but it's killing her. She needs people. She needs someone."

"... I think I hear Svéta..."

"Oh my gosh, Caroline, I am so sorry I am late! Dr. Hofstadter, hello!"

"Hello, Svéta!"

"But you know I had one half of a mind to not show up at all? To take a person who is a real person and turn them into a computer software! It is not right! This is what I have been telling to myself. Hmm. What is this?"

"Tea?"

"Caroline? You have given him tea right before the surgery?"

"Relax, Svéta, he only had a few sips."

"A few sips, a lot of sips... but I guess in this case it does not matter... hmm... but it is terrible that I say this! What matters and what does not matter? Do you know,

Dr. Hofstadter, that out of six patients this procedure only worked with four?"

"Oh, well, two out of three ain't bad! Caroline told me it was more like 50/50."

"You said this, Caroline? Hmm. It is not quite so bad as that, but still it is bad! Maybe you think two out of three is not so bad, but in brain surgery, let me tell you Dr. Hofstadter, it is very bad."

"He knows the risks, Svéta. If he wants to bang against the outer edges of life, who are we to stop him?"

"Bang against...?"

"Never mind, Svéta. I think we should get started."

"Are you ready, Dr. Hofstadter?"

"Please, Svéta, call me Julien. I am ready."

"Okay. Julien. I will put on, so to speak, my 'Game Face.' Hmm. Just a moment, I will be back in a jiffy."

"What do you mean by that, Caroline, that *I* am banging on the outer edges of life?"

"Aren't you?"

"Well... if I am it is only because we all must, sooner or later."

"I think you're more like Scout than you let on. Lonely and proud of it."

"I like my alone time, and pride has nothing to do with it. I've had my fill of people in this life."

"Have you?"

"I meant that much more gratefully that it sounded. Scout, on the other hand..."

"I am back, guys. I am sorry, did I interrupt?"

"Svéta, have you met my daughter, Scout?"

"Oh... yes... I have met Scout once or twice."

"Julien! Do you see what I see? I believe our Svéta is blushing."

"Blushing?"

"Okay, guys, maybe I blush a little because it is the reason I was late. I had lunch with Scout."

"What, like a date?"

"Oh, I don't know... sort of."

"I think this is serious Julien. I would have to consult my color chart, but I believe she has moved past 'rose' and has entered 'crimson' territory."

"Caroline, do not make fun."

"But tell me, Svéta, did Scout approach you, or the other way around."

"She approached me, in the institute cafeteria. It was so cute. I must have been rushing and muttering and looking at my watch, and it was so crowded. Hee hee! She came up beside me and she said, 'Follow me,' really quietly, and she made a path for me right to the register. Hmm. People are afraid of her, but why? She offered to pay for my lunch, but I said no."

"This is earthshaking news, Svéta. Don't you think, Caroline? And then you ate together?"

"Oh, yes, and we talked and talked. She is funny..."

"Funny? Really?"

"Yes. Why is this a surprise? And so smart. Then I called Caroline to say I would be late."

"What did you talk about, if you don't mind my asking? My daughter is not known as a conversationalist."

"All sorts of things. We talked about you a little, of course, because of the surgery. She is very proud of you, you know?"

"Yes, I know."

"And she talked a lot about her niece, who has had a baby. Hmm. Jimmy Dean?"

"Johnny Bing."

"Ah, that is it! She showed me pictures and she seemed somehow sad, and so I asked, 'Why are you sad?' but she made a joke and pretended that she was not sad. She is lonely, your daughter, no?"

"I'm afraid so, Svéta. Will you see her again?"

"Oh, yes! I like her. We are going to dinner on Friday. A real date."

"Well, what do you think about that, Caroline?"

"I think you're looking terribly pleased with yourself."

"I *am* pleased. I'm very pleased."

"..."

"So, let's do this thing."

"Caroline?"

"Proceed, Svéta."

"Okay, I am going to put this mask on you, Julien... There. Oh! You want to hold my hand, that is fine. Now I want you to count backwards from ten."

"(Ten, nine, eight, seven, six, fii...)"

"..."

"His grip is loose. I am sad, Caroline."

"'Game Face,' Svéta."

"Okay. 'Game Face.' I will help you with the clamp."

About the author

David Hammond studied English in college and thought he would be a novelist, but writing was hard, and eventually he gave it up. He worked at a copy shop in Northern California for a while, but, fortunately, he escaped to Boston, fell in with a crowd of computer nerds, and became fascinated by the web. This led him to a rewarding and enduring career as a web developer. For many years, through marriage and parenthood, he neglected but never forgot his passion for writing stories.

What got him to start writing again? The approach of middle age? Could it be that simple? Regardless, write again he did, and he found that increased discipline and/or decreased ambition allowed him to settle into a level of productivity he had never achieved as a young man. Now most of his waking hours are spent in front of a computer writing code for work and stories for pleasure, with the balance spent laughing, eating, and arguing with his wife and two teenage daughters. To read some of his stories, go to oldshoepress.com.

One of the Cities

Damien Krsteski

The City of Ionos Prime hung in its orbit like a ripe peach.

The urge to pluck it overwhelmed us; to rid our cosmos of rot, expose and exterminate the source of so much suffering. We were but a gamma ray burst away from turning Gomorrah's qubits into an unreadable scramble, but Captain stayed her hand, allowing this drop of poison suspended in vacuum to continue coruscating around its star.

The Bureaucrats on the vessel protested, but our complaints fell on deaf ears.

First we study the phenomenon, Captain countered, we analyze, examine, understand, before we even dare to suggest destruction.

So we Bureaucrats retreated to our quarters, where we debated amongst ourselves for 10^7 yottaticks before a modus operandi was reluctantly agreed upon.

When we submitted our proposal for consideration to Captain, her processes parsed it chunk by deconstructed chunk, optimizing on the fly before she spit out a treatise unrecognizable from our initial submission: while we were leaning heavily toward prudence, Captain was pushing for a thorough comb-through of the City, risks be damned. So back-and-forth we went for several cycles of submitting proposals and scrubbing Captain's heavily-edited drafts before we found middle-ground and an action plan took shape, neither too circumspect nor overly bold, which left both parties equally dissatisfied.

It was decided we were to keep our distance, reading the City's qubit states by measuring each constituent electron's spin, before reconstructing the whole polis *ex nihilo* within a heavily-compartmentalized quarantine on our own ship.

Safer, but harder than diving right into the City; like deducing the Roman Empire from scattered stones and centurion footprints, never once glimpsing Urbs Aeterna.

#

Our memories of the Program known as the Intelligence on Non-Organic Substrates were vague; the Truth Banks contained scarce information on the event, and so much time had passed that the Program enjoyed the status of myth among us emigrants.

A myth which told of the dawn of the machine age millennia ago, when humans—with their layers of biological tissue still unshod—gave up their physical lives for the purpose of the great migration, for solar winds to carry human minds outwards to fertilize the cosmos.

A myth of how the Program turned sour.

Of a disease which emerged from a diseased mind to spread from one established colony to the others, threatening the very existence of humanity. Our very own bogeyman.

We were all born with this fable-as-warning embedded in our minds, an internal moral compass that always swung to Caution whenever we found ourselves at a technological crossroads. But we all knew it was only a story, and the great migration had been carried out without a hitch.

That is, until branches of humanity began dying off, imploding under the weight of their own misanthropy. Then we could only hope we weren't too late.

#

We sieved through heaps of data rot to pick out nuggets of useful information, to piece together the story of Ionos Prime behind quarantine doors.

"Manifest is at one-third legibility," a colleague informed me. "Cannot say how much more we'll be able to extract."

"I'm loath to deploy the approxies," I said, "before we have at least three-quarters of the data. Risk of fuzziness might overwhelm the benefits."

Our hopping through the cosmos had finally led us to the culprit; we were going nowhere. So we took our time, sifting through muck, air-brushing what potsherds we managed to excavate from the dead hardware.

I split my exaticks evenly between the restoration effort and prolonged dreamless sleep. Those stretches of nothing rested my mind as little else did, with the worry of what we were bringing back to life no longer looming over me like a mountain's cold shadow, and whenever I woke I woke as if for the first time, opening my eyes wide, eager to do work on what we deemed patient zero; but toward the end of each shift I found myself drained and sad and despondent, counting out the kiloticks to my next period of sleep, as if the City's disease were seeping through the layers of gauze, infecting my mind.

When it became clear we weren't going to extract much more than half of the manifest's data, I reluctantly unleashed the approxies, and those little daemons began to scour through the City's DNA, constitution, and *raison d'etre* all rolled into one, to extrapolate from existing information and pad the story out, fill in the blanks wherever necessary.

The crew and Captain seethed with excitement while a part of the ship locked away from the outside world set to work, rewriting history.

#

The Manifest of Ionos Prime
    Character A's sitting in the waiting room.
    He rubs his eyes; he doesn't want the news; he waits.

When a nurse comes out of the room, for a moment he suspects she might be carrying good news, surely they would've sent one of the doctors had the outcome of the operation been bad, but her face says otherwise, and her brisk but solemn step confirms it, and her mouth moves but he hears no words, he just follows the movement of her lips, the shapes and grimaces which convey that Character B is dead.

Outraged, he paces the hallway. Clenches his fists, threatens to use them. He demands to speak to those charlatans who have learned their craft from diploma mills, who have but one arm with which to operate, who have no right to call themselves medical professionals, who are blind, idiotic, progeny of promiscuous she-dogs, and subject to other such insults his enraged and begriefed mind can come up at this instant.

Another nurse brings him a cup of sugary water to calm him down, but he slaps it out of the nurse's hand before storming out of the waiting room. Outside in the hot summer air he sits at the steps and buries his head in his hands. He lets out a long scream, which mutates into a growl, then he cries, tears leaking from between his fingers.

When Character A finds his way home the apartment welcomes him like a womb. He's surprised to learn that he's sleepy, that he's capable of wanting sleep at all. Surprised, too, to discover there's no ceremony to it all: he's just back home, while Character B isn't, and that's that. He pads to the bedroom, grabs a blanket and drags it to the living room, where he passes out, curled up on the couch for hours.

It's on the evening of the funeral that the cloning company reaches out to him.

They show a modicum of tact, he thinks, by calling only after his partner's body is underground. A soft-spoken representative offers condolences, then reminds him their child is mere weeks away from being delivered, by offering discounts on services and a promise to slash the already agreed-upon price, framing this call as a sort of consolatory present from the corporation, but Character A, tired and pathetic as he may be, sees it for what it truly is: a subtle reminder of the terms of the cloning agreement, about which, now they have gotten wind of the tragic news, the company agents fear he might be getting cold feet.

Which, he realizes as he hangs up, isn't too far from the truth. How will he react when he sees Character B's eyes in the child's eyes? Character B's sharp intellect, wit, Character B's sense of humor? He presses his knuckles against his forehead, and assures himself, as convincingly as he's capable at this moment, that he will do all he can to learn to appreciate the reappearance of B's traits, however viperly they might uncoil from the child's physiognomy to strike at unexpected moments of A's weakness; that he will try his best not to despise the child for being a walking statue of the dead—yes, he assures himself he has no intention of backing out of the agreement, assures himself he's eagerly awaiting his child.

The room is empty, him a big hole in the middle which drains it of its former warmth. For the first time since he found out about Character B's disease, he feels helpless. Back then, poring over the blood results together, discussing options, mapping out the hard road that lay ahead—all of it was difficult, sure, but they'd done it hand-in-hand, together always, and there had been no room for desperation, for helplessness.

But now that it's all over and he sits alone in Character B's study, he feels he has earned the right to treat himself with a brief depressed moment. Earned the right to feel like shit.

To contemplate dying.

There's a knock on the door, and a colleague of Character B enters.

A small group of B's closest colleagues from the Program had hung back to keep Character A company after the funeral, a token gesture which Character A finds touching.

The colleague asks Character A if he's okay, and when Character A nods, the colleague tells him he's going to take off soon, gesturing with the jacket in his hand toward outside, and that he's come to say goodbye.

Character A still has the phone wound around a finger. He swivels the chair away from the colleague, whose cringing makes him, although physically quite bulky, seem impish in the door frame. Instead of a goodbye, Character A impulsively unloads his burden and tells him about the child.

The colleague just stands there.

Character A can hear him shifting his weight from one foot to the other, the treacherous old parquet creaking with each minute movement, then the colleague walks over to him, places a hand on his shoulder.

He says everything will be all right. The child is Character B's last present for him, which he should cherish and love, and when overwhelmed, he should share the burden with him and the other colleagues from the Program, all of whom are willing to take up their roles as aunts and uncles to help with the raising. But his tone is odd, stiff, so Character A turns to face him again, and asks him how long he has known about the child.

The colleague purses his lips. Since the diagnosis, he admits.

There is silence then, and both of them become conscious of the conversational murmur which seeps through the partly open door. The colleague walks over and closes it, then sits down on the reading chair opposite Character A, leaning forward with his elbows on his knees as if awaiting a chastising.

But Character A isn't interested in dredging up bitterness at this particular moment, nor has he the willpower to do so, so he sighs, lets the phone uncoil from his forefinger on the mahogany desk and asks the colleague how it has happened that Character B had confided in him, when the two of them had decided not to speak of the child to anyone, especially after they'd learned of the disease.

The colleague's eyes dart across the study as if trying to find an object to hang onto without much success. He's conscious of the pain of this revelation, and his face is painted with the guilt of this additional heartbreak inflicted on Character A, but after a moment of mental recalibration, he seems to decide it's in Character A's best interest to tell him the whole truth. So he tells him how after one particularly busy afternoon at the lab, he'd found Character B sobbing, propped against a hallway wall. The colleague had approached B carefully, inquired if he could help in any way, and after some goading Character B had shared with him the bad news about the sickness, but also about the child A and B had already conceived together.

They had hugged, not having spoken another word, and thus a barrier had come crumbling down. After this incident, Character B and the colleague met to talk on a regular basis, with B offloading B's worries on the colleague, one evening even, the colleague says, by coming over to the colleague and the colleague's wife's house to spend the night, because B had been too shaken to return home.

This depiction of Character B comes as a mild shock to Character A, who's always considered B the pillar of strength in their relationship, because B'd barely ever frowned, let alone shed a tear for B's own ill health. Character A keeps quiet, digesting this. He smacks his dry mouth. The colleague offers to fetch A something to drink, even gets up, takes a step toward the door, but A shakes his head, motioning for the colleague to remain seated, and to tell Character A more.

Later there had come a tipping point, the colleague tells him, after which Character B's behavior had altered once more. B'd become more focused on the work at hand, discussing less B's inner life with the colleague but rather delving into the technicalities of the Program with which B was intensely involved, taking every opportunity to go over mathematical and/or neurological problems that had been bothering B. The colleague admits to Character A that this change had come as a relief to him, too, who'd found it easier to console (so-to-speak) B by proffering solutions to technical puzzles in lieu of relationship or life advice.

Character A fiddles with the wire-thin coil which is the phone. The colleague takes notice, and pauses. They look away from each other. Occasionally, somebody's voice from the living room goes up a notch and makes its way to Character B's erstwhile study as a nondescript aural comma punctuating their silence.

The colleague says he's sorry, but Character A refuses to accept there's anything about which the colleague should feel remorse. Character A says that he's the one who should be apologizing to the colleague, to B, for not being perceptive enough, for letting himself be so engulfed in his own pain that he's managed to not see the extent of B's suffering, how much B'd kept locked in B's-self, how much effort B'd put in to protect Character A, to protect him and their future child—

This train of thought is stopped violently—each sub-thought a car crashing into the one in front—by a gigantic slab of concrete of a realization which suddenly emerges in Character A's mind: that change of behavior in Character B that the colleague had noticed didn't coincide with anything in their life together, couldn't really be mapped to B's behavior with A, which was a constant background noise of doctors, therapy, and planning for either the best or the worst scenario, so what had made Character B's mood take such a swerve? Whence that dedication to work on the Program? Was it just something with which to occupy the mind? Or, perhaps—

The colleague's relieved (thinking erroneously that the topic has moved away from Character B) when Character A asks him whether the Program has already decided on the prime pilot.

The colleague says that the search is still on, that there's a surprising scarcity of volunteers which pass all intellectual examinations, yet the scanning and abstracting technology is almost ready, in part thanks to the last push by Character B. B's last gift, the colleague says, for B's colleagues and for humanity, and he bows his head slightly, thanking B by thanking A for it.

Soon afterward the colleague leaves, taking the others with him, and Character A's alone in his apartment.

He haunts the apartment like a ghost, room to room, not perceiving anything, only thinking.

Fully-clothed, he gets in the empty bathtub and lies there, as he always does when in need of a clear mind, the cold from the porcelain chilling his muscles, his bones, like in a mausoleum or a crypt, stopping time.

He stares at the tiled ceiling. There's no doubt in his mind what B'd been meaning to do, been working toward, just as there's no doubt that he doesn't blame B for it in the slightest. He thinks of where Character B would've been had Character B'd lived for a few additional months. Around Mars? Beyond Neptune?

Character A's eyelids are drooping; he thinks of the child. The part of A and B that, he's now decided, will be born and remain on this rock, and carry the memory of A and B in its blood.

He closes his eyes, sees himself treading on what could've been B's footpath across the cosmos, and drifts to sleep in the cold tub, nestled as if in one of those cryo-pods from the covers of old paperbacks.

When he wakes up, he knows he's already on his way.

#

Once the manifest was reconstructed, recorded, and cataloged, we let the ship cannibalize it, destroying all qubits before reclaiming this formerly-quarantined matter as part of itself. Ionos Prime was destroyed, too, by way of a gamma ray salvo.

The disease was made clear to us; despite the high-level of approximation in the reconstruction of the manifest, the main vectors of humanity's latest bane, borne by the prime pilot, became immediately apparent: narcissism, shying away from responsibility, an obsession with one's own problems, navel-gazing, reckless emotional myopia, all of which had come together in an incredibly viral mixture, and as such had already propagated in child-colony vessels from the City of Ionos Prime throughout the cosmos.

We were the only ones who knew, and therefore had to hurry. Out of this despicable blend of pathos we crafted (in memetic and neurological terms) the polar opposite: a vaccine. Using the language of the manifest cobbled together by our approxies, one could say we created the state of non-A for A.

A's negation.

#

There is no way to reach all affected colonies on time. So our vessel will split itself a trillion-fold, then each chunk, scraping matter from the immediate surroundings, will split itself another trillion times over.

Each shard will contain this record of our work along with the vaccine—a dose of optimism, a shot of Chin-Up to the collective arm of those afflicted.

There's not enough matter to go around for us and Captain, despite already having consumed the nearest star, and time is of the essence. Therefore, Captain and we will sleep soon.

We hope this reaches somebody. We hope somebody pays attention.

We'll sleep now, and so won't greet you in humanity's future, but to those there and still despairing, don't, and remember:

You are not alone.

###

About the author

Damien Krsteski writes science fiction and develops software. Some of his stories have appeared in *New Myths, Metaphorosis, Plasma Frequency, Flapperhouse, Kzine, The Future Fire, Devilfish Review,* and others. Originally from Skopje, Macedonia, he lives and works in Berlin, Germany. His online home is monochromewish.blogspot.com, and he tweets @monochromewish.

In the Absence of Time

Pauline Yates

T – Minus thirty-six hours and counting.

The labyrinth of corridors that runs through the Johnson Space Centre is as puzzling as John's musings. Is the summons the start of his transition out of the limelight and into obscurity? A crew member has died. A widow needs answers. Is his new role to be the face of diplomacy? In the three weeks since he lost his bid to captain the *Dynasty111* on its maiden voyage to Cyteria in the Centauri star system, he's had no input into the mission's final preparations. He's spent that time staring at placards of achievements that hang on his office wall while questioning whether youth was chosen over experience. It's true he's six months from retirement, but that doesn't mean he's lost his capacity to embrace an age of technology that will thrust mankind past the era of deep space exploration and propel it to one of interplanetary colonization. Considering the depth of his knowledge, today's summons smacks of hypocrisy. But beneath the surface of what he hasn't been told lies a deeper concern. Any setback this close to launch could threaten the mission. It's hard enough knowing he'll never personally see the fruition of his life's work. If the launch is delayed and this window lost, the next opportunity for this mission's planned trajectory isn't for another seventy-six years.

With conflicting thoughts of justifying the quest for humanity's continuance to a dead crew member's wife, he walks faster along the corridor. He stops at an office marked Doctor M. S. Steel. He raises his hand to knock, but the door opens and the man responsible for pushing him into the backdrops of anonymity steps into the corridor.

"Captain Gleeson," John says, lowering his hand.

"Captain Mitchell," Gleeson says. His eyes flash irritation. "I didn't realize you'd been called."

"Did you think your promotion to captain the *Dynasty* included delivering perfunctory condolences?"

Gleeson sneers. "If you're here to interject, don't bother. The *Dynasty* is as good as dead." Pushing past John, he strides down the corridor.

Frowning, John enters the office without knocking. His friend and colleague Mike Steel is seated at his desk.

"Upsetting pilots again?" John asks, not unkindly.

"In a manner of speaking." Standing up, Mike walks around the desk and clasps John's hand. "Thank you for coming at such short notice."

"I've known you too long to ignore a call on my private line," John says, returning the handshake. "How bad is it?"

"One of the Hyper-Life pods malfunctioned during a final test run," Mike says, returning to his chair. "Harry Matherson, second in command. Incinerated beyond recognition." He pauses. "It wasn't pretty."

"Good God." John sits on a chair opposite Mike and wipes his hand over his mouth. "What happened?"

"A technical glitch; I'm unable to ascertain a cause. But better I find out now than four and a half light years away."

John glares at him. "Better for you, perhaps, but not for the widow." Seeing Mike flush, he relents. "I'm sorry. Spouses are well informed of the dangers of our profession. I should consider my wife lucky she was spared the grief." When Mike remains silent, John continues. "Am I to assume you'd like me to speak to Harry's wife?"

"That's not why I called you," Mike says.

John raises an eyebrow. "No? What then?"

"Even if the Hyper-Life pods are replaced with the earlier SX model, the recalibration necessary to sync the SX to the star ship's mainframe and complete a full round of testing will push the launch date out by eight weeks." Mike pauses. "We'll lose the launch window."

John leans back in his chair. "Do you have a contingency plan?"

"I do, but—" He glances at the door. "It's not being well received."

"By Gleeson? He's used to his chair plumped and fluffed. What do the rest of crew think?"

"I'm yet to approach them, though I expect Gleeson will beat me to it."

"Damn it, Mike. Who's in charge here? You, or Gleeson?"

"He has good reason to question."

John holds up a hand. "Let's pretend, for a moment, he's capable of having good reasons. Personal opinion aside, what is your solution?"

"As you know, *Dynasty111* is equipped with sophisticated software that's designed to implement placement of the satellite communication link en route to Cyteria and initiate robotic construction of the civilian base upon arrival. The team of twelve crew members has little input other than to oversee the base construction and help assimilate the first group of passengers to their new environment when they arrive."

John rubs his thumb over his lip. "With this software, how necessary is the crew?"

"Other than a manual launch and land, they don't even have to press an on button. One crew member would suffice but a team of twelve will alleviate the mental pressure of deep space isolation."

"So send one. And use a pod that did pass the testing."

Mike clasps his hands together. "After Harry, I doubt any member of the crew will step within two feet of a Hyper-Life pod." He leans forward. "I can reconfigure the software to take complete control of launch and land, which will eliminate the need for any crew. But to do that,

I need to download my AI extension program. I haven't trialed a download, but simulations show an eighty-six percent success rate."

John lowers his hand. "So download the program. With your diligence, I've no doubt you'll sift through any problems before launch."

"It's not that simple," Mike says. "The AI extension is unique in that it converts neuronal synapses from the human brain into recordable data which is then downloaded into the ship's mainframe in the form of a virus. The human body will not physically survive the download process. But the human will live on as AI. As part of the software of the star ship, the AI extension will have full control over *Dynasty111*, and control over the satellite placement and robotic construction of the civilian base once landed on Cyteria."

There's a long silence.

John leans forward. "What exactly did you ask Gleeson?"

"I asked him to volunteer for the AI download."

Clenching his fists, John stands up. "Are you insane?"

Mike stands with him. "I thought you were at odds with Gleeson for pushing you out of a stellar end to your career?"

"Not enough to kill a man," John says. "What the devil are you thinking?"

"We don't have time to think," Mike snaps. "The success of this mission depends on finding a pilot to volunteer for this AI download. Which is why I called you."

"What?"

"Come on, John. I know how much the *Dynasty* means to you. This mission was to be the culmination of your life's work. I don't know why Gleeson was chosen over you but I'm offering you a chance to take back what's rightfully yours. Be the download." He pauses. "You're about to retire anyway. What have you got to lose?"

"My life? Oh, but I suppose that's inconsequential to our greater goal." He steps to the door and yanks it open. "If this is what we've regressed to, then perhaps it's past time I retire. And don't worry about Harry's widow. I'll see her myself. Somebody has to apologize for our poor judgment when it comes to priorities." Walking out of the office, he slams the door behind him. It's a rare occurrence but he has to admit he agrees with Gleeson. This mission is well and truly dead.

#

T – Minus twenty-six hours and counting.

Amidst scattered documents and scrawled notes, John closes his laptop and leans his head in his heads. No matter which way he looks at it, finding another launch window earlier than seventy-six years is impossible. Even if the *Dynasty111* follows the planned passenger ship trajectory path in two years' time and planet-hops from the refueling station on Mars, they'll skip past the third satellite placement, which is crucial to setting up the communication link to Earth. There's no way around it. For this mission to succeed, the *Dynasty111* has to launch now.

Leaning back in his chair, he rubs his hand over his mouth. The silence that surrounds him is as harrowing as the silence he endured when he met earlier with Harry's wife. He would have rather she'd screamed or cried; either he could handle. But her tight-lipped silence took him back ten years to when he'd announced to Patti he was embarking on another exploration to the outer reaches of space. That trip stole six years from their marriage. The tearing part is questioning whether he would have gone had he known they'd only share one more year together on his return. Guilt tells him he would have.

Is he so consumed with this obsession for continuance he'll cast aside the value of time spent with a spouse? For without partners, how does life continue? Has Mike, and perhaps Gleeson, fallen victim to the same obsession that makes losing the launch worse than losing a crew member? What hope is there for any civilization on any planet if the value of human life is reprioritized? On the other hand, what if AI is the hope humanity needs? If that's the case, who is he to fight fate? But if Mike's seed is planted in the wrong person, what kind of future will be cultivated?

Opening the laptop again, he brings up the data on the Hyper-Life pods. He recalls an earlier delay in production that caused an argument with Mike about changing from the already proven SX models. In hindsight, that delay spelled trouble. But what did he know? He's too old, apparently, to embrace new ideas.

There's a knock at the back door. It could only be Mike. They've been friends too long for a heated argument to last. Standing up, he steps to the door, but when he pulls it open, he stands back in surprise.

"David?" he says.

His son stands in the doorway. "Hey, Dad."

Three years of silence stretch between them. The initial shock passing, John opens the door wider. "Forgive me," he says. "Please, come in."

David steps inside and stands behind a kitchen chair. "I called your office," he says. "Your secretary said you'd left for the day."

"Yes."

David glances at the scattered documents. "Working late?"

John gestures to a chair. "Can I get you something? Tea, perhaps?"

David sighs. "Please."

John busies himself boiling a kettle. "You look—" He's about to say older, but his son grew into a man long ago. "—well. Sugar?"

"One." David pulls out the chair and slides into the seat. "Cathy sends her regards."

John smiles. "How is she?" Returning to the table, he pours tea into one cup and passes the sugar bowl.

"She's well," David says, clasping the cup. "She's pregnant."

John raises an eyebrow. "That is good news."

David sighs again. "Dad. I know we haven't spoken since Mum died, but I'd like to make amends."

"Hmm. Fatherhood does that."

David leans back in his chair. "I'm not entirely at fault here."

John looks at him. "No. You're not. The fault is mine." He takes a seat at the table. "If you can accept a father's apology for not being present when I should have been, I'd be grateful."

"Your work was your life. Sometimes I wondered if Mum and I were in your life at all."

"A fair statement. But one I'm past rectifying."

"In other words, you have no interest in fixing anything."

"Those are your words, not mine."

Shaking his head, David spoons sugar into his cup and stirs his tea. "Cathy and I have discussed moving closer to home." He pauses. "We'd both like our baby to have a grandfather in its life."

John frowns. "I was barely there for my own son. What makes you think I'd be any better at being a grandfather?"

"It's not like you won't have time. You'll be retiring soon."

"Ah, yes. And then I'll have all the time in the world to correct the wrongs in my life." He leans forward. "Did you ever consider whether there was purpose behind my long absences?"

David leans back and throws up his hands. "How would I know anything about purpose? You were never around long enough to explain it to me?"

"I won't make excuses for my career choice."

Pushing back in his chair, David stands up. "No. You left that to Mum, didn't you?" He shakes his head. "You know what? Forget it. You weren't around after Mum died. Why would retirement be any different?" He strides to the door but pauses. "The only thing I ever wanted was a father. But I guess that's too much to ask of you, isn't it?" He walks out, slamming the door.

John slumps in his chair. "Well, that went well."

He runs his hand over his head. If he were more adept at handling suppressed emotions, he'd have been able to drop pride and admit his son was right. He doubts he'll get another chance. How many years will go by this time before one of them makes another attempt to reconcile? By then, he could be dead.

He glances at the laptop. What good is purpose if it amounts to nothing? Surely some good must come out of the sacrifices he made. First his wife. Now his son. What about Harry? If the mission is lost, Harry's death will be in vain. Standing up, John picks up his phone and calls Mike. What has he got to lose if he's already lost everything?

#

T – Minus eight hours and counting.
John's cheeks ache from smiling at reporters. He wonders how much damage was done to his retinas from the camera flashes. Publicity before a launch is not new, but his thoughts are far from his scripted responses to questions about the last-minute change in *Dynasty 111*'s captaincy. This could be the last time he'll see the sky. It's a beautiful shade of blue.

Back inside the space center, Mike gives further instructions while escorting him to the laboratory.

"Once you're on Cyteria, it's imperative you take steps to protect the computer software. The crew for the passenger ship will be debriefed in due course, but I don't know how they will respond to taking instructions from AI."

"What about Gleeson?" John asks. "He's privy to your AI extension idea."

"And now that you've volunteered, he's kicking himself for not accepting the offer first. As far as the rest of the original crew is concerned, you've agreed to man the *Dynasty111* alone using one of the Hyper-Life pods that passed testing, as per your suggestion." He pauses. "Though Gleeson has agreed to keep quiet, he's put out that he didn't suggest that idea himself."

"It wouldn't take much for him to feel put out," John says, stopping. "You're putting a lot of faith in this procedure considering it only has an eighty-six percent success rate."

Mike turns to him. "It will work. I'd stake my life on

it."

John resumes walking. "Not your life, Mike."

"Regardless," Mike continues, matching John's strides. "Gleeson has insisted he captain the passenger ship." He lowers his voice. "Between you and me, I wouldn't put it past him to try and seize authority when he arrives."

"Isn't war supposed to remain on Earth?" John asks.

"War is a natural part of evolution," Mike says, stopping at an elevator. "Even at the most basic cellular level."

They take the elevator to sub-level 4A. When they arrive at Mike's laboratory, John expects an elaborate setup, but there's only a single reclining chair in the middle of the room with two monitors on rolling trolleys positioned on either side. A technician crosses the room and stands beside Mike.

"My research assistant, Doctor Susan Halliway," Mike says.

"I'm honored to make your acquaintance, Captain Mitchell," she says, extending her hand. "Your previous deep space explorations are impressive."

John returns her handshake. "Not as impressive as this procedure, should it work."

"We're behind time," Mike says, glancing at his watch. "Susan, get John prepped."

"This way, Captain Mitchell," she says.

John follows Susan to the reclining chair. "Ironic, don't you think, how time, or lack of it, has the ability to force our next action," he says.

Susan frowns. "You don't have to do this. I've run your suggestion of using a tested Hyper-Life pod through a simulator. The odds it will withstand the trip are high."

"As high as Mike's odds?" John shakes his head. "There's a risk in whatever choice we make."

"You should also know that as the AI extension, you may still succumb to the emotional pressure of deep space isolation. I've read through your medical file. The latest psychoanalytical report from Doctor Menzie is a concern."

John frowns. "Odd. He knows better than me that I'm more at home in space than on Earth." He wonders whether a discrepancy in the report contributed to his loss of the captaincy bid. But he dismisses the idea. Mike would have mentioned it. He smiles at Susan, who eyes him with unnecessary concern. "There are lonelier places than the depths of space," John says. "Now, why don't you explain what it is I'm about to experience?"

"The procedure will take approximately fifty-five minutes," she says. "You'll be sedated, so you'll be unaware of the electrical stimulus applied to your brain. If the initial conversion is successful, you will fall into a coma from which you will not recover. Brain activity will cease and your organs will shut down."

"I can't imagine a more peaceful death," John says. "What about the sixteen percent failure rate?"

"In the event of a conversion failure, it will feel like your head has been placed in a microwave and the setting turned to high."

"Hmm." John clasps his hands behind his back. "Well, let's hope Mike is on his game today."

Mike, now wearing a white laboratory coat, returns to his side. "You can remove your jacket," he says. "I'll generate a pixilated digital image from recordings of the press conference to use as your profile picture." He gestures to the chair.

"Lucky I shaved," John says. He removes his jacket and hands it to Susan, then sits down on the chair and lies back. Mike steps to his head and attaches electrodes to each side of his temple.

John looks up at him. "If by some unlucky chance this does not work, do an old friend a favor and don't let me cook."

Mike grimaces then addresses Susan, who shrugs her arms into a similar white laboratory coat. "Draw up twenty ccs of Prentanine. Have it ready."

John stares at the ceiling while Susan attaches a catheter to his wrist and Mike tightens a restraint over his waist and ankles. Another set of electrodes is pressed to the base of his skull. He flinches at the prick of a needle but otherwise remains still. His eyelids droop. He thinks of sitting with Patti beneath a blue sky.

"Stabilize base line one," Mike says to Susan.

Susan steps to the computer and types in a command. "Base line one stabilized."

Mike looks down at John. "John, can you hear me?"

Beneath an increasing heaviness in his body, John forces his eyes open. "Yes."

"You'll feel a strange sensation before you fall fully under the sedation. Don't be alarmed. It will pass."

John's tongue thickens. Response becomes impossible. He turns his attention to the monitor to his left, but then a feeling like being thrown from a window of a twelve-story building rushes over him. Pins and needles shiver through his head. His eyes widen of their own accord. The last thing he sees is the erratic spike of his heart line on the monitor.

"Open base line two," Mike says.

Susan enters another command. "Base line two opened."

"Prepare for capture."

Apart from the beep of the heart monitor, silence descends on the laboratory. John is in the hands of a computer now. His eyelids twitch, but the rest of his body lies deathly still. Mike glances from John to the monitor on his right then to the computer. Data flashes across both screens. As the minute's tick by, the crease in Mike's brow deepens. A command box pops up on the computer screen.

"Synaptic activity registering," Mike says. He steps to the monitor on John's right and places his finger on a button. "Enter the capture code. SYZ115YC89."

"SYZ115YC89," Susan repeats, typing. "Capture code entered." She glances at Mike. "Ready to run."

A bead of sweat rolls down Mike's cheek. "On my count. Three. Two. One. Capture."

Susan presses ENTER on the keyboard at the same time Mike presses the button on the monitor. There's a pause, then John's whole body spasms. His back arches, but the restraints hold him to the chair. The heart rate monitor explodes in a siren of beeps.

"Base line ratio?" Mike asks.

"Fifty-two, forty-eight," Susan says.

"Increase the current by two amps on base line one."

"Implementing increase."

John's body spasms again. The heart rate monitor races in irregular beeps.

"Fifty-three, forty-nine," Susan shouts. "Negative stabilization."

"Damn it." Mike rushes to the computer. "We're losing him. Prepare to inject the Prentanine."

Swapping places with Mike, Susan jumps to John's side and inserts the needle of the syringe into the catheter in John's wrist. Her hands shake. At the computer, Mike's fingers fly across the keyboard. The heart rate monitor steadies to a series of fast beeps.

"Fifty-one, forty-nine," he says through gritted teeth. "Come on, John."

A second command box pops up on the computer screen. Mike clicks on NEXT. The spasms in John's body stop. His body slumps into the chair. Mike sighs. "Fifty-fifty. Capture successful." He types a new command into the computer. "Implementing conversion." He presses ENTER.

Algorithmic data flashes across the monitor on John's right. Mike wipes the sweat from his brow and watches the screen. Susan withdraws the needle and steps away from the chair. Neither speaks. On the computer screen, the algorithms convert to single rows of data, but at the speed of the conversion, the lines are unreadable. Mike glances at his watch.

"Forty-two minutes," he says. "What are John's vitals?"

Susan presses a button on the heart monitor to bring up an alternate reading. "Body function consistent with non-responsive coma," she says. "Brain activity slowing." She glances at Mike. "What if he dies before the conversion completes?"

"He'd better not," Mike says. Turning to the computer, he types in a command and opens a line of data. "Memory banks have been accessed," he says, reading the data. "Conversion rate is consistent with neural functioning." He pauses. "He just learned he was to be a grandfather."

Susan wipes her hand over her head. "Yet he went along with this anyway? Why would he do that?"

"Whatever his reasons, they'll be here," Mike says, nodding to the computer screen. He watches the data continue to roll down the screen.

At fifty-three minutes, the data slows. A final command box pops up.

Mike clicks on FINISH. "Conversion complete."

Behind him, the heart monitor shrills one long, uninterrupted beep. Susan steps to John's side and presses a stethoscope to his chest. Hearing nothing, she turns to the monitor and brings up his vitals. "Cessation of brain activity. Internal organs shutting down. Neurological activity negative."

Mike inserts the disk into the computer and downloads the conversion. When the disk ejects, he holds it up.

"Let's revive him," he says.

#

T – Minus sixty minutes and counting.

Captain John David Anthony Mitchell. Husband. Father. Friend. Born to a potato farmer, his interest in deep space exploration started when he dug up a meteorite the size of a football at the age of eight. Wondering about the rock's origin led him to discover matching dust samples from an asteroid belt extending from the Centauri star system. Now, with the tick of time stopped, John sees how the questions he asked propelled the choices he made, and how the consequences of his actions shaped his life journey. He's exactly where he was destined to be.

"Are you there, John?"

The words intrude into the blackness of his world but not as sound. He's doused in algorithmic data that cascades over him in broken lines of symbols. It's not unlike lying in an open field watching a meteor shower ignite a star-speckled night sky. But human senses don't exist in this world. He has evolved. He is energy. As he absorbs the data, a new awareness unfolds. He has never felt so—alive.

Excited by the possibilities, he extends himself throughout the *Dynasty*'s mainframe and captures more data. The cascading lines of symbols shape to form digital images. In a nanosecond, he realizes what he has become and where he is. But from deep within the remnants of his human self, he recalls the possibility of a threat to his existence. With no defense mechanisms in place, he is vulnerable.

Channeling his energy to the systems of the ship, he locks down all programs and initiates the ship's unique security measures. With external access denied, he uses a function in *Dynasty111*'s mainframe to scan the cockpit. Detecting foreign entities, he zones in on the intruders. A mass of neurons registers as seven biological life forms. Until he learns otherwise, he must consider them a threat.

"Identification of unknown biological life-forms initiated." Through the audio device in the cockpit, his voice sounds robotic. Ignoring it, he activates the infra-red scanner. A beam of red light jets from the instrument panel and sweeps the cockpit. Genetic data is analyzed and cross-matched with the collated data through a direct link to Mission Control. Identities verified, he adjusts the computer-generated voice to one of his own.

"Welcome aboard the *Dynasty111,* Doctor Steel," he says.

Mike steps forward. "Captain Mitchell."

Activating a roving EMF scanner, John detects immense relief. And sadness. He addresses Susan, who stands to Mike's left.

"Doctor Halliway. Rest assured that my—departure —was peaceful, as you promised," he says to her.

Susan exhales a long breath, but she doesn't smile. Behind her, John detects jealousy. And something else—

"We must clarify identification," Gleeson hisses at Mike.

Mike looks up at a monitor above the control board. "Can we have a visual to confirm identity?"

"Certainly," John says.

The monitor sparks to life. Static crackles on the screen. John creates a link to Mike's computer in the laboratory and uploads the profile picture Mike generated from the press conference: a head shot of him, dressed in uniform. The background shows the entrance to the Johnson Space Centre. Adjusting the settings, he switches the background to a shade of blue sky. Locking his profile, he addresses Gleeson. "Captain John David Mitchell. Identification code AN349DSE55NAS88. AI Commander of *Dynasty111,* destination Cyteria, Centauri star system."

Mike clasps his hands behind his back. "Captain Mitchell. Can you confirm control over *Dynasty111*'s operational systems?"

"Of course," John says. There's a pause. "Implementing operational systems check. Stand by for verification."

Lights on the instrument panel in the cockpit explode to life. John's profile is replaced by running data. The speed of the system check makes the officials standing behind Gleeson murmur in approval. Susan shifts uncomfortably on her feet. Mike remains silent.

John's profile reappears on the monitor. "Systems check complete," he says. "All systems fully operational and in my command. Launch code confirmed and locked in at T- forty-five minutes." He pauses. "I've detected a wiring sequence anomaly in two of the eight Hyper-Life pods. Replacement of Hyper-Life pods will not be necessary." Data flashes across the screen. "I've sent a download for the correct wiring sequence to your private log. I suggest you cross-check the wiring sequencing on all pods preceding launch of the passenger ship."

"I'll review the data," Mike says. He turns to the officials. "Gentlemen, might I suggest we resume communication with Captain Mitchell from Mission Control?"

Gleeson steps forward. "If all but two Hyper-Life pods work, there's no reason not to send a partial crew on this ship. This AI extension may appear successful, but there's no guarantee the software will maintain its integrity for the duration of the trip. I insist we send a crew for manual backup in the event of system failure."

"There's no time to call in and prep the crew," Mike says. "We launch in thirty-eight minutes."

"Then I'll go alone. Someone has to be in authority on Cyteria when the passenger ship arrives."

"Captain Mitchell has been given instructions to the effect," Mike says.

"You can't expect an AI abomination to govern a new planet!"

Mike looks at the control panel. "John?"

"Once construction of the base is complete, my purpose will be to maintain the communication link with Earth and assist future arrivals in assimilating to their new home. However, as authority over Cyteria appears to be a concern, might I suggest that no fewer than three crew members be given a special clearance code which will grant access to my security systems, identification codes verifiable through the communication link."

Gleeson turns on Mike. "I will not be held accountable to a piece of software." He turns to the other officials. "There's no precedent for this. We have no guarantee this AI extension will hand over control of the Cyterian base."

"This AI extension may be the first of its kind but do not forget who it is," Mike says. "It's because of Captain Mitchell's discoveries that we stand on the verge of the greatest space feat of all time. And now, with the success of this download, the scope for traveling to the far reaches of the galaxy extends beyond our imaginations. We are not only on the brink of a new era of interplanetary colonization but of a future incorporating the use of AI to further our existence. If there is one person capable of leading us over this threshold, it is John Mitchell."

Gleeson fumes. "I was nominated captain of this mission," he says. "Control over this ship and authority over Cyteria belongs to me. Now enter the unlocking code and give me access to the mainframe before I have you detained for breach of protocol."

If he was all machine, John doubts the roving EMF scanner would understand the new emotion that radiates from Gleeson. But having had a life-time of human interactions, John knows a grab for power when he sees it. But how far back do Gleeson's narcissistic tentacles reach? Using frequencies he never knew existed until he became them, John extends himself through the portals of Mission Control and sifts through records and logs of every interaction involving the mission. His search doesn't take him far. He finds the oddity he detected when speaking with Susan prior to his—rebirth.

Evidence collected, John displays a page of data on the monitor for all to see.

"On analysis of Captain Gleeson's request," he says to Mike, "individual statistical data from Doctor Menzie's report corroborates a zero percent possibility of an episode of psychosis caused by the mental stress of deep space isolation."

Gleeson steps forward. "There," he says, waving his hand at the monitor. "It's been proven I'm more than capable of embarking on this mission alone."

Mike frowns. "Where are you getting that information?" he asks John.

"From the last psychoanalytical report conducted on all crew members as part of the selection process for the crew of *Dynasty111*."

Gleeson smirks. "And are we privy to your result?"

"Thirty-seven percent risk," John says.

Mike frowns. "There must be a mistake. You've recorded zero percent for the past forty years."

"Odd, don't you think?" John says. "However, according to the data I've collected, Doctor Menzie's report was accessed two days prior to the decision on captaincy from an external source linking to Captain Gleeson's private computer." A second document flashes on the screen. "This is an original version of Doctor Menzie's report as logged with Mission Control on completion. You can clearly see the conflicting statistics." He pauses. "It appears the data used for determining captaincy selection was altered."

Mike reads the document then turns on Gleeson. "You switched your results with John's? I questioned why John wasn't given this mission but I never suspected malicious intent." He turns to the other officials. "Escort Captain Gleeson from this ship."

When two officials step forward, Gleeson lunges at the control panel. But when his hand touches the instruments, a shock of electricity renders him immobile. Stunned, Gleeson drops to the floor.

"Security systems are activated," John says.

Mike grabs Gleeson by the collar of his jacket and drags him to his feet. "Get him out of here," he says to the officials. "And clear the cockpit. We launch in—"

"T – Minus twenty-two minutes and counting," John says.

"God speed to you, John," Mike says, as he escorts Susan to the door. "*Dynasty111* is in good hands. That much I trust."

"Never let it be said that trust between true friends falters in the face of adversity," John says. "Doctor Halliway?"

Susan pauses in the doorway. "Yes, Captain?"

"I sense your conflict with my decision. Would you be so kind as to help me with one last request?"

#

Launch + Ten days.

Susan traces her finger over the name written on the envelope and then reaches up and knocks on the door. She only has to knock once. She's expected.

When David opens the door, she smiles at his resemblance to his father. She thrusts out her hand.

"Doctor Susan Halliway," she says. "It's a privilege to make your acquaintance."

David shakes her hand. "Would you like to come in?"

"No, thank you. I can't stay." She hands him the envelope. "Your father asked me to deliver this in person." She pauses. "What did he tell you about his latest space mission?"

David's frowns. "I didn't know what mission he was on until I saw the press release. I watched the launch on television." He hesitates. "Has something happened to him?"

"Your father is fine." She plucks a business card from her pocket. "The access code is your birth date. The phone number on this card is to Doctor Mike Steel's private line should you have any questions."

"What's going on?" David asks, taking the card.

"It's not for me to explain." She nods to the envelope. "The information I've given you is highly sensitive. It would be best if you didn't mention this to anyone. Your father said you would understand." As she turns to go, she pauses. "Your father is—the bravest man I know."

After Susan leaves, David goes to his living room and opens the envelope. Inside are his father's personal documents: birth certificate, passport, will. Along with these is another, smaller envelope. Opening it, David pulls out a computer chip. Frowning, he goes to his laptop and inserts the chip into a port. Prompted to download the contents with a password, he enters his birth date. A line of data flashes across the screen. When the download completes, the screen's background color changes from black to blue, then John's profile picture appears and his voice speaks through the laptop's audio device.

"David," John says. "By the time you receive this, I'll have left Earth's thermosphere and I'll be steering the star ship *Dynasty111* to the planet Cyteria. It is with the heaviest of hearts I tell you I will not be returning to Earth. My life there is—complete. If I have one regret, it was to allow a childhood fantasy to stop me from experiencing a life with my own child. But had I not sought answers to my own childhood questions, I would not be where I am today."

"The time we lost over the last three years was an unfortunate consequence of your mother's passing. I fell into a darkness through which I could not see. How does one get over losing the love of one's life? But if one thing came from her death, it was the realization that death is inevitable for all of us. With that in mind, I want to leave you with more than memories that fade. After all, I have a grandchild to think of who may one day need wisdom and guidance from a grandfather."

"The data you downloaded encapsulates my memories, my life experiences, my entire being. You need only type in your question, and I will answer. It is only now, in this absence of time, that I can be the father you deserve. I hope it makes amends for the father I never was. As for my future grandchildren, their gift will be waiting for them four light-years away, should the need ever arise."

"If I can leave you with one thing, it's this: do not regret your choices in life. It could be destiny steering your path. You will, one day, realize your destiny, as I have realized mine. I am—the beginning."

###

About the author

Pauline Yates emerged as a writer late in life after putting her aspirations to pen a novel on hold while she raised a family. When the opportunity arose to start her writing career, she found herself in a world where a keyboard replaced the pen and on-line submissions replaced the post. Undaunted, she trained her fingers to type as fast as she thought, but she always keeps pen and paper at hand.

She spends most of her day with one foot in another world and loves to let her imagination run wild with ideas for the next story. Her passion to learn more about the craft of writing led her to short story competitions which she continues to use to hone her writing skills.

She admits the pressure of writing to a prompt and a time limit is addictive, but her success in this area has led to publication with *The Casket of Fictional Delights, Abyss and Apex, Every Day Fiction, with longer pieces appearing in Fiction War, Metaphorosis* and *Short Fiction Break.* An opportunity to step into the digital interactive media arena arose with her real-life 'choose-your-own-adventure' story, *Rumours Uncut,* produced by Story City, Brisbane.

She is a member of Writers Rendezvous, an active local writing group, and enjoys flexing her writing muscles in areas she has yet to explore. Currently living at Ocean View, Queensland, she takes full advantage of the insomnia that has plagued her life since an early age, and can be found writing late into the night in company with her dog and cat, her faithful writing buddies.

To find more about the world of Pauline Yates or read her latest stories, follow her on Facebook at www.facebook.com/pauline.mcauliffe.

The Long View

Karl Dandenell

Jacob Isaacson's wristpad lit up with an incoming message at 4 a.m. At this hour, the system would allow only three people through, so he thumbed the display.

It wasn't from his daughter, Carol, or her wife, Devali. It was from his friend, Vinod Kulkarnis.

Come in. We have to talk.

Now? Jacob replied.

Car downstairs in 5 minutes.

Okay.

Vinod wouldn't have called him unless it was really important. And *that* worried Jacob. He threw on sweats, tied his gray hair back in a rough ponytail, and stumbled downstairs. This early on a Monday, it only took fifteen minutes for the autonomous cab to reach Sunnyvale and drop him off at Long View Ventures.

Jacob waved his wristpad at the surprised security guard, then made his way to Vinod's office buried deep in the building. His flip-flops echoed loudly in the empty halls. Lights switched on ahead of him, and faded behind, as the building tracked his movements. When he reached the CEO suite, he pushed the door open and headed straight to the drink bot in the corner. The machine mixed steamed milk and espresso into a heavy mug printed with the company's logo: a stylized mariner's telescope against a starry background. Jacob sipped, then turned to Vinod's desk.

"Jeez, Vinod! You shaved."

Vinod rose slowly from his big leather chair. "You sound disappointed."

Jacob shook his head. "Just caught me off guard. Haven't seen your face since you went to rehab."

"Fifteen years." Vinod walked with careful steps to the drink bot and ordered up a hot chocolate for himself. He rubbed his chin. "I knew I was going to lose it once they ramped up the chemotherapy, so I thought, what the hell? Give Squatter the finger." *Squatter* was the name he'd bestowed on the tumor wrapped around his thalamus.

Once he had his hot chocolate, he said, "Hit the mute button, will you?"

"Sure thing." Jacob closed the door and flipped a switch. Magnetic bolts slid into the door and soft red lights blinked around the frame. Their wristpads chirped, unable to get a signal past the suite's Faraday cage.

"So what's up?" Jacob asked.

"Have a seat." Vinod eased himself down onto the couch. Jacob sat opposite him and glanced at the office displays.

Normally the smartwalls ran weather cams, news feeds, and project schedules. Today, however, they cycled through personal photos: Vinod's graduation from Stanford, his doctoral robes lined with Engineering orange; Vinod in a tuxedo, offering a toast at Jacob's wedding; Vinod and Jacob shivering on a foggy day at Mt. Tam, their mountain bikes spattered with mud; and Vinod on the TED stage, discussing the limits of interstellar travel and his failed cryogenic experiments.

"I wanted you to be the first to hear," Vinod said, rubbing his eyes. "We're going to launch in six days."

"You know, I read the same reports you do," Jacob said. "The *Joshua Slocum* is at least three weeks from final QA."

Vinod shook his head. "It's ready now. Last month I leased time on Noble Dragon's orbital lab printers, and their crew ferried the last roll of aluminum polymer to the L2 orbital warehouse on Friday. They spent all weekend rigging the main sails." He grinned. "They were happy to bill the overtime."

"Jesus H Christ, Vinod! I can think of eighteen reasons why this is a stupid move. Do you want me to list them in alphabetical order?" Jacob stood and grabbed an electric marker from the desk.

"No."

"Then what the hell?"

Vinod leaned forward and steepled his fingers together. "If we don't launch this week, if we don't have a goddamn perfect launch in front of a million reporters and bloggers, the board is going to kick me out. "

"No way," Jacob said.

"It's true. Maxfield and Wu gave me a heads up. The lightsail's burned through too much cash and engineering time," Vinod replied. "When the board meets a week from tomorrow, I'm out."

"Ah, shit, I am so sorry," Jacob said. He could see it now: a public statement expressing their concern for Vinod's health, a generous golden parachute, and a commitment to focusing on the company's core mission, etc. "It always comes down to the stock price, doesn't it?"

"What else? Between my cancer and Senator Geary's campaign ads, the investors are freaking out."

Jacob sighed. "Geary's a dinosaur and a protectionist. Even if we'd given General Electric the contract, they'd still be closing that plant."

"Probably, but not everyone's happy we're using a Chinese company to build the boost laser."

"Give it a few weeks," Jacob said. "I can spin up a viral campaign, and then—"

Vinod tapped two fingers to his head. "I don't think Squatter is going to give me time for that. Besides, I called in a favor from Elon Musk last night. He's going to bump their satellite launch this week and lift our cargo module instead."

Jacob rolled the pen between his fingers. "Okay... that still leaves us without a pilot. Last time I checked, you weren't happy with the beta AI."

"It's decent," Vinod said, "but we need something better."

Eighty of Long View Venture's best engineers, representing the top one percent of the company's total workforce, had volunteered to wear tight-fitting caps laced with superconducting cables that recorded their brain activity while they interacted with a VR simulation of *Joshua Slocum*'s projected 85-year journey to Alpha Centauri B. Unfortunately, the data from these passive recordings produced very simplistic AI templates. They were sufficient to follow the complex navigation program of the lightsail, but didn't adapt to well to changing conditions.

"So you want to go through with an active deep recording," said Jacob.

"I already asked the neurologist. She won't sign off on it," said Vinod. "So I was wondering if you could, you know, take my place?"

The display in front of Jacob was running a video of Long View Ventures' founders wearing yellow hard hats, grinning as they broke ground for the building where he now stood. Then it switched to a series of photos of Vinod dancing with Jacob's daughter Carol at her *bat mitzvah.*

Vinod took a deep breath, then continued. "You know as much about this project as anyone. And you know *me.* If my brain can't pilot the ship, you're the best alternative."

Jacob wasn't sure what to say. He knew how difficult this must be for Vinod. Decades of planning knocked down by a few cubic centimeters of aggressive cells. "I'm... flattered."

"Here are last night's project updates and all the paperwork for the procedure." Vinod pulled a data chip from his pocket and offered it to him.

Jacob tucked the chip into his pocket. "I'll need some time to review this."

"Of course," Vinod said. He stood up and shuffled over to the door. "But not too long, okay?"

"I'll call you tomorrow." Jacob hugged Vinod briefly, then let himself out.

#

By the time he got home, Jacob was wide awake. His body seemed to need less REM time since his seventieth birthday, and today was no exception. He fried up some eggs, took his vitamins, and parked himself in his home office with a fresh pot of coffee. He unlocked Vinod's data and spent the rest of the morning bringing himself up to speed.

He didn't agree with the board's decision, but he could understand it. For the past year, about the time he was diagnosed, Vinod had been systematically siphoning resources from other projects. Digging deeper, Jacob discovered additional consulting hours that appeared under the computer hardware division, but in reality were completely dedicated to the lightsail's AI team. But what truly shocked him was Noble Dragon's invoices. Vinod had plundered his private accounts to pay them, essentially bankrupting himself to finish the ship.

Jacob turned to the data chip's second directory: medical release forms and an animation of the active brain recording process.

The "experimental, elective medical procedure" would employ a surgical robot to cut 15 one-mm holes in his skull, stopping just shy of the dura mater. Then the recording filaments—bundles of carbon fiber a hundred times thinner than a human hair—would corkscrew their way into the "proper" brain matter over the course of several minutes, forming a recording mesh.

Not at all creepy.

Once the recording mesh was online, they'd test Jacob on the lightsail programming to map his brain's responses. They would also intersperse cognitive tasks with more relaxing input, like music and videos, to help them calibrate the creative portions of his mind.

The documents also laid out the potential risks: reaction to anesthesia, infection, memory loss (temporary or permanent), blindness, cognitive dysfunction, partial paralysis, and of course, death. No wonder Vinod's neurologist had nixed the idea.

It was a lot to absorb. Jacob considered taking his surfboard up to Pacifica to clear his head, but the beach was closed again due to high levels of bacteria from a broken sewer line. He settled for 100 laps in the condo's pool, pushing himself hard. By the time he pulled himself out of the water, shaking with exertion, he'd made a decision. After they launched, he'd take a leave of absence, and show Vinod all his favorite spots in Fiji, Belize, and the Great Barrier Reef.

And after that? He couldn't imagine going back to Long View Ventures without Vinod. Maybe it was time to give retirement another thought. He had stock options stashed away to keep himself on the water for a long time.

After a shower, Jacob contacted a notary, had them confirm his signatures on all the release forms, and sent Vinod a simple message: *Put me in, coach.*

Jacob then cleared his calendar, and caught the train to San Francisco. There, he rented a limo and picked up Carol and Devali for an evening of old-school Italian food and a revival of *Hamilton.* Jacob normally avoided musicals, but on this occasion he couldn't help getting caught up in the crowd's joy. They stayed out late, ending up at the Four Seasons bar for overpriced cocktails. When Jacob suggested they plan a spring camping trip to Joshua Tree, Carol gave Devali a side glance.

"I don't know, Dad," she said. "We've got a big project coming up."

"Life's too short, honey," Jacob said, feeling the buzz of gin and bitters. "Someone else can cover for you."

"It's complicated," Devali said. "But I would like to see the wildflowers."

"Then it's settled," Jacob said.

Carol gave him a fierce hug when he dropped them off. "Love you, Dad."

"Love you, too, kid."

She sighed. "Dad, I stopped being a kid when I turned forty."

Jacob laughed and stepped into the limo. Before the driver closed the door, he called out, "Parental privilege!"

Two days later, Jacob sat down to a surprisingly polite coffee with his ex-wife, then flew to Texas, where he sampled some excellent local bourbon. The next afternoon, a driver whisked him to a private surgical suite at a hospital that normally catered to celebrity plastic surgery patients. He appeared to be the only patient on the ward.

At 6 a.m., the prep nurse gently knocked on Jacob's door. He was already awake and scanning the news. So far, Long View Ventures had stayed out of the feeds. The nurse took him to another room, where they snipped off his ponytail for Locks of Love, then proceeded to shave his head.

They gave him a light dose of Valium to calm his nerves, and wheeled him into the main surgical suite. There a technician named Diego waited with a stainless steel drilling framework. Over the next half hour, Diego attached the framework to Jacob's skull, tightening all the nylon screws by hand. Every now and then, Vinod poked his head into view, checking on their progress. Jacob was wondering if he could order some Valium for his friend.

Eventually, Diego stepped away, and Vinod took his place. "How are you feeling, old man?" The transparent face shield slightly muffled Vinod's baritone.

"Fine," replied Jacob. "Like I was the last time you looked in. And the time before that."

"Sorry," said Vinod. "Wind's picking up over Brownsville. I'm worried Space X will scrub the launch, and they don't have another window this week."

"Let's focus on the positive," Jacob said. "You've run the AI growth sim twenty-six times since Wednesday. I think we're good. "

"Twenty-seven."

"Excuse me?"

"I ran another one while they were shaving you," Vinod said. "The sim looks nominal."

Jacob smirked. Vinod once declared during a tech conference that *nominal* was "the nebulous state between broken and fully functional." His friend probably wasn't *nominal* himself after his latest round of chemotherapy. He really should be resting at home, but had insisted on accompanying Jacob. "I won't hold it against you if you want to rest, Vinod."

"I don't think so. It's not every day I get to watch a robot laser holes into my best friend's brain."

"Not quite *into* the brain," said Diego.

"Close enough for government work," Jacob said.

"So what are you going to watch between sections?" Vinod asked.

"What do you think?" Jacob smiled, feeling his lip tug against the nasal cannula. *"Endless Summer."*

He loved that movie, screening the restored version every spring in the company's theatre, and kept a copy on his home media center for his Memorial Day barbecues. He also carried the original soundtrack on his wristpad. "Wish I could have popcorn." He couldn't eat, of course. He'd have to make do with the smell of artificial butter pumped into the suite to better stimulate his parietal lobe.

"Next time." Vinod pursed his lips.

"Next time," Jacob said, *"you* get to play Medusa."

Vinod's wristpad beeped loudly. He glanced down.

"Everything okay?" asked Jacob.

"Sure," Vinod said. "I'm going to check on the core."

When he opened the door, Jacob could hear the faint thrumming of the pumps next door. They were circulating liquid helium, keeping the racks of Mills-Chilten memory units at -269 Celsius. The ship's core computer and cooling units would fill a standard cargo module: 1 meter by 2, though you could hold the primary memory unit in the palm of your hand. Hard to believe they were cramming nearly 3 zetabytes in there. Once the whole thing was fitted into place aboard the *Joshua Slocum,* they could take advantage of the lower ambient temperature of deep space, saving the liquid helium for emergencies.

"We're good," Vinod announced a few minutes later. "One of the memory clusters was throwing an error, so I took it offline."

"Good thing we put in a few spares," Jacob said.

"Two point three billion active units," Vinod said. "Room enough for even your ego."

"Ha, ha." At two hundred terabits of data per square inch, they had room for a century of scientific data, plus a half a million hours of high-definition video. Jacob's digital self wouldn't be bored.

"We should get started. The superconductors are rated at 50 petabytes a second, but we're using much lower amperage to be on the safe side—"

"I know, I know. Eight hours," Jacob said. That was their worst case scenario. More than likely, the AI compiler would parse the personality data faster once it had a basic framework established. In some of the simulations, they finished in only four or five hours.

"One last thing," Jacob said.

Vinod leaned down. "What?"

"When this is over, we're going to that Brazilian steakhouse. Your treat."

"They're going to want to keep you overnight, but sure. We can do brunch tomorrow." Vinod nodded to the nurse, who called the surgeon.

"Okay, Jacob, we're going to put you out for this next part," said Diego. "Mr. Kulkarnis, it's time to leave."

Vinod reached down and squeezed Jacob's hand. "I'll be monitoring from next door." His wristpad beeped three times, then twice again.

"You better take that," said Jacob.

"In a minute," Vinod said. "See you later, old man."

"I'll be here," Jacob said. Propofol dripped into his veins, and the world went away for a while.

#

He woke to an odd prickling in his scalp, and a dry mouth. "Water?"

"Here you go," said Vinod, holding a paper cup to his lips. Jacob swallowed. When the cup was empty, Vinod gave him an ice chip. "Can't give you too much."

He tried to nod, but couldn't move his head. Of course. "Okay," he said.

"The recording mesh is online. We can start whenever you're ready," Vinod said.

Jacob blinked a few times. One of the nurses rinsed his eyes with saline. "Thanks," he said.

They switched on the monitor suspended over the

surgical table, and the lightsail's system menu appeared. As Jacob read each item, the monitor tracked his eye movements and displayed text and controls. He was working his way through the onboard printer troubleshooting when Vinod's wristpad beeped six times in a row, paused, then repeated the signal.

"Jacob, I just got a text from Carol," said Vinod.

"Everything okay?"

"See for yourself." Vinod transferred the message to the monitor:

Hi Vinod. Sorry to bother you, but Dad's not answering. Guess they took away his wristpad. ;-)

Please tell him the stork is coming. Since I won the toss, we're naming him Jacob.

Jacob felt himself lurch, trying to take in both statements. Carol had been trying for *years* to conceive. He remembered driving her and Devali to the fertility center, and giggling as they paged through the donor sperm web profiles.

"I'm going to be a… grandfather. Wow."

"Mazel tov!" Vinod said. The surgical team applauded. After a moment, Vinod switched the monitor back to the lightsail simulator. "We're still on the clock, people."

"Right," Jacob said. He tackled the printer section, then moved on to the microsats they planned to launch once they reached Alpha Centauri B. However, he couldn't stop thinking about Carol. "Vinod, I… need a minute. Maybe more than a minute."

Vinod pulled up a chair. "Just hang on a little bit longer. The AI is starting to parse data on its own."

"I'm just having trouble concentrating. This is a big deal."

"I can imagine," said Vinod. "You want to call them?"

"Sure." They tried Carol's number, but it went to voicemail. They had no better luck with Devali. "Maybe I could send some flowers. She loves those glow-in-the dark roses."

"Great choice," Vinod said. "Who doesn't like flowers spliced with jellyfish genes?" He looked up a florist in San

Francisco. "What shall we put on the note?"

"Congratulations. And love to both of them. And tell them I'll babysit since they chose a good name."

"That's mighty big of you," Vinod said.

Jacob continued. "Tell her I'll see them soon."

"Anything else?"

"No. Go ahead and place the order." In that moment, he remembered his own grandfather, Herschel, who wrote every grandchild a letter before it was born: heavy paper sealed with wax, composed with a fountain pen in precise strokes despite the old man's arthritis. Each letter contained ten dollars and "a little wisdom" to start their lives. Perhaps Jacob could continue the tradition, although he'd have to make a few changes. His own penmanship was so bad Vinod told him he should have been a doctor.

"Start a list, will you?"

Vinod said. "Okay, go."

Jacob thought for a moment. Then he said, "Life lessons for my grandson Jacob:

1. Be kind.
2. Be charitable.
3. Study hard.
4. Listen to your mothers, even when they make you crazy.
5. Learn to cook. It brings people together.
6. Take risks, especially in love.
7. Learn to sing. That way you always carry an instrument.
8. Forgive your enemies.
9. Follow your dreams... and
10. Stand by your friends."

Vinod gripped his shoulder. "Thank you, Jacob. That means a lot."

Jacob felt he should add to the list, but he couldn't think of anything at the moment. "Okay, I'm ready. Let's not keep Space X waiting." He called up the microsat data, and worked his way through the launch sequence.

#

"The template has stopped requesting data," Vinod said. "I think we're done here."

"Good thing," Jacob said. "I'm toast."

"Just sit back and relax for a bit. I'll let you know if we need any tweaks." He dimmed the overhead lights.

"Not going to stay for the movie?" Jacob said, his throat dry.

"I'll be back in a bit." He left the suite, and a nurse gave Jacob more ice chips. The monitor filled with images of clean-cut young men strapping surfboards to their car and driving into a saturated orange sunset. The surf-guitar riffs of The Sandals came over the speakers while the scent of popcorn filled the suite.

Jacob left himself drift.

#

Clicking of keys. "Hello, Jacob? This is Diego, remember me?"

Yes, I remember.

"How are you feeling?" the technician asked.

Nominal

Diego said, "Can you be more specific?"

I'm very warm.

"Too warm?"

No. Feels good. He was windsurfing in Alameda, wearing his wetsuit with the built-in heating elements to ward off the chill of the Pacific Ocean. He could feel the breeze cutting across the bay. The sun lay behind him, casting his shadow on the water. He leaned, lifted a shoulder. The board cut across foam.

"You're doing great, Jacob. Everything is lining up."

Glad to hear. He drifted for a time, riding one wave after another. The sun beat down on him and the breeze remained steady. How far was he from shore? Then he remembered his daughter.

Hello?

Diego?

"I'm here, Jacob."

Can I talk to my daughter?

An awkward laugh. "It's 2 a.m. in California, and

you're still asleep."

What? The breeze weakened. Jacob checked the water ahead for obstacles. Sometimes old Styrofoam coolers floated in from the bay. Everything seemed clear for the moment. *Am I dreaming?*

"That's a hard question to answer." Diego's voice transformed into a doppler of gull cries. "We're not sure if AIs actually dream."

Jacob pondered that for a moment, then grinned as a pelican dove into the water next to him, surfacing with a fish. Despite the constant tug of the sail, his arms felt strong. His feet gripped the rough polymer surface of the board. He wasn't hungry, or thirsty for that matter.

Diego, where am I?

He counted animals while he waited: thirty-six gulls, two pelicans, and a harbor seal.

"Just checked. You're currently passing lunar orbit, and accelerating."

I see. He closed his eyes. Against the darkness, system updates pulsed: photonic pressure on the lightsail, computer core temperature, telemetry data streaming back toward earth. *We did it.*

"You did! Your grandson is going to be very proud of you."

Where's Vinod?

There was another long pause.

"Mr. Kulkarnis died a few hours after the lightsail launched. The neurologist thinks it was a stroke," Diego said. "I'm so sorry."

Oh. Jacob wasn't distressed by the news. One advantage to his current state, he supposed. *Diego, can you let me know when I—the other Jacob—wakes up?*

"Sure. The communications lag is only about a second now."

Thank you. It was going to be hard on Jacob, losing his friend. But there was new life to cherish now. Perhaps he would suggest that Carol name the boy *Jacob Vinod Isaacson.* Had a nice ring to it.

"Can I ask you something?"

Sure, Diego.

"What does it feel *like?*"

Jacob looked to the horizon. *Have you ever seen a pod of dolphins leaping through the water?*

"Yeah, in Hawaii."

It feels like that.

He leaned into the wind.

About the author

Who the heck is Karl Dandenell?

A survivor of Viable Paradise XVI ("Fire Wombats!").

A First Reader for *The Magazine of Fantasy and Science Fiction*.

An Active member of the Science Fiction Writers of America.

Long-time resident of an island near San Francisco with my family and cat overlords.

Someone who is fond of tea in the way most people are fond of oxygen. (I like whiskey, too.)

Where can I see more of your work?

My writing site is www.firewombats.com. I'm pretty good about posting links to my recently published short fiction, and there's an archive back to my early days, when I wrote under my birth name, Karl Schlosser.

Birth name?

Well, that. When I decided to get married, I didn't want to inflict my Germanic name on my future wife, nor was I thrilled about her last name, so we compromised. We ended up with my maternal grandmother's name, Dandenell, which is Swedish but has origins with a bunch of artists in Belgium (near the village of Andenelle).

Incidentally, one of my ancestors, Noël Dandenell, served as a silversmith and iron worker to Swedish royalty. His work can be found at Drottningholm Palace near Stockholm. Drottingholm is also known as "Little Versailles" since its architecture and appointments were inspired by Louis XIV. In fact, the Swedes were so keen on Versailles that they hired a number of craftsman who worked on the original, including Noël, who emigrated to Sweden in the 17th Century. (The Dandenells apparently knew a thing or two about artillery, and introduced several improvements in Swedish cannons when they weren't making aesthetically pleasing castle gates.)

What's your writing process?

Slow. Painful. Chaotic. Occasionally brilliant. *Metaphorosis Magazine* gets some of the good stuff.

What's the best thing about writing?

Having written. Seriously, the best thing is making that connection to the reader. We're all readers at heart, and we love it so much we can't help but share it.

What's your dream job?

Retirement. Or bookstore flunky. As long as it doesn't involve sitting in a cube.

Anything else?

If you liked this anthology, spread the word.

High Fantasy

<u>Stories</u>

Blood Feud

Paul A. Hamilton

Gideon burst in, his bare chest heaving, the intricate pattern of his scars glistening with sweat.

"Highness, please. You are needed on the northwestern gate. Urgently."

Empress Jessaya released the clasp of her son's cloak and smoothed it over his thin shoulders. "Simply dashing," she said, as if Gideon were not present.

"You don't think the green?" Yuren asked.

"The silver is much more elegant." She leaned closer, feigning the removal of a speck from his collar. "And more likely to catch the eye of a nobleman's daughter."

"Don't start with that again," Yuren laughed.

"Highness! I'm afraid I must insist." Gideon took a few more steps into the room, drawing a sharp glance from the Empress.

"Gideon, honestly. I think we have more important things to attend to than a status report. The ceremony is in less than an hour."

"I am aware, your Highness. Most aware. I would not intrude if the matter were not—"

Yuren laughed and patted his mother's shoulder.

"I'll go see what's gotten him so excited," he said. He crossed to his aimea, and clapped him on the back. "What's the matter? Did we forget to extend an invitation to the Gran Tumortia again?"

Gideon let himself be led away, casting a regretful glance back over Yuren's shoulder at the Empress. "But sire, you asked me not to extend her an invitation."

Yuren barked more laughter, louder. "And rightly so! That old crone has been fishing for a proposal since I was still in swaddling cloths! Come, let's go see what the fuss is about."

Jessaya watched them go, a thin smile on her face. He would make a good Emperor, in time. He might need a war or two, in order to stanch his wide unserious streak. Something to remind him that the job was not all grand balls and chasing scullery maids into dark corners of the palace. *A wife would do him wonders*, she thought.

She reached for the vial around her smooth dark neck and lifted it. Nearly empty.

"Bilbert!" she called.

Her own aimea appeared at her shoulder.

"Highness," he said. It was one of only ten or so words he ever spoke.

"I'm empty," she said, not turning to look at him, but rattling the vial between her thumb and forefinger.

"My blood is yours, Highness." He extended a scarred arm, fist clenched, turned down.

"No, dear, I'll need something a bit more potent."

"My blood is yours," he repeated. He turned and hunched forward, offering his back, crisscrossed with raised, pale knobs of scar tissue.

Jessaya unclasped the bullwhip from the gilded belt at her hip.

#

"God's blood, man, you're practically sprinting," Yuren panted.

"Highness, please."

Yuren shook his head and matched the pace of his aimea. Unlike most, Gideon had volunteered for the role. As children, they had been playmates; friends. Mother often chided Yuren for allowing Gideon to speak as openly as he did. Aimea were not advisors, she was fond of reminding him. But Yuren couldn't bring himself to rein Gideon in tighter. They weren't friends anymore, naturally, but neither did they have the sort of crisp and businesslike rapport of most bloodmages and their aimea.

They arrived at the northwestern gate with Yuren gasping for air. He didn't like the grim expression on Gideon's face.

"Are you trying to soil my coronation costume?"

"Up," Gideon said with a tone of command that might have gotten another aimea excommunicated, "quickly."

Yuren followed up the winding staircase, sweat soaking the back of his garment and dampening the collar of his cloak. "This had better not be some coronation hazing ritual," he warned darkly. Gideon was nearly a dozen steps ahead, taking them two at a time.

He crashed through the tower door toward the parapet, almost as if he intended to fling himself over the edge. Yuren followed, spots dancing in his vision from the exertion, cautious of the edge and determined not to look straight down.

"There," Gideon said, thrusting a pointed finger to the horizon. Yuren took a moment to glare at him before looking out. In his peripheral vision, he saw the glances of the posted guards. He'd have to have another conversation with the aimea about proper tone, especially in front of members of the military court.

The city-state of Claretion spread out below, the gold and crimson leaves of early autumn lit like fire in the afternoon light. Sprawling farmlands lay in the low valley to the East, ordered rows of green outlined by irrigation canals. The Gundra mountains to the West stood tall, like snow-peaked sentries against the untamed lands beyond. The sand-colored walls of the outer city meandered over the low foothills for miles in every direction around Overwatch Palace. The vista never ceased to stagger Yuren, mild acrophobia notwithstanding. *Tonight I shall be crowned Emperor of this gorgeous land.* The weight of his duty and his desire to surpass even his father's achievements quickened his still-racing pulse.

When his eyes settled on the incongruity in the

landscape to the North, his speeding heart accelerated further. He wondered if the exertion had set him hallucinating.

Gideon's arm pointed directly at the distant encampment. Columns of smoke rose and joined the scattered clouds. The unmistakable sight of a forward line being dug and fortifications being hastily erected chilled his bones.

"What?" Yuren stammered. "Who? Who would *dare?*"

Gideon lowered his arm and inclined his chin. "Highness? It's Aphora."

#

Gideon watched as Yuren stiffened, then paused, then relaxed, and finally began to laugh. It was a low chuckle that grew into great, loud barks.

"Highness?"

"Aphora?" Yuren asked, wiping his eyes and gathering himself. "And what does our favorite dissenter intend to do with this little display? Disrupt the coronation?"

"She won't say. She has taken the runners into custody."

Yuren shook his head, amused. He patted Gideon on the shoulder.

"I have to say, I think this is the sort of thing you could have told me about back in my chambers."

"Highness?" Gideon spluttered. Sometimes the reality of his station was impossible. He knew his place, of course, was honored by his position and title. But the way Yuren chose to prioritize his time and attention was something Gideon could not fathom.

"Come, now, we can't let this little showpiece delay the coronation, can we? Apprise the generals. Once I am Emperor, squashing this silly little—"

"Rebellion?" Gideon interjected. Yuren cast a look at the fidgeting tower guards and glared at him.

"Let's just call it a demonstration, hm?" He pulled on Gideon's shoulders, ushering him to the door. "And tomorrow it will be my first act to speak with the ex-priestess and come to some amenable terms that will send her back to her post again."

"But—" Gideon began.

"Enough, now," Yuren said more firmly as the door closed behind them. "We have a celebration to attend."

#

"Postponed until tomorrow?" Yuren protested. "For what? Aphora and her saber-rattling? Is that what we've come to?"

"That you cannot seem to take a show of military force seriously in the face of your ascension to power is a strong indicator you are not ready for the mantle of leadership," Jessaya said. Her tone and manner were cool, but anger and disappointment slithered underneath the facade like a nest of vipers. Yuren scowled, the spoiled child inside him barely checked.

"I've spoken to the priests and generals."

"And?"

"The Vein will be here momentarily to—"

Jessaya was cut short by the liquid gurgle of a bloodgate opening. A portal spun into existence in the air before them, the grisly severed arm of one of The Vein's acolytes tossed in first, hitting the stone with a wet slap like a gruesome red carpet being rolled out.

The Vein—high priest of the bloodprestige—stepped through, wiping blood from his hands onto his stained white robe and waving the bloodgate away behind him. Jessaya caught a glimpse of the acolyte who had sacrificed an arm for The Vein's expediency. All of the cultists were pale and drawn from their constant fasting and bloodletting, only allowed to dress in swaddling cloths like babes. This one had been ghostly, close to death, in the Empress's opinion. The Vein had not taken much precaution or shown his usual level of mercy to the lad. This fact alone, that The Vein had not deemed his time leisurely enough to care for his subjects, sent a shiver down Jessaya's spine.

"Hail, Empress," The Vein said with a short bow.

His bald head was encircled by an unending spiral of scar tissue, which Jessaya knew wound sixteen times before straightening and traveling down his spine. She'd made the cuts herself.

"Hail," she said. When The Vein had straightened and locked eyes with her, she flicked her gaze to her son.

"Hail, Highness," he said to Yuren, without the bow.

"What's so important you couldn't take a mount to the palace?" Yuren demanded.

The Vein did not suffer many fools, but he had suffered Yuren for decades. Whenever the subject came up, Jessaya danced around The Vein's concerns for the empire once it was fully in Yuren's hands. But she knew the High Bloodpriest would serve loyally despite his misgivings. She admired the way he hid his annoyance with the jibe by motioning for the guard to clear the spent focus—the severed, bloodless arm—from the room.

"The army to the North is led by Aphora—"

"I know this already," Yuren interrupted. "What are her demands this time?"

Jessaya didn't like the look on The Vein's face, and saw from Yuren's frown that her son was discomfited by it as well.

"She's not here to negotiate this time, Highness."

"So what does she want?"

"Unconditional surrender."

The room was silent, and cold in spite of the bloodfires and large hearth. A dozen heartbeats passed and then Yuren burst out laughing.

"Surrender?" he asked, incredulous. "Well, I'll give her this, she's not lost her moxie."

Jessaya watched her son's body relax. He still did not give enough credit to the traitorous woman he'd once called a playmate, and later a lover. But he claimed to know her. He had brokered the deals granting her and her band of like-minded sycophants land, amnesty for crimes, trade rights, and most recently the right to create their own laws and organize a militia specific to their province. Yuren was still over-proud of the militia deal, which he claimed had saved the empire thousands of bloodmarks in outposts and patrols on the Northern borders. He'd sub-contracted the work out to Aphora and paid for it with tax credits instead of expenses. It was true he'd turned a threat into an asset. Perhaps, if he was confident, she should be as well.

Still, something felt off.

"Will she sit down to a meeting?"

"Not until tomorrow."

"Highness," Gideon broke in, "perhaps her goal is to delay the coronation? If she sends assassins in her stead to the parlay table, you could be removed before you ever took the—"

Jessaya cut off her son's aimea with a sharp gesture. "That's enough of that."

Gideon looked at Yuren, but her son—for once—sided with Jessaya. "Mother's right. She's not trying to keep me from becoming Emperor. She just wants attention." He drew a deep breath. "Every time she performs one of these little skits, she gets us to the negotiating table and she gets something she wants. Even if we get the better end of the deal. But she always leaves with a few more commoners than she came with."

Her message is alluring to the masses, Jessaya thought.

"Maybe she's got a big ask this time, and she needs a bigger gesture to set the bar high. Maybe she's got something else in mind. Either way, we'll meet her tomorrow, find some way to restore the peace, and then proceed with the coronation." He turned to Gideon and put both hands on the aimea's shoulders. "Trust me, this is no cause for undue alarm."

"Highness," The Vein began. Jessaya touched his arm.

The Vein cleared his throat. "Highness has spoken. With your leave then, I'll speak to your mother in private. We'll meet again in the morning."

"As you wish, bloodpriest. Thank you for your service."

"My blood is yours," The Vein said, and Jessaya couldn't ignore the drip of insincerity in his voice.

#

Yuren could not sleep. He knew his disappointment at the coronation's postponement had annoyed his mother. He hoped his speech, supposedly meant to allay Gideon's fears about Aphora, had done its primary duty to address his mother's fear that he was power-mad and petulant. But in truth, Gideon's fears had hardened into a ball that sat in the pit of Yuren's stomach.

He pulled a fresh vial of Gideon's blood from the drawer next to his bed. The aimea was never cautious about the extraction, always putting a little extra bite into the knife across his belly or the runnel-blade into his thigh. Still, self-draws were never as potent as withdrawals. The sleep charm he could fashion from this would be effective for a mere few hours at most.

If he were to cut his aimea himself, perhaps a surprise cut while Gideon slept, it might have enough trauma in it to ensure a solid night's sleep. He rose and went into the adjacent room, pausing to collect a thin knife from the rack mounted just outside Gideon's door.

Yuren moved quietly, the night-surprise cut a practiced extirpation of power he had discovered as a boy. A meter from Gideon's simple bed roll, Yuren froze. Gideon was not asleep. He wasn't even there.

The calm silence of the palace was broken, just barely, like skin parted on the surface level by the sharpest of blades, before the blood seeps up. A scream? One of the palace hounds? A horse down in the stables? Yuren stood to his full height and took several quick steps back into his room. He put the ceremonial knife back, but exchanged it for a long dagger, curved dangerously at the end. He hefted the vial of Gideon's weak offering, considered going to the trunk to retrieve the flask of potent face-blood. He'd harvested it over a year prior, beating it out of Gideon's mouth and nose with a cudgel.

But no. The trunk was locked, the key was in the bureau, and the sample was old. He was just being paranoid. Whatever he needed, the fresh vial would suffice.

He moved toward the door, but one last wave of paranoia hit him and he stopped with his hand inches from the latch. Without a sound, he turned and slunk back to Gideon's room. He gave it another quick but thorough check. His aimea was not there, no sign of where he might have gone. *You'll find him in the privy and have a long laugh about it*, he thought as he eased through the door to the main corridor.

Notions of mirth and self-admonition for his paranoia vanished at once. A few running steps up the hall, outside his chamber door, a pair of unfamiliar brutes stood. Weapons ready, they were fixated on his room. An ambush.

All his dismissiveness of Aphora's motives, Gideon's whereabouts, and his future as Emperor washed away. It was as if a great sea surge had risen up around him and taken everything he'd worked his whole life toward, lifted it, and pulled it back into the inky depths. What he was left with were numb limbs, that hard ball of Gideon's worry in his guts, and a cold fear that made his bones feel like ice.

The brutes must have heard him moving toward the other door. Yuren risked a glance behind him to see if any others were coming, or if Gideon's body might have been hastily moved just out of sight and into the shadows where the wall sconces didn't reach. He saw only the dark corridor, a few more dots of light from braziers at the end of the hall where it intersected with another passage.

Yuren turned back to the brutes. It was only a matter of moments before one of them looked around and saw him half-in and half-out of Gideon's room. He fabricated half a plan, then stepped out, the rest of the plan snapping into place as he moved.

He stayed low and took quick steps toward the closest brute, who had his back to Gideon's door. The pad of his bare feet on stone was soft, but it attracted the attention of the soldiers.

"Uh?" the nearest one said, whirling around. Yuren took one more step, just enough for the grunt's training to kick in and for him to start a swing of his large, one-handed axe. The rise of the man's arm broadened the chest and Yuren leapt, using his forward momentum to carry him straight into the man's middle. He planted a foot on the brute's chest and kicked off, flipping himself over backward. He squeezed the vial in his hand as he did so, crushing the glass and releasing Gideon's blood. The glass sliced into his palm, the pain of it elevating the potency not only of his own blood, but the weak blood from inside the vial as well.

Yuren focused his will into this handful of plasma, felt the elements of it crystalize under his mind. His back arched as his feet flew past the ceiling, and Yuren ran his bloody hand along the shaft of his blade, smearing the liquid energy from hilt to tip and letting the sharp edge slice another cut into the pad of his thumb, giving himself a little something extra to work with. It ensured his balance would stay true, his aim would be precise, and his muscles would be strong. He landed softly, transferring the momentum of his spin into his sword arm, bringing it up from the floor to the brute's groin.

But his kick-off had staggered the large man, and the dagger would have been too short if not for the spell. Yuren bore his mind down on the gore caking the blade, and the dagger elongated even as he continued its upward arc. The first hand-height up from the groin only sliced the brute's leather breeches, opening them and exposing the man's privates. It might have been comical except that once Yuren's blade-enhancement kicked in, the sword buried itself deep into the guard's bowels, then tore upward, bisecting him clean through the ribs, the heart, the throat and up until it neatly split his brain into separate hemispheres.

Blood, rich and powerful and teeming with agony and violence sprayed everywhere, coating Yuren's face. He withdrew his sword and watched as the man's halves pried open and fell to either side like a banana skin, revealing the blood-spattered face of the second brute behind him.

Riding a blood high now, Yuren grasped the energy, dumped his rage and betrayal and fear into the screaming life blood all around him. It ignited in a purplish ball of flame and searing heat directed at the remaining guard.

When the roar of flame was gone, all that was left standing in the corridor was Yuren and a scorched bastard sword, spinning on its point before clattering to the ground. Yuren turned, focusing as best he could under the thrall of bloodmagic to think strategically. *Where have they taken Gideon?*

#

Yuren made it a few steps toward the South stairs leading down to the vaults. It was the most logical place to keep a prisoner, regardless of whether the palace had been completely overrun or had merely been infiltrated. However, Yuren knew he alone would not be able to stop a large number of enemy combatants. It pained him not to run straight to where he felt certain they were holding Gideon, but he had at least one stop to make.

He moved to the floor above and into the chamber wing. He took a side hall used almost exclusively by the serving staff and found it empty. However, the grand hall that led to the Emperor's chamber was filled with armed soldiers. He didn't see any of the palace guard, but there were a few stains on the ornate carpeting which looked fresh and told of a swift, decisive victory by the insurgents.

Cursing his choice not to retrieve the flask of powerful blood from his chest after all, Yuren stayed deep in the shadows, using a bit of blood remaining on a sliver of glass from the broken vial to further obfuscate his movement. At the far end of the dusty hall was a rarely-used serving entrance. Previous Emperors had preferred their messages and meals be delivered discreetly via the side entrance, but Jessaya liked the pomp and elegance of a visible serving staff coming through the main door.

His mother was still alive, that much was certain. Their blood-bond, renewed every year on his birthday, would have alerted him if she were in mortal peril. But that didn't mean she was safe or even unhurt.

Instead of risking the door, Yuren knelt down and ran his fingers along the wall next to the door. He found a deep groove in the stone, crusted thick with dust, thinking the tray-drop slot (for those Emperors who didn't just want discreet servants, but invisible ones) was his best bet.

As children, Yuren and Gideon had used the slot to sneak berrywine from his father's cabinet and eavesdrop on his parents as they discussed their day or debated policy decisions. They had stopped their snooping after the time they'd heard his parents' activities move from the official to the amorous.

Yuren carefully unhooked the portal and lifted it enough so that a rush of warm air came into the cool corridor from the room. He peered in.

Empress Jessaya sat in the center of the room where the great desk usually stood, bound tightly to the desk chair. His mother was naked, the ropes squeezing her flesh painfully, her efforts to move and adjust leaving cruel-looking red burns at her shoulders, wrists, thighs and midsection.

The room looked to have been tossed, almost as if someone had been looking for something in particular and didn't care what they upset or destroyed in their effort to find it.

Despite her binds and her state of undress, Jessaya was not wilted. She sat straight-backed, her regal bearing undisturbed by her undignified situation. Her eyes glared passionate rage and she wasted none of it, saving every ounce of her loathing for the two people in front of her: Jessaya's aimea, Bilbert. And Aphora.

"If you don't have it or don't know where it is, then I'm afraid you're of no further use to us," Aphora was saying.

"I am not a thing to be used," Jessaya said. Yuren recognized the calm, collected exterior that masked but somehow also highlighted the poison beneath. "I am your Empress. If you release me now and end this charade, I will grant you a swift and painless execution."

"Painless?" Bilbert asked. He seemed amused.

"Unless you would prefer otherwise," Jessaya said, eyes narrowed to serpentine slits.

"Silence," Aphora said. "You're not in the position of power here, Highness. Tell me what I want to hear or I'll start to make things really uncomfortable for you."

"I already told you, I don't have it or know anything

about it. I honestly believe it is a myth, in truth. You might as well be asking me where we keep the unicorn stable."

"Don't toy with me," Aphora said. "I know you know where it is." She leaned closer to Yuren's mother and smiled unpleasantly. "I have had a spy right under your nose for the last ten years." She gestured at Bilbert and laughed.

"A spy? Is that what you've been?" Jessaya asked Bilbert.

"I have been a loyal aimea. I have done as you have asked without question or hesitation. I have offered you council and companionship." Yuren didn't like the emphasis the aimea put on that last word. "My blood has been yours," Bilbert finished.

"Oh, it has? Well, my *loyal* aimea, let me tell you what this blood you've given so selflessly has meant to me. Nothing." Bilbert stopped and blinked. Jessaya tried to lean forward and the ropes chafed and held fast, but she did not relax. "Not only has your offering been anemic and weak, even when I've had to brutalize you to get something the least bit workable out, but it has been tainted. From the moment you split your allegiance, from the second you thought of yourself first and not me, I have known of your betrayal. You don't surprise me with your revelations and justifications. I know all about you. I let you live and I let you serve because you don't matter enough to me to care. You aren't a threat enough to me to expend the effort it would take to replace you. I am strong enough to use your pitiful blood and run this empire with or without it." She began to struggle against her bonds, as if she were trying to get her hands free so she could choke the life out of her aimea.

Yuren frowned. That wasn't right. She was undermining her point with her effort to get to Bilbert. Her words had chilled and intimidated even him, and he couldn't imagine how Bilbert must have taken them, but —

And suddenly Yuren understood. His mother's struggle was sawing the ropes against her arms and legs. The redness was scarlet now and the burns must have been agony.

But soon the blood would come.

"You have failed in your duty. You have sullied your order, and you will never be a bloodpriest again. The Vein will cleanse your power, and the Blood-Gods will curse your family for eleven generations. And I?" Jessaya strained forward one more time and Yuren saw the trickle of blood run down her arm. He smiled. He knew what was coming.

#

"I will not pause long enough to wipe you off my heel when I crush you under my bare foot," Empress Jessaya said with a cold finality.

Bilbert didn't see the rivulet of blood. He was staring at his Empress, tears staining his face, his body trembling all over. *How could she?* he thought.

"She's got blood!" Aphora shrieked, and reached to her belt to draw her sword.

It was too late.

Bilbert had taken the Empress's bullwhip when they stripped her. The whip she used exclusively on him when she needed some powerful blood. It was in his hands in a flash. The whip was leather, old and supple. Woven throughout the intricate braid were short blades, bits of coiled iron filed to points. The better to ribbon flesh. The better to draw pure, agonized blood. Bilbert knew these sharp edges. They were so intimate he had begun to think of them as friends, perhaps as lovers.

And before anyone could do anything, he lashed the whip forward and it wound its way around Jessaya's neck. It held there for one heartbeat, one frozen moment. The blades and points cut into the Empress's throat, holding her, holding the room hostage.

Then, with a tear-soaked sob, Bilbert jerked back hard on the whip and the coils tightened. Jessaya looked up into his eyes. Had she only saved one part of her pride. One flicker of remorse or sorrow. Even pity. There was nothing but contempt.

The aimea's wrist flicked, and the whip unwound in

a blur and a spray of blood.

#

Yuren scarcely had time to scream, much less react. The blood-bond sent a sickening wave of pain and heat through his body.

Even more than the bond's breakage, the shock of seeing Bilbert—Bilbert!—murder his mother nullified Yuren's mind. He could not have found the focus required to use his mother's blood on a helpful spell any more than he could have brought her back to life once the whip's savage blades got ahold of her arteries.

He felt heavy hands on his legs and back and saw the grim faces of Aphora and Bilbert turn to him as he hollered and thrashed against the soldiers who hefted him and marched him around to the main corridor and into the room. His mother's limp and undressed body still sat in the chair, slack now, but nothing so limp as her head as it lolled on the remaining gristle of her ruined throat.

The four guards held him aloft, one to each limb, while he thrashed futilely against their iron grips.

"Ah, the boy who would be Emperor," Aphora said. But there was no macabre glee in her voice. She shrank away from a once-again stoic and silent Bilbert. A distant part of Yuren's mind recognized that the interrogation of his mother had not gone according to the plan.

"You damn fool," Yuren said through gritted teeth. "Look what you've done." He thrust his chin at his mother's corpse. He tried to focus, to reach out to the lifeblood of his mother. Even if he had to bloodbomb the room with himself inside, it would be worth it. But he could find no power there.

"What difference does it make?" Aphora asked, glancing momentarily at Bilbert. "She would have been redundant in a day's time anyway. A relic of the tyrannical past. You are the true future of this empire, are you not?"

"You don't have a single clue—"

Aphora waved him off. "Spare me, Highness. I know

you, remember? I know the kinds of games you used to play in the wine cellars. I know the clefts of your body. I know how your mind works. You're a coward. A cruel coward. A cruel, brilliant, craven maman's boy. So just put your bravado down and remember you're talking to the woman who deflowered you. The one you so pitifully adored you had to strip her of power and cast her out of the palace once you understood it was possible for someone to have a will apart from your own."

Yuren stopped fighting against his captors. "Is that it? Is that what this has been about all these years? You're resentful that I made you go?"

"Banishment seems like a pretty heavy sentence for breaking your heart."

Yuren laughed. "You were banished because you were stealing palace finery and selling it finance a rebellion!"

"A truth you were more than happy to overlook so long as I was willing to share your bed."

"I didn't know where the money was going."

"Tell me, *Highness*: would it have mattered?"

Yuren stared her down. She didn't look dangerous, once you understood that her stark red hair was not flame or even hot. As a young boy he'd thought his red-haired playmate to be something unique and mystical, like a creature from his nan's storybooks. She'd laughed when he confessed that he was afraid of her hair. Now he had to admit he did still have a mad impulse to reach out and touch it now, just to see. Maybe to remember. But he knew that despite her soft, perhaps alluring appearance, she was ice and iron inside. Their banter and negotiations had been flirtatious and playful, but the substance and details were always deadly serious. She believed in her cause, in the people who called her their governess, and he knew she was not afraid to die for either.

"If I had known you were trying to start a war, yes. It would have mattered."

"Well now I've gone beyond trying, Yuri. I've started one. And, considering I have killed the Empress and captured the Emperor-in-waiting, not to mention having taken complete control of the palace, I'd say I've also won it."

"So why are you wasting time? Kill me and get on with your new empire already." The words felt satisfying to say, something bold and noble should she take the bait and kill him. But inside, Yuren quailed. His most common recurring nightmare was that he'd been re-born as an aimea, bound by duty and honor and station to be cut and bled and hurt and tortured to provide his bloodmage with all the material necessary to run the country, protect the empire, and lead the people to prosperity. He didn't pity aimea like Gideon. He was awed by them.

"Perhaps I should. But first I'm going to need something."

"My blood is yours," Yuren sneered. Another good line. Another patent lie, cresting on a swell of fear.

"Good, but I need your mind more than your blood. For the moment."

Yuren said nothing, waiting for Aphora to blink first.

"I need you to tell me where the Heart of Charopos is."

#

It took Aphora less than ten minutes to grow exasperated with Yuren's insistence that he didn't know about any mystical relic. She ordered him thrown into the oubliette.

He found himself in the dank stone hole next to a half dozen wounded palace guards. "Where's everybody else?" he asked one.

The guard only groaned, nursing a broken arm. Yuren sighed heavily and sank against the wall.

"How could this have happened?" he asked aloud.

"They had help on the inside," a familiar voice responded.

"Gideon?"

An unmoving lump in the gloomy corner coughed. Yuren fell to his aimea's side and clasped his arm.

"What happened?"

"You didn't listen," Gideon deadpanned.

Yuren could barely make him out, but there was a sticky slickness beneath his fingers. He focused and found a powerful trickle of blood covered his aimea's arm. He used it to cast a directed light spell. Gideon was far worse than he would have guessed based on the strength of his voice and the persistence of his wit. A scarcely bandaged wound in his side had soaked the rag wrapped around his middle, but it was hardly the lone serious injury. It was top-quality blood, borne of betrayal and sadism. Its presence infuriated Yuren.

"I'm sorry," Yuren said, trying to prop Gideon's head up on Yuren's rolled-up dressing gown. The dungeon pit was damp and chilled. Yuren began shivering immediately, but he ignored the discomfort. "We'll get out of here."

"No," Gideon wheezed. "I don't think we will."

"Oh come on, this is Aphora. She's misguided, maybe—" The memory of his mother crashed back. How had he forgotten? It didn't seem real, but the vision of the Empress's shredded throat was too stark and vicious to be a dream. None of it made sense. Bilbert? Murder? Betrayal? His voice faltered.

"Look, dammit," Gideon said harshly, snapping Yuren back to the moment. Yuren peered around the oubliette in the crimson glow of the bloodlight spell. Maimed and dying palace guards moaned and wept softly. There were close to two hundred guards in the palace at any given time. Represented here were less than two dozen.

"There are so few."

"They didn't take many prisoners," Gideon said bitterly.

"But why?"

"Because she's not the harmless pest you always believed her to be!" Gideon's voice rasped painfully. He choked out a few coughs but wouldn't let Yuren protest. "She's been playing a game far more dangerous and subtle than you've been willing to see or admit. Now she's stormed the palace." Gideon's eyes flashed. "Your arrogance and folly have ruined you!"

Yuren had never relished bleeding his aimea. He

knew some bloodpriests took pleasure in withdrawals; the cruelty intensified the potency. But Gideon had been his friend before he was an aimea. Normally, their sessions were distasteful necessities. In that moment, though, Yuren wanted to hurt Gideon in a way he had never before.

"You watch how you speak to me, aimea. Am I not your Emperor?" His voice had the commanding air of a ruler, the cold arrogance of power.

Gideon was unimpressed. "What about your mother?"

"Bilbert has slain the Empress."

"Then you are indeed my Emperor." Gideon made a poor attempt at a sincere bow.

Yuren felt the fire of anger inside him flash out. His shoulders sagged. "My mother is dead," he said, throat catching on a sob.

"So what are you going to do, Highness?"

Yuren looked around. Stone walls bathed red in the light of his spell. The stench of festering wounds and emptied bowels from the guards who had lost their struggle to stay alive sat at the back of his throat. The vision of his mother's body swam in every bloody shadow and the void behind his eyelids. Gideon's face shimmered as his eyes filled with tears.

"There's nothing to do," he said. "I have ruined the Empire."

"As long as you still live, the Empire can be rebuilt."

"I won't live long down here," Yuren sneered.

"Perhaps not, then." There was something in Gideon's voice Yuren didn't recognize or understand.

"What are you trying to say?"

"Highness, forgive me, but if you know who killed your mother, how were you captured?"

"Aphora wanted to know where we kept the Heart of Charopos."

"She wants to legitimize her claim to power."

"But the Heart is a myth," Yuren protested.

"It's not," Gideon said, the burble of blood in his lungs giving the words a liquid quality.

Yuren gave him a look. "You're not thinking

straight."

"Unfortunately, Highness, I am. And I can help you retrieve the heart."

"You?" Yuren said. "You can?"

Gideon nodded.

"Well then, out with it, man! I have to get to the Heart before she does. I have to stop her," Yuren said. Even as the words passed his lips, he knew they were empty. What could he possibly do about it now?

"Yes," Gideon said, "you do." He caught Yuren's eyes, those dark mysteries glazed with pain and grief. But something else in them brought Yuren up cold. "But you're going to have to kill me to do it."

#

Gideon's time was dwindling. He hadn't felt his hands and feet for half an hour. He wasn't able to regulate his temperature, swinging wildly from sweating to freezing. If Yuren stood any chance of succeeding, he would have to grow up in a hurry.

Yuren's eyes were black pools in the sanguine glow of his bloodlight. It was extraordinary how long it was lasting; Gideon's own blood that powered the spell must have been crackling with his agony—both physical and emotional. Most of his wounds had been inflicted by Bilbert. He spat a curse to the traitorous aimea's name. It came up thick with blood.

"When I was very young, just before I became aimea, The Vein gave me a very special task. I was to hide the Heart of Charopos."

"Where did you hide it?"

"Far beyond the Gundra mountains, in a cruel land known as Blight."

"Okay, so as long as it remains hidden, Aphora's rise to power can't be legitimized. Right?"

Gideon shook his head. His vision was blurring. Time to speed it up.

"Not exactly. I still live because I have not yet revealed the location of the Heart."

"I'm sorry she did this to you—"

"It wasn't Aphora."

"What?"

"The Vein pulled me from my bed. He demanded to know where I'd hidden it."

Yuren's brow creased into deep, mistrustful furrows.

"The Vein? That doesn't make sense."

"He tortured me. I think he thought I'd be loyal to his cause."

"What cause?"

"The destruction of the Empire." Gideon coughed, and took a long moment to recover from the pain that radiated from the wound in his side.

"What do I do?" Yuren asked.

"You must let me die," Gideon repeated.

"But why?"

"Because part of the protections I put in place for the Heart was that only my heartblood could be used to open the portal to the place where it's kept."

"That's not fair," Yuren said.

"Is that what you think? That life is fair? That ruling an empire is just?" Gideon leaned forward so his face was inches from the would-be Emperor's. "Is it fair that I've spent my life bleeding for you? Feeding your whims and conveniences with my agony?"

Yuren's face melted into a complicated mask. "Is that what you think? I've been unjust?"

Gideon collapsed back. "No. Yes." He sighed, and pain sliced through his guts. There was so little time. "I do not regret my duties, or my service to you, Highness." He held Yuren's gaze for a long moment. "But if you ask if I believe the institution of aimea is fundamentally flawed? Yes, Highness. Yes, I most certainly do."

Gideon, perhaps more than any other, knew what this admission might do to Yuren. Yuren's separation from Aphora was at least in part due to a philosophical disagreement about bloodprestige; about the establishment of aimea and the laws restricting use of them—of any sacrificial blood—by lower castes. Gideon had overheard their argument the night Aphora left the palace and Claretion altogether. Of all people, Gideon was supposed to believe in the necessity, the sanctity of his order. But the beautiful pattern of his scars could not hide their hideousness. Gideon pulled Yuren's arm toward him, raising the sleeve and lining his own alongside it.

"Look at our arms, Highness. I was as clean as you, once."

Yuren's arm, smooth and nearly hairless, contrasted like a baby's skin next to a grizzled war general's. The sweeping arcs of scars, many self-inflicted but most laid on him by Yuren's own hand, were supposed to be badges of honor. Gideon hoped that once his lord could see past the dogmatic symbolism and through to the ugly truth: they were wounds. Wounds endured by a love borne from vows and loyalty.

"Why didn't you say anything before?" Yuren asked, tears sliding down his cheeks.

"This is what I have offered to you. This is what you needed from me. You have not asked for my counsel, only for my blood." Gideon coughed violently and felt his heart stop for a moment, only to resume reluctantly with a painful sputter. "But now I offer both to you, unsolicited."

"But—" Yuren began. Gideon cut him off with a raised finger.

"No. You must use my blood. Find the Heart of Charopos." Gideon reached into his tattered breeches and found the hidden seam inside the waistband. He slid his tiny reserve dagger free; a trick some of the newer aimea had taken to as a failsafe in case they were ever called upon for blood in a time of great need. *If ever a need there was*, Gideon thought.

He raised the small blade. "I do this for duty," he said through clenched teeth. The effort of holding the little dagger aloft made his arms tremble. "I do this for love." He looked Yuren in the eyes. "My blood—my life—is yours."

He let the dagger drop.

#

The blood that flowed from Gideon's mortal, self-inflicted

wound, crackled with power. Yuren staggered backward from his aimea's side, momentarily stunned by its potency. He readily admitted to being a middling bloodmage. But the potential trapped inside the heartblood leaking onto the cold stone floor sent his mind reeling with possibilities.

He reached out an experimental hand and dabbed a finger into the growing pool under Gideon's body. He closed his hand into a loose fist and waved it over the wounded guards. Gasps of sudden consciousness regained, of abruptly alleviated pain, of surprise relief filled the small chamber.

The sacrifice at the heart of Gideon's final act, the pain leading up to it, the depth of his devotion to and belief in his... friend? Emperor-to-be? Bloodmage? Yuren would have to ponder exactly what state of mind and circumstance could have led to blood this powerful. In the meantime, he would accept its gift and use it to right his wrongs. For his empire's sake. For his mother.

For Gideon.

"Those who can stand and move, I'm going to open a portal to the Eastern outpost," Yuren said in a clear voice. "I want you to go there, get medical help if you need it, and find someone loyal as soon as possible."

"Loyal to what, Highness?" said a youthful guard who was experimentally flexing a hand that had previously been crushed.

"The Empire," Yuren said.

"Yes, my liege."

Yuren paused and waited until the young guard looked him in the eye.

"You'll probably want to look away for this," Yuren said.

The work was ghastly, and undignified, but necessary. When he was finished, Yuren set the three pieces of Gideon's heart in a neat line on the floor next to Gideon's desecrated body. He'd wait for the final step until the soldiers were gone.

The pieces were not uniform. One was much smaller than the other two, and Yuren picked up this smaller piece, his head buzzing from the throbbing pulse of potential within it. He channeled his will, not typically a considerable thing. But in this case, it felt easier and far more natural than he was accustomed to. *No wonder The Vein radiates that aura all the time*, he thought.

And what of The Vein?

He pushed the question from his mind. He had tasks to perform, and a diminishing amount of time to complete them. Using the might of Gideon's blood soaking through the thick bit of heart muscle, he spun his arm in a wide arc and cut a hole in the air. The portal sprang into being more readily than even a simple bloodlight.

"Go. Now," Yuren barked, tossing the small bit of his aimea's heart through the portal to lock it open until he allowed it to close. In turn, the guards stepped through the portal until only the youthful one remained. Yuren caught his arm and leaned in close.

"Tell them what has happened here. And tell them The Vein is not to be trusted."

The guard nodded once and snapped his heels together before stepping through. Yuren allowed the portal to close, surprised to find himself no more taxed than if he'd heated his bathwater with a pinch of blood from a months old vial.

He hefted one of the remaining portions of Gideon's heart and traced a new circle in the still, dank air of the dungeon. A fresh portal sprang into being, and Yuren looked through. The sight beyond the gate he'd made sent a shiver down his spine, but he had one last thing to do before he had to go through.

Kneeling down, he reached into the ruined cavity of Gideon's chest and pulled up a palmful of the aimea's blood. It was tacky already, thick and syrupy, barely warmer than the room. Even still, it pulsed with primal strength. With a deep breath and a quick mind-clearing exercise his teacher had shown him, he centered himself and brought his hand to his mouth.

#

Blight stretched on forever, the cursed landscape spotted by bone trees, stripped of leaves and any sign of life, if they had ever borne it. Dull gray dust and colorless rocks filled the nothing between the skeletal trunks. Yuren doubted the land had ever been anything but dismal and oppressive. It might have crushed his spirit, were he not still buzzing from the taste of Gideon's final gift.

He made a slow turn, surveying the sameness of the landscape in all directions. Hadn't Gideon said the portal from his heartblood would lead to the Heart of Charopos? If so, putting the heart in the middle of the desert was a risky choice of hiding place. He didn't know if he needed to walk in a specific direction, or start digging, or cast a specific spell.

"Damn you!" he screamed, listening to the sound of his voice fall on the featureless landscape like a grain of sand dropped into tall grass.

"Damn me?" came a grating voice. Yuren started and spun around. A strange shape moved slowly toward him from the South. He would have sworn on his own blood there had been no one there only a moment before. "What did I do to deserve your damnation?"

"Who are you?"

The figure let out a low chuckle and Yuren relaxed a little. Some old fool on a long journey. "I'm just a courier, lad. No one to be afraid of."

"Who said I was afraid?"

"It's written on your face."

Yuren shielded his eyes to get a better look at the approaching stranger.

"I'm looking for something. It's supposed to be hidden around here."

The figure finally drew close enough to make out. Or as much as was possible. It was upright and unhorsed, clad in a thick robe and hood, face hidden well back in the shadows. The hands and feet were wrapped with dusty gauze, clutching a long walking-stick. The figure carried no pack or water skin.

"Pretty poor hiding spot," the figure said, looking around.

Yuren nodded. "Still, it is supposed to be here." He paused for a split second then added, "What did you say your name was?"

The figure stopped and seemed to regard him for a long moment.

"Oh, sorry," Yuren said. He stepped forward and reached out a hand. "I'm Yuren." Then hopefully, "And you are?"

"I have many names. The most common of them is Aldor."

"All right, Aldor, well met." Aldor took his hand and shook it once. "You said you were a courier?"

"That I am."

"And what are you delivering, if you don't mind my asking?"

Aldor paused and Yuren had the distinct impression there was a smile spreading across the shadow-covered face.

"A gift for the new Emperor."

Yuren's heart slammed in his chest. "A gift?" He took a half step back as Aldor moved a bit closer. "Wait. What are some of your other names?"

Aldor reached up and threw his hood back, revealing a face that was not dark like Yuren's, but black —pure black like the midnight sky. The eyes were pale green and seemed to glow in the hard light of dawn. Its teeth were pointed and yellow, showing through an intimidating grin.

"Perhaps you've heard a less common, but far more famous one. They call me Charopos."

#

Yuren drew his hands apart, fingers pinched, pulling hard on the rapidly emptying reservoir of Gideon's bloodprestige. A bloodblade materialized in the space where his fingers passed.

Charopos grinned and lunged at Yuren.

"How convenient that you're here," Charopos said, dodging a thrust from the blade, "I was just on my way to see you."

"Why? You want me dead as well?"

Charopos laughed. "I don't care about you, mortal. But I made a deal and I received the message. I tried to use the passage the bloodbag set up, but it was blocked. I guess you're more eager than I am."

Charopos swung a clawed paw at the human, who danced aside, powered by magic.

"Bloodbag? Who is 'the bloodbag'?"

"You call them aimea. The bleeding ones."

"Gideon?"

Charopos shrugged and sidestepped another swipe from Yuren's weapon. "I don't bother with your names, pest. But I was summoned from my long sleep to bring my Heart to the palace. As agreed upon many years ago."

"What passage?"

"The bloodbag had arranged a conduit from my realm to his. But when I went to use it, I found it impassable. Some foul prestige had corrupted it."

"If you were bringing the heart and were meant to be there yesterday for the coronation, why not just give it to me now?"

"My bargain is not with you, power-seeker. I serve only the bleeding one."

Yuren's demeanor shifted.

"Well the one you dealt with is dead. Betrayed."

"Then my work here is complete," Charopos said, its dry voice thinning out until it sounded like the rustle of fallen leaves. It caught Yuren by the wrist when his next swing went a bit wild. Charopos raised a foot and kicked out as hard as it could against Yuren's chest.

Its grip on the arm never faltered. The kick was so powerful the body of the Emperor-boy flew back and a squeal of bone and spray of blood left Charopos with a bloody arm in its claw and a fading bloodblade slipping from the limp grip.

Yuren looked at the ruined mess of his shoulder and screamed.

Charopos felt the anguish and pain and it filled the crystal lump on the chain around its neck with prestige of a less messy sort. The kind only harvestable by immortal daemons, such as itself. Charopos laughed. Humans were so much fun. It would have to be sure to visit a few outer villages before it returned to the veilrealm.

Charopos's laughter was cut abruptly short. It

looked down and saw the one-armed human clutching the Heart—its Heart—in the one remaining fist.

"How dare—" Charopos began, but Yuren didn't hesitate.

"You will honor your deal, daemon. For the blood of Gideon now courses through my veins. His blood is mine, and my blood is his." Yuren's words came through clenched teeth as he drained his well of considerable power to keep himself conscious.

"GiVe It BaCk!" Charopos squealed, its daemonic voice and language slipping through.

"No, I don't think I will," Yuren said, his face ashen and pinched, but his voice clear and firm. With a slight hesitation due to the awkward off-hand movement, he withdrew the remaining piece of Gideon's heart from a satchel and focused on it. He spun his arm in a high arc and Charopos pounced.

Halfway through its leap, the portal opened where the daemon was passing.

Charopos hit the dusty ground and tried to scramble to its feet. Human language had abandoned it and curses more ancient than the oceans spilled from its lips. It looked down and saw nothing where its cloven hooves should be. A portal to a verdant countryside stood just below Charopos's ribs. Black ichor pooled under the daemon's body where it had been cleaved neatly in half.

Charopos shrieked in agonized fury and tried to drag itself toward the smug human. Vile threats spilled from it, but Yuren couldn't understand and was unfazed. He stepped over the half-corpse of Charopos, dancing neatly away from its rending claws.

"If you'll excuse me," Yuren said as he stepped through the portal, "I have Imperial business to attend to. If you survive, and I hope you do not, I suggest you crawl back to your realm and stay there." He paused on the other side of the passage, where his voice was gauzy and distant. "I wouldn't want to see what happens to you if our paths cross again."

And with that, the portal closed.

#

Yuren had opened the portal deep into Aphora's camp, nearly on top of the rear guard but just behind the command tent. It was still early dawn, and the posted guards were meant to watch for threats coming from outside the camp. There was no one to watch if someone came, alone, in the middle of the fortification.

Yuren knew how risky his move was. He was out of portal-making talismans and the palmful of Gideon's blood was almost exhausted. He had used nearly all of it to recover after the grievous wound Charopos had inflicted.

But, as one point in his favor, he now had the Heart. He didn't know exactly what role it played in the coronation or what power it might hold. But Gideon had sacrificed his life so he could get it, and Bilbert had killed his mother trying to discover it. Perhaps he could find a way to leverage it to his advantage after all.

First, he had to confirm one thing.

He kept low as he approached the command tent. The rear of it was unguarded, but he suspected there would be at least half a dozen skilled fighters inside. He didn't want to think about how much worse it could be.

His missing arm was burning, as if a ghost of the limb were still attached and had been set afire. He couldn't afford to use any of his remaining heartblood to salve the wound or ease the pain. Instead, he took a deep breath and focused on it. The pain, the fear of a life without one of his limbs—his hand! his sword arm!—he let it wash over him in a cascade of panic and agony.

It centered him. There, in the calm eye of the storm of his sensations and emotions he reached for the last of Gideon's sacrifice and cast one final spell.

The command tent collapsed. The poles simply vanished, and the canvas flopped down, covering those inside. As predicted, the unexpected nature of the sabotage sent the guards inside into a frenzy. They panicked and lashed out, drawing weapons, sawing at the tent sides, shouting at each other, trying in vain to raise the alarm with no information. The canvas settled onto a brazier near the entrance. Because the rebellion was not royalty, it was filled with woodfire, not bloodfire. The tent began to burn, and the surprised and upset shouting turned to screams of fear and pain.

A guard crawled on his belly out of the back of the tent and looked up into Yuren's face.

"Oh," the guard said, "sh—"

Yuren stomped on the guard twice, and his body went limp. Yuren pulled the sword from the unconscious man's belt and moved slowly toward the front of the collapsed tent. Another guard staggered out, part of his raiment aflame. He was squealing like a boar in a legwire and batting at the flames. Yuren spiked the sword into the soft dewy ground and picked up a pitcher of water on the outdoor serving table. He upended it over the guard and the flames went out with a hiss. The guard looked up appreciatively but his expression froze when he saw who had saved him.

Yuren smashed the pottery over the man's skull and retrieved the sword. Two down.

The flames and smoke and shouts were drawing attention now, so Yuren knew his time was short. No more delay. He used a small bit of the blood trickling from beneath the brained guard's hair to cast a levitation spell and lifted the flaming tent off the remaining occupants as they scrambled for a second or two out of habit.

He quickly counted five remaining people thrashing about on the dirt floor that had been beneath the tent. Two of them—armed soldiers suffering from smoke inhalation and panic—took the opportunity to flee as soon as they realized they were no longer trapped.

That left three remaining. When Yuren saw the pale skin and soiled loincloths, he knew who the third would be without even looking.

"The one who got away," The Vein said as he stood and brushed the dust away from his white robe, brown streaks of dried blood ever-present.

Gideon's words echoed in Yuren's memory. *They had help on the inside.*

"So you're with the rebellion," Yuren asked.

"More like an alliance of aligned need."

"And what could you need, priest? Even more power? The Emperorship itself?"

The Vein scoffed. "Nothing so mundane. I believe in the Empire, unlike our mutual friend." He turned his scarred head as if he could hear something outside the range of Yuren's hearing. "Ah, here she comes now."

One of the cultists stepped forward and presented an upturned arm. The Vein grasped it and pulled a razor from a fold in his robe, running it quickly from wrist to elbow and up to the shoulder. The cut was deep and laid open muscle, arteries, and tendons. The cultist didn't even grimace, only rolled her eyes back and swayed slightly. The Vein whipped the blade in a wide circle, blood splashing in an arc, and a weak bloodportal opened just long enough for a familiar figure to stride through.

"Aphora," The Vein said with a cruel grin. He pushed the cultist woman back, and she staggered off toward the chaos of the camp, which still did not seem to understand the threat in its midst.

The ex-priestess looked around and fixed her stare on Yuren.

"That was an interesting trick back there in the pits."

"And how did our young would-be ruler escape your grasp, general?" The Vein spat the honorary title as if it were some sort of private jest.

"It was the Heart-keeper. His aimea. The one you said would grant us aid. 'Readily,' I believe was your word."

The Vein stared at Aphora for a moment, then turned his full attention back to Yuren.

"Well," he said, wiping the blade he'd used to summon Aphora and gesturing to the remaining cultist, "it looks like our misguided friend's efforts were in vain." He chuckled as though he'd told a subtle joke. "Our Emperor-to-be can barely stand up."

It was true. Yuren's loss of blood and the shock of the wound Charopos had inflicted were making him woozy. The convergence of betrayal from The Vein and the depth of Aphora's machinations to take his title were overwhelming his foggy mind.

"Then finish him off and let's get back to the palace."

"Patience," The Vein purred, "with the Heart-keeper's unreliable allegiance, we need to know if we can still recover the Heart of Charopos."

"For blood's sake, will you forget that foolish trinket?" Aphora shouted, startling both Yuren and The Vein. "The Empress is dead; her son is mortally wounded; the palace is ours and the militia is primed to surrender. The Heart doesn't matter."

"Are you truly so daft?" The Vein snapped. "What is it you think establishes and perpetuates the Imperial order? Do you think I would need your help to conquer Claretion if it were just a bauble? Me? With all the power at my command?"

"You said you needed my expertise..." Aphora looked shaken. This was good. Infighting gave Yuren a window of opportunity. He inhaled sharply, prepared for one desperate strike. He could take one of them if he acted quickly. But which? The Vein was clearly the greater threat; he was the most powerful bloodmage in the land, by definition and title. But he had been a loyal subject. Perhaps Jessaya and The Vein had not always agreed on all matters of state—and why would they? The bloodprestige's priorities didn't necessarily align with the Empire's. But they'd had a working relationship. Perhaps that could be re-established... once Aphora and her armies were no longer a factor.

It was a risk, but it was worthwhile.

Yuren lunged at the ex-priestess. His motion caught them off guard, and his sword found its mark, piercing the weak spot in her armor just above the hip. He leaned his weight against it and the sword punctured her body. *Perhaps I can use this blood to subdue The Vein*, Yuren thought. Aphora's scream suggested a potency of her blood similar to that of Gideon's. *I can't get used to this, though,* he thought. He would not allow himself to become a murderous blackprestige by matter of habit. The Empire had weathered enough of those in its long and turbulent history.

Yuren looked up into Aphora's face. "I'm sorry," he wheezed, pushing against the sword hilt with his one remaining arm. "But this is the price for treason."

Aphora's face twitched into a cold rictus. Her eyes glazed over. Yuren reached out to tap the blood he'd spilled, hoping to direct a desperate binding against The Vein. Maybe he could find enough power to escape with his captive and restore order. But the well of power he expected to find was empty. It was like stepping up the top stair only to find he'd miscounted and his foot was stepping onto open air.

A cold, dry laughter started low and grew behind him. Yuren looked down at the sword thrust through Aphora's side. Instead of the gory wound leaking jugs of blood, the sword penetrated the flesh with no more substance than a cadaver's.

"What?" Yuren asked stupidly. The Vein's laughter grew.

"I don't know what's better," the high bloodpriest said, moving closer to Yuren's back, "that you thought you could defeat me, or that you dispatched my puppet for me in an effort to do so."

"What did you do to her?"

"I didn't do anything to her. She came to me begging for it. She gave her life willingly to become a phantasm. She was a *believer*."

"In what? In you?"

"Oh, it had nothing to do with me. She believed in the complete dissolution of the Empire. In the ruination of bloodprestige's caste system. She believed in ridding the world, specifically, of *you*."

Yuren looked into Aphora's glassy stare. She could have been made of wax. Is that what she had become? Is that what he had created?

"You stripped her of her power, boy. You broke her heart and took her station, cast her out and made the most dangerous of enemies."

"I'm sorry," Yuren said to Aphora's corpse. He meant it.

The Vein was close behind him. The rest of the camp had finally realized what was happening and they were converging. Yuren felt if it weren't for his missing arm and the untreated wound left where it had once been, he would have been petrified at the prospect of his impending death. As weak as he was, though, he nearly welcomed it.

The Vein leaned forward and whispered into his ear, "I ought to thank you. But instead, I'll just end you."

Yuren heard the slick ripping sound of the high bloodpriest's blade parting the skin of his remaining cultist. He could smell the blood, feel the distant power pulsing, knew what it meant for him.

The Vein uttered a forbidden curse. A death curse. The cultist must have died, but he had done so silently without protest or even a groan. The strength of the spell slammed into Yuren and threw him clear of Aphora. It didn't hurt any worse than Yuren already felt. He was glad about that.

He didn't know how many seconds passed before he experimentally opened his eyes. He wasn't sure what to expect, exactly. Blinding red light, perhaps. The faded forms of his lost family members. Jessaya, he hoped, or perhaps his father.

Instead, he saw the gathering crowd of Aphora's troops coming out of their tents, investigating the ruckus.

"What? How?" The Vein's words mirrored Yuren's own thoughts. He did a quick inventory. Heart beating. Breath moving in and out of his lungs. Arm still missing, shoulder alternating between burning, stinging, aching, buzzing, and numbness in the same instant. He could still smell, see, hear, feel, even taste the earthy tang of dust in his mouth.

Yuren rolled over and saw The Vein approaching, rage flashing in his eyes. "This is not possible!" the priest roared. "You would have to be protected—"

And suddenly Yuren understood. He pushed himself into a sitting position and fished the small stone on a chain from inside his tunic. The Heart of Charopos. The ultimate check to the prestige's power. Immunity from The Vein's mysticism. The morning sun caught the unassuming gem and The Vein stopped in mid-stride.

"Give that to me," he hissed.

"You know I won't."

"You have no idea what to do with it. It won't protect you forever."

"No," Yuren said, "you're right. It won't. But it's already done enough."

Yuren steeled himself for a short second and then reached up and jammed his right fist into the gory socket that once held his arm in place. He pulled from the power of his own blood. He felt the wound twitch and collapse, the intrusion of his hand ruining any chances for the prestige-healers to restore his arm. It didn't matter.

The binding spell he created from the pain and violence of his spilled blood whipped around The Vein, and Yuren felt certain his mother would approve of the symmetry between her demise and The Vein's capture. He yanked his remaining hand free and conjured a portal right behind the traitorous high priest. On the other side of the portal he could see the oubliette's interior. Gideon's body still lay in the dark corner.

"We'll talk again soon," Yuren said and planted a hard kick into The Vein's chest. The priest staggered back, hampered by his magical bindings, and fell hard on his back onto the stone floor. He tried to cry out but Yuren snapped the portal shut, cutting off the sound as if he'd snipped it with shears.

He turned to face the camp. They were rebels. They were an invading force. But they were also his people. Or at least they were meant to be.

He pulled the Heart of Charopos up over his head and held it aloft.

"Hail, hardy folk of the North. Followers of General Aphora. This stone is the protecting force of the Empire. While I hold it, I cannot be harmed by stone or spell." He paused and looked at their faces, cold with fear and mistrust, the battle of their preconceptions and their observations plain on each feature.

With a strong motion, Yuren swung the Heart of Charopos to the ground and dashed it against a stone. It shattered into a hundred pieces, and Yuren immediately felt its absence. The blanket of serenity he'd never even noticed followed him around like a piece of jewelry rendered invisible by years of wear vanished. His first instinct was to turn and flee. He was facing an army, alone, and he'd just given up his only means of protection.

Instead he eased himself down awkwardly onto a rock. "Now, I am unguarded. I am at your mercy. You may attack. You may strike me down. You may torture or kill me, as you choose."

He sniffled and smiled warmly at the nearest trooper. "Or, you may ask me your questions. And tell me your stories. And I will listen. I will answer. I will do better. Or I will do nothing at all.

"But I will make you one promise. From now on, I will no longer hear the oath of the aimea directed at me. From this day forward, *my* blood is *yours*."

There was a long moment where the gathered soldiers did not move. They stared at him, or turned eyes to the side to catch each other's gaze. And then, slowly at first, they began to move toward him, their eyes full of suspicion, but tinged with hope.

###

About the author

Paul A. Hamilton is a writer, editor, and engineer living in Northern California with his wife and two daughters. His stories feature broken people, reassembled worlds, beautiful monsters, and hideous love. He gets his inspiration by impersonating an old-timey bartender, listening to stories told by lonely strangers. When not writing, he can be found reading, drawing, taking photographs, or riding roller coasters. More from him can be found at ironsoap.com, and @ironsoap.

Child of Flowers

Sean Robinson

There were a thousand seasons in the rose-city of Velinar. For planting the bulbs and trimming the hedges, for sharpening the blackthorn, and celebrating the fall of quince petals. For mulching mansion-beds, and spinning butter cups into thread, and weaving of rose canes for boning, and making aster gowns for Summerfinding. On and on and on as the city grew and bloomed and stretched ever-closer to the sun.

Across the Velinar, men and women, gardeners and shop boys, fragile blooms and deep-rooted lords made ready. Summerfinding had come to the city and the streets were alive: with music, with dancing, and the fall of petals from the mansions—the softest rain in the world.

At the heart of the city, where the thorn walls rose in the labyrinth core of Velinar, a girl waited at the edge of womanhood. She wore a gown as fine as any other, and she held her breath as any might. This Summerfinding was different for her and she watched the people of Velinar gather, leave their homes and their shops, and dance their way up the Street of Foxgloves, across the Bridge of Peonies, winding their way through the Orchid Markets, up and up and up. Coming to see Velinar's newest daughter.

She was pale, like wisteria. The skin of her hands

faded to indigo, as if her fingers had been stained. Her hair was done up, and her gown was stitched hyacinth, purple and blooming and lovely. But she did not feel lovely. Her name was Berai and she watched the city gather at the base of her father's palace and then push forward through the open gates.

"I'm scared," she said, laying a hand on the wall; careful not to crush the blooming irises. They had been her mother's flower, but even the scent of them was not enough to chase away the terror in her gut.

"All will be fine," said Doaine. The man was her oldest friend—companion and caretaker and keeper of Berai's secrets. Even after the many years of friendship between them, Berai didn't believe him.

He leaned out the window. "Lots of people today."

A cheer came up from the crowd below. No one else in Velinar would wear an overcoat of laurel flowers, blooms out of season. It matched the paleness of Doaine's skin and the color of his eyes.

The cheering continued. Summerfinding was a holiday overseen by the greatest in the city. Three people made up the pantheon that ruled Velinar—king, phoenix, and unicorn. Berai's father was king. Doaine was phoenix, and to see him from the window made the crowd roar.

"Show-off," Berai said.

The man shrugged his shoulders and smiled. "They're good people. If waving from the topmost turret makes their days a little brighter, why not?"

The girl in her hyacinth gown held her thoughts to herself, but smiled. Doaine could claim altruism and public good all he wanted, but she knew well enough that the vain bird liked the cheering and the waving. He had been a good friend to her for a long time. And nothing she said would change the fact that Berai wanted to run screaming from the tower, through the streets and not return for at least a decade. Maybe a century.

She had watched Summerfinding year after year. She'd watched her father take his throne, blanked by Doaine and Shanna: phoenix and unicorn. Had heard the call for the turning of the seasons. Watched with everyone else as magic lit up the palace, crawled its way along the streets, and set Velinar flowering again. It was beautiful every time.

But this time, Summerfinding would mean crossing the threshold from childhood into adulthood. Girlhood to womanhood. She shuddered. On the great lawn that was her father's throne room, she would stand and declare herself a child of Velinar. She would be named heir to the city and her magic would join her father's and the rest of the city—a flower of her choosing to weave its way through the rose-mansions and bloom houses and seed shops.

She touched the iris that had been her mother's addition, on the day she married the king. The iris was all that remained of Imelda Rosewarden. She was dead and gone to dust. It had left Berai's father alone and quiet on the throne, with an infant Berai to grow up in the shadow of her mother's loss.

Doaine was watching her. "Ready?"

No. No. She was not. She was not ready at all. And the truth of that made her heart ache.

"Yes," she said. Berai gathered a handful of the dress her father had had made for her. She eyed the window and the space beyond the city, where roads and other places waited. Places where she would not be bound to buildings and people and Velinar. Where she could be something other than Princess Berai.

Instead, she left the tower room, the city's phoenix still watching her with eyes that saw too much.

#

Velinar was an old city. It had grown where the Ossean Way curled south toward the caravanserai at the heart of the Rigel Plains. The people that settled there had been flower-makers from Marad Tir and if another city might have had battlements of stone and timber, Velinar's were made from withies and nettles. It had had many kings, and many queens—each called the Rosewarden. And if its phoenix was young, that was fine, the city's roots were deep. And if its unicorn had gone East—that had happened before. Another would come someday.

Berai had learned all these things as she learned her letters, and the many seasons of the city. The only thought in her head as she descended the stairs to the great court was that she did not think she could do it. She knew how. Knew the magic beneath her skin and how to send it out like a root, or stem, or a flower. When it was over, her roots would keep her in the city, next in line to be the Rosewarden. And with the roots, every child and man and woman now clustered along the lawn would know her, see her. And any hope she had of finding new roots, a new place to shine, would be over.

Berai would be the newest topiary in the most beautiful city in the world.

Her father sat on his throne. His eyes were black hellebores, with a spray of white at their center. He wore hyacinths as well, and his pale lips curled up into a smile as his daughter descended the stairs. The cheer that rose up from the throats of the gathered people was louder than any cheer before it. The city had loved Imelda and it loved the Rosewarden. It had watched Berai grow to this moment—they cheered.

The crowd cleared a path for her. The grass was soft and thick no matter how many feet trampled it, and when Berai stood, knees shaking beneath her hyacinth gown, before the dais and the throne, they watched in careful excitement.

The Rosewarden stood. Doaine a step behind the throne. Space open for the missing unicorn, the pantheon of Velinar watching.

"Who comes before the throne?" the Rosewarden asked.

"I do," Berai said. Her heart beat too fast. Could she? Could she really do it? And what was the thing she would do? Her feet begged her to run, her fists dug into her gown, crushing one of the flowers.

Her father smiled. "Why do you come?"

"To cross the threshold," she said. "I am Berai Rosewarden and I—"

She stumbled. She'd practiced the words for months. Doaine had quizzed her until she dreamed about the words. The action, the magic that would follow. She'd watched the palace kitchens prepare the feast that would follow and had let herself imagine the dancing to be her reward for all of it.

But the words didn't come. For a breath, then two, then more. Until her father's smile faltered, until the phoenix stepped forward. Until Berai opened her mouth to speak.

But the silence was broken first.

"I hope I'm not interrupting."

#

The eyes of every person on the lawn moved to the sound of that voice. It was throaty and dark and burned like nettles. Even Berai, who had stared into her father's face, hoping he would understand, looked behind her.

She wore red the color of poppies. Her skin was pale, as though it had never seen the sun. Her hair was the red of daylilies at sunset, and her lips were stained like pomegranates. And no one was brave or foolish enough to stand between her and the dais. As the crowd parted, it stared. The woman was a stranger but a few— the most travelled—began to murmur.

Hadn't there been a story, once? Hadn't there been a rumor? It was said that there was a queen all in red. How had the song gone? And a few more fled, because there had been talk on the trade roads of an army growing in the north. One lead by a woman who painted herself with heartsblood.

The Rosewarden was not a hard man. But the city was his and he glared at the newcomer. "You are unwelcome here, stranger."

She smiled, and it was beautiful and terrible. Berai found herself backing away, making space for the woman and her father. It was a reprieve from having to face that she wasn't ready to grow roots beside her father. But there was a new type of fear growing in her stomach.

"I have come to make new friends," the red-gowned woman said. "I am called Althair."

The whispers in the crowd said echoed the name.

Althair. Althair the Red. A Queen of Orissa. The one cast out. The crowd began to thin. Summerfinding and the Rosewarden's daughter would not keep them safe when war came. And for those who knew best, they knew that Velinar was no safe place anymore.

"I know you," the king said. "Althair. You think the city does not know you? Cannot feel the blood on your hands? Get out," the king said. Doaine flanked him, and Berai could see the magic growing between them. King to phoenix to city.

Althair smiled. "That is hardly being friendly. I've just come to make a deal."

There was silence.

"I am looking for a seed. Surely in the rose city of Velinar I might find a single seed?"

"Out, witch," the Rosewarden roared. The gathering screamed as the ground erupted and vines poured out from the earth. Each was taller than the tallest building in the city, thicker than a person was. Each was studded with thorns like swords. They curled and swung toward the woman in red.

But rather than cut her to pieces, they stopped short. "That is no way to treat a guest."

There was a flash of crimson light and the vines crumbled. The palace walls died, as if they had been brushed by winter. Berai felt the flowers die, and screamed. The Rosewarden screamed too, and what little was left of the once-happy crowd stampeded into the streets, until there was only Althair, Berai, her father, and Doaine.

Fire came next, because even though the phoenix was wrapped in the blossoms of laurel, he was a creature of flame. Berai's oldest friend opened his mouth and the sound that came out was the cry of the tiercel. The blast that followed set the girl back on her heels, tripping over the hem of her gown. But the fire didn't touch Althair the Red. It split around her and engulfed the dying rose-mansion.

"Apparently there isn't much courtesy around here. I'm very disappointed. I came to trade fairly, and here I am, attacked. Give me the seed I've come for,

Rosewarden, and I will leave you unharmed. It would be a shame for your daughter—"

She turned her eyes to look at Berai. And paused, as if what she saw within Berai made her laugh.

"Oh, poor Papa," she said. "Give me the seed and you can talk to your child and learn their truth. It is a gift I was never given, and never let it be said that the Queen does not have at least some sense of propriety."

"You are not the queen here," the Rosewarden said. His daughter watched the magic gather in him again. "You will never be queen here."

Althair sighed, as though she were confronted with a child who refused to do his chores. Or a servant who did not understand a command. She raised her hand, palm toward the Rosewarden. The man who had buried his beloved Imelda, who had woken in the morning with joy in his heart, because his daughter was everything he had ever wanted in a child. Althair's hand rose, and Althair's magic rose. And like the walls, like the vines, the Rosewarden's hellebore eyes turned brown, withering. His face went next, like flowers left too long in the sun.

Berai couldn't find the air to scream as she watched her father wither, turn brown, and die. The wind took what was left and scattered him as though he had never been.

#

The world slowed. Berai ran forward, toward the red queen. There was death in her heart. Her own, or Althair's, or the worlds. Between one breath and the next her life shattered.

But Doaine was there. Her oldest friend, her father's companion pushed her back, fingers like talons on her wrist.

Althair the Red turned her smile to Berai. "Now. Perhaps with a change in leadership, I might get better service. I have come to your little corner of the world in search of a seed. It's a very special seed. A magical seed. I want it. You will give it to me, you will be queen or king or anchoress or pope or chatelaine or whatever you choose to be. Wear a gown of ivy, or a doublet of sunflowers. A skirt, trews. Style yourself how you want, sweet child. Be the true version of yourself. Once I have the seed. It is the greatest gift anyone will ever give you."

Too many thoughts went through Berai's head. Her father had just...crumpled...withered. Like he was not the man who had sung her lullabyes and taught her how to plant tulips and took her across the city. He was her Papa and he was gone.

"Run," Doaine hissed. His laurel flowers were crushed and falling. The blight on the walls was spreading. The petals and leaves were falling, and Berai's father was dead. It was Summerfinding and it was supposed to be a day of celebration. "Run."

Berai did not want to run, but did. There was another gout of fire, another scream from the phoenix, another flash of light the color of blood. The stairs that had been so terribly long sped by in a flash. Berai went down a hallway blooming with buttercups, skirted a stairway that lead to the lowest depths of the palace and paused.

The Rosewarden was dead. The Rosewarden was dead. And a worse thought followed. Berai was the Rosewarden. The city needed a ruler and Berai was it. A scream started to form, but was broken by the sound of footsteps. Not Berai's father's, or Doaine who walked on soft feet. There was a click, click, click. Wooden soles on the floor.

"Seven Queens to Orissa came. Indigo and blue, yellow and green, blue and purple, and red," Althair sang. "I've never been truly happy with that song, child. Now where did you go?"

Berai ran down the stairs, bare feet making no sound.

But the clicking followed.

"I see you," the Red Queen said. "I *saved* you. Your father died never knowing the truth about you. That you weren't the pretty princess he thought you were. Wanted you to be. You'll never have to tell him. Never have to explain that in your heart of hearts, you aren't a princess. That you are something both and neither."

It was the closest secret Berai held. She stopped and leaned against one of the walls. She needed to hide, she needed to think. Her father was dead and the woman who did it knew what she had only told Doaine.

That her father had mourned her mother's loss and raised Berai to be the Princess, Daughter of the Rosewarden, Heir to Velinar. Dressed her in gowns and taught her the history of the city. Introduced her as the Rosewarden's daughter. To the saffron weavers, and the withy spinners, and the gardeners of aster and poppy and lilac.

Something both and neither.

Althair's face was beautiful and Berai had stopped running, caught on a landing, surrounded by flowers. For a moment, Berai thought to fight. It would be a small magic to bring the plants to life, to cut and bind and smother. Another thought, that the Rosewarden was dead and his great magics weren't enough to stop this interloper.

"Why?" Berai asked. "Why are you here? What did we do to you?"

"Do?" she smiled. "Nothing, sweetling. But once upon a long ago the very first Rosewarden came to this little stop on the trade roads and set down roots. Made a whole garden. I want the seed, sweet child. Now be good and fetch it for me."

"I don't—"Berai stammered, "I don't know—"

Althair, who had been a queen once, and who had slain the Rosewarden with barely a gesture, looked at Berai. The hyacinth gown was crushed, Berai's pale skin shaded at the fingers. The queen stepped forward, but a noise echoed through the halls.

It was Doaine. Screaming.

"Ah," she said. "It sounds as if my entertainment is ready. Bring me the seed and I will leave you to your roses, or your roads. Fail me, and I will be forced to be less respectful a guest."

"Leave him alone!" Berai screamed. But didn't dare magic. Didn't dare strike the woman in her red gown and red hair. Berai watched Althair walk away and felt herself go limp. She fell to the floor. Helpless.

#

The first Rosewarden had been Tisa. And in the way of all heroes, she left the city of Ias with nothing but the clothes on her back, and the magic of growing things in her fingertips. The line she planted had grown over the generations to Berai Rosewarden, whose father was dead, whose mother was dead, whose world had ended.

The would-be princess who was, at their heart, not a princess. Or a prince. Just Berai. Like an orchid or a sunflower. And hadn't Berai woken up this morning, dressed as the princess the Rosewarden wanted Berai to be, and been prepared to play pretend forever?

Berai's tears slowed. Hadn't Berai dreamed of running away, to a place where no one had heard of Velinar or the orphaned child who was its Heir?

But that was not the same as leaving Doaine to scream, the rose-mansions to wither, the people who had gathered to celebrating the coming-of-age of their princess and instead had watched the city's guardian die within moments of fending off a woman who, whispers said, wanted to destroy the world.

Berai leaned back against the wall and almost cried again. The hellebores were blooming beside the irises. The Rosewarden was dead and Berai was his heir.

Still sitting, Berai placed a hand against the flowers. The petals were soft. Like silk, or roses, or something. They were the color of Berai's father's eyes. Eyes that would never look at the child who had been born his daughter again. Berai would never be his daughter again.

Not this side of death.

That thought stayed inside Berai growing slowly. Like a seed that wasn't sure if the ground in which it was planted was fertile. But it was. And it grew inside Berai's heart, sent tendrils down Berai's arms, and eyes and tongue. When it struck the rage that burned inside Berai's stomach, the world changed.

Since Berai was a child, there had been lessons. How to speak correctly, carry on a conversation correctly, to garden and to grow. To know the seasons of Velinar in their many different blooms. And, as all the children of

Velinar before her—to use magic.

Her father had talked about it as a surrender. To give yourself to the city itself. To put down roots, to the heart of the city, from where the rose-mansions grew, and the people. It had scared her, terrified her. But her father was dead, the screams that echoed up through the palace said that Doaine was dead or dying. And the laughter from the queen was a blight at the heart of Velinar.

She pushed her hand into the wall, by the irises and hellebores and lilacs and lilies. There were roses as well, and where they cut her, she bled. Onto the flowers that made up the walls, the roof, the city. And with the blood came magic.

For a moment, Berai was afraid, still. Afraid of setting down roots. Afraid of being something other than the daughter of the Rosewarden. Of knowing that what she had been and what she would be could never be the same. Her father was dead. Her mother was dead. And whatever she might or might not be—

Berai's head echoed with the words Althair had spoken as her father withered and died— be queen or king or anchoress or pope or chatelaine or whatever you choose to be. Choose to be. Choose to be. Choose to be.

And she felt it, deep below, in the dark warmth of the earth, the power that waited to know. Waiting with the patience of flowers that grew. That knew each bloom that grew inside the city's boundaries. For her. And what she would choose to be.

She could choose to run. To be like dandelion fluff on the wind and scatter as far as she could go. Or settle roots and live and be in the city that her family had called home. Could it be both? The city, with it's heart beating in time with hers, had no answer. But it could feel the red blight, and so could she.

Blood was bad for flowers. For cities. For Berai.

And that was the answer.

She would be whatever she wished to be. But first, Berai would be Rosewarden.

#

The sun was starting to set. The palace lawn had been trampled. The open space where there had been flowers in the morning cast everything in red. Althair sat on the Rosewarden's throne. Doaine—who had been Velinar's phoenix—lay face down. Whether he was dead or alive was unclear. If he breathed, it was the shallow breath of a man who had a daylily's bloom left to live.

Berai was barefoot.

Gone was the gown of hyacinths. In its place were rose canes—bleak and flowerless. Her hair still hung like elderberry—black and dark and long. And her skin was pale, bleeding toward blue at the fingertips. She held something in her hand as she took careful steps across the lawn. She took in Althair, with the long length of her bare leg hitched up on the arm of her father's throne.

Berai held the heart of the city in her hand. It sang up her finger tips. Every wish, every prayer, every dream from every heart in the city of Velinar fed it. Made the city grow and prosper. It was power and magic and possibility and with it in her hands, Berai could feel every thoroughfare, every building, every footstep. More, the seed in her hand had been the connection between Rosewarden and city. It remembered the touch of every one of her forebearers. In holding the seed, she felt the touch of the people who had come before her. Father, grandmother, great-great aunt. Back to a girl with hair knotted through with roses, who had stopped at a place that looked quiet and felt like home. She had planted the seed and nurtured it, so that it could pass hand-to-hand down the line until Berai.

"My girl!" Althair said, smiling. Her face was beautiful when she smiled. "What is it you've brought me?"

Berai wanted to kneel beside the phoenix, who had been her friend and confidant and secret-keeper. But she felt the woman's magic. Her blight. And blight had no place in the rose-mansions of Velinar.

"This is the seed," Berai said. "It is the heart of the city."

"It is power," Althair said, standing. "With it, I can shatter the world."

"As you shattered my father," Berai said. "Shattered the joy of the people who had come to see Summerfinding. You—"

"I? As I saw at your little party, you were balking like a horse to an unfamiliar bridle. Were you going to turn yourself into the topiary they were expecting? One look, little one, and I knew that you were not the princess they'd dressed up in pretty flowers."

It was true. And Beria accepted it. Because Velinar accepted it. Because running up her arm, she knew that whatever she chose to be later, the city would love her. And braided tight through that love was the love her father had felt for her. No matter what.

"Give me the seed," Althair said. "Be free."

Berai tightened her fingers around it. It was the size of an apple, smooth like a stone. Its power felt like summer sun on her skin. She drank it in and let it fill her, tilted her head back, shutting her eyes and took in the magic and the love that she had never felt before.

The smile fell from Althair the Red's face. "Now, child."

When Berai opened her eyes, the color of them had changed. They were roses, as her fathers had been hellebores.

"My name is Berai Rosewarden," she said. And then she unleashed the sunlight.

The palace roared.

In a breath, the walls were in full bloom—but were roses. Roses the color of Berai's eyes. The canes around her body bloomed—roses again. But for every gentle petal, there was a thorn, long and sharp and ready to drink Althair's blood.

The red queen shook her head. "Think before you act, Berai."

There had been time for her to think, as she gave herself to the flower of Velinar. As she'd sunk into the wall of her family's palace, and passed into the dark, secret, heart of the city. In a room with roots thicker than her body woven into a lattice work, and the seed glowing in the quiet. The seed that had brought the stranger to her city, to kill her father, to hurt her friend. There had been time to think.

Lily of the Valley. Hemlock. Stinging nettle. Sea holly.

They erupted from the walls at Berai Rosewarden's command. Like a thousand arrows shot at once. But as Althair's hands moved in warding gestures, more followed.

Ivy. Wisteria. Bindweed. Vitis.

"Give me the seed, girl."

The vines erupted. From the ceiling. From the walls. From the lawn in a thousand, thousand vines. Not single ones, like great snaking tendrils. Too many for even someone as powerful as the woman who had killed Berai's father.

Althair used more magic. Withered vines as they touched her skin. And there was more. Velinar was a garden made into a city. There was not a plant in the world not grown somewhere in the avenues, in the shops, the private gardens. In a mansion, along an alley, in one of the great flower-houses. And they were Berai's to command.

Pine. Bayberry. Dandelion. Sedge.

The air exploded with pollen. Yellow, white, and cloying. It pelted down like rain. The space before the throne disappeared under the storm. It coated Berai and Althair. The red queen's eyes went wet with tears, her breathing changed. The beauty fell from her face as her perfect features reddened, the snot dribbled from her nose.

Berai had learned the seasons of Velinar and called each one to mind before speaking again. "There is no season here for you."

Althair tried to spring forward, as more shoots fell, more vines coiled, more dust fell like rain. But there was more. So much more.

Beanstalk. Rampion. Blackthorn. Rose.

"I would kill you if I could," Berai Rosewarden said as the oldest plants in Velinar dragged Althair away. The oldest and the most storied. Ones that held magic as surely as the queen, as the line who had founded the city.

Althair screamed as she was over powered; her skin pierced-through, limbs bound, mouth silenced.

She was taken into the walls, disappearing. To be cast out somewhere down the trade roads, perhaps. Berai didn't care.

Doaine was looking at her. His laurel blooms were gone, but he breathed.

Berai fell to her knees beside her old friend, clinging to him, crying, letting the seed of Velinar slip from her fingers, to the ground, back into the dark heart of the city that was now hers.

"I thought you were dead," she whispered, pressing her face into the crook of the phoenix's neck. "I thought I'd lost you too."

"Not so easy as that, little one," he said, holding her close.

And as the sun set on Velinar, Berai helped Doaine to his feet and thought of the future. Whatever came, would come, and Berai would choose who and what to be.

###

About the author

Sean Robinson is an author of fantasy and science fiction. His work has appeared in *Daily Science Fiction, Apex Magazine, Unlikely Story,* and is forthcoming from *On Spec* and *Diabolical Plots.* After a decade spent as a social worker, he's recently begun to teach English to high school students. You can find him (with growing frequency) on Twitter @Kesterian

The Tongue of the Chimera

Sandi Leibowitz

The last fiery swallow of ruby wine warmed Dev's throat. The magicked drink merely granted her courage—everything else depended on her skill. Her words would become a whirlwind, sweeping her audience away. She came into her majority tomorrow, when she would leave the dull court at last to become a llassrikh, bride of none but Story. Tonight she would receive a blessing from her parents, King and Queen of the Havanti-Sher, and tell the court her last story. Tomorrow she would don the veil of the Dream-Givers and travel the world, collecting and telling tales. Akri, her aged serving-woman, signaled to the guards to open the doors.

The court stood at her entrance. Dev wasn't used to such attention. She was no beauty like her mother, despite Queen Adramanth's more than a thousand years of life. It was only when she told her tales that the princess gathered notice.

"All salute my daughter Deveshlai on this, the eve of her eighteenth birthday. Drink a toast to her health!" King Kedemon commanded.

Candlelight glinted off jeweled goblets lifted in her honor, the objects of her sister's craftsmanship. Tekann, older than Dev by two years, was a goldsmith, no doubt soon to be named their parents' successor. Tekann had a mind strong as metal, and kindness radiant as gemstones. Her rings granted their wearers sharpened minds, and her goblets bestowed long, healthy lives on those who drank from them. The rule of the realm might as easily go to Dev's younger brother Melarus, a gifted potter. People who ate from his bowls dwelt in happy homes brimming with sons and daughters. If either reigned, the kingdom would continue to prosper in peace.

"We have made our decision," Queen Adramanth stated. "We will not wait for our youngest child to come of age to announce who will rule after us."

Dev could almost feel her sandals on the dunes of Saranay, her boots on the snowy mountains of Rasheen, her veil whipping behind her in the wind. Even if the crown were inherited in the old ways of her father's people, the Havanti, she would not be chosen, because she was a girl. If her parents used the old ways of her mother's people, the Sher, the eldest daughter would inherit. Either way, Dev would be free to compose the tale of her own life.

"We name as our successor," her parents intoned, "the princess Deveshlai."

"Mother! Father!" she cried. "You know that I am destined to take the veil of the llassrikh. Both Tekann and Melarus are better qualified to rule than I, who have no special powers. What's more, they wish to stay at home. I beg you to reconsider!"

"You are not *destined* to become a llassrikh, Dev," her father said; "it's merely what you want. And sometimes what you want isn't yours to take."

"Both of your siblings would have made admirable sovereigns," her mother said. "But the Serpent has spoken to me in a vision and told me to choose you. There is no gainsaying it."

Her siblings congratulated her. Her parents hugged her tightly, all the while keeping an eye on her to make certain she didn't argue or run away. In her mind's eye Dev saw the Veil ripped from her face. Her braids would not be tugged by the wind but confined by a golden crown.

Because of the great news, the feast lasted longer than usual. Dev chose to tell no tales; she lacked the heart for it. She longed for her bed, for a quiet space in which to weep. She drank more wine than she was accustomed to, as did everyone else. Courtiers slumbered under their tables, or retired to dark corners to disport with someone charming, or caroused loudly. Outside the windows, a timid dawn leaked through the darkness.

Dev heard a strange clicking. The sound increased.

Outside all was dark again. A storm must be on its way. The tapping persisted. Was it rain?

Something crawled in from the window. A black beetle. It had found a crack in the glass and squeezed itself through. Another beetle followed it. More wriggled through the crack in the glass, and then through tiny fissures in the stone wall. Myriads poured through. The darkness was a mass of beetles swarming the window, the clicking their legs against the glass.

"Father! Mother!" Dev cried.

"What—?" her father mumbled.

"Look!"

Her parents stood, holding hands, their exterior hands facing outwards. A thousand years ago they'd joined their hearts, their kingdoms and their powers; together they could destroy any threat. Fire pulsed from their free hands, and hundreds of beetles burst into flame. But more kept coming.

Dev pitched a jug at a knot of insects. It crushed some, the spilled wine drowning others, though many merely upended, legs wiggling until they righted themselves and crawled away. A lord saw what she'd done and began throwing jugs at the insect tide. A lady pulled a torch from the wall and set a swarm on fire.

The commotion roused those who'd slumbered. Any with magic powers sent out streams of fire against the unearthly invasion. But no matter how many beetles were killed, more poured in; and the window was still black with them.

The creatures swelled, like ticks gorged on blood, and elongated. They clambered upright and continued to grow till they were the size of men, black-armored knights. Red eyes peered out from their visors. The black knights drew swords from their scabbards. They slaughtered the weaponless courtiers till the hall ran red.

Dev's parents' leant on each other to keep from falling. Their magic had been drained dry.

The guards ran through the door, a paltry ten. The kingdom had suffered no threats in a thousand years; guards were posted for form's sake only. They unsheathed their swords and brandished them at the knights, even as more beetles streamed in.

Two dozen black knights came at the guards and mowed them down.

The last living courtiers rushed at the beetle-men. Those not decapitated by their swords were pierced by their mandibles. All but the royal family were dead. The insect-knights surrounded them, weapons drawn, but didn't attack.

The last phalanx of beetles swarmed through the window and poured in a stream before the dais. They swelled en masse, transforming into a tall knight, distinct from the rest. His black armor wasn't metal, Dev saw, but carapace. He wore no visor but a mandible-horned helm over a soot-black face, barely humanoid.

"Rhagji," the queen husked. Dev had never seen her mother pale and quaking. "How did you get free?"

"Well you may ask," the invader said in a voice like drought married to scream. "You buried me alive, bound in iron chains. Long ago, I'd protected my spirit with a preservation spell—as you knew. Day after day, year after year, I felt the agony of my flesh and sinews and organs rotting. My pitted eye sockets knew only darkness. My mind had no company but hatred. In a hundred years, the rusted chains fell slack against my naked bones.

"And then fortune came my way. A larval grub tunneled near my corpse, searching for food. I reached into its mind, striking a bargain. 'Bring me half your litter. Sacrifice them to me, and half again of each generation. In recompense I'll give you and your kind strenghth and power and long lives.' He agreed and fed me the life essence of his kindred. Each generation delivered half their offspring to me. For centuries I fed, and put on flesh and carapace and worked myself free. The survivors will soon reap their reward. As will I."

"Spare us," King Kedemon pleaded. "Take our kingdom. We will flee, grieving beggars, out into the wilds of the world."

Rhagji laughed. "As if that were all I'd ever wanted." He approached the queen. Dev's father attempted to shield her, but the sorcerer pushed him to the floor. "I'd offered you love. I was as powerful as him, with a kingdom as great and bountiful. You denied me." He stroked her face with a chitinous hand. "A thousand years later, still beautiful.

"No, I will not spare you. I will not bury you so you may return in a few centuries, safe and sound; I will kill you outright. But your children, your lovely children, them I will keep and use as I see fit. They will suffer eternal dying, as I did."

"No!" The queen fell to her knees, weeping.

Rhagji vomited a stream of green acid, which burned away her mother's flesh. Dev screamed. The giant struck off her father's head with his sword.

"Bind the heirs and bring them to the dungeons. We will feast tonight, as I promised."

Dev tried to run but there were beetle-knights everywhere. They caught her, their iron-like hands biting into her flesh. She struggled till she bled but couldn't get free. Beside her, Tekann and Melarus also struggled. *Still alive. As long as we three remain alive, there's hope,* Dev thought. They were dragged to the empty cells beneath the castle, each royal child locked alone in the darkness.

"Tekann? Melarus!" Dev called. She could hear nothing through the stone. She hurled herself against the iron door, banging, clawing, shrieking.

The gory scenes played out in her mind. Again and again, she relived her parents' deaths. She slumped to the floor.

Something roused her: not warmth nor light nor hope. Sound: a rustle, like paper being thrust under the door. Cold scales touched her skin. A snake wound around her arm.

"Dev," it whispered.

"Akri?" Her serving-woman was a priestess of the Serpent and could take Her shape.

"Not much time," the snake hissed. A dim aura lit her face. "Once I free you, take the northern road. Find the chimera. Loose its tongue. It's the only way to save the realm."

"You've come to the wrong child, Akri! Send Tekann or Melarus. They're more powerful than I."

"The Serpent has told me you alone may take this quest. Fail, and Tekann and Melarus will suffer eternal torment, Havanti-Sher belong to the enemy, evil reign."

"Even if some means should be found to unlock the cell, Rhagji and his knights would soon find and recapture me."

"Only accept," Akri hissed. "I will manage the rest."

"Yes."

The serpent reared up and sank her fangs into Dev's neck. She sucked and sucked.

The princess's body contracted in wrenching spasms. Her bones cracked and split. Her vision clouded. She felt limp and achingly cold. She had become a serpent. Beside her, Akri's snake-body expanded, grew skin and hair. The features took on an odd familiarity—a face Dev had only seen in her mirror.

"Why do you wear my face?"

Akri-in-Dev's-body sat up. "If they discovered you gone, they'd search for you. Rhagji must believe he has all three heirs in his grasp."

"But he'll torture you! I can't ask you to take on my fate."

"Yet, my dove, you must. I would give ten lives to save our realm, to save you, who are all but in name and flesh my daughter. Go. In twelve hours you will regain your true form, though I will remain your twin. May the Goddess speed you."

Dev-the-serpent squeezed under the door and slithered through the stone corridors. She kept to the shadows of the servants' quarters where the beetle-men were scarce. When she found a wide enough crack in the stone, she poured herself through it.

She slithered over the road, into the woods. It was slow going, a snake's pace, mere pebbles impediments in her path. She paused only for brief rests. Night fell. Hours later she scented a mouse; her weakness bade her hunt. She swallowed it whole before continuing her journey. Sometime before dawn, when she could go no further, she coiled into a ball and slept.

Dev woke in her own body. Her human legs strode quickly northward. Hours later, she saw smoke and headed toward it. When she came upon the village, she found only a ruin. Mutilated bodies proved that the beetle army had secured Rhagji's promised feast.

She aimed for the next village north, praying the beetles hadn't swarmed the entire realm. Part of her wanted to curl up in the leaf-litter and let death take her. But Tekann and Melarus needed her. All of Havanti-Sher needed her. She stumbled forward with a feral whine. Again and again, her father's head was lopped from his strong shoulders. The acid dissolved her mother's face.

The next village, a small and humble one, had so far been spared from invasion. She forced herself to rap upon the door of the first cottage. "Please," she begged. "Help me, in the name of Queen Adramanth."

A plump woman opened, fed her hot soup, and gave her warm water to wash the grime from her face and hands. Dev begged her for something clean to wear; the ragged finery from her feast was splotched with gore. The woman asked no questions but gave her a shirt and trousers that belonged to her son.

"Evil is coming," the princess warned her. "Arm yourselves against the beetle-men. The royal house has fallen to the ancient enemy but I seek a remedy." The woman blessed her, and pressed on her a woolen cape and a small sack filled with bread and cheese.

For days Dev walked north, finding charity where she could. The northern part of Havanti had not yet glimpsed the enemy; she warned each town and village, praying that foreknowledge would grant them the ability to stave off the invasions. Though it was only mid-autumn, the nights grew cold. Dev abandoned the road and used the steep forest trails that cut straight north.

On the seventh day of journeying, she crested Bamarik Mountain and looked down onto the city of Ysp, where the ancient relic, the Bronze Chimera, was kept.

How to pry the tongue loose? she wondered. She would require the help of someone skilled in metalwork.

She found her way to the nearest smithy. Five men waited for their horses to be shod. She pushed ahead of them. When they protested, the blacksmith moved away from the fire. Dev fell to her knees.

"You are needed, smith, for the salvation of Havanti-Sher. The capital has fallen. The king and queen are dead, the royal heirs imprisoned. Will you help?"

"There's been news of trouble, but it was hard to believe," the young smith said. "We're always wary of rumors from the south. What do you need?"

"I need you to cut off the tongue of the Bronze Chimera."

The smith's customers laughed. "That all?" one said. "How you gonna find it, girl? And if you do, you think the councilmen will just let you damage the city's greatest treasure?"

"She hasn't talked yet of payment," another man said.

"I've nothing to offer," Dev said. "Except myself. To be apprentice, servant, what you will. "

The first man cackled. "Now that's a bargain! She's crazed but not ugly."

"You sell yourself too cheap, my lady," the smith said. "Aye, I'll take your job. Without pay. Send for me once you locate the relic." He extended his hand to her. She grasped it in both of hers and shook it vigorously.

Dev staggered through the cobblestoned streets of Ysp like a sleepwalker. Her steps slowed till she had to lean against a cold stone wall to keep from falling down; she hadn't eaten in two days. She needed to take care of her body or she'd be useless. But no one in Ysp gave her a crumb, maybe because she wore clean clothes or because they were those of a laborer instead of a distressed noble. Dev gave up the search for bread and headed for the guildhall. Its dome gleamed in the sun, symbol of the city's prosperity. She presented herself there, begging for audience with the mayor. If he didn't know where the treasure was housed, he'd at least know who to ask.

"Petitions are heard every Seven-Day," the guard informed her. "Wait till next week and—"

"There isn't time!" Dev cried. "I come on behalf of the crown. The safety of the kingdom is at stake!"

The guard laughed. Another sentry came over, this one unamused. "Probably mad. You'd best watch out. Next thing you know, she'll bite you."

Dev straightened, summoning the bearing of a princess and the voice of a llassrikh. "Take me to Lord Ashaweer. He will recognize me despite my disguise. If he hears you delayed or treated me ill, he'll be angry."

"Better do it," the second guard said.

Dev waited in the hall outside the council chambers. The guards escorted her through the bronze doors. Lord Ashaweer, Mayor of Ysp, sat ensconced on a throne in the gilded audience chamber. He sneered as she approached.

"Ignore the mean garb and truly look at me," she commanded. The llassrikh's voice held power, and he looked. "You saw me this spring, Lord Ashaweer, and complimented me on my tale."

The lord examined her face. "Your Grace," he stammered, rising and bowing. He sped down the steps from the throne to greet her. "What brings you here alone and in this state?"

To tell him what had happened to her parents, to speak the words and confirm those events real, almost broke her. But if Dev couldn't speak for sobbing, she wouldn't fulfill the quest; she pretended her veil descended over her face and she spoke with the voice of Story. It had become an ancient tale: a kingdom beset by evil, a questor seeking help. It only needed her voice to spin it to its right conclusion.

Lord Ashaweer paled. His cheeks were wet. "We were always told that the Chimera guarded Ysp, that it was sacrilege to destroy or mar it."

"If the realm falls, so does Ysp," Dev stated flatly. "Will you help?"

"How could I deny my queen?" It took Dev a moment to realize he meant her.

The mayor brought her to the chamber reserved for

visiting dignitaries, insisting she be fed, bathed, and brought new clothes, while she waited for the smith. He begged her to rest in the canopied bed but she refused.

"Do my sister and brother sleep on swans' down?" she said. *And Akri, what is faithful Akri suffering in my stead?*

She was so tired. It helped to sit before a fire, clean, her hunger sated. No longer walking. But in the lull she heard that horrible click-clicking, saw the beetles swarm through the window, the blood of the courtiers, her parents...

Finally, the smith arrived, a satchel of tools on his back. "I am ready," he said, kneeling before her.

Lord Ashaweer led them to a backroom of the guildhall, unlocking a nondescript door. When it opened, the cold air made Dev shiver. The mayor obtained torches from a servant and led them down dark stairs, locking the door after them.

The narrow steps wound down a great distance, ending at last in the middle of a large, circular room. The floor was composed of concentric marble circles, black alternating with white. The walls contained a series of locked doors.

"Which one?" Dev asked.

"I've never been here," Lord Ashaweer replied. "No one's entered this place for centuries. We'll have to try them all." He carried a brass ring with odd-shaped, rusted keys.

The first door opened onto a small room without even a rug or a chair. The next room was also empty. Eleven doors opened onto nothingness. There was no twelfth key.

"Is this some sort of joke?" the blacksmith said.

"Not joke. Test," Dev said. She knew the ways of Story; tales preferred crooked paths. "Open them again. Keep them ajar. Search for the twelfth key."

Ashaweer fumbled with the keys again, cursing. He opened the first door, flashed the torch inside and huffed. Dev entered. Maybe they'd missed some small detail. "Help me look for a catch, or a loose brick that might hide a key." Each of them took a wall and felt along the damp stone. Nothing. Eleven times they did this, to no avail.

"You're certain it's kept here?" Dev asked.

Ashaweer nodded. "Every mayor and senior council member is shown the door and the keys, told in secrecy that the Chimera may be found here if it's needed. It can be nowhere else."

Dev rubbed her arms in an attempt to keep warm. The smith removed his cloak and offered it to her. She accepted it gratefully.

They stared at the doors, listening to the distant drip of water.

"It's a clock!" the smith exclaimed. "Look. Twelve doors in a circle, like the twelve hours."

"But no hands," Dev said. "The clue has something to do with time, then."

"Well, what time is it?" Ashaweer grunted.

"It was near the fifth hour when the lady arrived at my smithy, the sixth hour when we came down here. It must be nigh on seven."

"No," Dev said. "It's not about the time of day. It has some deeper meaning." *What time was it?*

She moved to the center of the room, to the tile white as a moon. She lifted the torch above her head with both hands. "I am Deveshlai, daughter of King Kedemon and Queen Adramanth, of the blood royal and designated heir of the slain rulers. I come to the Bronze Chimera for aid in vanquishing Rhagji, our ancient enemy. Now is the hour of need!"

The torch threw her shadow onto the moon-tile. She positioned her free arm till its shadow pointed like a clock's hand to the locked door. Beneath her feet something vibrated. Gears ticked—a great machine waking. The central tile moved. Quickly she stepped off it onto the outermost black ring. The moon-tile ascended. It was a canopy, with columns attaching it to a marble base, upon which stood the Bronze Chimera. The statue was about the size of a small horse, so finely crafted that the curling locks of the lion's mane looked like a woman's soft tresses. The gilding had worn thin, revealing patches of the bronze's mossy patina.

"Which tongue?" Lord Ashaweer asked. The thing

had three heads—a lion's at the front, a goat's rising from the creature's back, and a serpent's to cap the snake that served as its tail. All three thrust out their tongues in obscene leers.

"Start with the serpent's," Dev said. "The image of the goddess."

The smith opened his pack and took out a chisel and mallet. He chipped away at the statue, filling the room with the sounds of metal scraping against metal, and a pounding like being inside a pealing bell.

"Go slowly! You'll damage it!" Lord Ashaweer cried.

"Do you care more about the realm or your pretty statue?" the smith asked.

"Let him work!" Dev cried.

The lord nodded. Finally the serpent's tongue came free. The smith handed it to Dev.

"Save us," she said to the object.

Nothing happened.

"It must be the wrong one," Lord Ashaweer said.

The smith removed the lion's tongue. He gave it to Dev, who repeated her plea. Still nothing happened.

The smith shook out his cramped hands before beginning on the goat's tongue. When it came free, it clattered to the floor. Dev ran to retrieve it. She centered her thoughts and prayers on her need. She felt no spark of warmth indicating magic's response.

"This can't be!" Lord Ashaweer cried. "The Chimera will be the key to the salvation of Ysp in the hour of its need! It was promised!"

"The key!" the smith exclaimed. "Let me see that last tongue." He examined the shape, especially the tip. He went to the twelfth door and fitted the goat's tongue into the lock. The door swung open with a groan.

Dev peeked in. Not a room. Another set of stairs leading down. Were they supposed to descend? Where would this take them? "Let me see the key."

The smith pulled it from the lock.

Dev held it under the torch. "Something's inscribed on it:

'Seek the wild woods of Rysh,
hapless Key-bearer.

Under earth to mountains high
find the beast Chimera.'

"But it's only a story!" Lord Ashaweer exclaimed. "There's no such creature!"

"Many truths lie buried in the vaults of Story," Dev said. "Most people stopped believing in our ancient enemy, and yet Rhagji is no mere bogeyman to frighten naughty children. I must find the true chimera." She moved toward the door.

"But the beast is deadly," the smith said. "How could you possibly defeat it, milady?"

"The Serpent has decreed that this is my quest; no one else will succeed. It's the only way to save Havanti-Sher."

"You can't be meant to go unarmed, with no provisions, dressed in a princess's silks," the smith said. "Allow me to secure you a hunter. I know someone who's traversed the Forbidden Forest of Rysh. Ask Lord Ashaweer for provisions."

"I cannot allow you to go, Your Majesty!"

"It is not your place to allow or disallow me anything. Make it so." The mayor scowled but bowed obediently. "Bring me your hunter at once," Dev told the smith.

Lord Ashaweer brought her to her room. In moments servants fluttered in and out with packs of food, blankets and water skins. Dev secured better fitting men's clothes suitable for a hard journey, complete with a small sword and a dagger. In less than an hour she was ready, restlessly awaiting the smith's return.

He came back with a hooded boy in hunter's garb.

"This lad can take down the chimera? And protect the lady?" Lord Ashaweer demanded.

"This youth is the best hunter in the precincts of Ysp, and knows the Forest of Rysh better than anyone living. And I will protect the lady."

Lord Ashaweer made as if to object, but Dev silenced him. "Let us go then, we three. Now."

The mayor escorted them to the secret room, past the mutilated statue. At the entrance to the twelfth door, he paused. "Why would it take you underground? It's a few days' ride to the forest, and the way is up the mountain."

"There are several hidden tunnels to the forest that speed the way," the youth said. "Clearly this door leads to them."

"The Goddess speed your quest," the mayor said.

The youth took a torch and descended. Dev followed with her own torch. The smith, torch in one hand, Lord Ashaweer's sword in the other, brought up the rear.

It took a long while for them to reach the bottom. The low-ceilinged tunnel smelled of damp earth. Tree roots wove together to form the roof. They were deep below ground, as if buried in an enormous tomb. Dev struggled to breathe. As they walked, she stared at the young hunter's back or focused on the path; everything else belonged to shadow. Sometimes new tunnels branched away, and Dev glimpsed light from exits to the world above. The tunnel sloped upward, then gave way to steep stone staircases.

"Here!" the hunter exclaimed at last. He pushed open a door. A gust of fresh, clean air blew in. "There's a good spot for camping not far from here." He strode more purposefully, as if the thought of the campsite gave him renewed vigor. Dev struggled to keep up.

They reached an open glade. The sight of the clear night sky, bright with stars, gave Dev a small spark of hope. She heard a stream nearby. Signs of life.

"Sit, milady," the smith said. "We'll gather the wood. You've traveled far today."   *And many days before that,* Dev added internally. Ordinarily, she would have minded the special treatment, but her exhaustion didn't even allow her to answer. She could only nod her thanks. Her weary arm held the torch aloft.

Her companions returned and built a fire, onto which they all threw their torches. They ate.

"I'm Keel," the hunter offered.

"My name is Deveshlai, but you may call me Dev."

"Like the princess," the youth said.

"Not like. She *is* the princess," Jess said. "Majesty, we are at your service."

"Please call me Dev. Here's what's at stake." Again she was forced to recount the scenes of terror she'd witnessed. She waited for her listeners to recover. "How is it, Keel, that you have the temerity to hunt the Forbidden Wood?"

The hunter snorted. "The chimera's just a story. I'm not afraid of make-believe beasts."

"You had best believe that it exists, or Havanti-Sher is doomed," Dev said. "Do you think you can kill it? They say it has the ferocity of a lion but is larger and far more dangerous. The goat-legs at the rear can easily kick a man to death, and the serpent-head spits venom."

"I can kill anything that lives in the woods," Keel boasted. The quick turn of his head made his hood fall back, revealing a long gold plait and a face too delicate to belong to any boy. "But I'd have to find it first, and I've told you, I've never seen tracks that might belong to such a creature. I don't even know where to begin to look."

Dev reviewed her mind's cache of tales about the chimera. "The beast hunts by day. It's partial to deer. It inhabits a stony den high in the mountains. In one tale— no, two!—the chimera is known to worship the sun, so it emerges early in the morning to salute its deity."

"We're using fairy tales to hunt?" Keel huffed. "This whole thing is ridiculous."

Dev ignored the dismissal. She remembered, dimly, another chimera tale and closed her eyes to bring it into focus. "According to 'Tez the Bold,' the chimera once had a family. To achieve his quest, Tez had to slay all but one. While one adult was out hunting, Tez killed the other with a magic arrow, forged in the fire of the sun. He drowned the cubs. The surviving beast remains near that lake, which is silver as a mirror, says the tale. The stones there weep for the chimera's loss."

Keel snorted.

Jess elbowed her. "Is there such a lake?"

"I don't know about weeping stones—what nonsense!—but there's a lake whose waters are very clear; I suppose they look silvery. I've only ever come at it from the west. We could head there first."

All agreed. They sat watching the fire, or the stars.

Dev thought of her family, her home, worrying whether all their plans would work out right...

#

She felt something heavy on her shoulders. Jess was covering her with her blanket; she must have dozed. She curled up into the warmth and fell asleep again.

"Lady, it's time to rise." Someone shook her gently. It was Keel. Dev sat up and stretched. The hunter roused the smith, who immediately rose to his feet.

They found three stout branches for torches before Jess doused the campfire. Keel led them on in the pre-dawn darkness. Sometimes Dev heard a rustle in the underbrush, or caught the flash of yellow eyes—hunters like themselves.

An hour later, they came to the shore of a lake. The fading stars shimmered in its crystal-clear waters, turning them silver. They walked along the lake's circumference, searching for the weeping stones.

"There," Jess said quietly, his voice filled with wonder. Dev's arms pimpled with chills. He pointed to the small cliffs on the northeastern edge of the lake. A waterfall so slight it barely deserved the name spilled silver droplets, like strings of tears, onto the earth below. They fed a shallow rivulet that wove through the reeds to the lake. Farther on, Dev spied an opening in the cliff.

"A cave," she said; "no doubt the chimera's den."

The three companions headed there. They sat facing the cave entrance, weapons drawn. Dev heard the wind stir the reeds and the water behind her. The sky brightened.

The chimera emerged from the cave, blinking at the light. Unlike the statue, it had no mane; it was female. It sniffed the air—then stared straight at the companions, serpent-tail twitching.

Keel rose and loosed an arrow. Her aim was perfect, but the chimera's reflexes were lightning-quick. The hunter kept shooting, but the beast flew here, then there, eluding the onslaught of arrows. Finally, Keel's quiver was empty and the chimera bore not a single wound.

"You can't kill me," the goat-head taunted. "Don't bother trying."

Dev thrusted at the beast's flank, managing to inflict only shallow wounds. Jess hefted his sword above his head, swinging the blade at the lion's head. The chimera leapt away, slashing the smith's arm. Jess groaned. Keel had given up her bow and was slashing her sword at the writhing tail. Dev heard a shriek. Keel clutched at her face, which dripped with the serpent's venom. Her sword clattered to the ground, her senseless body dropping beside it.

Dev yelped as a blow shattered her shin. The chimera had reared back and kicked her with a powerful hoof. She hobbled out of striking range, putting most of her weight on the other leg, and resumed fighting.

How long before they were defeated, she and Jess? He was covered with gouges from the lion's claws, his chest and shoulder bleeding profusely from a deep, possibly mortal wound. They had no sun-forged arrows. But—what if they could drown the chimera as Tez had its cubs? They would have to trick the beast into entering the lake.

"Jess, switch with me!" Dev yelled.

She engaged the chimera from the front, whirling her sword in crazy, random movements, all the while heading backwards towards the lake. The lion's head snarled in frustration. Jess drove the beast from the rear. Dev's feet slipped in the mud, but she righted herself, the injured leg complaining. She kept feinting at the lion's head and chest, still slowly, slowly, backing up. The cold water seeped into her boots. The chimera raked her sword arm but she willed herself to ignore it. The water now reached halfway to her knees.

She heard Jess scream. He collapsed in the mud and didn't get up.

How could she keep luring the beast into the lake? Could she count on killing the beast before it killed her?

The chimera had the power of speech; it mourned its dead. It had a mind, therefore, and a heart. Could she appeal to its better nature? Would it understand the difference between good and evil—or was it by nature evil? The tales said no such thing. Would it care about the fate of the kingdom it inhabited, a creature of the wilds that knew nothing of humanity except perhaps the violence it had suffered at human hands?

"I don't need to kill you," Dev said, her breath coming hard as she continued to whirl her sword, keeping the beast at bay. She no longer stepped backwards. "But I do need a sacrifice from you. You hate humankind; understandable. But my companions and I haven't hunted you for sport. The only hope for my kingdom is if I cut off your tongue—I don't know why." Three sets of yellow eyes glared at her.

"Countless numbers of my people have already died. I'm all that's left of the royal court. My parents, the king and queen, are dead. My brother and sister have been kept alive for the sole purpose of perpetuating their torture. Our enemy, Rhagji, is a sorcerer with the power to keep them alive in that state for centuries. I require only one of your tongues. I can stitch the wound, staunch the bleeding. It will hurt, I know, and I'm sorry, but you can live without it. You've killed my companions; can we call your maiming the price for their deaths? I wonder if you can you feel pity. Can you give of yourself so others may live? The kingdom of Havanti-Sher, the land where your forest is located, will otherwise perish."

"Why should I help you, human?" the serpent-head hissed.

"I don't know!" Dev cried. "Maybe for the sake of goodness. Maybe to spare others from losing the children and spouses they love, as you lost yours. Mercy! I beg you for mercy!"

The chimera stopped advancing. It reached around to lick its bleeding flank, an action that reminded Dev of her pet cat.

"I don't want to kill you. But if you don't let me have your tongue, I'll have to."

"You don't need to maim me," the lion's head answered. "That won't help you. Think, what were the exact words of your prophecy?"

"Lord Ashaweer said, 'The chimera will be the key to the salvation of Ysp in its hour of need'—but that's not what the Serpent's priest told me. Akri said, 'Loose the tongue of the chimera.' We thought it meant the tongue we removed from the statue, which was indeed a key. But the inscription on that key *told* me to seek you." Her sword arm dropped. She caught herself and raised it again.

"You don't need to slice off any of my tongues."

"Then you'll fight Rhagji? He's a sorcerer of almost limitless power. Can you defeat him?" Dev asked.

"You've misunderstood," the chimera said. "I can save you, and I don't need to suffer to do it. It just requires my choosing to help you. And I have yet to decide. Perhaps it's time for me to call an end to mourning. Perhaps I should interest myself again in the affairs of humankind; I did once, long ago, before those I loved were taken from me."

Dev wasn't sure she could trust the beast, but she lowered her aching sword arm. She remained poised, ready to strike if she had to. The chimera seemed wary, too. It backed out of the water and sat on its haunches, its tail thrashing behind it.

"What do you know of tales?" it asked.

Dev's mouth opened in surprise. "I was about to take the veil of a llassrikh. I know many stories."

"How many?" the creature catechized.

"I—I couldn't say. Maybe a few hundred."

"A mere drop in the ocean of Story. And what do you know of the origins of all tales?"

"They don't have a single origin. People make them up. Stories come to them, if they are the sort who make up stories."

The goat-head bleated. Dev supposed it was a laugh. "Some do that now, though only because Story existed first. I am the Mother of Story. The first tales were my first offspring, the babes I produced out of myself before I discovered my mate."

Here was a tale Dev had never heard, and she marveled. "If the fates had been kind, I would have wed myself to Story. So you are, in some strange way, almost a mother to me." She knelt in the shallows and flung her sword away into the depths of the lake. "Will you not save me and those I love? I beg you, Mother Chimera, help us."

The lion's eyes misted. Even the goat-head lost its mocking expression. "It has been long, long years since any creature's called me Mother. I will help you, child, since you ask so humbly."

"Thank you," Dev whispered, bowing her head. "How will this be done?"

"Though thousands of my tales have died, many of my progeny live on. I will call upon the heroes of Story and they will come, armed with swords and axes and bows, armed with lightning and magic and fire, armed with goodness and pure hearts and strong purpose. Rhagji will become the evil all must vanquish, and vanquish him they will. I have had centuries to dwell on what I should have done when Tez murdered my mate and cubs. I fought with claw and fang, with hoof and venom, and was defeated. If only I'd called upon my first children then! Since the death of my beloved, I have only roared and screamed and groaned and bleated and hissed, but until today I've never spoken. I will now loose my tongues and call my children to aid you, princess. Let it not be said that the last of the chimeras lacked compassion."

Dev had no time to thank the beast again before the lion's bass voice rumbled, "Once upon a time there were three brothers…" The goat's tremulous tenor started, "Long ago, in a kingdom without song," and the serpent-head hissed, "Listen to the tale of Askalar and Sureth.'" Dev strained to understand the words, but the voices spoke quicker and quicker, the sounds blending into mere cacophony. Did the creature pause to breathe?

Dev heard a splashing. She looked to the lake. Three armed men in ancient dress emerged, their faces almost identical. A woman with a diadem of stars followed them, flaming arrows in her quiver. A man and woman of exceptional beauty stepped forth next, their hands clasped. New stories spilled from the chimera's mouths, and the shore grew crowded with men, women, centaurs, naginis, giant spiders with human heads. Dev saw a dragon, a winged lion, and a host of creatures she could not name.

While the chimera's other heads continued telling tales, the lion's addressed the throng. "Go into battle, my children, to the capital of Havanti-Sher. Travel by land, underearth, or by air. Find Rhagji, the Villain of All Villains, and destroy him."

The brothers mounted three winged wolves, the diademed woman an enormous stag, and they raced away. Dozens of others climbed aboard the dragon's back, which lifted its enormous wings and took to the sky. Giants scooped up other heroes in their hands and ran off, the ground thundering beneath them.

The chimera's goat and serpent mouths continued spewing forth tales, calling forth new heroes. "Mount me," the lion's head commanded

Dev climbed aboard the creature's wide back, clinging to its neck as it galloped through the Forbidden Forest. Before them, behind them, above them, heroes ran or rode or flew toward the royal palace.

The streets of the capital were strewn with the bodies of slain beetle-knights. Heroes still engaged others in battle. Everywhere Dev looked, a warrior-queen or satyr or hippogriff speared or trampled an invader. They were unstoppable; not being flesh and blood, they couldn't be injured or killed. Dev cheered them as the chimera battered down the doors to the palace and rushed to the throne room.

Alone, Rhagji fought off a minotaur, hurling bolts of blue fire at his shaggy chest. The palace walls crashed down, as a roc hurled itself through the stone, forcing the chimera to scramble out of the way of the cascading debris. The giant bird grasped the sorcerer in its talons; he was pinned, helpless. The minotaur drove his horns into Rhagji's chest. Blood gushed from the foot-long rent, the rib-cage pulverized, the heart reduced to pulp. The sorcerer laughed.

A red giantess dismounted from the roc. Four of her arms wielded swords, another two notched an arrow to a bow.

"You can never destroy me," Rhagji cackled.

The giantess smiled slowly, revealing gleaming fangs. She brought her last two hands forward from behind her back. They cradled a green egg.

"No!" Rhagji shrieked. "My spirit!"

The giantess crushed the egg in her hands, a putrid, steaming liquid spewing out. Rhagji burst into flames. A pile of smoldering ashes soon remained where he'd stood.

"The dungeons!" cried Dev. "We must free my sister and brother and the Serpent's priestess." The chimera nodded to the minotaur and the giantess. They broke down the cell doors and released the prisoners from their bonds. Dev cried out at the sight of the broken bodies. *Broken, but alive.* Tenderly she embraced Tekann and Melarus. Akrit still bore Dev's likeness, only grossly wasted. When Dev kissed her, the beloved maid regained her true form. Akrit's eyes flickered open, and she smiled.

"Say your farewells," the chimera said. "They will be healed. But you must come with me."

"Reign well," Dev whispered to Tekann. "Restore the realm to peace." Tekann managed to nod her head.

"I will return to the Lake of Tears," the chimera said, "and you will join me. Havanti-Sher will carry on without you. No, not entirely without you, for you, Princess Deveshlai, will be remembered. Though I am the Mother of Story, you are right: my children are not the only tales that now exist. People bring new ones into being without me. Your brother and sister will sing your name, your people will tell their children of your bravery, down through the ages."

Dev climbed onto the beast's back. She wished she could bring with her the llassrikh's veil she'd spent so many years embroidering with figures from her favorite tales—Vatta the Brave, Fearless Garamir, the lovers Agraia and Fayrem. But she was their sister now, and would know them better than she would have as a llassrikh. And so Deveshlai—princess, questor, briefly queen—became Hero, and passed from this world into Story.

About the author

Sandi Leibowitz lives in a raven's wood, next door to bogles, in New York City. After a variety of careers and jobs (including ghostwriting for a monsignor and working behind one of the caribou dioramas at the Museum of Natural History), she is now an elementary-school librarian, which enables her to hook kids on reading, tell stories, and use puppets and funny voices. She also sings classical and early music and plays recorders. Her speculative fiction and poems may be found in *Liminality, Through the Gate, Luna Station Quarterly, Mythic Delirium, Kaleidotrope, Gaia: Shadow and Breath 3, Mirror Dance, Liars' League London, Ellen Datlow's Best Horror of the Year 5,* and other magazines and anthologies. Her poems have been nominated for the Pushcart Prize, Rhysling, and Best of the Net awards; "Weathering" tied for second place in the 2015 Dwarf Star Awards, and "Loss" won third place in the 2016 Dwarf Stars. Sandi invites you to visit her at www.sandileibowitz.com.

Song and Sacrifice

Rob Francis

The Spire shivered to the chorus of a thousand voices.

"Asaia! Asaia! Protector! Asaia!"

The crescendo of adulation swept through the Onyx Hall, redoubled, came back on itself and hammered against the crystal windows. An inkwing flittered madly amongst the rafters high above, desperate to escape into the calm of the night.

Asaia watched the creature with sympathy from her thornwood throne. It was going to be a long evening, and already she wished it were over, done with, all the formalities and obligations met. Her thaumaphonic song was almost finished at last, after almost a dozen years of work. The composition on her people's flight into exile would astound everyone with its perfect blend of sorcery and music. The renewal ceremony was a distraction that chafed at her badly, despite its importance. Her fingers itched for the comforting strings of her lyre.

Her parents stood at her side. As the chanting rose, they placed their hands on hers and raised her up, presenting her to the massed ranks of Tainted that filled the floor, steps, and balconies of the vast chamber. She was pleased to see the twin red cloaks and matching hair of Maribius and Stappia, her closest friends, amongst the crowd. She hoped Maribius had brought his lute. Stappia certainly had her pipe; she carried it wherever she went.

Asaia stood awkwardly, her left leg still weak from surgery, scar tissue tight where the chirurgeon had removed a patch of necrotized flesh. She shook her head to clear the hair from her right eye and did her best to smile. She'd meant to prepare better but the song had consumed her lately, day and night. Even grooming her ratty half-head of hair had been too much trouble.

Her father raised his other hand for silence, and gradually it was given.

"Brothers and sisters! It has been three hundred years since our escape to this quiet isle, our Blightholme. Three hundred years since great Loktanella give of himself to work the most astounding sorcery ever performed to shelter us from the Tarlanites and their persecution."

A thousand faces turned to the statue that dominated the hall, a towering man in flowing robes, his expression fierce. Loktanella himself. Each of them bowed their thanks.

"We still decay. Some of us have died. More have been born to us, and grow old slowly." He smiled at Asaia. "Like my daughter Asaia, now full grown over a hundred years, and ready to take on some of the burdens of court and rule." The people cheered and applauded again. Father beamed.

"And look at what we have achieved! Our skills of sorcery and enchantment have grown tenfold. We have raised buildings to the sky, created works of great beauty, sculpted perfection from an old, abandoned city. The governors of Tarlan cast us out to die; the diseased, the malformed, the Tainted. And Loktanella saved us, gave us shelter. Though death was his reward."

Two guards moved forwards, their thin moonbronze armour shimmering in the torchlight. The three sacrifices walked calmly between them, heads high. Their serenity impressed Asaia. It was an honour to be a renewal sacrifice, and all came willingly, but Asaia wasn't sure she would be so content in their place.

"And now, on the anniversary of Loktanella's feat, we sacrifice to renew the sorcery so that our small city, an enclave of paradise itself, may remain ever sheltered.

Magus Labrys?"

The magus stepped forward, still tall and proud despite the ravages that the Taint had visited upon his body over the long, slow years. One hand was little more than a withered claw, but the other held a large bronze key that he raised to blistered lips to kiss, just once, before moving to stand before the sacrifices. He cleared his throat. Talking pained him these days, but still he gave hours of counsel to Asaia's mother and father, and hours of lessons to her each day.

"Beloved sacrifices," he rasped, "we thank you for your gifts. Your willing surrender of life will help all of us survive, and we owe you a great debt. Now our Protectors, Thioclava and Nereida, and their daughter Asaia, will begin the sorcery that will carry you peacefully into eternal sleep." The magus bowed to the sacrifices, and then began a low hum. Moments later, her parents began to sing.

The music flooded her body and she added her voice to that of her parents, feeling the air become heavy with sorcery that sparked against her skin. She gazed at her sacrifice, an old lady with a face so ravaged by the Taint that her features could hardly be discerned. Asaia thought a smile hid there. The lady gasped and rocked backwards, the song beginning to steal her vitality so that it might be used to power Loktanella's spell of isolation for another century. Her father's sacrifice was already toppling, her mother's beginning to buckle.

She thought of her composition, unfinished but so close to perfection. Could some of these notes be worked into it? Perhaps a lilt, an inflection in the third bridge suggestive of terrible melancholy...

"Asaia!" Labrys was striding to her, eyes wide in alarm. With a sudden rush of shame, she realised she had lost focus. The lady's face was screwed up in pain, the full impact of the spell breaking her, stripping her flesh from her bones. She fought to regain control as Labrys added his voice to the song, and slowly her sacrifice toppled to the floor to rest alongside the others.

The magus regarded her furiously, and her mother's hand tightened on hers. The hall was silent.

"I'm sorry!" She bowed her head. "I don't know what..."

"A weakness," hissed Labrys. "A break in the spell. We are fortunate that it went unnoticed–" He stopped as the statue of Loktanella groaned, the stone seeming to tremble and twist slightly. Then it cracked, fractured, burst open to reveal a swirling shadow, and from the shadow stepped a woman of burning white. Asaia gasped.

The woman towered over Labrys, clad in thick crystalline armour that shimmered in the torchlight and cast rainbows over the stunned crowd. Her hair was a blinding furnace, her skin pale yellow. In her left hand she held a staff shaped as entwined snakes, and in the right a sword of translucent blue.

The woman looked at Asaia and smiled beautifully. "Thank you." Her voice was the sound of raindrops on ice. "I have been waiting a *very* long time."

"Caracal." Labrys looked tiny before the blazing apparition. "How can it be? So many years..."

Guards ran at the intruder, but she ignored them, striding instead toward Labrys, who fell back, the key held before him like a ward.

From the swirling shadow leapt half a dozen other figures, all alike, serpentine masks covering their faces, long white robes streaming. Spears whirled in their hands with astonishing speed. A guard fell, impaled, then another.

Caracal continued her advance.

"Oh, Loktanella was more powerful than even you knew, little magus. This foul island was not just stolen from Tarlan, it was moved to a place where time bleeds more slowly, each moment becoming a thousand. You have been gone from us barely a decade. How many years has it been here? A hundred? A thousand? And yet here you are, rotted but not dead. Yet. How wonderful his sorcery was."

Now more guards were falling, and the ranks of Tainted in the hall beginning to flee, to escape into the night, throwing themselves against the doors and windows in panic and desperation.

Power crackled along the blade in Caracal's hand.

In the crowd, someone was calling Asaia's name.

Her father strode forwards, hands high, a haze of black lightning building between his palms. Caracal turned to him and smiled.

"Thioclava! And your beloved Nereida. Still together after so long? I was told you had fled to Brightholme. I didn't believe it. Having lost so much, I thought you would rather have died than take shelter with the other Tainted."

"Would you have given up, Caracal?" Father hissed through gritted teeth. "There was still hope. And now look — we have made a new life here!"

"This is not life," Caracal said sadly. "This is a mockery of existence. You are as good as dead already." She turned her gaze on Asaia, its intensity a scourge on Asaia's flesh. "You and... your daughter! My, we have been busy, haven't we?"

"Leave!" Father sucked in a breath. "Leave us be, now! Or be destroyed."

Caracal smirked. "Still so melodramatic, Thio, after all these years? Impressive."

The dark lightning flew from Father's hands, joined an instant later by another blast from Mother. Caracal stumbled backwards, the force of the blows shocking her and crazing her crystal breastplate with fine fractures. One of the masked soldiers standing beside her froze, then crumbled to ash. Her parents began to sing, to add strength to the sorcery that enveloped the blazing woman. Asaia opened her mouth to join them, but hesitated. What if she made a mistake, as with the sacrifices? She stood, a tangle of indecision.

Caracal snarled. She seemed to scream silently, but after a moment a pure note that Asaia had never heard before began to echo around the room. Her parents' lightning faltered, flickered. Caracal raised her staff, and the note grew, filling the hall. Those few Tainted who had not managed to escape stood still, staring in terror.

Then Caracal began to sing.

Raw power tore through the room, and one by one the Tainted fell, seared through with sorcery. Asaia's father met Caracal's eyes fiercely as he died, while Mother cried out in anguish as her vitality was burned away. And the truth of the song came to Asaia's mind, in images born of Caracal's sorcery — a land of mountain and forest, rivers and lakes. A home that might have been, that she would never see. A people diseased and frightened. A struggle for survival. A story not unlike the one she had been composing these last years, but she knew, she was certain, that this was not the story of her people, the ones Loktanella had brought to the island of Brightholme, before they renamed it and took it as their own. This was happening to the ones left behind, the Tarlanites. Right now.

"You seek a cure!" Asaia said, and Caracal's eyes snapped to her. The song stopped, the silence dropping like a stone into a well.

"Yes!" she said. "The Taint destroys us, and Loktanella was so close to understanding it. I need the knowledge you have here, in this place, in yourselves."

The masked soldiers joined their mistress. Labrys shuffled in front of Asaia, holding the key tight in a trembling hand.

Caracal raised her staff. "Tell your people to cooperate. We only want to learn, to save Tarlan and the thousands of innocents that suffer. They were your people too, once. It is for the greater good."

"We suffer too, sorceress," said Labrys. "And we are not here to serve you." The key blazed like sunlight on glass.

Caracal shook her head. "Fool. You are already beaten. Accept it."

Labrys closed his eyes. "Not yet." The magus gave a cry of raw anguish, a sound like an animal casting its soul to the wind. The key burst into flames, the room turned about itself, and all was darkness.

#

Silence. An aching of nothingness that held no music, no song. Death, perhaps.

Then a rush of wakefulness, of broken harmony, and Asaia was staring at the night sky and the low moons, feeling the wind rasp her raw skin.

She stood, pushing back vertigo, and found herself atop a cliff, at the bottom of which the dark Forever Sea plunged against rock in violent madness. From the coast of Blightholme stretched only darkness, rising to meet the stars. Asaia turned to look inland and saw the Spire, smoke rising wormlike from it in the moonlight.

"Asaia."

She followed the sound of her tutor's voice back from the cliff edge and down through whispering grey grass to a wind-blasted thornwood, against which the magus slumped, propped on one arm. The old man's other limbs poked from his ragged robes, pale and withered. His breath came hard.

"Labrys." Asaia knelt and gave him her hand. "You saved me." And as she said it, she allowed herself to understand what had happened just a few moments ago. Her parents were dead. The world had been torn in half. The knowledge crushed her heart, squeezed it so tight in her chest she was sure she would die too.

"No." Labrys shook his head weakly. "Bought some time is all. At a high price." He lowered himself to the ground and lay staring up at the two huge moons, shadows of the thornwood branches covering his face. "I'm all ashes. Now it's up to you. Caracal will take those she can back to Tarlan to examine, to experiment on, to dissect. But she doesn't understand. The transition alone will kill them; away from Blightholme and its preserving sorcery, the Taint will complete its work in moments, turn them to rotten meat before they can draw breath. Only one thing can stop Caracal."

Asaia wiped the tears from her face and grasped the magus's hand. It was cold and dry. "Tell me."

"Loktanella wasn't trying to save us, when he sang his final song. Only his daughter Aonyx, dying of the Taint. She was hiding in Brightholme, a refuge then as it is now, hiding from Caracal's purge. Loktanella came for her. He brought Stellaria with him."

Asaia frowned. "Stellaria? What–"

Labrys squeezed Asaia's hand hard in his own. "Stellaria, Asaia, is a lyre, made from the bones of a fallen star. It has great power, but it *takes*. It takes from anyone who plays it, to work its sorcery."

Asaia's frown deepened. "I play the lyre."

"Yes!" Labrys smiled. "Ever since you were a child I have cultivated your music, and your sorcery. I chose your instrument of practice, when you were very small. This is why. A ruler needs to be ready to use any weapon in desperate times. I hoped such times would never come, but I prepared you. And now here we are."

"So I must use this... Stellaria?"

Labrys closed his eyes. "Loktanella's sorcery took the entire island to this place, between worlds, where time is warped and twisted. But the casting burned him through, and not just him; Aonyx was immolated, seared into nothing. Loktanella died shortly after; you know of his tomb, on the shore. The lyre lies within."

"But ... I don't know what to do! I couldn't even complete the sacrifice properly. I'm to blame for all this!"

"Your parents are gone, Asaia. Soon I will be too. You are the Protector now; the only one. It has to be you." The old man released his grip. "Go now, child. Find the lyre and help your people. And remember: it *takes*."

Asaia opened her mouth, then closed it. Swiftly she bent to kiss Labrys's forehead, and then she limped through the darkness, leg aching, seeking the cliffside path and a tomb of black stones.

#

It was a modest resting place for a great sorcerer. A pile of basalt rocks, roughly carved, huddling above the strandline like a sleeping animal. There was nothing to indicate its significance, or whose bones rested within. A lone inkwing perched atop the tomb, watching her approach. It burst into flight as she neared.

There was a sound of boots on soil, close by, coming fast. Asaia turned, and through the long grass came two figures, running low. She started to hum, drawing power to herself that she could use to hide or to strike, but she faltered at the sight of a shock of red hair.

"Maribius? Stappia?" She grinned as Maribius

poked his head up, then burst from the grass into the dunes, stopping a few steps from Asaia and looking her up and down, breathing heavily.

"You're unharmed," he gasped. "Thank the stars."

"Maribius!" Asaia rushed to hug him. The Taint had yet to affect her friend, beyond a scattering of skin lesions and a withered ear. Over his shoulder, she saw Stappia approach, face pained. Stappia had been less fortunate than her twin, her flesh riven with fissures, her bones brittle. She moved more slowly, sucking in air, grasping her thin silver pipe tight in her hand.

"Asaia!" Stappia smiled in relief and placed her arms around her friend and her brother. "Labrys told us he had sent you here."

"How did you escape the Spire?"

Maribius nodded to his sister. "Stappia worked a fine song to keep us hidden, at least for a time. We tried to reach you, but the sorceress's power pushed us back, and then when your magus cast his spell, well … everyone had to get out. The tower is gone, destroyed. Stappia knew where Labrys had taken you — she's so sensitive to sorcery–" He stopped, awkwardly.

Stappia waved his concern away. The Taint had made her sensitive in many ways, but not to words. She was used to people pointing out how frail she was, intentionally or not, and rarely took offence.

Tears spilled down Asaia's cheeks. "This only happened because of me. I was thinking of my song, I lost my focus on the sorcery, the sacrifice. All those people. Mother and Father. What am I supposed to do now?"

Maribius squeezed her tight again. "Caracal was waiting; it was only a matter of time before she found a way in. It can't be helped. And whatever we need to do, we can do it together."

"I'm so glad you're both here," Asaia said quietly. Then she turned to the tomb, and sighed. "I have to get inside."

Maribius raised his eyebrows. "Because…"

"Labrys said Loktanella had a sorcerous lyre, an instrument of great power. Stellaria. Apparently it's the only thing that might stop Caracal, before she kills everyone by taking them back to Tarlan. It's why Labrys always insisted to my parents that I play the lyre to forge sorcery. Thought it might come in handy."

Stappia nodded. "Well, it might, if we can get to it." She shuffled forward, staring at the wall of the tomb. She cocked her head, ran a hand along the smooth stone. Sniffed at it. She shrugged. "No enchantment, as far as I can tell. No door either," she added helpfully.

"I suppose they didn't want anyone taking the thing, if it's as powerful as all that." Asaia placed her hands against the black stone and pushed, as if hoping a door would suddenly reveal itself, or the wall would topple at her command. It failed to oblige, instead standing as solid as a cliff. "Any ideas?"

Maribius scratched thoughtfully at his chin. "The stones were set, so there are gaps between, no matter how fine." He slipped his lute from his back and quickly tuned it. "If I work up some water, and you two work on freezing it..."

He began to play, a sweet, crystalline tune that spoke of rivers and streams, of flowing rivulets of clear water running through mountains and forests. Maribius sang, and the wall of the tomb before him was bleeding with water, the stones themselves dripping.

Stappia's pipe added a staccato tune to the sorcery, and Asaia added her voice, singing of the hard, cold darkness of ice that lived in the glacial heart of mountains. The water began to freeze, hardening suddenly into a sheet that cracked the stones within it. A moment later the blocks slumped to the ground, the wall falling with a dull rumble to expose the black emptiness of the tomb.

The three companions looked at each other in silence. The twins smiled.

Asaia led the way.

The moonlight did almost nothing to lift the darkness inside the tomb, so Asaia sang the notes that would birth a little light. And it illuminated little: a low basalt slab with a ragged bundle of cloth atop it, and nothing else.

No withered, mummified remains, no enchanted

accoutrements that might once have belonged to one of the most powerful magi that ever lived. A conspicuous absence of sorcerous lyres.

"It's not here," she whispered. Maribius swore and drummed his fingers on the body of his lute. Stappia chewed at a fingernail anxiously.

Asaia crossed to the bundle and teased the folds of cloth apart. Only an empty robe.

You have come for the lyre.

The voice came from nowhere, reverberating within Asaia's bones.

"Loktanella?"

Maribius and Stappia turned to her in concern. "Asaia? What's wrong?"

She held up a hand to quiet them. "Loktanella, we believed you dead."

There was a faint crackle that might have been laughter.

I am little more than a residue of my final song. The lyre keeps me. My Stellaria. She has taken so much, and now she won't even let me die.

"It's here? The lyre?"

The shadows shifted, and Asaia saw it. In a small alcove against the far wall, a lyre with a body made from the burnished shell of some animal she had never seen, with arms and yoke of what looked to be a dull grey metal. Silver strings shone in the light.

Underwhelming, isn't she? But you, of all people, must know the importance of looking beyond appearances. Inside your blighted shell, there is great power and beauty. So it is with Stellaria, too.

Asaia reached for the instrument, but recoiled at the heat radiating from the strings.

Not just anyone can play her. She is alien to us, and you must give of yourself to work her sorcery. She is like the mountains that can carry a few words for leagues in a great echoing leap. A little power becomes a great tide. But you are less after. You and... yours.

"How do I take it?"

Do you have a song to play? One that is yours alone?

Asaia thought of her composition and the horrors her obsession with it had caused.

"It's not finished."

That does not matter. Play it, then. Show Stellaria that you are worthy. And you have my sympathies.

Asaia grasped the lyre, and for a moment it felt like her fingers were afire, her palms blistering in the scorching heat. And then it was as if she had held the instrument all her life, and nothing could be more natural. It was cool and smooth to the touch.

She lifted the lyre with hands that shook only a little. Took a deep breath in the dead air of the tomb. Her fingers found the strings.

She sang.

#

The Spire was gone.

Where it had stood, on a spit of land that stretched into the Forever Sea, there was now only rubble, smashed and scattered like the bones of a great leviathan.

Asaia wept to see it. She picked her way slowly through the broken blocks where the Onyx Hall had been, stepping over pieces of furniture and the blackened remains of people that a short time ago had been cheering her name. She could feel the anger bleeding from the twins behind her.

Anger and pain. Her own body was sore, bruised on the inside. Singing her song, channeling it through Stellaria, had hurt her, scourged her muscle and bone so that even walking was painful. Her half-head of hair was gone, her scalp bare in the moonlight.

Maribius had suffered too, his back bowed, the almost-clear skin of his body now streaked with necrotic tissue.

Stappia walked in a storm of agony, blood flowing freely from her flesh, cheekbones poking white through the skin of her face.

But still they walked, looking for Caracal where they knew she would be.

The Tainted were gathered on the shore of the

Forever Sea, huddled together, hands clasping hands in fear while they gazed at the black ocean. The Sea was torn, rent in half almost to the horizon. Caracal stood a short distance away on the silty bed, sorcery wreathed about her as she worked, forcing the elements apart, making a way back to Tarlan so that the Tainted — Asaia's people — could be made to return to their deaths.

She began to push her way through the crowd, and once people saw that she was alive, that she had returned, they began to part. She walked between them and stood, facing Caracal across the distance, she amongst a small ocean of Tainted and the sorceress surrounded by the elemental power of the Forever Sea that separated worlds.

Two of Caracal's serpentine soldiers burst from the crowd and charged, sand fountaining in their wake. Asaia hesitated. Was she prepared for this? Her song wasn't even complete. Did she have enough power to counter Caracal's might, even with Stellaria?

Her fingers tickled the strings and the music of the lyre screamed out to engulf the first soldier in white flame, sending him rolling and thrashing on the beach. His companion hurled his spear but another plucked note sent it spinning into the sky. Still he ran, until Maribius sent a petrifying blast that stiffened his limbs, causing him to stumble, topple, and finally stop at Asaia's feet.

She bent to remove his mask and stood silently, gazing down at his face. A handsome face, covered in lesions and patches of dead, desiccated, Tainted flesh.

"I told you!" Caracal's voice rang across the beach in a magical torrent. "We are dying. I need you, I need to understand what Loktanella did, how he hoped to defeat the Taint. I must take you back. All of you."

"We will all die if we go back!"

"You are already dead! At least for us, for many, there is still a chance." Caracal raised her arms, and two great wings of fire sprouted from her back, pounding against the air. Her sword blazed, and lighting rippled around the snake-head staff that she held to the sky. "You cannot win, child. Accept your fate, and help us."

"This is not my fate. This is not *our* fate."

Caracal flew across the sea bed, raw power ripping it into a wall of sand before her that whipped and lashed, scattering the Tainted across the beach as they sought to avoid it.

Asaia sat and began to play. Her song was discordant, erratic, telling the tale of her people as they sought to save themselves from the Tarlanites and their attempts to eradicate the Tainted. She sang of struggle, anguish. The wonders of Loktanella and the sorcery he wrought. The sacrifices made. She wove images of her parents, the lands and family they lost to disease and persecution, and the love that endured it all.

Her mind was focused on the song, her fingers picking the chords to create it, to weave its sorcery, but she could feel her body breaking, her flesh burning in a distant agony. Behind her, Maribius was playing his lute, Stappia her pipe, adding their power to the song. Stellaria shone like a star in her hands.

Thunder roared as her sorcery met Caracal's, and the impact rocked her back. The Tainted began to run, leaving the beach to hide amongst the ruins of the Spire.

"You cannot win!" The sorceress' voice was a screaming rush in Asaia's head.

Asaia sang of Blightholme, and the life she had lived there. Of the things the Tainted had done with the time they were gifted, the beautiful things they had crafted, the lessons learned, the knowledge gained. Sang of happiness. Her fingers worked the strings and sent the music soaring, accompanied by her friends.

Caracal stopped, unable to push further against the combined power of the song and the lyre. The two figures struggled, waves of sorcery thrashing against each other, held in balance. Pain raked Asaia's flesh. She faltered.

"Your song is not finished." Caracal's voice was a hiss, the strain clear.

"I have an ending now," Asaia whispered, and told a story of sacrifice. Of the loss of family and friends, and the survival of a people who deserved it. She wept as she sang, knowing what she did, and the notes rang clear across the Sea. The lyre burned incandescent, and Asaia was no longer sure if she was playing it, or if she was merely a puppet, fingers jerking to the music it made.

She felt a great pain in her chest, and knew she was going to die. Behind her, Maribius and Stappia fell silent.

Caracal whimpered, and a sudden stillness rushed across the world. The sorceress's blazing fire was extinguished in an instant. Asaia fell to her knees and watched as the Forever Sea joined its two halves together, crashing down on the tiny figure lying on the sand.

In the terrible silence, she looked at her hands. Her fingers were gnarled and blackened, curled into her palms. She couldn't move them.

Her joints ached as she stood, her clothes sloughing away in a fine ash. Her skin was blistered and raw. She turned, dreading what she might see but knowing that she must look.

The twins were gone. Ash cut across the sand in the breeze, drifting slowly towards the Sea. Asaia began to walk, painfully shuffling down the beach to the shore, Stellaria abandoned on the sand.

Three of Caracal's soldiers stood at the strandline, spears held defensively before them. Asaia raised her hand weakly. If she was the Protector now, the only Protector, then it was time to start doing some protecting.

"There is a thornwood tree atop the cliffs on the other side of the island, overlooking a tomb of black stones. The body of my magus lies at the bottom. Bring it here, and cut the tree. I want to make a new throne."

The soldiers turned their serpent masks to each other, and then by unspoken accord nodded, and each knelt before her. Then two of them stood and raced up the beach, toward the remains of the Spire and the other side of the island.

She walked past the remaining serpent, and crouched at the edge of the Sea. She reached out to place her hands in the cool black water, feeling the power it held.

"Bring her back to me," she said.

She waited, kneeling on the sand with her hands in the water while her body protested. The Tainted began to gather on the beach, whispering to each other, amazed and uncertain.

In time the rolling waves crept higher, and then Caracal was at Asaia's feet. The sorceress looked smaller, her hair duller, face pale. The fire gone. Her armour hung in fragments from her neck and shoulders. Asaia raised trembling fingers to her throat and felt for a pulse. It was faint, but there.

She turned to the Tainted on the beach. "Bring me rope."

The serpent soldier stepped forward and removed his mask. His face was pitted, the upper lip half gone. He dropped the mask to the sand and knelt.

"My lady, please... do not kill the sorceress. She was acting from desperation, to save our people."

Asaia raised a hand to silence him.

"I do not mean to kill her. She will be restrained at first; I am sure she retains great power, even without her staff. Once she has recovered, she and I will talk. Caracal will learn all she can from us. And then I will allow her to return home. Only a short time will have passed in your world, after all. You will be welcome to return with her, if you wish. Or you may remain here."

Asaia turned and began walking back along the beach. After a moment, the soldier took her arm to support her. She raised her voice, so that her people could hear her. "We will rebuild the Spire. We will preserve Blightholme, and carry on. We must. There is no other choice."

They came to where Stellaria sat on the sand, covered in a fine layer of ash. An inkwing perched on the lyre's yoke, its head tilted as it stared at Asaia. She thought she saw pity in its eyes.

The soldier spoke softly. "What will you do with it?"

Asaia looked again at her ravaged hands. She sighed. "I will hide it. Perhaps one day someone will need to play it again. But not me."

She limped on up the beach, ashes swirling around her. Her people watched.

It started small at first, then grew, each person adding their voice to a chorus that seemed to shake the ground and shiver her bones.

"Asaia! Asaia! Protector! Asaia!"

She closed her eyes and concentrated on putting one foot in front of the other.

About the author

Rob Francis is an academic ecologist and writer based in London. He started writing short fantasy and horror in 2014, and since then has had over twenty stories published in various magazines and anthologies. Recent pieces have appeared in *Metaphorosis Magazine, Broadswords and Blasters, You Are Here: Tales of Cartographic Wonders, Syntax & Salt* and *Tales of Blood and Squalor* by Dark Cloud Press. He lurks on Twitter @RAFurbaneco

The Gentlest River

Karolina Fedyk

The deeper I walk into the river, the more memories peel from my mind and float away. I see them glimmer under the surface: images unfurling in water like ink, until they lose all semblance to people and places. One blink of my eye, and they're gone.

"Don't stop", Ayz urges me, clinging to my back with eir only arm and the scarred stumps of eir legs. "Kass, don't look at them. Don't stop in the water."

The river sways gently against my legs. Warm. Inviting. I've spent my whole life living in the sky, but it's this water, its earthy smell, that reminds me of home. I want to sink, to go home. Forgetting is our Queen's greatest kindness.

I don't listen to Ayz. I look at the freshest memory: my own face blushing, hand concealing a self-satisfied smile. Behind me, my favorite sibling, Nanna, beaming like e just spilled some great secret.

\#

"You will be the next king, Kass," Nanna murmured, braiding my hair before sleep.

Startled, I looked at the rows of beds in the hall and beyond. The room was still mostly empty, save for few motionless shapes wrapped in their blankets. There were figures of guardians, black-clad, moving through the balconies behind the resin windows, but no one seemed to mind Nanna's words.

"No," I said, suddenly shy, too afraid of my hope voiced so clearly. Now that the king was dying, one of us would take eir place; and all of us dreamed of it, desperately. I wanted Nanna to be right, but I had to deny eir words. A king has to be humble. I needed to contain this huge, destructive hope burning in my chest. Keep the flame in. Scared of what would happen if it became true.

"Who, if not you?" Nanna finished braiding and patted my arm gently. We both looked around at our siblings, readying for sleep in the hall.

I pressed my lips together. Couldn't be certain who was listening. Our rooms were quite high in the Tree, the rivers' churning waters barely a murmur, not enough to drown out conversations. Until now, I had always felt safe: protected by the guardians, embraced by my siblings. But in this one moment, I saw the room as full of opponents: each of the sleeping bodies belonging to someone who could take the throne from me. I couldn't know if Nanna was just teasing me, or playing a dangerous game.

"I'm not here to guess whom the Queen will choose," I said. But I'd make sure she'd notice me. The hope was now burning higher than ever, white-hot. I had to cling to it.

Because — if I were not chosen king, where would I go?

"Spoken like a true king would!" Nanna giggled. "Modest and pretty. I wish I had my amber to show you. The Queen won't look at anyone else when she sees you…"

"You lost it?" I turned to em. The guardians wouldn't be happy to know had Nanna lost their token, that perfect honey orb carved out of the Tree sap. They didn't give those away freely.

"Just can't find it," e said dismissively, wrapping eirself in blankets. "It must be somewhere. Sleep well, princeling."

#

The memory disappears underwater, Nanna's laughter still echoing in my head. I shiver in the shade of the World's Tree. It looms over me, blocking the sun and the sky and the world: nothing but the enormous, partly ossified trunk, gnarled roots boring into the soil, drinking in the river of memory, the river of dreams, their angry sister river of lamentations. Above, in the crown, veins of wood and amber marking the empty, skeletal branches. I force myself to look up, to the whirlwind of ashen flakes. Massive limbs lurch in the wind, threatening to snap and fall.

I should be afraid of the Tree. It's sick, but still violently, relentlessly alive. It could shake us off and we'd be nothing but a scratch in its ancient bark. It'll do just fine without us treading the corridors carved in its trunk.

I can only think about how long will it take the Tree to heal. It's already been a long winter. Nothing indicates it will end.

I thought I could bring an end to that winter. All it takes is, after all, walking from one massive root to another, separated by the gentlest river. I could feed my memories to the river, let her take everything before the Tree, all the pieces of my earlier life tugging at my heart. There is barely one meander between the roots, and the water isn't very deep. It runs slow and patient over sandy riverbed. But the currents want us back, and they curl around my shins, pulling us towards the Kind Queen's halls.

"It's not our time yet, Kass." Ayz begins to sing to distract me from memories falling apart. I should remember the song, but the words unravel in my head as soon as they leave Ayz' lips.

#

The next days passed in a haze. My grief was half-hearted; the ambition outshone it. I've seen the Queen: she arrived to escort her king to her halls.

Her cloak and veil were spun from the sky,

embroidered with human dreams. Her dark eyes glimmered. There was something old and terrifying about the knowing gaze of someone who had seen everything, who had never blinked at the universe, and had witnessed, stubbornly, its every breath. But when she reached out to hold the king, her hands were ordinary, smooth and soft.

She gathered em in her arms and walked out on the balcony, her robes billowing in summer breeze. And then they were gone, the Queen and her king.

On the branch whence they left, the Tree grew a fruit: a single golden orb like a miniature sun. Every day I walked past that branch, seeing the fruit swell and darken, waiting for the day it ripens — and fell into my hands, marking me as the Queen's chosen one, her guardian. The one who will stand between her and the living world, keeping them apart. The Tree was our gate.

In our shared rooms, we siblings eyed each other anxiously. Hatred was not known to us; but we could fear each other, and we did. The guardians moved about the rooms, accompanied by the rustle of leaves. I trusted them to intervene if we rediscovered anger and violence, the things they worked painstakingly to uproot. But I also kept my head low, lest the guardians accuse me of being too proud.

I couldn't read their faces. I knew them well; they taught us and made sure we had everything we needed. Until recently, they had been our companions, even if I never knew whether they, like us, had had a life outside of the palace. I liked some of them. But looking at them now felt like opening a book just to find its pages blank.

My face, in turn, was a page overflowing with hastily scribbled lines. I wanted to be chosen. That was the only fate I knew. And I knew I would be a great king. A splendid king. Bringing the light and sun to the land above, keeping my Queen safe from the demands of the living. A union to make both realms peaceful.

I imagined the Queen's delicate fingers over mine, the veil lifting from her face, those unblinking eyes holding me in their steady gaze.

The apple hung above our heads, leaves turning to

fragile bone around it. We could almost touch its surface, brimming with life — but it wouldn't fall to our hands. I could graze it with my fingertips, but couldn't coax it to fall. Nanna barely flicked eir fingers at the fruit. E stepped back with a secretive smile. I could swear e winked at me.

Next morning, Ayz entered the dining hall. Short and plump and shaking with anxiety, e was still a kid. Arms hunched, feet dragging. Wild dark curls covering eir face. E held both hands to eir chest. Finally, e revealed the glow of gold in eir palms.

I held my breath. Ayz held to the gleaming apple like it was eir anchor. E looked for answers in our faces; but we had none, equally shocked that such an honor should fall to eir hands. To an anxious, stuttering kid.

The king, I told myself. Ayz was now our king.

#

Disappointed guardians glaring at me across the room. Their faces pale like driftwood. Nanna gasping in disbelief. The past draws me in — and dissolves when I try to get a closer look.

Ayz pulls my hair to make me look up.

#

Anger or not, I still had to attend to my duties. Defeat carefully tucked away; head high, eyes shining bright. I was supposed to be happy for my sibling. So what if my smile was a little pinched?

"What happened?" Nanna whispered as I took place by eir side.

I shrugged, not looking at em.

"The Queen chose Ayz. That's what happened. You've been there. You saw it."

"Yes, but..." Nanna frowned. "Ayz? How? E's a child, and... why would the Queen choose a child?"

"How would I know?"

E shook eir head.

"It should have been you." The words that have

been burning in my heart the whole night. "The Queen must have grown impatient with this procession of... insufficient heirs. And she found Ayz and eir innocence appealing? That's the only possible explanation."

"Nanna." I pushed eir hand away. "No one asks us to guess Queen's choices. If she wanted Ayz, who are we to disagree?"

"But it should have been you." E insisted.

Queen, Queen is one matter; but earthly politics is another. Too alien for her; she wouldn't understand. And neither did I, until that moment.

Did I really think no one would ever be tempted to influence her choice, push her hand?

So used to seeing her as the all-powerful. Forgetting how she bound herself in the agreement with us, bound with mortal blood, the one thing she could never resist. And, I learned, some of our habits outgrow death. We keep going in circles.

#

I think I see her standing on the other root of the Tree, the one I'm trying to reach for, with Ayz clinging to my back.

I, I, I. When we reach that root, there will be not much of me left. Just the outer shell, an empty body. Ayz repeats something that must be my name.

But. The Queen.

She's standing there, tall and proud, veil lifted. She's wearing my mother's face, then Nanna's face, Ayz' hopeful gleaming eyes, all of them at once. Amber on her brow, collar of garnets around her neck, dreams dripping from her cloak.

Then I see her real, unblinking eyes, and there's kindness in them. And love. That's reserved for Ayz. I think I know now what she saw in em. Ayz resisted the guardians, was never lured by their promises. Maybe e saw them for what they were.

#

At the edge of the mortal world, we can't free ourselves from politics. Ambition is too deep an instinct. Even the guardians can't forget it.

I couldn't sleep, so I listened to nervous pacing in the ossified corridors. Guardians and siblings were running up and down stairs carved in the trunk. Favors exchanged in hushed words. I knew they said my name.

In hindsight, I know all the questions I should have asked. Why would they want me to be king? I came from nowhere and, in all honesty, took longer than most to shake off life from before the palace. They say I was wailing to the high heavens when they marked me with the Tree's sap. They say I was too weak. Did Nanna truly believe I would perform well by the Queen's side? Did she think she was doing me a favor?

And does it matter? The harm's done, either way.

#

I must remember. I try to tell Ayz.

"There was this moment." My mouth feels dry. "When I saw Nanna talking to the guardians. If I had only listened, I'd know what they were plotting, but I chose not to."

Ayz combs my hair with eir fingers.

"Conserve your energy, Kass."

"No. I have to say it. You need to know. I was complicit. I know Nanna was saying — e was saying — something about you, and about me, and how you wouldn't be — be right..."

"Shh." Eir hand clenches on my braids. "No more of this. Don't tell me. I don't want to hate you."

E leans over my arm. Eir face, soft and kind. Eyes that give away everything.

"Let the river take it," e whispers into my ear. "And keep going."

I can keep quiet, but I'll repeat it to myself silently so that it takes many tiny roots in my mind. The river won't be able to tear this one away. I need to remember.

#

It spreads around me in the water, over and over and over again.

A night in the hall. Most of our siblings already asleep in their beds. I lay in a pool of moonlight, eyes half closed, anger still burning in my chest. Nanna rose from eir blankets, quiet like a ghost. I watched em move into the shadows under balconies carved in ossified bark. There were two other silhouettes. Dark robes, unlike the soft grays worn by the royal siblings. Family guardian cloaks.

"How is Kass?" I recognized guardian Varuna's voice.

My muscles went taut. I had liked Varuna.

Nanna whispered, "Confused, I think. Angry. Disappointed in emself."

"But Ayz? That child? You've never spoken of em to us."

"I know." E bowed eir head. "No one considered em... important."

A quiet scoff. "All this effort, and for nothing. We can't get rid of em now."

I stifled a gasp. But Nanna still stood there, eir hands clasped, like e didn't know what "getting rid of" could possibly mean.

"But maybe we could still show that Ayz is unsuitable." Guardian Meshe. "Couldn't we, Nanna, dear? Was it really the fruit e was holding?"

Nanna breathed deeply. E would wake the whole hall, I thought. But, of course, no one even stirred.

"My amber," e whispered. "Your gift."

"Haven't you been saying around that you can't find it?"

My heart froze. Nanna was telling me this very thing.

"But... the fruit?" E asked, shaking.

"Was there a fruit? Or did Ayz destroy it?" Meshe said.

Guardian Varuna touched eir arm. Nanna didn't flinch, but eir body was stiff as a statue.

"Clever princeling. You knew we might need it."

"What if the Queen mistook the brightness of that

artifact for the brightness of Ayz' heart?" Meshe asked gently.

I stared at them through the night, but no one thought to look at me. Black, silvery white, black again. Nanna was surrounded by the very people who were here to ensure our safety. E looked fragile, like a wisp. One move could shove em out through the carved balcony and down, down to the Tree's roots, where the underworld met the living.

My heart was beating wildly. I knew what I should do — but I didn't. I didn't call for help. Didn't ask Nanna about that meeting in the night. Didn't try to stop em. Didn't tell Ayz.

I lay, paralyzed with fear, once again feeling Nanna's fingers braiding my hair and eir soft voice telling me that I would be king.

#

"Kass, we're almost there." Ayz' hand holds my chin and brings it up, to the sky, to air, to the world I belong to. E's lying. We're far from the root. I'll never get here. Not as myself — I noticed how Ayz repeats my name so that I know, this heavy body is Kass, the fleeting mind is Kass. But Ayz can still make it. Safe, the amber in eir hand, ready to show the truth.

#

It was morning when the guardians — not Varuna and not Meshe, they were too smart for this — went over Ayz' meagre belongings. The to-be-king watched them, pale and immobile. The sad showcase of eir previous family: a farmer's sickle and glass beads e would be too ashamed to ever wear in the carved Tree-halls. A cloak woven by some sibling or cousin, wool coarse and uneven. And in its folds, Nanna's amber, which you couldn't tell from the Tree's fruit if you haven't felt its pulse. Or so Ayz had claimed, but no one believed em.

E sought help in our faces, but we united against em; all of us hurt, deceived by the Queen, shamed by a child who knew only corn fields and orchards.

E thrashed on the floor and cried, and swore eir innocence. They took em away.

But I knew the Tree palace is not a fair place, didn't I? It's cruel. It plays games. It seems stern and unmoving, but look at what hides in the shadows.

We never ask the right questions. We don't listen enough to the rustle of its leaves. And that night, the leaves were repeating Ayz' name.

#

"What did they do to you then, Ayz dear?"

Ayz breathes out.

"I don't want to talk about it."

"Tell me something. Distract me. We'll bring down — bring down — what were we supposed to bring down?"

"The guardians, Kass. The ones the Queen made to protect us. But they didn't."

"They almost killed you. This I remember."

Ayz sighs deeply against my back.

"They tried to. But in the end, they could only give me to the Tree."

#

This I remember. On a surprisingly chilly day, we all gathered on the carved balconies. Beneath us, rivers of the underworld hurled their angry waves at the roots. I thought I could lose my mind in the violent currents, churning memories of the recently dead. My throat became tight. And this, I thought, I wanted to be my kingdom.

I wanted it a little less as I watched the procession walk down the chiseled staircase. Dark-robed guardians, and among them Ayz. At some point Ayz looked up, right at me, with such despair I forgot about my ambition. As if my sudden magnanimity could unmake all that was happening to em. But the guardians held eir hands, and e had to turn to the narrow carved path.

The procession moved from one bridge-root to

another. They were treading on ancient paths, the wood turned by thousands of feet into polished, slippery substance. Any wrong step could send them falling into the Kind Queen's embrace. I shivered. Shouldn't she save her chosen one? But she wasn't there. Just the hungry waters breaking over smaller, younger roots and spilling into the depths of her domain.

They tied Ayz to the Tree. E extended eir hands, but tried to reason with the guardians. You could as well talk to the ossified tree bark. Fresh shoots knotted themselves around eir wrists and ankles. I knew I couldn't hear em wailing, but I was certain I did.

The guardians could, though. And yet they turned away.

And the Tree started dying.

In an eyeblink, summer turned into fierce winter. I sat in the windows, watching darkened leaves fall and hit against the trunk. They weren't the usual color of rust and Queen's gold, but bleached, sick green speckled with black. I witnessed their sudden decay with sleepless eyes, never being able to move past Ayz and into calmer, kinder dreams. In each dream, I found em calling for my help. The guardians gave me some brews, but those only made my thoughts woolly. I started spilling them when no one was watching.

We soon started noticing dark veins trailing up the still-living tree, crawling along the youngest shoots. Carved bark became brittle. Dark as the guardians' cloaks. I should have noticed the similarity then.

A bridge fell. The Queen took five of my siblings.

No, that's not right. That's not how I remember it. The Tree shook us off.

As if we were the disease here, the black tar flowing from under our hands. As if we were the poison.

But we became sick as well. Brittle like the Tree. Only our guardians seemed unaffected. If anything, there seemed to be more of them.

Five new guardians.

I looked through cracks in resin windows. The Tree could just get rid of us, and still go on, new tissue growing over carved corridors and splendid halls. Tree flesh would fill out my favorite nook near the kitchen, and the treasury. We wouldn't survive. We were fragile. Unwanted visitors.

I knew, even before the second bridge broke, that soon we would be gone. Or: not gone, but clad in dark, shadows of past selves, let out from the Queen's realms to tend to her tree. Going in circles. Still ambitious. Human, but not quite human.

I found Nanna in one of the empty halls. E was without eir usual company of guardians, and eir guilty look told me e'd been avoiding me.

"What do you want from me?" e asked, eir eyes darting towards the doorway. I stood so that I was blocking it.

"I need to know where they took Ayz."

"Let me go." E tried to run past me, but I wouldn't budge. "Ow!"

"Not until you tell me." I looked em in the eye. "You, and them, are killing the Tree."

"I'm not!" E laughed nervously. "What do I have to do with the guardians, anyway?"

"What? How about this 'you should be king, Kass' nonsense?"

Nanna turned pale.

"You really think I'm most qualified? Do you know anything about me — or is it enough for you that I'm pretty?"

E stepped back.

"Just tell me, please," I asked.

Nanna kept silent for a long, long while. Was e waiting for the guardians? I half expected them to run into the room and ruin my sad excuse for a rescue plan.

"I'll take you there," e finally said.

#

"Nanna?" Ayz sighs. "I never thought..."

"An infatuation the guardians used against em," I say through clenched teeth, pretending it didn't flatter me, and didn't hurt when e admitted there was nothing more to it.

"But e took you down the Tree."

"Yes." Among the myriad paths carved throughout centuries, I could have wasted days looking for Ayz. If I didn't get lost in the oldest, collapsed corridors.

My fears sink to the bottom of the river. More and more of us dying. My siblings' faces float past us.

"And you came for me." Ayz' hand is soft and gentle.

I clench my teeth and keep going.

#

The outer sides of the tree were the oldest, most delicate constructions carved by our predecessors centuries ago. The steps were fragile like old bone. Nanna led me to the top of the stairs and looked down, lantern dangling in eir hand.

"I'm not coming with you any further," e said, stepping back. "The guardians will find me."

"Fine." I didn't look back at em. I hoped e would join me, but couldn't demand it. Wouldn't force Nanna, even if it might be safer for em than returning to the halls; I couldn't begin to imagine how guardians could punish em.

"But take this." E pushed something into my hand. It was eir amber orb, glowing with faint light. "And come back? With Ayz?"

"You think e'd like to see any of us ever again, even if I find em?" I bit back laughter.

"Do either of you have anywhere else to go?" E asked in response.

No, we didn't. We belonged to the Tree. Our guardians slowly chiseled paths into our minds and hearts, until the only thing we knew was the Queen's realm.

So I walked down.

Halfway, I slipped and tumbled down in a cloud of dust. The worn steps broke under me. I screamed, scraping the floor for purchase. I held by my arms. My fingers burned and my nails broke. I tried to climb back up, but my hands gave in. I fell. The next floor held me, but the impact knocked air from my lungs. I curled into a ball and sobbed, hiding my bloodied fingers. In that moment, I only wanted the guardians to find me and bring me back.

It'd been hours. I rubbed at my eyes and looked up, at the broken staircase. The more I threw myself at it, the more I risked stabbing myself with splintered wood. I was only getting more tired. I yelled at the tree until my throat was raw.

I could go down, but not back up. We'd have to find another way. I was thinking, "we", although I didn't even know if Ayz was still alive.

I kept going.

And then I found em, not tied to the tree, but grown into it.

"Winter's breath, Ayz." I fell to my knees next to em, nearly slipping on the wet, smooth bark. E rolled eir eyes. Eir legs had disappeared entirely in the tree. Eir one hand hung limp, the other half-devoured by the Tree. When I touched it, Ayz winced. Flecks of eir fingers fell away.

"Ayz. Ayz, look at me." I held eir face in my hands. Eir eyes were hazy and unfocused, but finally, Ayz noticed me.

"Kass?"

"It's me. We're going home."

"Is it over? Or are you a ghost wearing eir face?"

"No. Winter's breath, no, I'm real."

"I saw many of our siblings here." Ayz looked at me, suddenly lucid. "They all died recently. You could be a ghost."

"I'm not. And I'll take you from here."

"I can't walk." E smiled at me sadly.

"I'll carry you."

It was the obvious, only solution to me, but then I thought of consequences. We couldn't use the staircase. On my own, perhaps, I could climb — with a bit of luck. But not if I was carrying Ayz. I looked over my arm. We'd have to get to the next bridge-root and from there — through water.

The river between the roots was murky and calm.

"Through there?" Ayz guessed my thoughts.

I shivered.

"Yes. Through there."

"You won't remember yourself."

"So what?" I bristled. "I made my choice already. Don't try to talk me out of it."

Ayz only regarded me with huge, shining eyes.

I walked away to say my quiet goodbyes to everyone I remembered. My family, back before I was born into the royalty. My ideas and hopes. The places and people I liked. In the end, to myself, the first eighteen years of Kass. The fool. *I won't miss em,* I thought, and knew I was lying to myself.

"Alright." I turned back to Ayz. "It's time for us to go."

E swallowed. "I'll remember you."

"Not much to remember." I shook my head.

"Now, don't be bitter." E stretched eir surviving arm, trying to stroke my cheek. "Just... tell me things? So that I remember for you?"

#

And here we are, now.

I've been telling Ayz things about someone named Kass. Ayz murmurs the name, Kass, Kass, a rustle of falling leaves, a whisper of spring when winter breathes out. My robes are soaked, and not white anymore. They're earthen, dark, not quite guardian robes, more like decaying foliage and autumn mud.

I keep walking. It's what I've been doing for as long as I remember. But soon I'll have to think of something else to do; we've almost crossed the water. That's fine. I'm empty and light inside. I need new things. A name, although Ayz convinces me that Kass sounds nice.

"And you..." Eir voice falters. "And Kass had an amber orb, remember? A gift from eir friend Nanna. Made by the guardians." E sighs. "Aren't we all made by the guardians."

"The guardians are us," I protest, insistent, although I don't know why.

"They were us," Ayz corrects me gently. "Look at the amber."

Indeed, I've been holding a round object in my hand.

"What do I need it for?" I look into it, and an unknown face frowns at me.

"To show the truth," Ayz tells me. "About the guardians."

"Would Kass do that?"

"Yes." E swallows. "E would. I think I can imagine how it would be. Kass and me, holding hands, walk into the main hall. Kass holds up the shining ball. And there are scenes playing out on its surface: guardians plotting in the dark, guardians talking to youngest siblings, the royal children shaped and molded like trees in an orchard. The whole room holds its breath. The world has never been so quiet."

So am I, caught in eir tale.

"There is justice. There is awe. And a great feast in the name of Kass and Ayz." E gives a dreamy sigh. "And I see thin bands of gold, Queen's gold, decorating their brows."

"Two kings?" I say, incredulously.

"That's not unheard of," Ayz replies, and I don't question em for even a heartbeat.

And I think I see someone waiting for us at the root, even if climbing up, weightless but with the weight of Ayz on my shoulders, is a daunting task.

Her robes billow in the wind, and she holds two golden apples in her hands like two newborn suns.

###

About the author

Karolina Fedyk: a wearer of many hats, of which the academic, the nerdy and the writerly are their favorites. They write in two languages and their works have appeared in *Strange Horizons, Star*Line, Metaphorosis,* and *The Dark.* They come from Cracow, Poland, but have been travelling across continents and countries since then. Currently they pursue a PhD in what might as well be science fiction subject matter. They like learning new languages, coffee, and owls. They can be found tweeting as @karigrafia.

Clayton Memorial Medical Fund

All proceeds from the *Reading 5X5* anthology benefit the Clayton Memorial Medical Fund.

Originally set up to help author Jo Clayton, the fund has since helped many other SFF writers. Their mission statement says:

"The fund helps professional science fiction, fantasy, horror, and mystery writers living in the Pacific Northwest states of Oregon, Washington, Idaho, and Alaska deal with the financial burden of medical expenses."

Find it at <u>osfci.org/clayton</u>

Copyright

Metaphorosis

Metaphorosis offers beautifully written science fiction and fantasy. Our projects include:

Metaphorosis Magazine

Metaphorosis, a weekly magazine of SFF short stories, including stories from all the authors in this anthology. Find out more at magazine.metaphorosis.com, and sign up to be notified of new stories.

Metaphorosis Books

Metaphorosis: 2017

All the stories from Metaphorosis magazine's second year.

Fifty-three great science fiction and fantasy stories. One for every week of 2017.

Metaphorosis: Best of 2017

The best science fiction and fantasy stories from Metaphorosis magazine's *second* year.

Snow queens and their daughters, invisible giants missing vanished lovers, transformations, quests, searches, and discoveries of all sorts.